# FULL TERM

# J. I. M. Stewart

# FULL TERM

A Novel

W · W · NORTON & COMPANY · INC
NEW YORK

PUBLIC LIBRARY, PLAINFIELD, N. J.

© J. I. M. Stewart 1978

First American Edition 1979
All Rights Reserved

ISBN 0-393-01282-4
Printed in Great Britain

A Staircase in Surrey

\*   \*   \*   \*   \*

FULL  TERM

794686

# I

THE COLLEGE TOWER was coming down. Already where its upper ranges had been there was only naked scaffolding. The sun dropped through this criss-cross vacancy every evening. If one walked round Long Field at night there was a point from which the moon was to be observed similarly disposed, like a sickly prisoner behind bars.

Not that we put in much time staring. Building operations of one sort or another were commonplace; during term and vacation alike they went on now in this quad and now in that; the fabric was extensive and most of it dated from centuries back. Yet we didn't much like what we were now seeing. Although there was money for a complete restoration, from which there would only be lacking a certain weathering that it would be absurd to attempt to reproduce, we'd still own, we knew, an irrational sense of loss.

I suppose nobody's consciousness of this was oppressive. Yet everything taking place during the academic year now beginning was to occur against a background of dust and rattle as the tower crumbled away, and when tensions built up they were a little exacerbated by that.

Matthew Arnold thought of his colleagues at Oriel College and elsewhere as men of 'petty pottering habits', and a century earlier the undergraduate Edward Gibbon judged 'the monks of Magdalen' to be 'decent easy men, who supinely enjoyed the gifts of the founder'. Gibbon's stricture would scarcely have been applicable in the Oxford of Arnold's time—a place from which the general strenuousness of the

7

Victorians was not absent. Nor could Arnold's words be used with fairness, a century later again, of the university I knew. For if the interests, say, of Albert Talbert might have to be described as petty and pottering they were at the same time marked by a quite monumental industry, and by and large I was steadily aware of being in the society of intelligently active men and women.

This predominant tone was so secure a possession of the university that people were slow to trouble themselves before the spectacle of apparent idleness here and there. In many English public schools those boys are most admired who achieve intellectual or athletic distinction with the least appearance of effort, and in college we were ourselves prone to applaud able youths who collected university prizes and an impressive First Class in their final examination with no trace of application whatever. It was the same with their seniors. Men would gossip with witty aimlessness in common room until a late hour and then return to their college rooms or North Oxford dwelling, there to turn up the lamp on strenuous research through deeper watches of the night.

Within this area of not quite authentic *insouciance* appeared to fall the first formal meeting of the college tutors in each term. It was the duty of my colleagues to answer a proxy roll-call certifying that each of their pupils had returned into residence. Inevitably by no means all had done so, and the Senior Tutor read out to the meeting such excuses as the absentees had sent in. These were various, but with common-place ailments and accidents little in evidence. A premium seemed to be set on invention. One man would be awaiting serviceable aircraft in Nepal and another a snow plough in Scotland. Organizing a mother's garden party or a grand-mother's wedding, attending upon the birth of hound puppies, awaiting ransom after having been kidnapped by bedouin in the Sahara: these are representative of the exigencies presented to us. Cyril Bedworth passed them on to

8

the meeting with an air of discreet amusement handed down to him by predecessors in his office.

The absurd letters and telegrams and telephone calls were treated, then, as a traditional beginning-of-term joke. There was rarely the hint of a headache in them. The youths involved very well knew the rules of the game. Saturday's captive of the Sahara would be around the place on Monday morning, and hound puppies were born regularly on time. And so also in other matters. We scarcely bothered to preserve among ourselves the humorous fiction that undergraduates are childish, impervious to reason, inexpugnably lazy, incipiently alcoholic, and so on. It was the dull fact of the matter that they were a reliable crowd, well able to get smartly off a mark when the pistol barked. A strain of complacency lurked in this persuasion. Hadn't we hand-picked the ablest boys in the kingdom? So what would you expect?

We had also hand-picked ourselves or each other. Nobody in the world could wish a colleague on us. We decided on our needs, advertised, interviewed, deliberated, and finally elected into a fellowship a man whose tenure became at that moment virtually for the remainder of his working life. A small closed society of this self-perpetuating sort might be expected to exhibit a conservative collective mind. But in fact the college was sometimes venturesome and eccentric in its recruitment, as if there were an assumption that the strength of that mind depended upon its incorporating at least a strong dash of heterodox views. This matter of the mind of a collegiate society is a tricky one, which I am very little able to elucidate. I would have described the majority of my colleagues as being, individually, diffident men, who through their intellectual endowment were very sufficiently aware of the perplexingness and treachery and uncontrollability of things in general. But collectively they had a serene confidence in themselves. They reposed this confidence, indeed, not

9

merely in their own conjoined wisdom but also each man in the other individually. Or, if they didn't do this last, there was a convention that they should profess to do so—a convention barely to be breached even in the conversation of intimate friends. Hence that enviable assurance which I have always tended to associate (perhaps mistakenly) with the notion of a crack regiment.

But to such time-tempered societies breaking strains can come unsuspectedly, just as they can to the fabric of an ancient tower.

The roll-call meeting was an after-dinner occasion, rarely lasting more than fifteen minutes. Pipes and cigarettes were in evidence, and prosperous or improvident men lit cigars. At the end of the proceedings the more sociably disposed usually returned to common room to drink and converse. This had become my own habit. My vacations were tending to be solitary affairs, given over to the writing I had little time for during term. As a consequence, when a new term began I behaved in a clubbable way for some weeks. It was in these circumstances that I had my first encounter with David Graile.

Graile came up to me in front of the decanters, waited until I had poured a tot of whisky, and then introduced himself. He had been a fellow of the college for fifteen or twenty years, and I hadn't met him because, during my single year as a member of common room, he had been absent on sabbatical leave. This was an institution stoutly upheld among us. Every seventh year a man might disappear as he pleased, continuing to earn his pay solely in virtue of his private research, and not at all for any continued labours in the way of educating the young. Opinions appeared to differ as to whether a man availing himself of this provision ought to present any formal intimation of what he proposed to be about. One man would turn in a detailed programme and another do little more than bleakly announce his impending disappearance. Those college Statutes by which we were all supposed to live attained a maximum of obfuscation on this point, since they spoke of a fellow as 'entitled to permission' thus to vanish. But this dark saying, like many others in this book of wisdom, was of no practical consequence.

'What did you make of that meeting?' Graile asked.

I don't know why I delayed for a moment before answering this casual-seeming question. If there was one thing that my recently acquired colleagues had never suggested to me it was that of adopting the role of examiner or inquisitor *vis-à-vis* their neophyte. It was indeed their constant attitude—lightly but unmistakably intimated—that any cadet in their midst was at least by some crucial margin better-informed than they were—and this even in regions so arcane, so shrouded within the particular mysteries of his novel ambience, that only the most pronounced clairvoyant faculty would have made any such knowledgeableness conceivable. I suppose there may still have harboured in my mind the ghost of a juvenile persuasion that all dons—and in particular freshly encountered ones—were disposed to subject one to the rigours of viva-voce assessment. And in Graile's tone I had perhaps detected some hint of challenge.

'It appears to be a meeting designed for purposes of amusement,' I said. 'I don't feel I came away with any very useful accession of knowledge.'

'One learns who's not around.'

'That could be put on paper.'

'Well, no, Pattullo. Or not comprehensively. Consider Watershute.'

'But I heard that name, and his tutor answer for its owner. Quite rightly. He's certainly up. In fact he's a decent-looking lad who has just moved in on my staircase.'

'Ah, that's the son. I'm talking about the father. One couldn't very well have a Senior Tutor being gently ironical over some facetious communication from *him*. But, for that matter, Watershute—William, that is Watershute *père*—would never bother his head to turn in any communication at all.'

'I've barely heard of William Watershute, and didn't connect him with the young man.' I was finding myself a little at sea over these exchanges. 'He's actually a fellow of the college?'

'Of course he is. And an extremely able nuclear physicist.'

'He certainly can't have been much in evidence since I turned up last October. If I set eyes on him, it was without being aware of it.'

'Well, Watershute did have a couple of terms' leave. But he's been so seldom on view since then that you might think he had miscounted, and stayed away for three. One would expect a higher degree of numeracy in a scientist.'

'I suppose so.' Graile's last observation had been quite in the common line of academic humour. 'Are you telling me that this roll-call meeting is in aid of spotting who's not round the table—which of us, in fact, is on French leave?'

'It has inescapably that function, wouldn't you say? It's sometimes made a joke of. One wouldn't dream of taking the suggestion seriously. This is a damned rum place, Pattullo.'

'I sometimes feel it that way, I admit.' I still felt a little out of my depth, or at least uncertain of the extent to which Graile and I were just being funny together. 'It does strike me as odd,' I said, 'that I've hardly heard of my young neighbour's father. Am I right in thinking that there's felt to be a situation about which a little reticence is to be observed?'

'Yes, you are.'

'Then why, Graile, do you come at me with it? I'm a very new arrival here, and massively junior according to the rules of the place.'

'Perhaps I have it in mind that, as a fresh observer of our

12

cloistral scene, you may preserve and present a usefully objective point of view.'

'I've no point of view whatever—or not on the matter we seem to be talking about. For one thing, I haven't a notion of what sort of person this William Watershute is, and in the circumstances it doesn't look as if I'm going to have any large chance of finding out. Or not, at any rate, at first hand. And I don't know that I have much impulse to go inquiring around.'

'Haven't you, Pattullo? You disappoint me. Aren't you a dramatist? I'd suppose it was your thing, rather—discovering how somewhat out-of-the-way people tick.'

'He's out-of-the-way, is he?'

'Ah, that's better! And I'd say he is, decidedly.'

'Just as a don? An irresponsible and rather frivolous type?'

'I'd scarcely have said that until recently. But he does seem to have been moving that way. Coming to have the look of a loose fish, if you ask me. Tell by a fellow's mouth, don't you think? Kind of saggy effect. Belated playboy, perhaps, kicking out as his youth sinks over the horizon. Question is, could he be yanked out of it by being pulled up sharp.'

These remarks, unexpected as offered about a colleague in this place, held me dumb. So Graile was able to continue.

'Something freakish about him, too. You could never feel certain—or I couldn't—what he might be up to next. But the devil of it is you *can* be certain—at a mere whiff of the man you can be certain—that there's a purposeful creature there as well. Thorough, too. Never does things by halves.'

'It's a useful endowment.'

'He couldn't have got where he has, without it. But it looks as if that particular Watershute is being squeezed out. Playing fast and loose with his duties in the most startling way.' Graile was silent for a moment. 'But I mustn't plague you with uncongenial gossip,' he then said a shade maliciously.

'What you say seems a little beyond that. Are you telling me there's a real problem looming?'

'Within a month, I'd say. Will you put a bottle of port on it in the wager book? We could fudge it to look quite innocuous.'

'No, thank you. It's not my kind of bet.'

'Bloody glad to hear it,' Graile said. 'We get all sorts here now.' He put down his glass and walked away.

When I myself left common room a few minutes later it was with a displeased sense that there had been an examination after all; that I had been subjected by a totally fresh acquaintance to a process of sizing up. Just how this had been meant to work wasn't clear to me. But my behaviour in face of the unexpected had certainly been in question. I'd been offered, for instance, the choice of a right or wrong response to that proposal about a wager. It was something I could scarcely be other than resentful about.

The Great Quadrangle washed this feeling away in an instant. It was a composing place, particularly at night. And this was a frosty mid-October night in which a clear sky was powdered with stars. The most brilliant of them appeared to have congregated together in the west; they might have been suspended from the scaffolding round the tower as lamps on a Christmas tree. The central fountain was still playing, perhaps for the better refreshment of the college chub, and its gentle plash was the only sound to be heard. The Great Quadrangle is given over in the main to senior persons of a sober habit. One would not have expected from it any sharp impression that after summer slumbers the college had filled up again, was murmurous and pulsating like a vast and intricate honeycomb of caverns into which there had once more flowed some codling-crowded sea. Yet the impression did

14

hold, and fairly enough. Of the several hundred young men who had been dining in hall a couple of hours before, the majority were still within bow-shot of me now.

I walked on into Surrey and paused to take a look at it. From file upon file of lighted windows, for the most part uncurtained, a diffused illumination defined at least the outlines of the scene. It was like a large stage upon which the curtain has risen with the rheostats turned low; in a moment a speeded-up dawn would reveal some tremendous spectacle—Diocletian's palace or the Taj-Mahal—with a numerous cast of actors posed before it. This didn't happen now, but at least I discovered I was not alone. A young man had overtaken me, and was going by with a tentatively interrogative glance. He was my new neighbour on Surrey Four, whom I had just discovered to be the son of one William Watershute, a fellow of the college. I hadn't yet spoken to him, and the appropriate moment to do so had turned up. I believe I hesitated for a second, nevertheless. There had just gratuitously come to me reflections on his father of a derogatory sort. I felt (irrationally) that I'd be chargeable with a kind of fishing in the matter if I hastened to make the son's acquaintance immediately thereafter.

'Good evening,' I said. (For reason had prevailed.) 'Your move has made neighbours of us. My name's Pattullo.'

'Good evening, sir. I'm Giles Watershute. How do you do?' Making these orthodox responses, Giles Watershute fell into step beside me.

'Is it a move at the start of your second year?' I asked.

'Yes. Last year I was doubled up in Howard with a man called Emerson. We got on pretty well, but when we both had a chance of single sets we thought we'd take it. Both of us were at schools that are a bit lavish with study-bedrooms for senior boys. So the chumming-up thing had been rather a throw-back in a way.'

'I suppose it would be.' Giles Watershute had been a little

more informative than might have been expected, and I felt it was up to me to strike a similar communicative note. 'When I came up to the college ages ago they shoved me straight into a set of my own. It was the set you have now.'

'Then you must have been a scholar.'

'Yes, I was.'

Giles seemed to have intimated that he was not. The odd business of scholars and commoners, with their differing gowns and privileges declaring a kind of élitism within an élite, seemed to me a merely archaic feature of English university life (as it is of some English public schools). It could be slightly galling to the marginally less favoured. Perhaps Giles felt that way.

'I flunked that scholarship fence badly,' Giles said, confirming this guess.

'You flunked it and I fluked it. Language is very odd. Does it tell me that you were at school in America for a time?'

'Yes, when my father worked there. I was at a place called Groton for a couple of years.'

'Were you, indeed?' To say 'a place called Groton' when you mean 'Groton' is like saying 'a school near Windsor' when you mean 'Eton'. So this appeared to be a defensive young man. I had resolved to put his father out of my head, but now found myself wondering whether the paternal reputation I had been hearing about had reached him and worried him. 'The last man to have your rooms'—I hit on this by way of changing the subject—'was a certain Nicolas Junkin.'

'He produced that sprawling play.' Giles had revealed himself as taking a poor view of the dramatic ability of Christopher Marlowe. 'But at least it was rather splendid when the lights went out on the first night. There was all sorts of talk about it. Sabotage and heaven knows what.'

'So there was.' We had reached the entrance of Surrey

Four. I halted before my door. 'Would you care to come in and have a drink?'

'Thank you very much.' Giles made no bones about this. 'Junkin,' he said as I switched on lights, 'is a frightfully good producer, isn't he?'

'He may become one. He's no end enthusiastic. I see quite a lot of him, partly because the theatre has been my own concern.'

'Of course I know about that, sir.'

With this prompt civility Giles accepted brandy. We sat down, and I took a fuller look at him. He was black-haired and black-eyed, with sharp clean-cut features. I told myself that he probably took after his father.

'Wasn't your father the painter?' he asked in what seemed a slightly telepathic way.

'Yes, he was. Lachlan Pattullo. The sketch over the grate was a study for one of his paintings. It's called *Young Picts watching the arrival of Saint Columba*.'

Giles jumped to his feet at once and examined the picture. There was a good deal of directness to him, a kind of openness he had perhaps picked up in the United States.

'I can see Columba. He's holding up a cross. But your father wasn't a historical painter?'

'He was what's called—or used to be called—a landscape painter. Occasional historical *motifs* were just pegs to hang his pigments on.'

'He hung them pretty well, didn't he?'

'It's generally thought so. But he wasn't too hot on his history. He has put those young Picts in kilts, as you can see.'

'Junkin has told me about the picture, and your father, as a matter of fact.' Giles appeared to feel that an admission of his slight antecedent lack of candour here was required. 'He says that the boy with the kilt blown back from his bare bottom is you. I was to look out for it, he said, if you ever invited me like this into your rooms.'

17

'Well, there it is.' It amused me to think that I must be known about the college as the don who kept his own bare bottom over his chimneypiece. 'Junkin had an alarming Japanese thing in the corresponding place in your room.'

'Yes, I've seen it. It's in his new digs in Walton Street.'

'You know him quite well?'

'More or less.' Giles spoke diffidently, as one disclaiming intimacy with a celebrity, 'He's rather marvellous, really. His father's a coal-miner.'

'Coal-miners can be rather marvellous.'

'Yes, of course.' Giles gave me a swift and lowering glance from beneath black eyebrows. 'I suppose we're always falling into rotten class-ridden ideas. Miners dig out the coal from somewhere quite close to hell, and then keep it in their baths.'

'So our grandparents believed.' I hadn't leisure to speculate on the political or ideological hinterland of these remarks. Again I changed the subject. 'What was an English school like after an American one?'

'Not too good at first.'

'The uncontaminated English boys felt it a duty to lick you into shape?'

'Literally that. It was quite surprising. But not more surprising than painful. Painfulness was the brute fact during my first year.'

'It sounds like a school not precisely in the avant-garde.'

'Right at the tail end in every sense,' Giles said with brief humour. 'What did you read when you were up, sir?'

'English. What are you reading?'

'Not Natural Science. That's what this place calls my father's thing, when it's not calling it Experimental Philosophy. I'm reading Modern Languages, which means French philology in the fourteenth century.' Giles gave me another sharp look. 'Why are you here?' he asked impulsively.

'Why? Well, why not?'

'You write plays. Why drift back into an Oxford college—which is a mix-up of a well-appointed nursery and a geriatric hospital?'

'It's rather a complex question. Perhaps I'll answer it another time.' I was silent for a moment, and felt I'd betrayed a sense that Giles Watershute wasn't being too polite. I didn't want to do this; too many young people were conventionally polite to me; if here was one cultivating a forthright note, that was something I ought to accept. 'Have you made a mistake in coming to the place yourself?' I asked.

'It's too soon to say.' Making this sensible reply, Giles smiled fleetingly. A smile was something he seemed to be sparing with. 'What I'm wondering about is something different, really. It's why so many people have to bolt to universities nowadays. Scientists, for instance.'

'A great many scientists work for industrial concerns, and for government in its various departments as well. But I suppose they may be rather pressed for practical results. The universities are havens for pure research. Or so it's said.'

'Havens for pretty well everything now. I saw that in America, and now I see it in England. Every sort of culture contracting within the walls of these institutions. Of course it happened long ago as well, with the decay of the great courtly societies. From courts to colleges. That's pretty dismal, if you ask me.'

'I don't doubt there's much in what you say. But there's a notion that you get a balanced sort of life in a college. Teaching and learning going naturally together. Do you think there's anything to be said for it?'

'For some things, I suppose, but damn-all for others. There are kinds of research that hitch on not to teaching kids in a stimulating scholars-together way, but to vast moral and political issues. Terrifying things.'

I resisted the thought of offering Giles Watershute more brandy. We had started off with talk about fathers—mine and

Nick Junkin's—and it looked as if another father might be hovering now. There was perhaps little probability that this self-possessed young man would break into untimely confidence. But I was at least determined to do no poking around. One gathered that it wasn't uncommon for a don to have a son up at his own college; there didn't attach to the situation the awkwardness felt when the same thing happened in a school; if it occasionally involved college officers in disciplinary embarrassments that was all part of their job. But if it was the father who was proving the problem child questions of some delicacy might no doubt develop. I had made from afar the observation that a father-and-son relationship is always likely to be ambivalent. If it finds itself within a context of exceptional difficulty there may be the devil to pay.

'We're both,' I said rather inconsequently, 'at the start of a second Michaelmas Term. But I've been that once before, so with me there's a certain effect of *déjà vu*.'

'The paramnesia mechanism.' Like all undergraduates that ever were, the younger Watershute could be lured into showing his paces. 'I've no sense, thank God, that I was up here in a former existence. Under Provost Pagden, say, or Provost Harbage.' This was more innocent showing off. Junkin would never have heard of these ancient college worthies. Giles, a fellow's son, would have in his head fragments of the place's history.

'It seems there are people who do receive intimations of a former existence. I've never felt it, any more than you have. But the simple "This has happened before" business always relates, surely, to something we think we've experienced in our present identity, not a former one.'

'Yes, of course.' Giles nodded briskly. 'And I think there are two varieties or degrees of it, and that the second takes even more explaining than the first. In the first you find yourself saying "Why, this has happened before!" And the experience ends there. In the second you feel yourself going one further, and about to predict what more will immediately follow. And then you feel you've actually done just that. *Déjà vu* with a strong lick of the precognitive thrown in.'

'It's elusive, isn't it? But I recognize what you're talking about.' I saw that Giles Watershute was a very intelligent young man. What he had said—and continued to say—on this random topic was perhaps unremarkable, but he organized it with the rapid confidence of those fortunate youths on whose examination papers alphas descend like snowflakes. Moreover he knew about the uses of the clock. When we had talked in a desultory way for a further half-hour he stood up with an air of inflexible purpose and said good-night.

## II

Mᴜᴄʜ ᴀs ɪғ hound puppies or a garden party had been detaining him, William Watershute turned up in college a couple of days later. It had to be concluded that his term's scandalous near-truancy had been prolonged only for so brief a further period that it didn't count. My colleagues took him in their stride, not remotely signalling a consciousness that in his conduct there had been anything out of the way. 'Duncan, have you met William Watershute?' Adrian Buntingford asked me casually before dinner, and what followed between the long-lost personage and myself was no more than an exchange of nods. I felt, indeed, that although Watershute was restored to us in the flesh he was liable to be intermittently absent in mind. But while dining, and in common room later on, I kept my eyes on him sufficiently to see that a number of people engaged him in amicable conversation to which he responded animatedly enough.

This might be a matter of our society putting on one of its punctilious turns, and behind these seemingly unaffected exchanges something different might lurk. Even Bedworth, although dissimulation wasn't his line, might be feeling that an entire term's delinquency had taken Watershute too far by a long way. Wheels might be moving in this delicate affair without the involvement of a peripheral cog like myself.

On the other hand it was possible that Graile had pitched his story at me too steeply. Various compromises and accommodations might have been resorted to in the previous term without being brought within the cognizance of the Governing Body. Perhaps some competent committee had stopped paying Watershute his money and turned his teaching over to somebody else on the proceeds.

My guess that Giles Watershute took after his father proved wrong. The senior Watershute was fair and freckled, with a featureless face of the concave kind which appears to be in the act of folding itself up along a line running from one ear-lobe to the other—an effect in his case a little obscured by a shock of depending sandy hair. There was nothing impressive about Watershute. It was the habit of some of our oldest members, at the mention of a man who had soared out of academic life into the Cabinet or other high place, to murmur 'I remember him as a perfectly undistinguished young don'. Watershute looked as if he had been a perfectly undistinguished young don. He wasn't, for that matter, all that old now. Roughly speaking, we were contemporaries.

Later that night I looked him up in *Who's Who*. He had achieved all sorts of distinctions, and in our own body only Ranald McKechnie, that eminent Classicist, had the appearance of being in the same flight. But the record didn't make me feel any lively interest in Watershute's standing in a scientific field I knew nothing about. His personality was another matter, and of this I was to have a glimpse a few days later. Before that, however, I saw him at the first Governing Body meeting of the term.

There was a good deal that interested me in these formal and structured occasions. While they lasted we treated the Provost much as a bevy of barristers treats a judge, bobbing up when he came in and bobbing up again when he went out. The more contentious the matters in debate (but they were seldom all that contentious) the more temperately were views on them expressed. Moments of occasional snappiness apart, everybody paid studied deference to everybody else. There was a convention that one didn't speak from notes, but people seldom uttered without having given thought to what they were going to say and even the words in which they'd say it. So an effect of weighty deliberation frequently attended our discussion of trivial issues, the spectacle being rather like that of stately galleons gone fishing for sprats. An astringent critic might have said that we'd get through our job more rapidly by thinking less of our own consequence. But that wouldn't have been altogether fair. Our urbanity and decorum must have evolved itself over generations to some useful end.

It might be expected that amid these rigid conventions, by subscribing to which some fifty men of very varying ages and backgrounds constrained themselves as it were to parade in uniform, individual traits of character would tend to be obscured. But this was by no means so. Conformity in manners and address served, if anything, to high-light the quiddity of this individual and that. Every now and then one was aware of a man's personality as exposed in a fashion that might have escaped notice on some more casual occasion. And one could become aware, too, of the presence and movement of that corporate mind. Its operation was distinguishable from anything one had previously remarked in any of the individuals present. The corporate mind was capable, for example, of simply disregarding certain of our number; of virtually switching off when someone thus disfavoured began to speak—this in a manner inconceivable on any merely social occasion. A man who might be listened to with indulgence and even affection over our wine would be regarded as a dead loss the moment he opened his mouth on any question under formal debate. And this instant man-of-straw rating didn't, so far as I could see, correlate with the intellectual distinction or capacity of the person involved. It sprang from some group-judgement at the level of character. What seemed fatal was any querulousness of tone, any irrelevant self-reference in a stray sentence or two, even (I sometimes thought) something as trivial as a twist of the body accompanying speech. Once one had become sensitive to this strange group severity, it could be quite frightening at times.

But there was also operative another and milder degree of this switching off or non-reception of contributions to our debates. It tended to be directed upon people who, like myself, were not preponderantly involved with the work of the college. They were judged, I imagine, not to have their eye steadily on the ball. Unlike the first group, they might be admitted to be men of weight as well as intelligence, but their weight belonged elsewhere. Watershute seemed to be classed with these. He made two short interventions at this meeting, which were perfectly sensible although neither was on a matter of moment. We didn't much attend to him. But this was the only breath I could detect of any feeling about the inadequacy of his tutorial labours.

A few days later I had a short—and curious—conversation with Watershute. We had bumped into each other in a small room, not much bigger than a cupboard, used for the temporary storage of newspapers and periodicals. It was thus a markedly cheek by jowl encounter, such as might be judged favourable for picking up the vibrations of an interlocutor. It certainly favoured a close study of the physical man. I found myself, even while judging it an indecent thing to do, looking for the saggy mouth of Graile's description. I couldn't be certain that I'd succeeded. Watershute suggested less the saggy or soggy than the shagged—a word from my school-days designed to indicate less the physically unkempt than the fatigued or strained in some not readily definable way. One was shagged when, for one reason or another, one had come close to shooting one's bolt. Watershute's otherwise un-remarkable features did run to dark rings under the eyes. He might be a dissipated man. Equally, he might be a man working to the point of exhaustion on some difficult frontier of the finite human mind.

'Giles and I have become neighbours in Surrey,' I said. 'We've been swopping a certain amount of information about our careers.'

'I didn't know he'd had one. But I'm sure you have. You're the playwright, aren't you?'

'Yes, I am.'

'What on earth has persuaded you to come and teach? Hard times behind the footlights?'

'Not exactly. But the question puzzled Giles too. I had to leave him unsatisfied on the point. But no doubt we'll discuss it again. He's a conversable boy.'

'So he is. But do you like chatting up undergraduates? Don't let him be a bore.'

'I see no danger of that. And young people do interest me. I was rather short of their acquaintance until I turned up here again.'

'Where you were an undergraduate yourself?'

'Yes—and it can have been only a shade after your time. We may even have overlapped.'

'Perhaps. I don't suppose I'd remember you.'

This might have been discouraging, but I didn't find myself taking it that way. When I write a play there is a stage at which the characters start fumbling round for their roles. Or it feels like that—as if they are doing the job themselves, without much help from me. It is a process that has at least made me aware of a similar activity as sometimes going on in real life, and I now had a sense of Watershute as being up to something of the sort. I wondered whether he had decided really to quit the college, and had decided to have the fun of being variously outrageous in the process.

'As for young people,' he now went on, 'I suppose they have charm and all that, if you want to put in time with that sort of thing. But as undergraduates they're certainly a dead loss—at least when they require teaching. In more spacious days one simply sent them out to the hacks. And perhaps took them on in their final year for a week or so. It was a privilege they looked forward to.'

'That must have been a good deal before our era.' I wondered what the serious Bedworth would make of such doctrine. It certainly represented a flourish of theatrical *panache* in a man already chargeable with grave neglect of duty. 'Would you like Giles's tutor,' I asked, 'to feel that attending to him was a sheer waste of time?'

'Oh, that sort of chap has nothing more serious to bother about, has he? The pleasures of literature and so forth. A load of old rubbish! Saving your presence, Pattullo.'

'Don't mind me.' Into my head there flitted the extravagant notion that Watershute was mildly mad, and then the yet more extravagant one that—like Hamlet—he was disposed to feign such a disorder in pursuance of a further escape from irksome commitments. He was certainly inventive. 'Do you know,' I said, 'that the pleasures of literature are something I'd suspect you of being rather fond of?'

'Perfectly correct. I do read all the world's greatest bores until my brains turn to train-oil.' Watershute had moved to the door and I had followed him—so on this entirely absurd remark we both reached open air. 'I say,' he said cheerfully, 'they've been talking to you about me, haven't they? I can see it in your eye. Well, good luck to them!' Clutching a bunch of papers in one hand, he offered a rapid gesture of farewell with the other. 'Do have another word with Giles from time to time,' he called back to me as he walked away. 'He's not a bad fellow. Not a bad fellow at all.'

These, it seemed to me, were the first untheatrical words this curious character had spoken.

It was the Provost's habit to lunch in common room once or twice a week, and at the end of the meal to prevail upon one of those present to join him on the sort of rural walk that is still just possible round about Oxford. 'Prevail upon' was his own invariable expression; he would direct it indifferently upon the most eminent savant and the humblest junior lecturer. I imagine he employed it, and backed it up with similar courtesies, even *vis-à-vis* his oldest friends. I had ceased to feel critical of this sort of behaviour on the part of the head of our college. It was one way of coping with what couldn't be an easy job.

'My dear Duncan, can I prevail on you to take a turn with me as far as Iffley Lock? If your occasions, that is, enable you to indulge me so handsomely.'

My thus being singled out occurred for the first time, as it happened, on the afternoon of the day of my encounter with the senior Watershute. I accepted the proposal and we set out at once. The towpath bordering the Isis wasn't thronged, and we strode briskly forward. I thought of the perambulations upon which, as an undergraduate, I had frequently been taken by Albert Talbert. Talbert had been disposed to long and pregnant silences as he walked, nor had his dog Boanerges at all lived up to his name. In Talbert's case, indeed, one was always conscious that something was cooking, or that there was slowly concretizing in the depths of his mind a pronouncement which would surface (unnaturally, indeed) only when it had achieved a weight and density not of the common sort. Talbert would then say something like 'I am urging our librarian to remove Gosse's rubbish from his shelves' or 'The inn at Nuneham Courtenay is kept by an Ethiopian'. And silence would succeed for the following couple of miles.

Edward Pococke, contrastingly, believed in sustained rational conversation, so that one had the feeling of taking exercise at a peripatetic dinner table. His talk, if on the consciously polished side, was always interesting, and the more arresting because you could never be sure what he was about. He was not a man who favoured relaxation (unless on a tennis court or golf course) of an idle kind. More often than not he was winding his way into something impossible to foresee. This kept you on your toes, and was enjoyable in its fashion.

'You must be in process of forming clear views, Duncan, on the role of a university in society today. It can only be a changing role, since the times are so notably changing around us. Yet some of the older views—older controversies, one might say—would still appear to me as holding their relevance for us. Not, indeed, on theological matters. All that, whether happily or unhappily, is much in abeyance. We no longer spy on our John Henry Newmans to see whether they have got significantly into flannel trousers.' The Provost paused on this, perhaps to make sure that an ancient piece of Oxford folk-lore was not lost on me.

'I doubt,' I said, 'whether there are many John Henry Newmans around.'

'Quite so—and the more's the pity. But consider how applicable today is an anatomy of Oxford in terms still of Benjamin Jowett and Mark Pattison. Balliol and Lincoln. Rival camps! Pattison saw the function of the university through what have been aspersed as Germanophil eyes. As a place of learning and scholarship, at some remove from the world of affairs. Jowett, although himself so considerable a scholar, viewed it as an indispensable nursery of rulers and administrators. It was something of a Platonic approach, but allowing a good deal to the social conditions of the age. The young men of superior privilege were to be groomed and civilized as legislators. The others, if they didn't simply enter the church, were to be the backbone of the higher civil service.'

'And of the Empire, I suppose.'

'Indeed, yes. And something of these contrasting views—learning on the one hand and public leadership and activity on the other—still obtains with us today.'

'Yes.' I wasn't managing much more than monosyllabic

replies to the Provost—perhaps having a sense that, were I to pipe up on my own, it would be in the character of the troublesome sort of student who breaks in with questions at a lecture. We had reached Long Bridges, and had stopped to watch a nursling torpid making a splashy progress up-stream.

'Bow is late,' the Provost said. 'Slow in coming forward to the stretcher.'

I had no doubt that this was so. We walked on.

'But nowadays,' the Provost resumed, 'there is the complication of all the scientific and technological things. Many of our men are involved with these outside the university as well as within. It must be difficult for them, now and then. It is even conceivable that something like a conflict of loyalties may occasionally result.'

'Yes.'

'And this may produce situations in which it is necessary to move delicately and without precipitation.'

It is possible that at this point I had a glimpse of what lay ahead. It wasn't simply Iffley Lock and Iffley Church. And if I had any doubts about this they were quickly resolved.

'You will have heard,' the Provost said with a sudden clarity of intent, 'of the trouble over William Watershute. A brilliant man. We must hold on to that.'

'I've heard only a few words,' I said, 'and they came to me casually and by mere chance. They were to the effect that, as a tutor, Watershute has been judged to be rather cutting his corners. Incidentally, I've barely encountered the man himself. I feel I've got to know his son better. He's on my staircase.'

'Is he, indeed?' The Provost appeared to take a moment to reflect on this before going on. 'The situation, I can only say, has the ingredients of a scandal. There is something unstable in Watershute, or at least problematical. I have very little sense of where we may presently find ourselves.'

This uncharacteristic avowal on the Provost's part was

arresting. And in fact we had both come to a halt. Before us Isis—perhaps in this reach to be called Thames once more—flowed doggedly on from Oxford's calm to London's turbulence. I wondered whether Dr Pococke was envisaging a scandal which might carry that far.

'The natural thing to suppose,' the Provost pursued, 'is that Watershute has been finding his research so absorbing that he has rather broken down on the tutorial side. There would be nothing too scandalous in that. It is, as you may imagine, something that happens from time to time. A solution of the difficulty can commonly be found. Particularly in such an instance as Watershute would afford, where there is no question but that a fuller concentration on his own work would be greatly to the advantage of his subject. The genuine advancement of knowledge comes first, after all. Of course some element of material sacrifice is sometimes involved.'

'He'd lose out on the pay packet?'

'Just so. And this, as I have said, is the natural and proper assumption for us to make, in the first instance, in Watershute's case.'

'But he has never come forward with any inquiry as to whether something might be done?'

'Not, certainly, to my knowledge. And it is the circumstance that makes me uneasy, I confess. It may almost be said that he could have a straight research post in the university for the asking. Or so I believe—although with scientists, indeed, one never quite knows.'

'Then what other explanation may there be?'

'Money difficulties. Let us remember, Duncan, that dons are extremely badly paid. If a man is careless or improvident, he can quickly get into a serious scrape. And when he glances out at the community at large, he regularly sees men of no higher calibre than himself earning in industry or commerce four or five times his own salary.'

'He can get out, I suppose, and join the happy crew.'

'Indeed he can. But he may choose to compromise—and in a manner taking us far from that conflict of reputable interests which I have touched upon. He may retain his academic appointment, while at the same time taking on all sorts of remunerative jobs in a hush-hush way on the side. I recall a distressing instance in one of the provincial universities only a few years ago. The professor of chemistry was found to be devoting almost his entire time to the routine supervision of the manufacture of useless—it may well have been harmful—patent medicines.'

'How very dismal! You must know Watershute, Edward, much better than I do. Can you see him doing something like that?'

'It would depend on the degree of his need. Say, in a general way, that behaviour of that kind—indecisive and temporizing behaviour, among other things—must depend on the pressures at work on a man. If, for example, he were in those financial straits as the consequence of disreputable courses not readily to be avowed, then his judgement and sense of responsibility might suffer—shall we say?—disorganization. And something like Watershute's picture might result.'

'David Graile—who is the man who fired the problem at me—seemed to hint at something of the kind. He called Watershute a loose fish.' It was a certain impatience that made me come out with this. 'For my own part, I just can't speculate on the thing. Scientists are a closed book to me. They come into college to do some old-fashioned teaching—listening to essays, I suppose, although heaven knows what an essay on molecular physics can be like—and then they go back to some lab or other and get on with their job. What has been happening in the Science Area so far as the wandering Watershute is concerned? I'd imagine they'd have more of an eye on him there.'

'We certainly don't require the punching of a time-clock.

As for the scientists in their enclaves, they prove to be somewhat uncommunicative at times. And about Watershute it might be inexpedient too frankly to inquire.'

'But if he vanishes from our own ken for long periods on end, it should surely be possible to discover whether he takes himself out of Oxford altogether.'

'One would suppose so.'

For perhaps fifty yards we walked on in silence. If the Provost was indisposed to further communication, I wasn't going to make any bid for it. But then why had he started in on Watershute at all? The answer came with what he must have judged to be a prudent absence of excessive concern.

'The fact is, Duncan, that I sense a good deal of criticism of the situation among, in particular, some of our younger men. They see a gross abuse on Watershute's part of his secure position as a fellow. But it would be unwise of us to over-react. Open scandal in a college, even if it be rationally shown to concern only one man, tends to rub off on those around him. And even on the whole place.'

'Then just where do we go?'

'I have it in mind that we should have a small committee. Not a committee of the Governing Body. That would simply be the road to a maximum of publicity. Something quite informal. If it were known that a representative group of responsible people were collectively addressing their minds to the matter, that might at least mute anxiety for a time. And I should much hope to prevail on you to be one of us.'

'Edward, I can hardly think of anybody less suitable.'

'You are mistaken.' The Provost glanced at me with some severity. 'You are the most senior person to have thrown in his lot with us for some time, so that you command both mature views and a fresh mind. Your presence would serve to mitigate any impression the younger men might form that what they call the dark old cabal was at work.'

'So that the thing can be quietly sat on in the hope that it blows over?' I must have been distinctly rattled to produce this odd mix-up of images. I didn't at all like the picture of myself it served to create.

'But a yet more important consideration is in my mind.' The Provost had ignored my question. 'You were of the greatest service to us, Duncan, in handling that perplexed and ill-starred affair of the Blunderville Trust. It gave me the highest opinion of your discretion. Please forgive me for being so impertinent.'

This might have been called the full treatment, and I had to cast round for some further line of defence.

'You are very kind, Provost. But that was entirely a matter of my connection with the people concerned. Of course I had to try to help. But with Watershute I have no connection whatever.'

'At least you are on a basis of neighbourly accord with his son.'

It was a moment before I realized that this was other than a jocular remark. Then I saw that the Provost had been perfectly serious—judging that even some slight link with William Watershute on the family and domestic side might be useful in coping with him as a professional problem. This time, I was even more displeased with the role seemingly envisaged for me. Nevertheless, I couldn't blankly turn the Provost down.

'Of course,' I said, 'I'll join in any discussion to which you invite me. I wouldn't think of doing anything else.'

'Thank you, my dear Duncan. I shall give thought to what can be arranged. Shall we cross over by the lock, and refresh ourselves with a glance at that singularly beautiful little church?'

Romanesque architecture was our main topic of conversation when we came to walk back to Oxford. I was left reflecting that I knew little more about Watershute than when we had set out. Were his absences from college due to a

34

devotion to abstruse research, or had they a hinterland in purely private and personal matters? If the Provost possessed either positive information or a pronounced opinion here he was in no haste to come out with it. But in this he was only running true to form.

## III

In these first weeks of my second year as a senior member of the college I gained a lively impression of the transitory character of undergraduate life. Many of the young men now surrounding me were new arrivals. Of those among whom I had been domesticated a term before, some had gone down, nearly a third had moved out of college into lodgings either near-by or remote, many of those remaining had flitted from one quad to another. Over this moving pageant time itself could be seen flowing. Although no longer schoolboys, these young men could frequently be distinguished as having added to their inches during a long vacation. It is possible that they had also matured in mind and manners and assumptions, taking on greater self-confidence as a result. Certainly they themselves believed this. With no more than three or four years between the oldest and youngest, they were more aware of seniority and juniority among themselves than were my colleagues, although these ranged in age from the early twenties to the late sixties. This feeling among undergraduates must have been a hang-over from their schooldays, when each had lived at a stiff remove from either slightly younger or slightly older boys. The barrier, at this recent period of which I write, appeared at least as pronounced as any barrier of class. Nicolas Junkin of Cokeville permitted himself in that regard an entire freedom with the Sheldrake twins, products of a major public school, while at the same time maintaining in relation to them the reserve proper in a third-year man.

The senior common room showed little effect of flux. There were a couple of new fellows: one so young that he and

Junkin might have played cricket together; the other, bald and abraded, was understood to have escaped in middle age from some professorial assignment in the antipodes. David Graile and William Watershute, returned (the latter so belatedly) from leave of absence, were other new faces so far as I was concerned. Charles Atlas had gone off to America, taking his wife along with him—which left Mabel Bedworth indisputably in the lead among the more personable college ladies. I mildly missed Mrs Atlas at the parties that ushered in the new academic year. Janet McKechnie I missed very much. The McKechnies had concluded their period in the Princeton think-tank, but would not be back in Oxford for some little time yet.

Nobody had reached a retiring-age (although Arnold Lempriere, mysteriously preserved to us, was a long way beyond it). Nobody had moved on to another job. Of traffic of that kind there was little, since departure to a formally enhanced status at some lesser university was regarded as a demotion which only the direst penury ought to bring about. The unfortunate nobleman in Hilaire Belloc's poem, sentenced by his outraged kinsman to go out and govern New South Wales, might have been judged the archetype of any wretch of this sort.

Buntingford, whose note was the cynical, was fond of quoting a couplet of Pope's as applicable to senior common room life:

> Lo, where Maeotis sleeps, and hardly flows
> The freezing Tanais thro' a waste of snows.

We didn't freeze; in fact, we were uncommonly snug. But it was at least true that our tempo was not that of the young. The college was like a motorway on which lanes are provided for fast and slow vehicles. To the undergraduates their seniors must have appeared like lumbering lorries, or ageing cars hauling caravans of learning too heavy for them: alike to be flashed past by the bright speed of Morgans and Aston-Martins. We were either this or senescent contraptions vegetating on the soft shoulder provided for those who have altogether given up the race.

On Surrey Four I continued to be intermittently involved with the life of my juniors. Junkin had departed to what was probably a very modest abode, but not without making prudent dispositions for a *pied-à-terre* in college. This was a common practice among those moving into digs. In one's last term in college one cultivated some appropriate junior man, favouring him thereafter with a good deal of one's company, as also with one's gown, books, sports' gear and general impedimenta, to say nothing of drawing freely upon his electric fire and kettle. Junkin had noted my possession of a useless room, the same in which it had long ago pleased Henry Tindale, the White Rabbit, to study from his bed next door the graces of belated young men tumbling into college through the window. Junkin had taken over this room, to which he came and went with a decent unobtrusiveness. It was perhaps unusual to arrive at such an arrangement with a don. But Junkin's theatrical activities had by now made him a person eminent in the university, so licence might fairly be allowed him. It was only once or twice a week that he would burst into my sitting-room, dispose himself on the sofa, and politely inquire 'I say, are you fearfully busy?' as a preliminary to accepting drink and conversation.

My relationship with Junkin was so easy as to appear to stand in no need of analysis, yet its elements were not entirely simple. Our first meeting had been in circumstances making for intimacy, involving us as it had done in the joint muscular effort of lowering a young woman through a bedroom window into Long Field. The incident, although morally blameless, had been of an undergraduate order, and our companionship remained tinged by the exploit. We had elected each other as friends with much the same speed as Tony Mumford and I had done on the same staircase a quarter of a century before. But our ages were such that the association embodied to some extent a father-and-son component, although on Junkin's part there may have been no great awareness of this. As Giles Watershute knew, Junkin had a perfectly good father already—who had lately surfaced to poorer pay (as Junkin explained to me) after labouring for most of his working days at the coal face of his Yorkshire mine.

The easiness of the Junkin connection was the more grateful in that I was aware of less simple acquaintanceships looming on Surrey Four. As Nick had done, Giles felt the germ of a special relationship to inhere in the fact that he now occupied what had once been my own rooms. He was an able and attractive boy, and any cautiousness I felt about him had to be laid at the Provost's door. If his father were really to prove seriously at odds with the college, an older man in his own confidence might be useful to him. But it ought not to be one who had been called into some inner circle of persons deliberating on the matter. I felt this more strongly, I believe, than the present quite vague state of the case warranted.

The Sheldrake twins were another story. Mark Sheldrake, since he continued quartered in Ivo Mumford's former rooms directly above my own, was of daily appearance. Moreover, he and his brother Matthew, alienated from one another the term before but reconciled, were much in one another's pockets, and spent a good deal of time in each other's rooms.

A single long vacation had dealt strangely with the Sheldrakes, and in a fashion instancing that swift mutability of early life. They had gone away as youths so transcendently beautiful that it had been almost embarrassing to look at them, as if one feared that one's glance might linger in a manner only to be licenced before, say, a Phidian marble or a drawing by Michelangelo. They returned with their divinity shed, and simply as two good-looking boys whose chief attractiveness lay in a disposition to break into friendly and cheerful smiles. This last was a marked transformation, since in their demigod days they had been as aloof as their good manners allowed. Whether or not they were aware of themselves as beings from whom a burden had been lifted I don't know. I was chiefly conscious of their being cordially disposed to me. Quite early in the term I found myself in Mark's rooms and in the company of both of them.

I suppose that this, and several subsequent occasions of the same sort, could be regarded as odd. The brothers had quarrelled because my former wife had amused herself by adopting deplorable means to make them do so; each of them had been in bed with Penny, and this, I believed, with all the momentousness attending sexual initiation. They may have decided that I had been useful in returning them to good sense, but, even so, it might well have been their instinct discreetly to close our account. Yet here we were, all three, rather like men reunited after having long ago escaped from the same prison camp: conscious of a common bond, but not at all disposed to go back over unpleasant experiences. Perhaps the Sheldrakes, although they gave no hint of anything of the sort and talked to me only as a conversable senior man, were getting a certain satisfaction out of feeling seasoned and adult. We talked about cricket (although it was the wrong time of year) and about the theatre. Later on—and this was a great advance in intimacy—they told me about their parents and sisters and dogs.

I made another undergraduate acquaintance at this time—or, rather, he made mine. It happened one morning over breakfast, a meal which I had persuaded Plot, still the scout on Surrey Four, to turn on in my own rooms. The door opened after a perfunctory knock, and a young man stood revealed.

'Professor Pattullo,' the young man said. He spoke with a distinct suggestion of menace, much as if I had been an elusive and socially undesirable character whom he had run triumphantly to earth.

'I'm not a professor. I suppose you've seen my name over the door.'

'Exactly. My name is Chaffey. Boswell Chaffey. Boz. I'm the Press.'

'How do you do?' This dim civility was the best I could manage at the moment. As a mere appearance Chaffey was familiar to me. He was an undergraduate who occupied, two above me and one above Mark Sheldrake, the rooms long ago belonging to my Australian friend Martin Fish. Physically. Chaffey was so large every way that he everywhere collided with the framework of the door. My first impression was simply of his taking up far more space than was reasonable.

'And I'm in luck,' Chaffey said. 'I mean, your being free for interview. May I sit down?'

Chaffey had already sat down. This, although reminiscent of the imperfect synchronizations frequently exhibited by Junkin, was of different effect. I decided I mustn't instantly snub Boswell Chaffey. He was a boy, I told myself, harmlessly inhabiting some fantasy world.

'Is it *Isis*,' I asked, 'or is it *Cherwell*?' The zeal exhibited by undergraduate reporters was one of the minor nuisances of life. They would appear, often carrying tape-recorders and accompanied by stenographically-accomplished pretty girls or by amateur photographers, several times a term. But I hadn't hitherto known such a visitation unheralded in writing.

'*Isis*? That's kids' stuff,' Chaffey said with professional scorn. 'I'm starting an agency, as a matter of fact. Chiefly for the English national dailies. But I intend to syndicate a good deal in America. I intend to go over there and fix things up in the Christmas vac. Your father was an artist, wasn't he?' The young man had briskly produced a notebook. 'And quite well known in his time?'

'Yes—and I suppose so. Can I lend you a pencil?' My inquisitor had been fumbling in a pocket.

'Thanks a lot. But I've got one.' Having located this instrument of his craft, Chaffey made a tick in the notebook, thereby presumably confirming my father's artistic standing. 'And your mother's name was Glengarry.'

'Glencorry.'

'That's what I said. Who did your father try to paint like? What important artist, I mean.'

'A difficult question. As a young man, he was a great admirer of Monet.'

'A great admirer of Manet.' Chaffey wrote this down. 'Have you any brothers and sisters?'

'I have one brother. He's a judge.'

'Would you say he makes more than you do?'

'I am afraid the emoluments of his office are unknown to me.'

'Emoluments.' Chaffey appeared to transcribe this word phonetically, and then to scrutinize it with disfavour. 'I wasn't asking about his office,' he said. 'I suppose it's in some sort of law-court. I was asking about his screw. But never mind. What about favourite books? Do you read detective stories? Do you think there ought to be pornography? Have you ever been prosecuted over anything of that sort in your plays? The public likes to hear about that kind of thing.'

'No doubt. But, Mr Chaffey, I'm afraid I simply don't feel confessional at breakfast-time, and we're getting into a false position. If you really want to interview me, please fix an appointment beforehand. And it mightn't be a bad idea to

42

give the occasion a little preliminary thought. Getting your questions into some sort of coherent order, for example.'

'Oh, but that doesn't matter a bit. One always changes everything round. Before printing, I mean, and just as they do on radio and TV. An article or a programme can be made much more interesting that way. Even somebody quite dull can be livened up. It's an art.'

'Would you care for a cup of coffee?' It seemed to me that Chaffey, although talking rubbish, was taking my refusal to play fairly well. Moreover, he was a close neighbour, and seemed to own a mild eccentricity which might repay study. With this thought in mind, I had picked up the coffee-pot.

'I don't mind if I do,' Chaffey said handsomely. 'The stuff they give you in hall is pretty foul, as a matter of fact. I've been thinking of doing a piece on that.'

'Do you suppose it would be of general interest—in the national press, as you say? I'm not sure I wouldn't skip it myself.'

'Oh, but it depends on the write-up.' Chaffey didn't seem discouraged by my rather bleak remark. 'I expect you've found that with your plays. A crack falls entirely flat because you haven't known how to give it the right twist. Then somebody comes along and says "Just shift those words round in a way they don't commonly come". Something of that sort. And you do it, and you get your laugh.'

'Just so.' I didn't feel I need be offended by this simplistic view of dramatic composition—particularly as Boswell Chaffey didn't seem at all easily offended himself. 'Do you intend to make journalism your career?' I asked.

'Yes—but chiefly in the way of organizing things. My agency is going to have tentacles all over the place. That's why I'm proposing to get activities going in the States quite soon, as I explained.'

'Have you many connections there?'

'Well, not just at present. I'm planning to collect a bunch

of introductions from the Provost, as a matter of fact. He'll know everybody, don't you think?'

I found no reply to this question, and reflected on the extraordinary notions that undergraduates can form on the structure of things in general. I also felt some curiosity as to how Edward Pococke would receive so ill-judged an application. And Chaffey seemed to interpret my silence as conveying mild stricture.

'Of course,' he said, 'I know one has to begin in a thoroughly modest way. I've got to take a rattling good First in Schools. I'm setting aside a little time for that. Then the road's clear right ahead.'

'And meanwhile you supply Fleet Street with newsy bits about Oxford life?'

'Just that—and particularly about this college. It's got cachet, you know. A college can have cachet, just as a restaurant or a boutique can have chic. It was a bit of luck, really, my getting into this particular place.'

'It was, indeed.'

'But while the agency is finding its feet I have some other plans as well. You can't get all that way on social stuff. That's a wench's stamping-ground chiefly. I'd say the next step is investigative journalism. That's something entirely new.'

'I'd rather doubt it's being exactly that, Mr Chaffey.'

'It's entirely new.' It was rather magnificently that Boz swept aside my qualifying word. 'And one can make a name at it in no time. A single big scoop, and you're home and dry. Well, thanks a lot for the caf. I'll be contacting you.' And Boswell Chaffey got massively to his feet. 'I've got to see a don in another college. He's been had up for drunk in charge.'

'He'll be looking forward to your call.'

'Yes, of course. People just love to get into the news: dons, boxers, disc-jockeys, playwrights like yourself. It makes no odds. Mind you, tact is required. I never lose sight of that. See you, then.'

With this the ace reporter departed, and I thought no more about him. It was one of the attractions of the possibly stagnant waters of academic life that odd fish bobbed up in them plentifully enough. And that Chaffey could conceivably be a menace didn't enter my head.

# IV

Aᴛ ᴛʜɪꜱ ᴛɪᴍᴇ I had got back to believing that I very
seldom thought about Penny. Her shocking affair with the
Sheldrakes was now a thing of the past—even if of the fairly
recent past—and I had no occasion to burden myself with the
memory of her. This had been my settled attitude ever since
our divorce, and I believe it never occurred to me that I'd
have done better to face up to that past from time to time:
even again to pick up, as it were, those binoculars with
which, perched on the *Piccolo Gallo*, I'd discovered myself
married to a woman for whom sexual pleasure was enhanced
by the inflicting of sexual humiliation. That I'd swept all
this unadvisedly under the mat was perhaps instanced in
my having unconcernedly taken over, upon my return to
college, the former rooms of Henry Tindale, the humiliated
party.

It was Fiona who tackled me on this. Although she had
declared herself interested only in the broader outlines of my
intimate life she had in fact picked up more of it than that.
She may be said to have briskly inquired, and then briskly
concluded.

'The truth is, Duncan, that you've been ducking yourself.
Squandering a decade of your life on tepid episodes with tepid
women.'

'I'd call that a summary on the severe side. But, in any case,
it's over and done with. Are you and I going to be tepid,
Fiona?'

'You were badly traumatized.' Fiona's only reply to my
demand had been the swift and misdoubting look that,
nowadays, I detected in her from time to time.

'That's just a silly vogue word.'

'It's a vogue word, if you like, but it's also a real thing. Your marriage ended in that shocking mess. And you sat on its head and went all controlled and reticent about it when you'd have done far better to treat yourself to a jumbo-size freak-out. The result is that you're scared of sex to this day, and have to tag after . . . after safely inaccessible females.'

'Good God!'

'Yes—like that old flame of yours, Janet McKechnie, who's a completely married woman if ever there was one. And college ladies at their stupid sherry parties. And heaven knows who else. A kind of erotic shadow-boxer—that's you.'

We held extraordinary conversations like this, and there was something about them that I didn't understand in the least. It was true we never kept it up for long. Our encounters were for the most part of a rational and mildly affectionate sort. But then again there would be silences in which I caught my cousin glancing at me wide-eyed—much as if she'd never been confronted with a man before. It was coming to me uncomfortably that her own inaccessibility (if it existed) might be connected with the character of the *ménage* in the Woodstock Road. I'd never believed that Fiona and Margaret Mountain, although obviously fond of one another, were fixated in a relationship of an irregular sort. But J. B. Timbermill had believed it. And hadn't Timbermill been— and increasingly so at the time of his death—a seer preternaturally endowed? I could remember telling somebody— perhaps Timbermill himself—that I didn't care twopence what these young women might have been up to. But that had been no more than modish permissiveness—and no doubt belonged with the chronic sex-funk Fiona had been attributing to me. I'd never thought of myself that way, but perhaps she was right. At least it was true that in that region I was a burnt child who dreaded fire. Penny had scorched me;

perhaps I'd appealed to her as abnormally scorchable; perhaps I had a constitutional vulnerability of that kind. Hadn't I called out to Martin Fish—in our hotel bedroom in Ravello—to stop quoting Lawrence on awful experiences of women? I can't have soberly believed that I was preparing for myself any awful experience with Fiona. All the same, I was nervous. If I hadn't been, Timbermill's implausible persuasion couldn't have returned to my head.

'Duncan,' Fiona continued on this occasion, 'you ought to be married. You ought to be married and with kids. Why not?'

'If that's meant as advice, it's not exactly novel. Cyril Bedworth offered it to me a year ago on the very first occasion that I sat down to eat a dinner at high table.'

'Didn't you want Penny to bear you children?'

'Yes, I did—rather powerfully.'

'You were damned lucky she didn't.' Fiona snapped this out with unaccustomed passion. 'But you were clear of the hazard a dozen years back, and have been fooling around ever since. Getting deeper and deeper. There you were, at least out in the world, and with women liking you who can't all have been imbeciles or tarts. And what do you do?'

'Bolt into a monastery.'

'Just that. And you don't even choose a college that's gone rationally co-residential—with women around at last, even at high table. You ought to be giving a close look at half-a-dozen such. Ten years younger than yourself: not more, not less. Well short of the menopause, that is, and fit to bring you, say, a boy and a couple of girls.'

'Thank you very much. Now they're married we wish them joy.'

'Exactly. But what do you actually do? Waste quite a bit of time, I gather, chatting up young men who'll have forgotten all about you six months after they go down.'

'So they will.'

48

'It's almost as if you were like that feeble creature you say had these rooms once, or that funny old fuddy-duddy Lempriere. You're not, are you?'

'I've got no excuse in that direction at all. You know well enough that I'm susceptible quite fondly to female charm.'

'Then haven't you any desire left to get into bed with a woman?'

'Oh, shut up, Fiona—there's a good girl. You talk quite a lot of sense about me, as a matter of fact, and I'm duly grateful. But enough is enough.'

'For the moment,' Fiona said.

This episode (or rather my handling of it—for hadn't it offered me the basis for a show-down with Fiona?) was not encouraging. I had been indicted of measuring out my life with coffee spoons—and this with sufficient justice for the accusation to sting. And it wasn't just in the sphere with which Fiona had been dealing. In the Victorian age elderly clergymen, if unmarried, sometimes 'retired upon a fellow-ship'—meaning that they retreated into their old college and did nothing but a very little teaching and even less preaching for the rest of their days. It now seemed to me that I'd done something like this myself: breaking my career in two, and for the obscurest reasons bolting into what Fiona had agreed to call a monastery. Here I was, pretending to be a scholar who might still in his spare time divert himself with his pen.

These and similar reflections (which did me little credit) set me prowling round the room as soon as Fiona had left me. I found myself coming to a halt before *Young Picts* above the chimneypiece. Surely, I asked myself, those delicate washes were fading? The water-colour was never exposed to direct sunlight, but ought it not perhaps to live in darkness except during a few winter months? Hadn't the Turner water-colours in Edinburgh been treated like that? I seemed to remember that as a schoolboy I'd been able to wander among them only at such a season.

But *Young Picts* was as it had always been—alive with its own light. It was merely that my room was more crepuscular than I'd noticed. Surrey on a November late afternoon could be a dusky place; a shadowed stony box, frowning and magnificent, from which there was no escape except through tunnels and round corners. I was telling myself (in this dismal mood) that I disliked it heartily, when I was returned to reason by a knock on the door. I called to come in.

My visitor entered and paused by a window, so that for a moment he was the best-lit object in the room. I saw a stringy man of about my own age, bronzed in a manner that didn't suggest England, dressed in a manner that did.

'Duncan!' this person said. There was a fractional silence, since I was quite at sea. 'You don't recognize me, but you do remember me. I'm Martin Fish.'

'Martin—glory, glory!'

'I heard about what you'd taken to. I thought I'd just drop in.'

'You've come to dinner?'

'If it's going.' Fish smiled at me cheerfully—entirely the man I'd known (when in his right mind) on this staircase long ago. Nobody could have looked less like one prone to hysterical performances following girl-trouble.

'Of course it is! And you're going to be here for some time?'

'I'm in a motel beyond North Oxford for a few nights. Just to look round and see the sights. But I'm going to be quartered in London for several weeks.'

'Excellent news.' As I said this I went over to the telephone, since I'd have to talk tactfully to the college chef. 'Have you business concerns over here?'

'Cultural.' Fish allowed himself an inflection of mild irony. 'One can't spend all one's days with silly sheep.'

'I suppose not. But didn't you read Maths, and quite shine at it? You haven't become a professor of the stuff?'

'No such luck. I'm just what we're fond of calling a leading citizen—which is an odd way of describing a chap who lives hundreds of miles from any city. But I've been seeing a lot of urban life just lately. It goes along with buying pictures.'

'Ah! I always knew the Fishes swam in gold.'

'It's not quite that. I consult with people about buying things for a national collection. I say, Duncan, this is scarcely real, is it? Twenty-five years! And I've never given you a thought, you know. Or pretty well that.'

'No more have I to you.' I made my telephone call. 'We'll be entirely awkward with one another. That's inevitable.'

'So it is. But we can swop histories.'

'So we can. Do sit down. It's not too early for a drink.'

'Not a bit.'

'A sundowner.'

'That's South African. In Australia a sundowner's a tramp who arrives on you for the night. I'm not quite doing that. I say! One doesn't know where to begin. Who's dead? Mrs Triplett, I suppose?'

'Heavens, yes! They've knocked her house down and built a college.'

'That tennis court?'

'Probably turned into a ornamental pool with shubunkin. But I don't know. I've never been near the place. Shall I try to do a martini?'

'Yes, please. Bonzer, that will be.'

'Don't be idiotic, Martin.' I mixed the drink and wondered where we were going to get to, now or later in the evening. It was true that we knew literally nothing about each other's histories. I might ask casually, 'Did you ever come across that girl Martine again?' and find that I'd said the wrong thing. Fish might similarly come out with, 'By the way, have you any idea of what happened to Penny Triplett?' and a similar situation would result.

I sipped my martini and saw that this was to get the matter muddled. Tony Mumford had been my principal crony as an undergraduate, but it was with Fish that I had finally become much more an intimate—this because he and I had shared experiences, shattering at the time, of a sort that Tony certainly hadn't yet run across. (Perhaps, indeed, he was never to do so.) And this had established something for keeps between Fish and myself. There was no help for it. If we were to talk about ourselves each to the other at all, we'd have to try to tell the truth. And that, of course, is difficult in any circumstances whatever—solitary communion by no means excepted.

'Well,' Fish said, 'for a start take that tennis party. Have you any idea of what happened to Penny Triplett?'

'And now,' I said half-an-hour later, 'there's somebody else I'm coming to think I want to marry.'

'Good man, Duncan. Tell me.'

'She's called Fiona Petrie. She's a cousin of mine—but the sort of cousin who's a generation younger than oneself.'

'What they call once removed? You want to marry a girl young enough to be your daughter?'

'Yes. And it's whose daughter she really is that's rather funny. My cousin Anna Glencorry.'

'Why should that be funny, Duncan? If this Fiona is your first cousin once removed she has to be some cousin's child.'

'You're not remembering, Martin.'

'Yes, I am!' Fish spoke rapidly, and his eyes had widened on me. 'You wanted to marry your cousin Anna. Or rather you didn't. It was because she was pregnant, and . . .'

'Martin, you're a marvel—and one of the two people I've ever told the story to.'

'She was pregnant, and there didn't seem to be a father even in the offing. So you offered to stand in as one. You must have been about sixteen.'

'Eighteen—just.'

'Then the real father turned up and made your cousin an honest woman. His name was Petrie?'

'His name is Petrie. And Fiona was the unborn child in the story.'

'I admit that *does* deserve to be called funny.' Fish showed no appearance of actually being amused. 'Not, I suppose, *too* funny. If you waited another generation it might be that. There's a novel about it.'

'All right, Martin. *The Well-Beloved.* About a man who pays court to a girl, and has to confess he did the same thing to both her mother and her grandmother. Not a very good novel.'

'And not even a very good cautionary tale? Who's the other person you've told the story to? This Fiona herself?'

'Heavens, no! Janet.'

'Janet?' This time, Fish had to frown in an effort of recollection. 'The girl who married the fisher-lad?'

'Yes. The fisher-lad got himself drowned, and their sons with him. Janet is now married to a professor—here in Oxford. They're on their way back from America at this moment, as a matter of fact.'

'I see.' Fish looked at me steadily. 'The Janet thing was serious, wasn't it?'

'Quite quite serious.'

'And stuck?'

'And stuck.'

'I expect that while you were married to Penny you did rather a lot of thinking about Janet from time to time.'

'Yes, I did. I expect there would have been a decent girl you'd have thought of from time to time, Martin, if you'd had the ill luck to marry that awful Martine instead of just being driven briefly dotty by her.'

'I got off lightly, all right. And now it's about my turn to bring things up to date. But one thing first. You see quite a lot of Janet now that you're both in Oxford?'

'Yes, of course.'

'How does it make you feel?'

' "Muddled" would be the hard word for it. Or *fainéant*, perhaps.'

'Stick to English. Is Janet in a muddle too?'

'No.' I produced this instantly, and without bothering about Fish's thus accepting my estimate of myself. 'Absolutely not.'

'Then it must be all right, mustn't it?'

'I suppose so.'

'Duncan, you haven't thought up this Fiona Petrie for the same reason that you thought up Penny Triplett—to distance the unattainable Janet?'

'It may be a facet of the thing, but it doesn't appear to be how I see it. Fiona's quite a different affair. The appeal is different.'

'The appeal of a fresh young thing who's kittle and elusive?'

My only reply was to pour Fish another drink, and then I made him tell me about himself. I can't have recalled him other than as a reticent young man—reticent even when in the kind of torment in which I had first encountered him. During our wanderings in Italy he had got to know rather more about me than he had cared to confide in return. On this occasion he went full shares at once. Shadows of one sort and another had fallen across his path. But the chief accent, although he didn't obtrude it, appeared to be upon almost untroubled domestic felicity. His wife and two children were in England with him. I surprised myself by listening with more pleasure than envy to this recital. And it wasn't that I had a beautiful nature. It was simply that Penny and Martine, neither of them estimable persons, had indeed bound Martin Fish and myself together in a notable way. Yet we had allowed twelve thousand miles, or thirty hours in air, to sever all connection between us for a major span in both our lives.

'Would you like to wear a gown?' I asked at the end of all this. 'The butler can lend you one.'

'Bonzer, again. But—I say, you know!—most of your colleagues will be total strangers to me. Who's still around that I know? The Provost, of course. But he won't remember me.'

'You can bet he will. And his wife, too, if you have the grace to pay a call on her. And then—let me see—there's Cyril Bedworth. He's Senior Tutor.'

'Good Lord! He once walked me round Long Field, and tried to persuade me that I could alleviate my pathologically love-lorn condition by reflecting on the life of John Keats. Christ! How time distances things one felt were with one for good, Duncan.'

'Not quite everything, Martin. Then—let me see—there's Damian—Robert Damian. He practises in North Oxford. But he's also the college doctor, and dines quite often.'

'His plan—didn't you tell me?—was for dropping me down trap-doors to the accompaniment of loud noises. He'd been mugging up some crackpot behaviourist.'

'No, no—that was an opinionated amateur called Badgery. Damian was for electric shocks.'

'There's somebody else,' Fish said suddenly. 'Only I don't think you knew him back in those days. He must have gone down just before you came up—and returned to the college, just like yourself, after a longish interval. I remember noticing the appointment in the university news in *The Times*. We do get *The Times*, you know. It takes a day to reach Sydney, and two more to reach Wangarra.'

'Wangarra?'

'That's where the sheep are. A scientist called Watershute, who seems to have become quite a swell. Will he be around?'

'It's possible. Watershute comes and goes. He has a son called Giles, who's in residence now. Giles has my old rooms, as it happens, on the floor above this.'

'More *tempora mutantur* stuff.' Fish glanced around him. 'Didn't these present rooms of yours belong to an odd character called Tindale?'

'Yes, they did.' I hadn't mentioned Tindale's name in giving Fish an account of my past fortunes. 'Tindale died a few years ago. He entered a lay order of some sort, and ended his days in a kind of monkery.'

'He went in for popes and people.'

'Pope Zosimus.'

'That's right.' Fish appeared to feel that here lay the explanation of the White Rabbit's final choice of a way of life. 'But about Bill Watershute. I hope I'll meet him. We were quite intimate for a time, although I was much his junior in the college. As a matter of fact, I believe I had a glimpse of him not long ago. It was in Venice. I was stalking a Carpaccio, believed still to be in private hands there. But Watershute seemed to be stalking——' Oddly, Fish had broken off. Oddly, too, I remembered how I had been used to think of him as one of the miraculous youths who never put a foot wrong. 'Did you say Watershute has a son—a grown-up son?'

'Yes.'

'*Tempus edax*, again. I suppose Venice isn't a bad place to meditate that theme. But about the Carpaccio. I'd taken it into my head that the picture was his lost *View of Jerusalem*. There's a theory that its existence suggests that he'd been there. But it's my guess that it was a purely fantastic thing, a *veduta ideata*, like those urban backgrounds in the cycle for the Scuola di S. Stefano. Duncan, you must find it rather funny

56

that I turn up as a prosperous antipodean, prowling Europe for artistic loot, like that chap in Henry James.'

'I don't find it a bit funny. You always liked pictures. Have you still got that Sidney Nolan?'

'Yes, of course—and several others as well. Incidentally, I've got two of your father's pictures, and put several more into galleries. How do you find it, Duncan, having had a father who was a greater painter than you may ever quite become a playwright?'

'Not crushing, Martin. Chastening, of course. No harm in that. By the way, just how did you have that glimpse of Watershute in Venice?' I had marked how Fish shied away from this.

'It was in the Gritti Palace Hotel, as a matter of fact.'

'Well, well!'

'Yes—not my kind of pad. I happened to have one of our Ministers with me. They rather fancy commanding the best, and it's something to find one prepared to interest himself in the arts at all. New men, most of them, as you can imagine.'

This was the patrician Fish that I remembered. He would have been as chary of using class-slanted words as my Uncle Rory himself—who would have regarded 'gentlemen', for instance, as proper only over the entrance to a public lavatory. But Fish did sometimes yield to the temptation to assert that, socially as physically, his native country was not the un-yielding desert that some might suppose. His earlier account of himself had included the information, more or less humorously proffered, that he had married 'the girl next door' —the point of the joke being, I imagined, that 'next door' in his case meant three or four hundred miles away, there being no fellow-pastoralist's daughter nearer at hand than that. I was curious about life amid such vast spaces, but more curious—just at the moment—to learn a little more about William Watershute and the most luxurious hotel in Venice.

But further interest in this might appear out of the way unless I preluded it by confidence. And although Fish and I might have been said to be going in for confidences like mad, they had been our own confidences and not other people's. I wasn't entitled to tell Fish about the college's problem over its intermittently absentee fellow. But Venice remained in my head, and prompted my next utterance.

'Martin, isn't Venice rather a watery spot for you to be disporting yourself in?'

This was quite as frank as Fish's question about my attitude to my father's fame, and Fish received it with his own frankest smile.

'Do you know, Duncan, all that's just the same? *Not* diminished by time—not in any degree. If I was chucked into a horse-pond I'd still be in a blind panic. But of course nobody *does* ever chuck me into anything of the kind, so it doesn't affect my life in the slightest. It does affect my sons' lives. I've seen to it that they're the two best swimmers in their school.'

I glanced at my watch and saw that this must be, on the present occasion, our last nostalgic exchange. It had been a fairly notable one. There couldn't surely be another man in the world to whom I could recall anything like what I had been recalling here. For it was almost true that the first direct glance I'd ever received from Fish had been one of blind terror from just above the muddy sluggish surface of the Cherwell.

'Out, out!' I said—this having been the prescriptive manner in which our contemporaries had roused one another to action. 'If we go over now, I can introduce you to some of the dons before dinner. And the chef has prepared a fatted calf for the prodigal sheep.'

This idiotic remark—which may or may not have caught a note of innocent babble from long ago—took us out into Surrey. There was a skim of autumnal vapour, like very shallow water, over the grass, and beyond it the library loomed monstrously huge, like a stranded whale. Young men had not yet begun strolling towards the buttery and hall, and the quad seemed quite deserted. Immediately above our heads, somebody—it must have been Mark Sheldrake—was playing the piano; with a commendable striving towards perfection he was putting much *brio* into banging out the same chords again and again.

'Do you remember,' Fish asked, 'that chap who played the 'cello—or rather who couldn't play it?'

'Gavin Mogridge.'

'That's right. He became a great traveller, didn't he, and wrote an astonishing book?'

'*Mochica*. Yes, indeed. And he believed in the virtues of travel already. He judged it more efficacious in the event of nervous distress than no end of electric shocks. I'm not sure he didn't set you and me on our road to Italy.'

'Good on Mogridge! Do you ever see him?'

'I've run across him once. It was at the summer Gaudy a couple of years ago. He behaved as if we'd had dinner together the night before. I don't think he turns up very frequently at other times.'

We were now in the Great Quadrangle. The moon, as had been its punctual habit during the past few nights, was putting on its turn through the criss-cross of scaffolding where the tower had been. It was a waning moon, as if the prisoner were being under-dieted behind his bars. Fish paused to study this appearance.

'It takes a little getting used to,' he said.

'All is going to be as before. There isn't even a money problem. We sold a Piero della Francesca.'

'Pretty drastic, that. I heard about it.'

'But probably not the whole story. It was made off with by a mad cleric. And professional thieves had a go at it after that, and were foiled by a boy called Peter Lusby who's a freshman

59

in the college now. For various reasons we're rather keeping our fingers crossed about him, but he's said to be making do very well. There's a small history there that I'll tell you all about later.'

'Plenty of yarns for one another still,' Fish said contentedly.

# V

It LOOKED LIKE being a small night. There were no more than a dozen men standing about common room waiting to go in to dinner. The less abstemious were sipping sherry— by custom the only drink on offer at this hour. The more expansive were conversing. One or two shy or reserved persons were bending over newspapers, affecting more interest in them than they actually felt. There were also two or three strangers: probably old members who had taken it into their head to exercise the privilege of dining at high table without ensuring that there would be somebody present who knew something about them. The comforting of such people was the responsibility of Arnold Lempriere, who held a species of presidential office in common room. But Lempriere hadn't turned up, and would probably not do so. This part of the day had been his life for half-a-century, but he was no longer regularly up to it. Everybody realized the fact as revealing that Lempriere was failing fast. So these unknown guests stood awkwardly in corners until somebody else had the gumption to tackle them.

At the far end of the big room the little tables were ranged in a semicircle before the fireplace, with the wine-railway in front of them. Dessert was already deployed on the polished surfaces. A young lecturer whom I had noticed as going in for *outré* behaviour was prowling among them eating almonds and raisins. The butler wasn't watching this performance disapprovingly only because it had caused him to raise his eyes in agony towards the heavens.

A bell clanged briefly outside, intimating that in the college chapel evensong was over, and that anybody who had thought to attend it was now free to think of dinner. From hall, although it lay at some remove, one could hear the voices of assembled undergraduates. They would be talking to one another at a casual leisure as they lounged beside the long tables, but from here the effect of these exchanges was of a muted rapid chattering in some foreign tongue.

The Provost entered the room in a hurry, as if fearful that he might be discourteously late. Rapid motion contrived to impart to his gown the billowing amplitude aimed at by eighteenth-century portrait-painters when commemorating the higher ecclesiastical, judicial, and academic classes. I might have offered this thought to Fish as a connoisseur in such matters, had the Provost not recognized my guest at a glance and come straight over to us. Fish was properly impressed by so regal a feat of memory, and as it relieved me of any need to perform an introduction I looked round about me once more. Thus engaged, my eye happened to go to one of the strangers whose isolation I saw had not yet been relieved. He was standing in a shadowy corner of the room, and appeared to be staring fixedly through round spectacles at a spot near the ceiling. I had just put this down to a continued embarrassment discreditable to his hosts, when I was astounded to realize that I was in fact looking at Mogridge. And Mogridge was looking at me. He had been doing so, and in a relaxed manner, when I had been presuming otherwise—my mistake being occasioned by the ocular peculiarity he had always exhibited. And now he walked across the room to me just as I was rejoined by Fish, who had no doubt been bidden to place himself beside the Provost at high table.

'Hullo, Duncan,' Mogridge said vaguely and as if through some mild abstraction. 'Oh, hullo, Martin. Do you know? They say it's going to rain like anything. I'll have to borrow an umbrella if it rains like that. You can get extremely wet in heavy rain. If you haven't an umbrella or something, that is.'

Here in a very quintessence was what I thought of as the original Mogridge. That any other Mogridge (except, indeed, the inspired author of *Mochica*) existed was a fact unknown to any soul in the college except myself. Ivo Mumford had known—at least to the extent of conjecturing that Mogridge must be a member of the Royal Family—but Ivo had departed from us. Mine was the sole knowledge of the true Secret Service Boy. I felt, quite irrationally, that this constituted an unnerving responsibility.

'I suppose you still live in Australia?' Mogridge was saying to Fish in a more or less absent-minded way. 'It's quite a step to Australia. Australia really is quite a step.' Mogridge's eye glinted briefly towards the Tompion clock standing against a neighbouring wall—which in fact meant that it was glinting at me. It was as if he were murmuring, 'Duncan, just how far can I go?' 'Yes,' he went on, 'quite a step. Do you know the mustering camp at Deception Creek?'

'It's on my land.'

'That's very interesting. It's very interesting that you should own Deception Creek, Martin. I was nearly bitten by a camel there. One should avoid being bitten by a camel. I went north of that once—through the Macdonnell Range, in fact—but it was a bit too late for much of the real thing. The Western Aranda honey-ant ceremony—that was good. And the bandicoot actors with their *tnatantja*-pole. They're the ones up in the North, I think.'

'So they are.' Fish was pleased with these reminiscences, and I took this to mean that Mogridge knew his stuff. 'You must come out again and take another look round. Before quite everything of that sort passes away. You must come and stay at Wangarra. That's my house. It would be a good centre for months of exploring the whole region. Won't you, Gavin? And write a book about it. I'd love you to.'

This, as it came from Fish, didn't sound falsely expansive. He was really delighted at the idea of entertaining the eminent

63

traveller on a generous scale. The situation made me feel uncomfortable. Mogridge's travels had long since ceased to be more than a cover for other activities. Or at least it seemed to be nearly that, although he did produce not particularly distinguished books occasionally. These, for all I knew, were ghosted—Mogridge's time being regarded in high quarters as too valuable to be expended on cooking them up. The paradox inherent in an honourable man's consistently leading a double life which he was obliged to conceal even from his intimates struck me forcibly and not particularly agreeably, just as it had done on first being revealed to the senior Mumfords and myself when Ivo's crisis had blown in on us at the Gaudy. Here, for instance, was something that I'd have to conceal from Fish. And—unlike the Watershute business—it didn't concern a man to whom I was indifferent, but somebody whom I counted among my friends.

'It seems to be good luck meeting you tonight,' Fish was saying. 'Because Duncan says you don't turn up very often.'

'Well, no. That's true.' I saw that Mogridge was embarking on one of his most tautologous flights. 'There's some arrangement about M.A.s being allowed to come in and dine with the dons. Up to so many times a term, or something like that. Yes, so many times a term one can turn up if one wants to. But it wouldn't be quite the thing to take one's full whack. Even although one gets a bill for it, you know. Yes, there's a bill.'

'So I'd suppose.'

'But just for this term—or a bit longer, it might be—I've been put on a different basis. The Provost very kindly fixed it up with some committee. What's called, it seems, being made a temporary member of common room. When you're made a temporary member of common room you can drop in to lunch or dine and so on as you please. It's going to be awfully convenient. I'm mugging up, you see. I'm mugging up some history and anthropology before going off again.

64

I'll tell you all about it after dinner. It's a frightfully interesting project, and I'd like to explain it. But the point is that one capital place for this particular material is an Institute out on the Banbury Road. You probably know the Institute on the Banbury Road. I'll be dropping in and out of there a good deal.'

'*Dinner is served!*'

It was with some relief that I heard the butler make this announcement. Mogridge's conversational mode, although a certain nostalgic fondness attended my memories of it, took a little readapting to.

But now as we moved into hall he drifted away from me as casually as he had drifted up, and presently I saw him take his place beside Bedworth at a far end of the table. Here, too, he gave the appearance of labouring under a mild and chronic absence of mind, so that I wondered under what circumstances, if any, he was likely to be observed as acting in a purposeful manner. Perhaps he would do so when prompted to gate-crash a honey-ant ceremony among the Western Aranda of Central Australia. I wondered, too, whether it would be possible to contrive a situation in which he would show himself perturbed. My most devastating remarks long ago on his inability to play his 'cello in tune had certainly had no such consequence—nor had even that (to me) embarrassing occasion when I had opened the wrong cupboard in his room and disclosed his sacred books: Biggles and T. E. Lawrence, Allan Quartermain and Richard Hannay, and Sir Percy Blakeney the Scarlet Pimpernel.

Since the period of that almost juvenile episode—now at so substantial a remove—my only direct encounter with Mogridge had been on the night in which I had been peripherally concerned with his brisk rescuing of Ivo Mumford from the impending terrors of the law. But I had thought of him from time to time, since the contrast between the blundering 'cello-walloping boy of my first acquaintance and the rapid incisiveness in crisis which *Mochica* (although with an entire modesty) declared did appear to be worth any writer's brooding upon. Yet it wasn't the crux of the great Mogridge mystery. There was a straight line from the Mochica expedition to the hazardous and romantic role of old-fashioned gentleman spy. But the Mogridge that Mogridge exhibited to the world (even when, as on Ivo's occasion, he was a little constrained to lower his guard) was the Mogridge we had known before that eruptive or traumatic Peruvian moment. What on earth was the relationship between what must be termed, roughly, his two personalities? He was certainly no 'split' personality in the classical manner exhibited by, say, Morton Prince's protean patient, Sally Beauchamp. Alternative Mogridges didn't come and go in an involuntary fashion. It would be reasonable to suppose, rather, that the first Mogridge had been deliberately preserved as a mask—or 'front' in the current word—for the second. Yet Mogridge didn't, somehow, quite render to me the feel of that. At this moment, as he stared absently into the duskily raftered roof of the college hall (which meant that he was assessing the oysters on the plate in front of him) he came to me as owning some more complex mental lay-out than this. The first low-gear Mogridge continued to exist in his own right, and on terms amicably agreed between the first and the second. It was a psychological conundrum.

The Provost, having sat Fish down beside him, was inquiring about his present course of life—without, I imagine, betraying any recollection that here was a man who had once made a sensational nocturnal departure from college in an ambulance as an odd and sudden case of what used to be called actual neurosis. Presently he would switch to a courteous informativeness on the current Oxford scene, and these exchanges would probably take us half-way through dinner. So I talked to James Gender, the other man sitting beside me. Gender was concerned about the tower; as a member of something called the Fabric Committee he was well up-to-date on the subject; and it had transpired that unsuspected complications might attend upon the coming re-edification of this troublesome college monument. Even as late as Tudor times the foundations of major buildings had been rather casually regarded, and it might be said that the tower (like some English churches) ultimately rested on water. The water had been draining away—much as it had once done, Gender threw in, from under the campanile at Pisa, and was now said to be doing, with disastrous possibilities, from beneath the city of Ravenna. What appeared to be required, Gender went on with a shift from seriousness to whimsy, was a diver of the sort whose pertinacious labours had successfully shored up the entire structure of Winchester Cathedral. Responding to this, I nominated Albert Talbert for the job, as being a man eminently laborious and slow. We had got thus far in pleasantry when, in common with everybody else, we were startled by a blinding flash of light which cast the hall into a momentary brilliant illumination.

I believe that, for a similar brief instant of time, I expected a tremendous crash to follow—to the effecting of a general catastrophe such as might signal the detonation of a well-placed bomb. Nothing, however, succeeded but a silence, since the episode had been sufficiently untoward to strike even three hundred undergraduates dumb. What followed again upon this was a burst of boisterous yet distinguishably nervous laughter. The young men were taking it for granted that we had witnessed the perpetration of an audacious joke.

Because dinner took place in a very subdued light, mediaeval in suggestion, what we were returned to seemed for some moments a near-darkness. Into this the Provost, not a man to be disturbed by nonsense or annoyance, could presently be seen gazing with a brief calm severity before resuming his conversation with Fish. Fish himself could be relied upon to offer no comment on the incident. Mogridge

67

seemed to be looking at me, which almost certainly meant that he had instantly brought within his actual view the door through the screens at the far end of the hall. Gender was more visibly concerned; as Dean he was responsible for the discipline of the college, not an easy assignment among liberated schoolboys who were inclined to judge as merely archaic any airing of the conception at all.

'One is prepared to put up with that sort of thing at one of their wretched bump suppers,' he said to me with irritation. 'But out of the blue it's a bit thick. I hope that the hall manager or one of the other servants is able and willing to identify him.'

'Isn't that a bit tricky now, Jimmy?' I asked.

'Yes, it is. It used to be regarded as part of the game that the scouts and so on were on the side of law and order. There was even sympathy with them as underlings compelled to side with the dons or lose their jobs. Now they're treated like informers, and have to think twice before reporting, say, the most disgusting shambles on a staircase. It takes a tiptop warrant officer—our head porter, in fact—to stand up to them. He, mercifully, can still put the fear of God into the little brutes.' This speech showed Gender as rattled, it being his customary line that we had, on the whole, a very civilized crowd of boys. 'And why just that? You'd have expected the chap to let off one of those things called a thunder flash. Big bang, too. It's perplexing.'

'It's not perplexing at all.'

This flat contradiction came to us from the young man who had been so prematurely eating almonds and raisins in common room, and who was now sitting opposite to us. Gender, although no doubt displeased, at once assumed an air of diffident attention.

'Ah!' he said. 'Do tell me.'

'It was a chap taking a photograph. You need a pretty powerful flash in a big place like this.'

'My dear Ralph, you must be right. I'm most grateful to you. Some abominable tourist. There's no limit to their outrages.'

'They fart around, all right.' Ralph, whose other name remained unknown to me, said this so loudly as to catch the ear of the Provost, who afforded him a constrained smile as a result. 'But that wasn't a tourist. It was Chaffey.'

'Chaffey?'

'Calls himself Boswell Chaffey—a damned silly name. But he'll have bolted from the hall before anybody could set eye on him. He wanted high table, if you ask me.'

'Chaffey is a perfectly harmless eccentric. There are always a few undergraduates like that. And why should he "want" high table?' Gender was perplexed. 'It's quite senseless.'

'Nothing of the kind. Dons guzzling. You'll see it in some London rag in the next day or two.'

The young man was certainly right about what had happened. The taking of a flashlight photograph had been the sole occasion of so startling us.

'Chaffey's on my staircase,' I said to Gender. 'He's rather an odd man.'

'Then you think it was him now?'

'I've no opinion to express on that, Jimmy. He has journalistic ambitions, but I can't see they'd be much furthered by this sort of thing.'

'Can't you?' The aggressive character called Ralph had interrupted again. 'Don't make me laugh, Pattullo. Dons guzzling, I tell you. It will be on the front page.' And Ralph retreated busily behind his knife and fork.

## VI

Back in common room, and as the company was dis-
posing itself for the ritual that would result in the consump-
tion, among other things, of the surviving almonds and
raisins, I took charge of Fish again. We sat down at one of
the little tables designed to accommodate four people, where
we were joined first by Bedworth, who needed no introducing, and then by David Graile. Graile had not been around
in Fish's undergraduate days, but he always exhibited a
fondness for making the acquaintance of other men's guests.
This amiable trait in him was not quite trouble-free. His
manner could be more challenging than was compatible with
casual encounter; he would catechize strangers in an
embarrassing way; his notion of after-dinner chat was to
argue against anything being taken for granted by anybody
else. Buntingford declared that in these regards Graile
modelled himself on Lempriere, whose mantle he was
grooming himself to assume.

'Martin Fish and I,' I explained to Graile, 'were companions
here in youth. Port?'

'Sauterne.' Graile made this choice as if it were itself a
first clash of foils.

'And we've been reminiscing like Shallow and Silence.' I
unstoppered a decanter, having chanced on the seat in which
this preliminary action was required of one. 'Our youthful
fights with Sampson Stockfish, a fruiterer. That sort of thing.'

'Why should Shakespeare call a fruiterer Stockfish?'
Bedworth asked. 'It's perplexing.'

'Nonsense,' Graile said. 'Stockfish meant dried cod, and it
had to be beaten before cooking, and Sampson had been

given that sort of walloping. Shallow and Silence? I don't think, Duncan, that you come near qualifying as a Silence. Shallow's another matter. Would you describe your plays as shallow?'

'I hope not. Limpid, perhaps. I've always wanted to be limpid.'

'Quite right,' Bedworth said pacifically. 'Or lucid. You generally manage that. *The Accomplices* presents a complex state of affairs in an uncommonly lucid manner.'

'Thank you, Cyril. But I don't know that many of the critics would agree with you.' Bedworth was the only man who regularly made references—generally flattering—to my work in the course of any group conversation. I suppose it was because he regarded himself, quite accurately, as my oldest surviving friend in college. Most of my colleagues appeared to feel the topic one that a prudent man ought to treat with circumspection as belonging to a world alien to any field of learning.

'I saw *The Accomplices* played in Melbourne,' Fish said, instantly and easily. 'One of those rare occasions, Duncan, when my thoughts turned to you. It was an amateur company, and they weren't too good at it. But those of my countrymen with a taste for theatricals just love dressing up as dukes and duchesses.'

'Don't be silly, Martin. There aren't any dukes and duchesses in *The Accomplices*. In fact, I've never invented duke or duchess in my life.'

'Well, people with similar credentials.' Fish poured himself port, and passed the decanter to Bedworth. 'Quite right, too,' he went on. 'Serious drama ought to be concerned with people of more elevated station than ourselves. That's one of the grand canons, isn't it?'

'Stuff and nonsense!' Graile said this so vigorously that one might have supposed him to judge Fish to be talking seriously. 'This is the age of the common man—or at least we

71

began saying so round about the year 1900. That's another grand canon. So drama ought to be on a level with the common surfaces of life. Kitchen books and kitchen plays give a true reflection of our state. Look at the people in this room, all hard at work playing scholars and gentlemen. In fact, their lives centre in small ups and downs round the kitchen sink. Look at this little table; look at all these little tables. Exquisite affairs. You can see your own nose in them. But if they were truly to mirror our condition, they would have to be puddled with beer and ringed with the marks of pint pots.' Graile looked challengingly at Fish. 'Don't you agree with me?'

'I don't think I'm meant to, am I?'

'You mean you haven't the basis for doing so. I've no doubt that in Australia, my dear sir, you continue to preserve some vestiges of decent society. Your own standing is quite obvious, you know. You're the virtuous country gentleman living quietly on his estate.'

'I'm not that sort of person, at all.'

'Certainly you are. The very clothes you stand up in attest it.'

This inadmissible personal remark would have scandalized Lempriere, and it made Bedworth uneasy. Whether or not Graile was to be regarded as Lempriere's inept apprentice, I didn't know. I was wondering whether I ought to try to protect my guest from this mild hectoring when Bedworth intervened with a firm change of subject.

'Apart from the Provost and Duncan and myself, Martin, there can't be many people around here now whom you remember. Jimmy Gender, perhaps?'

'Not really. He'd just arrived as a junior fellow, I think, and probably didn't have many contacts with under-graduates. But there was Bill Watershute, who was a near-contemporary of mine, and seems to have come back to you. I was talking to Duncan about him earlier this evening, and saying I hoped to run into him. But he doesn't seem to be dining tonight.'

'No, he isn't. He was Bill, was he? He's William now.' As Bedworth said this he directed an alarmed glance at Graile, as if afraid he might come out with some unsuitable revelation of Watershute's reprehensible behaviour—mountingly in evidence, it seemed, during the current term. But Graile did nothing of the kind. His manner changed at once. He began to talk about Watershute on a note of sober regard.

'A brilliant chap,' he said. 'And interesting, too—which isn't the same thing. I sometimes feel I'd like to know more about him. Unfortunately, he's out of Oxford at the moment. Or at least I think he is. Cyril, do you happen to know?'

'Yes, he is.' It had been a moment before Bedworth, the most straightforward of men, had consented to take a cue from Graile's manner. And the look these two had exchanged, it occurred to me, might mean that the Watershute affair had taken some turn even more acute than hitherto. It was certain that Fish was going to be told nothing about it. But it was possible that, as an old acquaintance of Watershute, Fish might have something useful to say. This was what was in Graile's mind.

'I gather,' he said, 'that you haven't set eyes on Duncan since you both went down. Is it the same with Watershute?'

'Yes, it is.' Fish hesitated, which was something unusual in him. 'Or not quite literally that. As I was telling Duncan, I had a glimpse of Bill in Venice a number of months ago.'

'Scientists get around in the most enviable way. Perhaps he was working on a plan to save the place from sinking into the lagoon. Was he alone? He's a family man.'

'So I gather—and that he has a son up in the college now. I don't think he had his family with him.'

'I have a notion that his wife is, or was, an actress. Would that be right, Cyril?'

'Yes, an actress.' Bedworth said this to a faint effect of

73

disapproval. What he didn't approve of was being obliged to confirm a small blot on the Watershute name. Bedworth (so staunch an admirer of my plays) carried from some early phase of upbringing a sense that actresses, although to be admired by liberal persons when behind a proscenium arch, were not quite respectable when encountered on the hither side of it. 'And their son,' he added with a change of tone, 'is one of the best boys of his year. Backward in some things, because of having had most of his schooling in America. Otherwise, I'm inclined to think he'd have carried off the Timblethwaite.' The Timblethwaite was some particularly grand college prize. 'Yes, Giles Watershute is of Timblethwaite calibre, I'd say.'

'I'm not sure,' I said, 'that young Giles thinks all that of reading Modern Languages.'

'Disparages it, does he?' Graile asked. 'No more than a pose, probably. His father rather goes in for running things down.' Graile paused. 'Perfectly pleasantly, you know.' He had added this for Fish's benefit, and it was Fish he now directly addressed again. 'What kind of an undergraduate was William? I'd picture him as absolutely concentrated on the job.'

'So he was. But there was nothing dim or grey about him. He did know how to take time off.'

'In feminine society?'

'Oh, quite a lot, I think.' Fish produced this reply readily, but not without a hint of raised eyebrows. 'Bill would get political enthusiasms. Civil liberties, the Marshall Plan, Britain clearing out of Palestine—that sort of thing. He could project himself into distant situations in an odd way. I can remember him being all steamed up because somebody had deposed the President of Ecuador. He harangued me about it. I can even remember the rascal's name. I expect he was a rascal. President Ibarra. But it's probable we could neither of us have placed Ecuador on the map.'

74

'Distant passions and causes used to be very much an undergraduate thing,' Bedworth said. 'Nowadays, their horizons appear to have shrunk. Look at their graffiti at the present time. Parish pump stuff. It's rather depressing.'

'I don't see why you need say that, Cyril.' I came in with this by way of backing up Bedworth's plain wish that we should drift away from any inquisition into the youth of William Watershute. 'Don't you think those sort of charities ought to begin at home? Community and neighbourhood politics are much in fashion now.'

Bedworth made quite a speech in reply to this, and Graile accepted the hint thus given him. We talked about other things until dessert broke up and people began reassorting themselves as they moved into the next room. There I had some talk with the young man called Ralph—being anxious in an elderly way to show countenance to an awkward character who had told me not to make him laugh. Later on, I turned again to Bedworth, and got him into a convenient corner.

'Cyril, you and Graile were making faces at one another. When we started talking about Watershute, I mean. Has the man been playing up again?'

'Yes, he has. And, this time, I believe Edward is really worried about it. Watershute has cleared out once more— and quite noisily. I don't see we can avoid a rumpus. And I simply don't understand it. The man's a closed book to me. He seems positively to *want* a row. Why can't he conduct his wretched amours in private?'

'That's your reading of the matter? It seems to be David Graile's.'

'I see no other explanation. Think of it! With a son actually in residence.'

'Yes.' I judged it characteristic of the place that Bedworth should say 'With a son actually in residence' rather than 'With a wife actually in North Oxford', or something like that. 'But,

75

Cyril, I tell you at once that I don't see Watershute as a vulgar amorist. They don't behave that way. They play it cool, so far as work and jobs are concerned. It sounds rather more like a chronic liability to disastrous infatuations, which isn't at all the same thing.'

'I see the point.' Bedworth was receiving my opinion with respect. It was one of his firmest persuasions that a man who fabricated comedies for West End theatres must be deeply read in human nature. 'And Mabel says just that too.'

'I'd expect her to.' Accepting this disclosure that Bedworth discussed such college matters with his wife, I did feel that Mabel Bedworth was quite as likely to have a clear view of the situation as I had. 'But I see Martin winking at me. I must get him into a taxi and back to his hotel.'

'It has been nice to see him again. I hope he's going to be in Oxford for some time.'

'I haven't got it quite clear. He goes round buying pictures and things for the Australian equivalent of American City. Not that he strikes me as much like Adam Verver.'

'Nor like Prince Amerigo, either.' Bedworth wasn't the man to miss a reference to *The Golden Bowl*. 'You and I must have another word tomorrow, Duncan. I know the Provost very much wants you to keep in touch.'

'I can't say I thank him for it.' I made this graceless remark with some feeling. 'That idiotic Blunderville money was one thing. This is quite another.'

'I agree with you there.' And Bedworth nodded sombrely before saying good-night.

I collected Fish, and when he had restored his borrowed gown to the butler's pantry we went out into the quad. Fish made proper remarks about his entertainment. I saw with pleasure that he had enjoyed the evening very much.

'High table at last,' he said. 'And your overwhelmingly adequate Provost—and even Gavin Mogridge thrown in. I believe he really may come out to Australia. We had quite a talk about it.'

'Martin, it can't have escaped you that there's a spot of trouble about your old acquaintance Bill Watershute. And you've twice been a shade reticent about Venice. What was he up to there?'

'It's important?'

'Yes.'

'He seemed to be after a very glamorous young woman. Either after her or already in possession. And I had rather a notion that she must be married.'

'To someone else, you mean? What put that in your head?'

'Just a small, odd episode in a corridor. There was a chap who seemed to be spying on them. It made me think, somehow, of divorce courts and private detectives. It made it more of a shock to me to learn this evening that Watershute is a married man with a family.'

'Should you have predicted anything of this kind for Watershute? That's what that man Graile seemed to be after.'

'I don't think so. But I don't know. Messed-up affairs with women have never been my kind of thing.' The one-time victim of Martine said this with complete confidence. 'I say! Moon and stars where the tower ought to be. That's quite a shock too.'

## VII

It was on the following day that Janet revealed herself as back in Oxford. She did so by running into me in the High Street. Nothing could have more swiftly driven William Watershute and his affairs out of my head.

'What we need is a tea-shop,' I said. 'A tea-shop with a balcony and a view. That's our thing.'

'Hardly in this chilly weather. But we could have a drink.'

'So we shall. In fact, here's our pub. How is Ranald?'

'In despair. He feels that the garden has been neglected, and he's throwing himself at it like a maniac. When he ought to be settling happily into the Bodleian again.'

'Has he got that mechanical monster going?'

'Yes, and hitched on the contraption for gathering leaves. But I still can't think it's the right way round. The leaves go straight up in air, spiralling very fast, and then come floating slowly down again. It's quite pretty, really. But not all that useful.'

'Would you say Ranald is honestly fond of rural pursuits?'

'No. But he has convinced himself that I'm a country-woman. So there we are in our barn of a vicarage, with all those unkempt acres around us, and Ranald feeling he has done the right thing. What's more, he is really developing a taste for it. Or, if not a taste, a mania. It has its bright side, with the prices of fruit and vegetables what they are today.'

For some time Janet and I talked in this fashion. She thought it proper to remind me at times that she was what Fiona had rather crossly called her: a completely married woman. Making gentle fun of her husband achieved this perfectly. And I myself liked it so much that I was sometimes surprised when a momentary sense of awkwardness interrupted our talk. It was a matter, I believed, of a missing topic —at least of an elusive sense of something of that kind. *And how are the kids?* It worried me that this was a question that the McKechnies' childless condition didn't permit me to ask. I had no notion whether the situation worried Janet. She was a bereaved woman, but she hadn't been a barren one. Perhaps she felt tragedy to have long ago closed a cycle of experience upon which she had no impulse to embark again. I rather hoped it was so, not liking to think of her as walking about her laicized vicarage looking for what wasn't there.

'What's happening, Dunkie? How are things? Are you going to settle in as a don?

'I don't think so.'

'Don't you like it?' Janet was dismayed. 'I always supposed you do.'

'I think I've told you before, Janet—and I'm not sure that, for my pains, you didn't tell me that I dramatized myself. Or it may have been Fiona.'

'Good heavens! Am I becoming telescoped in your mind with that girl?'

'Certainly not. The fact is I'm fond of Oxford, but not too good with its denizens. It's something that's just been brought home to me in an odd way. Did I ever mention to you a man called Fish?'

'An Australian you knew ages ago?'

'Yes. He's in England. He turned up yesterday, and dined with me in college.'

'How very nice.'

'It was nice. But it has struck me he's the only man I've ever made a close friend of in this town. There was Cyril Bedworth, too, of course. And Tony Mumford, and a man you won't have heard of called Mogridge. I suppose I'm fond of all of them. But they none of them pass the test of complete mutual confidence. Tony, for instance, who was an absolute crony. I know almost nothing about his domestic life. And I've never told him a word about my marriage.'

'What has started this heart-searching, Dunkie?'

'Just your question of how it goes in college. I do feel a distance between myself and those people. I can be lively at times, and they like it in moderation. But I'm not, at least in the areas they respect, a properly serious person—as, say, Bedworth is.'

'Or that old owl Albert Talbert.' Janet said this with a tartness that should have warned me I wasn't doing too well. But I pressed on.

'All right—or Talbert. Or certainly Ranald. No, I'm here on a five-year initial term. When it's up, I won't seek a renewal of the thing.'

'But they're going to make you a professor. Prof. Pattullo. It would be smashing.'

'Don't make fun of me.'

'I'd rather make fun of you than tell you what I think.' Janet had fired up in the sudden way characteristic of her. 'But, no—that's not right. Listen. I don't care for that sort of talk from you. You've made yourself a career, and plenty of people like you quite a lot, whether or not you condescend to like them. So stop crawling.'

I had brought this wholesome speech upon myself, and I don't think I resented it. On the contrary, the trouble was that it told me rather powerfully whom I *did* like.

'All right,' I said. 'All in order and correct.'

'All askew, you mean. You're made for family life, Dunkie, and you won't do a damned thing about it. You infuriate me.'

'My celibate condition gets me told off wherever I turn. My

cousin tells me just the same thing—and it's damned perverse of her.'

'Fiona Petrie? How does that—well—relationship go?'

'It doesn't—or she wouldn't be telling me to go and get married, would she?'

'Have you proposed to her?'

'Well, no. There's a block. Perhaps it's our ages.'

'You might do better with that friend of hers.'

'Margaret Mountain? You must be potty. She's even younger.'

'Even so. And I only said *might*.'

'Are you declaring war on Fiona, Janet? Did you decide to after vetting our relationship on that river picnic?'

'Don't be frivolous.'

'But I've told you. I'm not a serious person.'

'Then so much the better. Oxford is jam-packed with serious people. It's as bad as Princeton. Let's elope, Dunkie, you and me, to some quite madly gay and irresponsible place.'

We kept up this joke for a little, but it petered out. I was conscious that in addressing themselves to the problem of Duncan Pattullo Janet and Fiona shared some common ground.

'Don't you think,' I asked, 'that I ought to move on—and do some honest writing?'

'I don't know. But in some ways you certainly haven't moved on. You still keep that house in the south of Italy, don't you, although quite wretched things happened there? And here in Oxford you're snugly back on your old undergraduate staircase.'

'It's a sad picture, isn't it? Let's go. May I come to tea or something on Sunday?'

'Come for the day, and in your oldest clothes. You can help Ranald with that baffling machine.'

From this encounter with Janet, at once enjoyable and

disturbing, I got back to college in time for luncheon. It was a meal a good deal frequented by the younger members of common room, and on this occasion I was taken charge of by two of them before I had helped myself to cold ham. They led me off and sat me down between them in a businesslike way. One of them, named Lenton, was a physicist. The other was called Hickman, and I had been told his subject was physiological psychology—information that didn't mean a great deal to me.

'You can help us,' Hickman said. 'We feel we're through with this. There's no future in it.'

'University teaching and scientific research,' Lenton explained. 'They're being strangled, aren't they? One has to face it.'

'Hard times, certainly,' I said. 'But how am I going to help?' It was clear to me that Hickman and Lenton were proposing no more than twenty minutes' nonsense.

'We're turning over to science fiction,' Hickman said. 'Much more money in it than in science fact. And you can explain to us how to effect a breakthrough.'

'I'd suppose it to be simply a matter of having a few bright ideas. No need to bother about the literary graces. Or even how to find a publisher, and so on. Just think up something sufficiently ingenious, and everything of that kind will sort itself out. No doubt the stuff must be given a lick of science sufficient to satisfy a lay mind.'

'Yes, of course.' Hickman didn't seem dashed by these dull remarks. 'What I've been thinking about is Eskimoes and Solomon Islanders, morphologically considered.'

'Morphologically. I see.'

'Why are Eskimoes dumpy and almost round? It turns on the surface area of the sphere. A sphere presents the highest ratio of volume to surface area that you can arrive at. As it's the prime need of arctic peoples to conserve their heat, the more globular they are the better. And conversely with chaps in a torrid zone. They need to shed all the heat they can, so they breed themselves long and lanky. At this point other-planet stuff comes in. The arrival from a cold planet of perfectly globular beings, and from a hot one of beings who are pretty well a straight line. What do you think of that?'

'Not terribly much. But I'm no authority.'

'You're probably right.' Hickman was not offended, and for some time we continued this sort of talk. I wasn't keen on it, having other matters on my mind—and notably the self-centred and poor-spirited show I'd offered to Janet at a reunion I'd been much looking forward to. I now did my best, however, to keep my end up, and presently Lenton and Hickman, growing tired of their joke, fell to talking seriously in a jargon of their own. Eventually Lenton looked at his watch and rose from table.

'Time to punch the clock,' he said—presumably referring to the time-clock which the Provost had remarked to me that we didn't go in for. 'I have to sort out Water-shute's brats for tutorials. The whole bloody lot are being pitched at me.' Lenton said this with an irritation he plainly didn't feel. Teaching for the college in an emergency was a good mark for men of his standing. 'I'll have to fit in some of them round about midnight.' He glanced at me. 'A spot of lucubration, as you learned chaps say.'

'Has Watershute gone sick?' I asked innocently.

'Not a bit of it. He's been put on some commission or committee or something. He said it would take him the whole week to fix himself up with it.' And Lenton looked at me sharply. 'What do you make of that?'

'That you scientists are a rum crowd. But no doubt it's all in the interest of the march of mind.' I felt I was giving nothing away. 'So good luck to him. And be kind to his brats, Lenton. I dare say you've forgotten. But young men can be extremely sensitive. They haven't toughened up like you and me.'

'I'll be very careful,' Lenton said with a grin. 'And thanks a lot for being so discouraging. Perhaps we'd better try straight thrillers.'

## VIII

I ought to have sought out Bedworth at once, and had myself reliably briefed on Watershute's latest disappearance. But I was still unreconciled to the Provost's notion that I was one who was to be particularly concerned with the matter. As soon as I had parted from Lenton and Hickman there returned to me the strong sense of personal perplexity that the meeting with Janet had prompted. I felt I couldn't care less about a vagrant don, and that what I wanted to do was to see Fiona—this in the specific sense of taking a look at her. I had invented people by the dozen, but was I any good at seeing them? Had I ever looked hard enough? I set off walking to the Woodstock Road with the confused notion of looking at Fiona as my father would have looked at a landscape in search of a vision to transfer to canvas.

The rain expected by Mogridge the night before had now arrived over Oxford. It sloshed down in the Cornmarket, where citizens huddled along dismally under umbrellas. The little paved area in front of St. Michael-at-the-North-Gate was silted up with pashed urban leaves, and its normally well-peopled benches were deserted. Water dripped and trickled over the elaborate miniaturized pinnacles of the Martyrs' Memorial. A graffitist had been recently at work on it with red paint—I suppose challenged by the technical difficulty of desecrating it in an intelligible manner. The rain had got to work on the still moist paint, so that the Memorial, appropriately enough, appeared to be liquefying like a relic on its appointed day. A group of young men swung past it in track-suits—sweating, panting, and with glazed looks suggesting that they had blindly strayed from some running-track unawares. Misguided Americans were scrambling into a big black car outside the Randolph Hotel, perhaps believing that they would find sunshine as well as Shakespeare's bones at Stratford-upon-Avon. An ambulance went wildly sirening into St. Giles', bearing the latest load of street casualties to succour in the Radcliffe Infirmary. Oxford seemed a desperate place, a chaos amid which the colleges barely maintained their ground, like forlorn last-ditch fortresses.

But the Woodstock Road was quiet, and I turned with relief into the little garden before Fiona's and Margaret Mountain's house. There was no point in knocking on the door or ringing a bell, since nobody ever attended to such a summons. I went inside and entered the sitting-room. Margaret was there, and so was Hatty Firebrace. The philosopher was on this occasion unaccompanied by her sons or dog, and so the better able to direct on me an undistracted scrutiny from beneath and behind her sibylline locks.

'Oh, hullo! Is Fiona around?' This question must have come from me with graceless haste, since Margaret, normally so impassive, glanced at me with what seemed to be social disapproval.

'Hullo, Duncan!' she said. 'You know Mrs Firebrace? Have some whisky.'

'No, thank you. Not quite teatime yet.'

'Then take off that mac and sit down. But it's a blank so far as Fiona's concerned. She's in Scotland. Or nearly. She took a morning train. She's going to Garth.'

'In the middle of term? How very odd! One of her parents isn't——?'

'Parents? Her mother has moved into the dower house. And Fiona is having a row with her two brothers. Over money, I expect. Or bits and pieces. It usually happens.'

'Good God! You don't mean that Andrew Petrie'—I scarcely knew the Christian name of young Petrie of Garth—'is *dead*?'

'Of course he's dead.' Margaret stared at me, and Mrs Firebrace stared at me as well. 'He died some months ago.'

I found this news, or rather the belated manner of its communication to me, distinctly curious. Fiona and I, it was true, had formed the habit of not referring to our family backgrounds. In her case I put this down to her consciousness of being a rebel against the traditions in which she had been brought up, and I supposed that she attributed something of the sort to myself. Her neglect of her people—if it came to that—might well be less censurable than mine, since I was deficient even in common curiosity about the Glencorrys and numerous other persons in my Scottish past. Ninian had for some time rather stiffly ceased to be informative; if I wasn't interested, my brother said, he wasn't going to waste time on outlying family news. But Andrew Petrie had been my cousin Anna's husband, and it was odd that his death had passed me by. Ninian, knowing that I had made contact with Anna's daughter in Oxford, must have taken it for granted that the news would have reached me.

'Does she expect to be away for long?' I asked.

'I shouldn't think so. She has rather a heavy programme this term, and she's terribly conscientious.' Margaret spoke as if a topic of minor interest were now disposed of. But Mrs Firebrace had something to say as well.

'I'm sure she'll have sent you a note before going off. I know you've been seeing a lot of each other.'

'Yes, quite a lot.' I told myself how much I didn't care for Mrs Firebrace, although she was a totally harmless woman. Perhaps Penny's brief domestication with her was at the bottom of the hostility I felt. Penny might well have communicated to her as a triumph her enthralment of the Sheldrake twins. This was a disagreeable thought.

'If Fiona is having a rumpus with her brothers over a family carve-up,' Mrs Firebrace said, 'I wish her luck. I don't expect a bean has come across the border to her since she left school.

Her bid for civilization would be resented, wouldn't it? And one knows her sort of people. Petty gentry—with sons shoved into the army and taking every shilling.'

'I think you may be a little hazy about over the border,' I said. Mrs Firebrace's remarks had been substantially correct, and it was no doubt comical that they had occasioned in me this spark of resentment. 'I've heard Fiona's grandfather—who's my uncle—called a wee laird. He's as wee as you please. But there's nothing petty about him.'

'Stout words, Duncan!' To my surprise, Margaret Mountain had given way to laughter, a weakness I couldn't recall her ever having fallen into before. Roughly speaking, she was the same sort of intellectual as Hattie Firebrace. But my childish speech (as I conceived it to be) had presumably touched some atavistic chord in her. 'Duncan,' she went on, 'finds no appeal in aspersions cast upon the landed classes. He writes plays in which it always becomes apparent that breeding tells.'

At this point I was reduced to inwardly cursing women at large. I knew very well that Margaret, whose literary interests were confined to the deliverances of *la nouvelle vague* in France, had never seen or read a play of mine in her life.

'I must be on my way,' Mrs Firebrace said, and reached for her umbrella. She might have been deciding that here was a favourable moment at which to leave Miss Mountain and myself tête-à-tête. 'The boys are off my hands till five, but I have to collect the dog from the vet.' She moved towards the door, and then turned back to me. 'Are you going to be at June Watershute's party?' she asked.

This unexpected question referred to something that had already caused me surprise. I hadn't met William Watershute's wife, but she had sent me an invitation to a sherry party which was now only a few evenings ahead. It had announced Mrs William Watershute as At Home, but I didn't take this to mean that her husband—if in Oxford, as he well might not be—wouldn't be present too. Almost all written communications I received in Oxford embodied either conventional forms of expression, as here, or archaic ones such as only learned persons would preserve. If I was summoned to a college meeting I was told that it would be 'holden' in this place or that. If we commissioned an artist to paint a portrait of an eminent colleague (as was happening in Arnold Lempriere's case now) it was referred to not as a portrait but as a 'likeness'.

In this same spirit of convention I assured Mrs Firebrace that I hoped to be at the Watershutes' party, although my actual feeling was that I couldn't decently avoid it. As for Mrs Firebrace's question, it had been in tone entirely idle, but there had been the hint of a sharpening curiosity behind it. I told myself that what was plainly going to be the 'Watershute Affair' had already become a subject of gossip in the university at large.

At least Mrs Firebrace did now go away. I was left with Margaret Mountain, the young woman whom Janet had lately commended to me in so equivocal a form. Janet had been doing no more than making fun of me, as she often did and as I normally liked her to do. But now I let this fact escape me, and began having solemn thoughts about the matter. Had Janet's second marriage—pretty well polar, it was clear, to her first—tended to insulate her from the baffling mysteriousness of the forces of sexual selection? For if I advanced on Margaret Mountain now in a perfectly civilized and sophisticated amative way—tilting up her chin, say, or laying a light hand on her either shoulder, or asking 'Do you mind if I kiss you?'—I should be blundering against that invisible barrier, at once so sharply palpable and as frangible as glass, which protects one from another person whose conjunction would be wanton because forming no part of Great Creating Nature's plan.

This was a home-made philosophy, evolved from my own

experience of wear and tear from time to time, and it was irrationally that I now asked myself why Janet didn't acknowledge it. Why was she against Fiona, between whom and myself some positive current must surely be sensed as flowing, and at the same time prepared, however lightly, to throw a casual vote for Fiona's friend, between whom and myself nothing relevant flowed at all?

'As Fiona isn't here,' Margaret said briskly, 'you'll have to make do with me for a small civil space of time. But you needn't sit glowering at me as if you were trying to work out my place among the women in your life.'

'No "as if" about it. It's just what I'm doing.'

I have noticed that people given to the utterance of whatever comes into their heads occasionally chance upon mind-reading effects of the sort just brought off by Margaret. She took my response, to which I had imparted no facetious colouring, quite in her stride.

'I'm going to be the woman who makes you tea,' she said, standing up and moving across the room. 'That's what you really want. And I tend to drift towards tea myself when Fiona's away.'

'You're very kind. I'll enjoy tea. Are you saying, Margaret, that it's Fiona who plants the bottle on the table?'

'Yes, it is—which isn't to say that she's an incipient alcoholic. Still, I suppose it could be worrying in a forward-looking way.' Margaret spoke in the most matter-of-fact manner. 'She's more at risk than I am. I get desperate about my work. But that's quite in order, and can be kept in hand. Every artist—or whatever one's to be called—gets like that, just because his best work is by definition beyond him. Fiona hasn't the resource of getting desperate about work. She works very hard, and obviously with steady success—everything getting ordered and sorted out typologically and all the rest of it in time. So she gets desperate on less tractable matters instead. Personal relations, as with that impressive old headache, the late J. B. Timbermill. And others. I'm afraid there's nothing to eat.'

'Just tea's fine. Desperation is rather an unfocused conception, Margaret, although one can feel it sharply enough.'

'Unfocused? It's a kind of magnetic north to some people, so that they just have to go that way and land themselves.'

'We all have a certain morbid desire for tough spots and hideous dilemmas, and I'm not eager to see Fiona as an extreme case. She feels the fascination of what's difficult, I suppose. Timbermill answered to that, all right. And she's a hard-headed girl, after all. Look at her now—apparently off to Scotland on a perfectly normal *post obitum* rumpus. Who's going to have the dear old parrot and the cage? That sort of thing.'

My entertainer probably judged this to be a coarse-grained remark, for she poured me a second cup of tea in silence. I came away feeling that it is probably a good idea to have only one woman in one's life, and have her early. This unfashionable disposition of things I had missed out on in what was now a distant past.

## IX

ONE QUICKLY BECOMES conscious in Oxford of the convention that all senior persons are known to one another. Of the letters coming to me on various academic accounts from men I had never set eyes on the majority began 'Dear Pattullo' rather than 'Dear Mr Pattullo'. It seemed only among junior people and recent arrivals that there was growing up an awareness of the scale of the modern university as rendering the assumption implausible. In the nineteenth century 'Box of Balliol' and 'Cox of Corpus' must have been instantly identifiable by anybody in Lincoln or St John's, and to a surprising extent this held still. Men and women belonging to related disciplines met one another on committees and boards of examiners, and those with totally distinct learned interests knocked up against each other at high tables and in common rooms or as fellow-members of convivial clubs. The conservative lamented that these latter channels of social intercourse were withering away under an adverse economic climate. Old assumptions as to what constituted the minimum requirements of civilized entertainment died hard, and people were coming to think twice before inviting a couple of acquaintances to dinner. In my own college, a stronghold of the old order, small nights were now a good deal more common than big ones.

These changes were arriving gradually, and didn't much disturb the general clubbability of the place. But the clubbability didn't mean, never had meant, that there wasn't a great deal of hierarchical organization among us. People floated on their several levels and revolved in their several coteries. An obscure intruder like myself and the head of a college who had been, say, an ambassador or a top civil servant met on what soon became a casual Christian-name basis—tinged, perhaps, by a consciousness that we had both been imported on the score of activities alien to academic minds. It didn't mean that my concerns were his, or his parties my parties. Parties, indeed, were in general set up in one of two ways, according as to whether they were university or college oriented. At one of Anthea Gender's one was substantially although not too obtrusively in the presence of grandees drawn from all over the shop. The Bedworths', on the other hand, were straight college occasions. This represented less Mabel's inclination than Cyril's. Mabel would have been prompted to go into highways and byways, since she had a taste for odd juxtapositions gratifying to what I still thought of as the tart Virginia Woolf side of her nature. Her husband's notion of a party was the contriving of a relaxed occasion for the sorting out of current *contretemps* of a local order. Mabel, as a conscientious Senior Tutor's wife, commonly deferred to this view of the matter.

I didn't know what Mrs Watershute's party was going to be like. It seemed surprising that it was happening at all. But one might anticipate its representing a kind of showing the flag, since William Watershute's concerns were clearly approaching a crisis.

I arrived at a clearer view of this, and at a first hint of a further dimension in which they might be involved, not from the perturbed conversation of Bedworth, but from an encounter which took place out of Oxford. I owed entertainment, as it happened, to Alexander Pentecost, one of the university's most eminent physicists, who had cultivated my acquaintance as a consequence of his absorbed interest in amateur theatrical affairs. Having found this an attractive trait in so severely intellectual a man, and discovering, predictably, that he was one of those who regularly went in for a 'London day', it occurred to me to invite him to luncheon at my club—one reflecting the odd affiliations which have long existed between the legal and theatrical professions. Pentecost knew a number of theatre people, but in the main, I supposed, as a matter of slight acquaintanceships; he might enjoy any further casual contacts of the sort likely to turn up on such an occasion.

My late walk across Oxford on a wet afternoon had made me think poorly of its latterday condition; now, on a wet morning, London struck me as a great deal worse. The advertisements were ominous and the shop-windows full of disheartening stuff; I didn't like the faces people carried around the streets; a small cinema into which, long ago, I had sometimes dropped to see rather dull news-reels was offering a film called *How to Seduce a Virgin*. The whole vast sprawl was like a kitsch version of the decadence of imperial Rome. I recalled my recent confession to Janet of discontent with my Oxford condition; now the folly of such an attitude, even if only a passing mood of the mind, quite frightened me. That I had lately abandoned my flat in town seemed one of the more sensible decisions of my life.

But London offers numerous havens to persons overcome by the sort of gloom that had assailed me, and with an hour to spare I turned into the nearest to hand. It was the National Gallery, which was no more than a few minutes from my club. A whole range of new rooms had lately been opened, and they were at present devoted to an exhibition affording instruction on the entire history of the Renaissance in Italy. It was an ambitious project, and admirably realized. Presently I found myself in a darkened auditorium, in which perhaps as many as a couple of dozen people were listening to a lecture. The text of this discourse on art was coming from a cassette —and at the same time the points being made were receiving illustration on a screen. It was like an old-fashioned 'lantern lecture' up-dated by modern technology. Only something—I suddenly realized—had gone wrong with a synchronizing process, and the confident cultured voice was calling upon us to admire in a portrait of Federigo da Montefeltro 'one of the most finely proportioned of Palladio's façades'. The audience —knowing, presumably, that protest to a living being lay not within their power—continued to watch and listen respectfully.

I ought to have found this small hitch in a majestic deployment of national treasures amusing, but in fact I left the Gallery feeling alarmed. All around me more and more things were being achieved by more and more complicated means, and with more and more hitches as a result. My father used to tell a story of how he had come to start smoking; he had put a penny in a slot-machine in the expectation of receiving a bar of chocolate, and what had emerged had been a sixpenny packet of cigarettes. Nowadays you expected information on a Duke of Urbino and got chat about the Palazzo Valmarana instead. In either case one might suppose that sundry little wheels hadn't been going round quite as they should. All over the place they were failing to do that. And sooner or later weren't they certain so to do in some manner inimical to the continued existence of things in general? This man to whom I was about to give luncheon, for instance. He worked, I vaguely understood, at the very heart of nuclear physics. What if he got day-dreaming of triumphantly producing *Titus Andronicus* for the OUDS, and gave a flip to some wrong little wheel as a result? Piero's pictures and Palladio's façades would alike vanish from the face of the earth.

This naïve vision of what somebody in *Macbeth* calls dire combustion and confused events was still in my head when Pentecost turned up on me. He looked reassuringly competent, and gave care to a choice between several varieties of madeira—murmuring without self-importance the while of a tedious morning among 'those confounded chaps at the

Ministry'. Supposing the Ministry of Dire Combustion to be in question, I listened to this in a respectful silence, and we soon turned to what he plainly regarded as the more significant subject of plays currently running in London—a review in which we enjoyed the assistance for ten or fifteen minutes of one of London's theatrical knights.

When Pentecost and I moved into the dining-room and to a table by ourselves our talk turned to Oxford. Pentecost believed like the juvenile Lenton and Hickman that the university was due for progressively starvation rations, English governments being chronically less concerned that knowledge should be made than that motor-cars which nobody proposed to buy should continue their obsolescent trundle along the conveyor belts.

'Now what about that maverick young man of yours?'

Pentecost thus abruptly ended our wandering talk while digging a spoon vigorously into a Stilton. I couldn't pretend not at once to pick up the reference. We were going to discuss William Watershute. I can't say that this hadn't been in my head, and the fact showed me as in process of reconciling myself to the Provost's notion of me as a contact man.

'Watershute?' I said. 'It's a point, perhaps, that he's not all that young. Years of discretion are his, or ought to be. But he's certainly causing concern.'

'Of course he is. But perhaps he has to be given his head—within reason. He's a star, you know—and within reach of becoming a big one. Never does anything by halves. On the contrary, his weakness might be said to be overkill. And he's a viewy type as well. There's all this damned eleutheromania, for example.'

'This what?' The learned word had momentarily baffled me. I think I associated it with the poet Shelley.

'Freeing people from dungeons in Chile, and that sort of thing.'

96

'Oh, I see! When he was an undergraduate it was Ecuador.'

'Was it, indeed.' I could see that Pentecost was impressed by my thus airing a piece of stray information gleaned from the conversation of Martin Fish. He probably thought I had been doing serious spade-work. I had a glimpse of myself, indeed, as a kind of amateur Mogridge, who had been engaged in the operation known in his line of business as taking somebody's name through the files. 'Of course,' Pentecost went on, 'one can't fault a man for having feelings of that sort. And Watershute has other public concerns of a thoroughly reputable order. The free currency of purely scientific information between workers in one country and another. He's just got himself on some highly respectable committee or other concerned with that. It has the backing of the Royal Society, and what have you.'

'I've recently heard about that committee.'

'Ah!' Pentecost was again struck by the fact of seeming to be in the presence of a knowledgeable man. 'All admirable, of course. Only it does most confoundedly take him out of his lab.'

'And away from his tutorial duties.'

'Bother his tutorial duties. Any tiro can manage all that. Try a perfectly competent lad of yours called Lenton.'

'We are. But it can only be a holding operation. And there's another side to the whole thing, isn't there?'

'There is—and a more obtrusive one. All sorts of hazards go along with that temperament—wouldn't you say, Pattullo? It seems that Watershute has always been a bit free about his women. Now they've got on top of him—metaphorically speaking, that's to say. We have to face it. The man has turned as lecherous as a sparrow.'

'I can't confirm that—or not in the extreme form in which you put it. And, in any case, is it any business of ours?'

'It is, if he goes to pieces on it. And it seems he's not content, for one thing, to get his goods reasonably on the cheap.' Pentecost paused on this expression—which struck me as on the brutal side—and contentedly finished his cheese. 'It wouldn't surprise me to learn that the man's badly in the red.'

'Plenty of people are in a bit of a hole that way. Most of them get out of it again when they've had a fright. Or they're extricated by firmly-dealing relatives or employers. It's something we've thought of, actually, in Watershute's case. Or our Provost has. It would be premature to do more than just docket the possibility of stiff financial trouble.'

'It can be dangerous.'

'Well, yes. No doubt a man blows his brains out from time to time. It must come hard on a family: bereavement with a dash of disgrace thrown in.'

'Suicide isn't quite what I'm thinking of.'

'There are other possibilities, no doubt.' I found myself staring rather oddly at Pentecost. 'Shall we take our coffee in the smoking-room? Port, if you care for it.'

Pentecost indicated that it wasn't his time of day for port, and we moved out of the club dining-room together. It was a process of threading our way between tables, and if we weren't going to talk down my fellow-members' necks it imposed an interval of silence between us. During this intermission several quite novel ideas went through my head. It would have been rather a thick head, I suppose, if they had not. When we sat down again I exercised a host's privilege and introduced a change of subject.

## X

THE FOLLOWING DAY brought round Mrs Watershute's party. I found myself making my way to it in the company of Tommy Penwarden, our librarian. Penwarden never seemed much to enjoy parties, but equally seemed never to miss them. He was a bachelor, and perhaps lonely; or his attendance may have been the consequence of a carry-over into social occasions of the conscientiousness distinguishing his professional activities. The Blunderville Papers, which I had glimpsed as an undergraduate on the fateful night which had seen my first glimpse of Penny too, were preoccupying Penwarden now as then.

He exhibited during our walk a certain agitation which I put down to a sense of the possibly awkward character of the party ahead. But this was a misapprehension. We were taking a route through the University Parks; it was dusk; and at dusk the Parks are locked up. We had gained ingress through one gate, but might not egress be denied to us at another? Should this happen, Penwarden appeared to envisage the necessity of our spending a chilly autumn night in open air. He quickened his pace. I found no difficulty in keeping up with him. He had become a portly man of sedentary habit, and thus quickly out of breath.

I endeavoured to divert Penwarden's mind from the terrors of our situation by introducing some conversational topic of commanding interest. At the moment, and in college terms, this meant Watershute. There was perhaps a certain lack of urbanity in canvassing the problems of one who might presently be pouring drinks for us. But I didn't think of this. My attitude to the Watershute puzzle was changing. I was coming to think that the more quickly we knew more about it the better.

'Has Watershute turned up again?' I asked.

'I don't know. I don't know at all.' Penwarden glanced at me askance over the edge of his under-sized spectacles. 'It's very worrying, Duncan—very worrying, indeed. We should do idly to ignore the fact. Not but that, on the present occasion, he appears to be engaged in a responsible and indeed laudable manner.'

'This committee or something?'

'A conference, I believe, and of an international character. Perhaps, Duncan, we should cut across the grass. It will be a little quicker.'

We cut across the grass. There were still a few people strolling about with an apparent absence of concern, but they were undeniably thin on the ground. Nobody rings a warning bell in the University Parks, or bellows rude injunctions to clear out. I had a notion that the man carrying the fatal keys made a final round on a bicycle in the interest of the dilatory or absent-minded. But this precaution, if it had in fact ever existed, might have fallen into desuetude. I began to be a little worried myself. Irrational anxieties are said to be the most catching.

'Is Watershute's conference about academic freedom?' I asked.

'Not exactly that, I'm glad to say.' Penwarden was now very short of breath. 'One has to disapprove of academic freedom. In practice, I mean. No doubt it's all very well in theory.'

'But we don't want to be bullied, do we, by Ministers of Popular Enlightenment, and Big Brothers generally?'

'Of course not.' Penwarden now actually stopped, glanced anxiously at his watch as if calculating whether we had thirty seconds to spare, and then took off his spectacles and polished them with a large silk handkerchief. His perspiring condition had resulted in their becoming misted over. 'But when people start making a song about that sort of thing'—Penwarden replaced the spectacles and strode forward again—'you can be pretty sure they're up to mischief. Demonstrations and resolutions and so forth—and after that come strikes and smashing furniture. There he is!'

A man in a peaked cap was certainly to be observed some way in front of us, and it was conceivable that he was up to no good.

'Yes,' I said. 'And I think I can hear the jingle.'

'The jingle?' Penwarden repeated.

'Of his keys.'

'Good heavens!' Penwarden, although he glanced at me suspiciously, was alarmed. 'Perhaps we ought to call out to him. But I suppose we can cut him off on his return.'

'And plead with him. It's a particular aspect of academic freedom, isn't it? Being entitled to be let out of our own park.'

'You're being frivolous, Duncan. And we're considering a serious matter.'

'So we are. I'm sorry. Do you suppose that Watershute might smash up Mrs Pococke's nick-nacks in the Lodging? All those pastoral staves, for example.'

'Certainly not. Watershute is not inclined that way at all. Or not of late. He was very left-wing for a time. I'm told he actually joined the Association of University Teachers.'

'Good Lord!'

'Yes, I believe it's perfectly true. But he has become much more conservative in maturity, as people with any sense commonly do. He has abjured such connections.'

'I see.' I felt that this piece of information (if it wasn't misinformation) afforded in some obscure way food for thought.

'Which makes it all the more shocking, Duncan, that his personal affairs should have fallen into such disgraceful disorder.'

'You don't mean this committee, or whatever it is?'

'No, no. That's a perfectly respectable affair, with sound backing. Not academic freedom, as I said. The freedom of ideas in a totally non-political context. Learned societies all over the world being allowed to get together for the advancement of knowledge. That's highly desirable. Watershute's trouble, as I've said, seems to be entirely a matter of his private morals. But look! That fellow has turned away towards the river.' And Penwarden gave a gasp of relief. 'He's not locking up the gates, after all.'

Even in the dusk it was possible to tell at once that the Watershutes were little given to gardening. Their house—probably college property—was one on a line of large detached villas from the charmlessness of which, you felt, occupants of any sensibility would have striven to divert attention through every resource of horticultural art. The Watershutes, however, appeared to confine themselves to hemlock and thistle. In the front garden, indeed, a rough clearing was being maintained round a shack or hovel which loomed forlornly in the gloom. Constructed in the main from a debris of packing-cases and abandoned sheets of corrugated iron, it suggested some refuge from the elements hastily erected by dispirited late arrivals in a shanty-town where all the more promising materials had already been used up. It certainly hinted no cousinship with the Gritti Palace Hotel. Yet a pronounced boldness of design, or resolute handling of the rubbish available, made me suspect that here was the juvenile handiwork of Giles Watershute, constructed as a hide-out from the rigours of family life, and now preserved as a bicycle-shed or spare bin for household coal.

It was Giles who received Penwarden and myself at the front door. Like any don's well-conducted son, he had eschewed the pleasures of college life for an evening's labour supporting a hospitable occasion at home. Even so, I'd have expected him to glower at us in a kind of civil hostility, as if intimating that he was stretching a point in rising to this virtuous behaviour. But nothing of the sort happened. Giles said 'Oh, hullo, sir!' to Penwarden and 'Oh, hullo!' to me—a distinction paying tribute, I supposed, to the solidarity of Surrey Four. 'So nice of you to come,' he added formally. 'You're about the first of the crush, as a matter of fact.'

I had already realized that this must be so, there being a notable silence in the Watershute house. Penwarden's haste to escape incarceration *en route* had been responsible for our thus over-promptly turning up. Penwarden proving to have nothing to contribute at the moment, I offered some remark on our walk and on the late-autumnal scene.

'A desperate time of year in Oxford,' Giles said. 'But one has to have joy while one may.' Giles was nervous. 'Let me take your coats. There aren't many proper pegs. We've never got them up. I'm sorry my father isn't here. He's out of Oxford, and we don't know whether he'll be back for the tail-end of things. But he's sent in a case of champagne.'

Penwarden, an honest man but socially not always reliable, gave me a glance of unnecessary significance over the little spectacles. Champagne had fairly recently become a legitimate vehicle of entertainment at Oxford parties, but was tacitly understood to be proper only in the houses of persons of confessed extra-academic affluence. Penwarden had instantly hitched it on to the general untowardness of William Watershute's behaviour.

'This way,' Giles said—and added, again with formality, 'My mother will be delighted.'

We entered a large room at the back of the house. It was perhaps its being so very large that made me feel that it was also oddly bare. But this impression may have resulted from its present virtually dispeopled condition. The Talberts were standing on either side of the chimneypiece, each with a glass in hand. They might have been a pair of grotesquely ill-matched china dogs, Emily Talbert being all elderly angularities softened only by a flutter of diaphanous scarves, and Albert ('Geoffrey' to his wife) a kind of pink blob largely obscured behind his enormous white moustache. The Talberts looked at us impassively and without motion, as if constrained by some high propriety to pretend they were part of the furniture. There was—this frozen posture intimated—a hostess for Penwarden and myself to make a bow to. But Mrs Watershute (whether or not she was to be 'delighted') seemed not in evidence.

The disconcerting impression lasted only for a moment. Then a farther door opened and the lady of the house appeared or reappeared. She advanced upon us—or rather she advanced upon me, since I suddenly found myself kissed and enveloped in a warm embrace. I even experienced some difficulty in keeping my feet—Mrs Watershute, scarcely a slender woman, having contrived to kick both her own feet simultaneously in air, depending from my neck the while.

'Oh, Duncan, Duncan,' she cried, 'what a marvellous thing! I've ached for you for years.'

Being accustomed to theatrical behaviour, I wasn't much put out. Under the disapproving gaze of Penwarden—but not of the Talberts, who looked on with benevolence at this exhibition from another world—I even kissed June Watershute on both cheeks. Giles seemed only slightly surprised, perhaps as being accustomed to extravagant comportment on his mother's part. Not that the lady lacked reason either for her greeting or for having invited me to her party. She would have been justified had she reproached me for years of neglect. I simply hadn't come across her, whether professionally or otherwise, for a very long time. But June Watershute was the June Trevivian who had played Anita in my first successful play, *The Bear-Garden*. She had been a quite uncommonly beautiful girl (a fact to which retrospection disposed me to attribute the play's long run) but had not gone on to make any particular mark on the stage. And one had to conclude from Giles's present age that she had married William Watershute while still very young.

Further arrivals at the party now cut short this reunion, and I put myself into general circulation by means of suggesting to Giles that I help him with the drinks—having, as I remarked to him, so old-standing an association with his mother that I must count as an established friend of the house. Giles accepted my offer uneffusively, but after a glance which, though not conspiratorial in itself, seemed to hint that conspiracy might be in order one day. I took encouragement from this, since he was the only Watershute I judged it likely that I could be of much use to.

It was with the Talberts that, bottle in hand, I now made my first contact. Mrs Talbert would not, I believe, have known whether she was drinking champagne or cider, even if one had obtruded on her gaze the label on the bottle. Talbert, on the contrary, although so abstemious when in the fastness of Old Road, was well-seen in such matters, and evidently pursuing his customary party-going policy of securing a fair share of what was going early in the evening.

'I haven't yet been greeted by, or even seen, our host,' Talbert said, holding out his empty glass. 'I believe he works very hard. Only the other day Bedworth was telling me about him. Bedworth spoke with a misplaced air of confidentiality, to my mind. I recollect him as merely saying —and you know, Duncan, that my recollection is seldom astray—that Watershute has a very heavy tutorial load at present, and is making great sacrifices in its interest.' It was with massive confidence that Talbert produced this wild distortion of anything Bedworth could conceivably have asserted. 'But some of our younger scientists,' he went on, 'are sadly unsettled. Only the other day one of them—Lenton by name—actually sought my advice on how to write a novel. I referred him to you, Duncan, since you still write novels yourself.'

'But, Geoffrey,' Mrs Talbert said—as always, on a single in-drawn breath—'Duncan still writes *plays*.'

'Ah, plays.' Talbert received this correction with disfavour, and even seemed a little nonplussed by it. 'Duncan may yet come to write novels. The transition from the one literary kind to the other is not uncommon in maturity. Fielding's career is a notable instance.' Talbert sipped his champagne; his gaze became a shade unfocused; I could see that he was no longer quite clear that we were not sitting on either side of his little square table. '1707,' he said informatively, 'to 1754.'

'And what else did you say to Lenton?' I asked.

'I advised him'—Talbert's voice sank to an enormous gravity, but in the same instant I heard that faint rumbling laughter, and glimpsed in his eyes the glint that was like the momentary lightening of a horizon as remote headlights sweep on their way—'I advised him, my dear Duncan, to essay the now well-established *genre* of salacious campus fiction.' Talbert, thus coming—most mysteriously—bang up to date, enunciated the word 'campus' with exquisite glee, as if it were a vocable hitherto current only among primitive beings scarcely yet down from the trees.

Mrs Watershute's party was now revealing itself as planned on a large scale. Giles's 'a case of champagne' had been an under-statement designed to play down the prodigality of what his father was offering us from some unknown remove. Nor was it preponderantly a college party. A good many university notabilities were present, accompanied by their wives, and there was a higher proportion of faces wholly unknown to me than I was by this time accustomed to meeting with on such occasions. It was to be hoped that nothing untoward was going to happen. If it did, it would be in a kind of open forum so far as the university was concerned.

My next port of call was Professor Babcock. The figure is appropriate to a lady who, at an advanced age, still bore herself like a galleon of which the nobly-breasted figurehead was the predominant feature. She had by this time retired from her university chair, and might thus be described as permanently in dry dock. But she had chosen to continue to frequent the Oxford scene, establishing herself to this end in a *cottage orné* at the discreet semi-remove of Wolvercote. What made the Watershutes' one of her ports of call I don't know, and at the moment she was adopting a detached stance in relation to the company at large. I replenished her glass.

'Good evening, Duncan,' she said briskly. She seldom addressed male persons other than in a formal way, and I realized that I rated for this more familiar address on the strength of having first encountered her in my Oxford infancy. 'Is there any news of the McKechnies?'

'Safely back from Princeton, I'm glad to say. I spent a day with them last week. You'd expect Ranald to be still dripping from immersion in that think-tank. But he must be described as distinctly dry.' This sprightliness of repartee was again a legacy from our first meeting; with Professor Babcock to the end of my days I'd be hard at work keeping my end up. 'I helped Ranald in the garden, while Janet cooked us a splendid meal. I tried to persuade him to constitute his whole terrain an artificial wilderness on the best eighteenth-century principles. He took the proposal seriously, but decided that an artificial wilderness would be particularly hard work.'

'He was never afraid of *that*.' Professor Babcock was reminding me that McKechnie had been her star pupil when I was an idle boy concerned to be smart at a dinner-party—

one, in fact, for whom a career in some entertainment industry might have been predicted on the spot. 'As for wildernesses, our present hosts may be observed to go in for one with nothing artificial about it.'

'William Watershute is a man engaged on several fronts, and he probably hasn't much time for gardening.'

'Nor for attending parties, so far as present indications go.'

'Physicists tend to have commitments to various government agencies and so on, as well as to their college and university department.' I made these remarks with a firmness which I felt the Provost himself would have approved. I was learning, I told myself, to be the complete college man. And the wretched Watershute, after all, was our host, even if *in absentia*. 'I suppose,' I added, 'you now have plenty of time for gardening yourself?'

One ought never to imply that retired people have joined a leisure class. But as it was well known that Professor Babcock knew all about gardening (as she did about everything else) she could take no offence at this hint of the *cum dignitate otium* character of the life upon which she had withdrawn. I received, indeed, an approbatory thrust from the forward part of her person.

'When you retire to your native Scotland,' she said, 'it is to be hoped that you will take up arboriculture. With favourable soil, you might establish a cottage industry in walking-sticks.'

This was a Johnsonian joke such as Talbert might have appreciated. We continued our snip-snap conversation amicably enough, like conscientious wits in a Restoration comedy. Then, Professor Babcock having been joined by another academic woman in the person of Mrs Firebrace, I walked over to Jimmy and Anthea Gender, who had just arrived and made their bow.

'It can't be maintained,' Mrs Gender said, 'that the larder is bare.' She held up for inspection a small canapé, which had been made the foundation of a liberal hillock of caviare. 'But the same mayn't be said of this drawing-room. Whatever can have happened to the carpet?'

'The carpet, Anthea?' I had vaguely supposed that we were treading upon some orthodox parquet affair, but I now saw that this was not so. 'Perhaps they've sent it to the cleaners.'

Gender offered his wife a deprecatory glance. This was fair enough, and the more so as her voice possessed a carrying character. Fortunately there was nobody near us except Geoffrey Quine, the college Bursar, who came to a halt and turned round at once.

'More probably in hock,' Quine said. 'And why not? So is the whole damned country, isn't it? To say nothing of most of what's under the North Sea. Leased out like to a tenement or pelting farm. Don't look now. But where's the piano?'

Being unfamiliar with the customary Watershute set-up, I had no reason to suppose that a piano ought to be on view. But a covert glance afforded evidence that this was so. There was no piano, but there was a piano stool. It was perched in obtrusive isolation in a large empty window embrasure.

'I think, perhaps,' Gender murmured, 'that we are *expected* to look. It's a horrible thing to say, but I feel there's a distinct effect of a demonstration about this untimely party. I wish Anthea hadn't dragged me along to it.'

'Don't be a fool, Jimmy. We can't start cutting these people simply on account of some stupid college rumpus.'

I had never heard Mrs Gender speak thus tartly to her husband before, and the effect was uncomfortable, like a first glimpse of a house divided. I wondered whether we were all going to divide over Watershute. And I also wondered whether it could conceivably be true that the Watershutes had been reduced to pawning their possessions. In this secure

North Oxford setting it was an idea, surely, that could occur only to a jester in a public bar.

'Anthea,' Gender said, 'if there's something sticky about this affair, it's just your sort of thing. Exert yourself. Go and talk to Watershute's wife. And then talk to their boy.'

Mrs Gender, accepting this as only a mild challenge to her social resources, went at once.

## XI

I NOW NOTICED that there was a small undergraduate contingent at the party. This was unusual. There were those who held that such festivities ought to be organized on a fifty-fifty basis so far as seniors and juniors were concerned; that undergraduates, since they are officially grown up, should be treated that way and expected to enjoy or suffer the company of older persons. Not much could be advanced against the doctrine on a theoretical level, but most people acknowledged that in practice it didn't work too well. The young men would regularly bring along young women, and the young women would sometimes bring along young men, with whom for various reasons rapport was not easy to establish, and who were inclined to consume whatever was offered them in a silence which was in all probability only an uneasy and despairing one, but which it was possible to misinterpret as of hostile intent. So on the whole it was left to the Pocockes to mount such affairs on a large scale in the Lodging—other people undertaking the entertainment of their pupils in small batches and over a square meal. There existed, however, one exception to this general rule. Where a household ran to undergraduate sons and daughters it was judged proper that some of their own friends should be bidden to parties like this one.

Such was the state of the case now. Giles Watershute had hailed along a number of his friends. The first I noticed was Junkin, and I supposed that an intimacy had grown up with characteristic undergraduate speed between them. Junkin had become a man with whom acquaintanceship carried prestige, particularly since an event of which the evidence was now before me. Moggy was at the party—and no longer as his girl-friend, at least in the technical sense. Junkin had lately announced his marriage, not as a forthcoming but as an achieved condition. Moggy was lawfully established in Walton Street.

It might have been expected that this bowing to convention would impair Junkin's standing with his contemporaries. But I had discovered that the reverse held true, and had regularly so held in similar instances reported upon by my colleagues. Young men who appeared to have solved all the problems of sex by finding a young woman to go to bed with on a basis of decent demi-semi permanence, and others, fewer in number, who had done so in terms of a bold promiscuity, alike now treated Junkin with a deference approximating to awe. Junkin had forged right ahead of them into a mysterious region of unchallengeable maturity. And it was as gratifying to know Moggy as it was Nick.

I went over to speak to them. Two young men attending upon Mrs Junkin, whose faces were familiar to me although I didn't know their names, made off slant-wise at my approach, rather in the manner of nervous old women fearful of being brought in contact with the bearer of a cough or a cold. This code of polite behaviour was now well known to me, and not to be taken amiss. Junkin (who was in his London suit) greeted me warmly. He had placed himself and his bride beside a well-stocked side table with the prudent intention of making a substantial evening meal.

'Nothing wrong with the fleshpots,' he pronounced, possessing himself of a miniaturized hamburger as he spoke. 'Rather a surprise.'

'At least a useful one,' I said. Junkin's opening remark belonged to the same area of speculation as Mrs Gender's, and I wondered whether William Watershute's scandalous situation was now a subject of comment among our juniors. But for the moment Junkin's thoughts were running on general lines.

'It seems dons are shockingly paid,' he went on. 'They haven't got together to demand the rate for the job. Moggy and I met a young one from Balliol the other day, and we worked it out he isn't paid anything like what my dad is—or would be if they hadn't kicked the poor old man up from the coal face to cleaning lamps on top.'

'He cleans them very well,' Moggy said. 'I've seen them.'

'I don't think dons are all that badly off, Nick.' I felt that I had to disclaim grinding poverty. 'They occupy what Robinson Crusoe's father called the upper station of low life: the best state in the world, he took it to be.'

'I don't believe it's anything of the sort, Duncan. Look at Giles and his father.' Junkin—thus plunging, after all, in a direction I didn't want—paused to provide Moggy with a smoked salmon sandwich. 'Giles hardly gets a penny in student's grant, because of the means test on his father's screw. And he doesn't think his father can really afford to have him up at Oxford at all. It worries him a lot, and every now and then he comes out with some pretty queer crack. Do you know what he said when he invited us to this party? That it was probably going to be the last day in the old home. He said it as if it was a quote. An old comic song, I expect.'

'It's not a song. It's a picture.' Moggy, who tended to be better informed than her husband, offered this correction indulgently—and along with it a plate of sardines on toast. 'By a man called Martineau, and you can see it in the Tate. A degenerate aristocrat is tanking up his small son with wine in his baronial hall, and in the background there are bailiffs and auctioneers and people preparing to sell the whole place up. Giles told me he was going to get a lot of postcards of it and send them round at Christmas.'

'That's it. That sort of thing. It ought to be looked into,

if you ask me.' Junkin gave me a quick glance, biting a sardine in two the while. I realized that he hadn't been idly divulging a friend's confidences—which would, indeed, have been contrary to his character. He had spoken in the robust but ill-conceived faith that I was the person to do the 'looking into' which he judged desirable. I was still wondering how to handle the immediate situation when a diversion occurred which, although not agreeable in itself, brought confidential discussion with the Junkins to a close.

'Good evening, good evening! Chaffey's the name. But of course you remember me.'

I was the recipient of this confident address, and unable to deny its accuracy. Boz Chaffey's mere bulk would have rendered him memorable, even if there were not facets of his personality conducing even more powerfully to that result. I must have glanced at him in some dismay. Although a neighbour of both Giles Watershute and myself on Surrey Four, he struck me as an unlikely person to have become one of Giles's friends, and it was to be feared that the only explanation of Chaffey's presence at the party was his simply having got wind of it and walked in. There could be no difficulty in doing that. And Giles would feel unwilling firmly to turn him out.

'Good evening,' I said. 'May I fill up your glass?' It wasn't for me to discriminate against a possible gate-crasher.

'I don't mind if you do,' Chaffey said on a robustly concessive note. 'Would you say that people are enjoying themselves? Who's that old man who seems to have had a stroke? Did you see the much younger woman he arrived with? Do you think she's not his wife? What's this about Dr Watershute —and why isn't he here? What's this about a piano? I overheard something about a piano—only I couldn't get quite near enough to pick it up. Do you know? I sometimes wish I was a less bulky physical object.' Chaffey laughed loudly, and seemed disappointed that we didn't join in. 'I say, Professor, could you introduce me to a few people in the swim here? I'd be most grateful. Put you right in the good books of the fourth estate of the realm.'

'You, Chaffey,' Junkin said with deliberation, 'piss off.'

'What's that you said?' It was evident that the ace reporter declined to believe his own ears.

'Piss off. What I mean is something-else off. But we're in the presence of ladies, and I'm being polite. So just get lost.'

'You're drunk, and I allow for it,' Chaffey said—I thought with some presence of mind. And he turned round and marched away.

'Bloody fink,' Junkin growled. 'Sell his mother's death rattle for five bob.'

From Junkin's earlier remarks, it appeared as if the domestic situation of the Watershutes, and its hinterland in William Watershute's extra-domestic activities, had reduced the son of the house to sardonic commentary at least to his closer friends of the moment. I looked round for Giles now, wondering whether this discomposure was betraying itself in face of his mother's guests. But he was going round the party with a box of cigarettes, and exhibiting the same polite and slightly formal behaviour as had greeted Penwarden and myself when he opened the front door to us. Here, I thought, was another of the oppressive number of human situations I knew little about. If the general Watershute disarray was due to William Watershute's spending too much money (and time) on amatory enterprises elsewhere it was unlikely that this could be veiled from a young man of Giles's intelligence. So how did a boy feel when involved in broken-home stuff? I had no recollections from the past to help me answer the question. The Pattullo household in Drummond Place had been regarded as disorderly by conventional people, but it had been far from running to anything of this sort. And again, even if this hadn't been so, would the 1940s be any reliable guide to the 1970s? The latter period belonged with a decaying society as the former had not. So would a boy in late adolescence today react in the same way as would a similar boy then to the discovery that his father was messing around with a bunch of amateur tarts? At least would he do so if, so to speak, you scratched him? What is perennial in our domestic constellations, and what is not?

I transferred my attention from Giles to Giles's mother, and with a curious result. It was almost as if I were no longer in a drawing-room in North Oxford, but back on the stage of a London theatre long ago. It was during a rehearsal of *The Bear-Garden*, and I was much too young and diffident to say much. But I wasn't really approving of the dazzlingly pretty June Trevivian. She wanted too much of the scene; was too anxious to make her name; and was, in consequence, over-playing her part. And this was what June Watershute was doing now.

About the part itself there could be no doubt. She was the injured wife, bloody but unbowed, gallantly keeping her gay little flag in air. Even if this was her true situation (and that it was I didn't positively know) she was viewing it as a role and projecting it in a distressingly histrionic way. And now another memory came to me: that June, although not broadly speaking a good actress, owned a sound technical command of timing. She was timing something now.

Oxford's early dinner-hour was as usual looming up on the party, and at any moment people would be beginning to take their leave. Mrs Watershute had her eye on this, and was building her climax accordingly. She was walking across the room, exhibiting a courageous smile, and contriving to draw general attention to herself in not too obtrusive a way. She came up with Giles. Without pausing, she put out a hand, clutched him momentarily by the elbow, and walked on. *You and I must see this through together, my darling boy.* It was almost, I told myself, as if the woman had actually uttered these words. Giles, who was rather pale already, turned paler still. He must have been accustomed to his mother's demonstrations. But one couldn't blame him for not relishing his position in the least.

This small performance might well have been designed to bring down the curtain amid applause. But it wasn't so. Mrs Watershute went on her courageous way. She now more openly sought to gather attention—rather in the manner of a hostess who feels that things have turned dull, so that some enlivening manoeuvre is required. It was true that something of a silence had fallen upon the company at large. And then, within seconds, the *coup de théâtre* was achieved. Mrs Watershute sat down on the piano stool, gathering our glances with the roguish look of one about to indulge in a charming caprice for the further entertainment of her friends. She poised both hands in air, turned her head, seemed to become aware for the first time that her piano was no longer there, and burst into tears.

Macbeth's thanes at the unfortunate turning up of Banquo's ghost, or the courtiers of King Claudius when their monarch called for lights and broke up the play, would perhaps have been extravagant images for one seeking to evoke the controlled consternation that this little tableau occasioned. For, all things considered, the final moments of the party passed off tolerably well. In no time at all Mrs Watershute, with Giles beside her, was standing at her drawing-room door, valiantly shaking hands with her departing guests. I didn't myself escape without a second embrace.

Penwarden had left early, and I walked back to college with David Graile, whom I had only glimpsed from afar at the party. I expected an immediate and stiffly ironic commentary on what we had been subjected to. But Graile was subdued. For some time we made our way in silence through a damp and dismal Thames valley fog. When he did speak, it was to approach the matter from a slightly unexpected direction.

'I was sorry for that boy,' Graile said.

'Yes.'

'No doubt the woman had ample reason for letting her hair down. It puzzled me, all the same.'

'Actresses,' I said tentatively.

'Yes, of course. It's what will be said. It's one of the things that will be said.'

'Undoubtedly.'

'A woman like that—if she's really like that—would make any man hit the bottle.'

'Good Lord! Is that another of Watershute's troubles?'

'I don't know. I don't know him very well. Nor his wife, either. I don't often go to these things. Nor to the theatre, for that matter.'

I considered this for some moments in silence.

'Theatre people,' I then said, 'do tend to act theatrically. Even when scarcely knowing it.' But I knew that I was speaking with an authority I didn't feel. In this whole affair there had been an element I had totally failed to get hold of. I couldn't identify it at all.

'I suppose so. Duncan, you don't think there may be something else? Aside, I mean from all this wretched professional negligence and stupid womanizing? Something that she knows about and is scared of?'

'There may be. But I don't see how it fits in with all that play-acting. And it's enough of a mess as it stands.'

'Yes. He'll have to go.'

'You really think that?'

'They'll say he has to go—most of them.'

I believe we spoke no further word until we reached

college. We were just in time for hall. Mogridge was dining —recruiting himself, it had to be supposed, after one of his sessions in that Institute on the Banbury Road. Afterwards, in common room, I had a notion that he avoided me.

# XII

WHEN MARTIN FISH had spoken to me about *The Madonna of the Astrolabe* I had said that Peter Lusby, the young man who had courageously resisted the theft of Piero's picture, was 'making do' as a freshman. But I hadn't then gone on to explain why this was something we were very much hoping for. Since he had been admitted to the college which his elder and abler brother had so tragically quitted, it would be very unfortunate indeed if he failed to hold his own.

Whatever Peter might be short on certainly wasn't character. The sort of backbone that this term connotes he possessed, on the contrary, to an almost inconvenient degree. He might prove to be a very uncompromising person, and what his conscience told him to put first he would take a good deal of persuading to place second for more than half an hour at a time. From the beginning of term this cast of mind had revealed itself in his relationship with Arnold Lempriere, the benefactor who had given him a helping hand into the college by privately providing tuition directed to that end. Lempriere's inveterate guile had come into play when Peter—as I suppose—had been hesitant over accepting this help from a stranger. Lempriere had represented himself as acting out of a high regard he had formerly entertained for Paul Lusby, whereas he had in all probability been unaware of Paul's very existence until the day before his suicide. Whether this should be called an innocent deception I don't know. It had increased Peter's sense of obligation a great deal. Very properly, he had presented himself to Lempriere on his first day in college, and discovered—I don't quite know how—

that he was not only an old man but a very sick man as well. And this, he soon found, was a secret he shared only with Lempriere's manservant, a taciturn person; with myself; and with Robert Damian—whom Lempriere had lately, and probably ungraciously, come round to admitting to the role of his private G.P. Everybody, as I have recorded, knew that Lempriere was in failing health, but nobody else had tumbled to the full state of the case. Damian himself would not be in any hurry to publicize it, colleges being notoriously apt to acknowledge themselves not well equipped to handle situations of the kind.

It was a state of affairs all too tailor-made for Peter Lusby's sense of duty. Peter owned, moreover, the kind of sensitiveness which enabled him quickly to understand a great deal about this difficult old man. For many years there had been two facets to Lempriere's life in the college. He had dominated our senior common room, at least on its social side, and in particular enormously enjoyed entertaining in it former pupils of his own, many of whom had risen to, or simply inherited, august positions in the land. At the same time he had interested himself in the lives of our undergraduates to a quite unusual degree: entertaining them privately; making interest for them of one sort and another; catechizing them as to their intimate lives; and loading them, it was said, with a great deal of admonition of the sternest moral sort.

All this had been Lempriere's life, and lately it had been dying on him. In particular the young men had ceased much to frequent his rooms. They can't be charged with being faithless. There was, after all, a new generation of them around every year; and year by year the sort of relationships which Lempriere had fostered must have seemed increasingly little in accord with the *Zeitgeist* blowing through the university at large. I don't think the changing social composition of the place was much involved. Lempriere was quite as good with boys like the Lusbys as with boys like the Sheldrakes;

and he had a taste for rebels and misfits even when, like the unfortunate Ivo Mumford, they had a leaning towards being bad hats as well.

So Lempriere was now a lonely man, and it wasn't a condition to which he was well adapted. There used to come into my head at this time the occasion upon which he and I had chanced upon the aged J. B. Timbermill perched like a tramp on a bench in Oxford's Cornmarket. By this vision Lempriere had been terrified. But they were two very different men—Timbermill being companioned to the end at least by the residual deliverances of his own imagination and the achievements of his own scholarship. Lempriere was without resources of this kind.

Here was what Peter Lusby, pitched into the strange environment of a great Oxford college, had taken on. It seemed that Lempriere, among other things, was having trouble with his eyes, and reading was becoming difficult to him. That he had ever been much of a reader may be doubted, but whatever solace he might now have gained from books was being progressively denied him. So Peter read to him. He spent hours sitting in Lempriere's gloomy study, reading aloud heaven knows what. And Lempriere, no longer much in touch with the interests of the young, would at other times talk to him at length on subjects and people that Peter knew nothing about. Sooner or later this laudable act of corporal mercy might begin to affect Peter's work.

I got to know about the situation, although sketchily, because I was, for the time being, Peter's only confidant in college. He admired his tutor, Jimmy Gender, who had been his brother's tutor too. But Gender was being cautious about seeking to breach his reserve—knowing from experience, I suppose, that personal relationships with a tutor wear best if built up slowly. So I had to wonder about Peter's college life in general. Was he, for instance, making friends? Both my own memories and my recent observations told me that this is something commonly achieved by freshmen precipitately and sometimes with comical results; on the whole, however, intuition or obscure affinity triumphs over chance, so that a man's first friends remain his friends for as long as they are in residence, and sometimes for a lifetime as well.

'Have you made many friends yet?' I asked, not too casually. Peter had dropped in to return a book.

'Oh, yes.' Peter was confident at once. 'I've got to know a man called George Tarpark. He's from a London school too. George is very nice.' That George Tarpark had become 'George' was obviously pleasing to Peter. 'We've been going about together quite a lot. When I have time. When we both have time, I mean. Might I bring him along one day? He'd like to meet you. He knows your plays.' Peter might have been saying 'He's well up in Sanskrit'. 'When you're not too busy, that is.'

'Bring him in for half-an-hour before hall, Peter. If you're both free.'

'That will be just right.' Peter seemed alarmed at this promptness of response. 'George is reading English with Mr Talbert. He finds him rather a silent man.'

I am afraid I looked forward with no particular enthusiasm to making the acquaintance of George Tarpark. It seemed probable that he would be as excessively serious as Peter himself, but without whatever it was in Peter and his history that attracted me. Tarpark, like Peter, would be one who regularly discharged his religious duties in the college chapel, and discussed worrying theological problems over mugs of midnight coffee. I would have to be careful with Tarpark if I wasn't to offend Peter—which I very much didn't want to do.

It turned out that there was no danger of anything of the kind. When Peter and his friend entered my room that evening—Peter announcing 'This is George, sir' with a mingling of diffidence and triumph—I realized almost on the instant that I had been out in my reckoning. George Tarpark was not going to suggest immediate recourse to prayer. On the contrary he was the kind of youth who commends himself shamelessly to one's regard on a basis of gaiety and cheerful disrespect. He was looking at me now as if exercising uncommonly quick wits to divise some bizarre practical joke at my expense.

'Oh, sir, I say,' he said, 'what a gorgeous room. Oxford's civilization glimpsed at last. And to think that I'm condemned to sweat out long hours in that Talbertian chicken-coop!'

This might have sounded silly and rather impertinent. But Tarpark was only concerned to amuse, and behind the effort was the modest implication that this was about his mark. Since I had myself devoted a long stretch of years to the same enterprise it wasn't for me to be critical. Moreover Peter was looking a little anxious, although I thought I also distinguished in his eye a sparkle not often to be detected there. So I made haste with small hospitalities, assuring Tarpark meanwhile that I had suffered in the chicken-coop myself.

'Has he taken a vow or something?' Tarpark demanded. 'The chairs! It's like the people who walk about on nails.'

'So it is. But you must remember that Talbert doesn't live in college, as I do. He uses that room only for teaching. He does rather a lot of teaching, as a matter of fact. And he has to keep awake.'

'I can't see why. He'd be no less communicative if he was fast asleep.'

This was a pithy utterance, and Tarpark put it to me in a man-to-man way that it would have been indecent to snub.

'You'll get used to the silence,' I said with candour. 'It's upsetting only at first.'

'Oh, but there isn't any silence. You see, *I* talk. I just have to! It must be so dull for Talbert—whom I like very much, you know—sitting there all day running a series of Trappist committee meetings. So *I* talk to *him*.'

'What about?'

'Literature, of course. It's his thing, isn't it? He *ought* to be interested in it. As a matter of fact, I think he's beginning to be—just a little.'

'I'm delighted to hear it.' I thought it well to offer Peter a reassuring glance, since this could scarcely be his idea of a proper conversation between an undergraduate and a don. But I saw that this was unnecessary. Peter must have encountered a clown or two at school, but not one qualified to play the Allowed Fool. He evidently admired Tarpark. If Tarpark proved to admire him (which was entirely possible) their friendship might be to the benefit of both of them.

'What sort of literature do you talk about?'

'Oh, the major novelists mostly. From, say, Gore Vidal onwards.'

'Good heavens! Doesn't Talbert disclaim all knowledge of such stuff?'

'He doesn't have to. I don't *assume* any knowledge in him. I just tell him. I've worked out what might be called a syllabus, as a matter of fact. I think he'll eventually shape quite well.'

'Have you included, by any chance, what might be called the latest gen on campus fiction?'

'Oh, yes—I made quite a thing of that.' Tarpark looked surprised. 'Only I'm afraid he really was asleep.'

'I think not. You ought never to trust to simple appearances with Talbert. What does he say when you've finished one of those teaching sessions?'

'He says something like "Your next essay will be on *The Repressor of Overmuch Blaming of the Clergy*. A very interesting book." Or some thrill like that.'

'Yes,' I said. 'I remember that one. But I'll tell you a striking thing. He'll ask you to tea three Sundays running, quite forgetting that you turned up first and second time round. It can be rather embarrassing when his wife opens the door to you. But he'll never repeat himself in telling you the books you have to read and write essays about. Which shows —doesn't it?—that he's a very learned man. And, of course, he likes you to dig deep.'

'In unfathomable mines.'

'Exactly. I remember what he commended to my attention the very first time I went to see him. It was something called *Camilla's Alarm to slumbering Euphues in his melancholy Cell in Silixsedra,* and he said it was a very interesting book or pamphlet or poem or letter or something.'

'Oh, God!' Tarpark exclaimed, and banged the top of his head with a despairing hand. 'Three years spreading awfully before me! Shall I ever bid these joys farewell? And in a monkery too—a kind of melancholy cell on Athos. Do you know what Peter and I are crying out for? A lovely wreath of girls, dancing their sleek hair into tangled curls.'

Peter didn't look to me to be at all in this Keatsian condition. On the other hand, he didn't look scandalized, or even disposed to drop on his knees and pray that his companion might be redeemed from so unregenerate a state. He was fascinated by Tarpark. The young Bedworth, an attic varlet hypnotized by the frivolity of Tony Mumford, came fleetingly into my head. I judged it a fortunate thing that in George Tarpark there was quite evidently no vice whatever.

'Do you know?' Tarpark demanded out of the blue. 'Peter very much disapproved of that chap Chaffey getting his photograph of the dons into a sixpenny paper. It was indecent, he says, to show a row of elderly men eating twice as much as the horde of famished growing boys sitting below them.'

'I never said anything of the sort.' Peter spoke up robustly and at once. 'We all get more than enough to eat—although it can't exactly be called home cooking. It's the whole thing that's quite wrong. Our all consuming five times as much as tens of millions of people ever get a glimpse of in the Third World.'

'Not to speak of the Fourth.' Tarpark was grinning wickedly. Then he glanced at Peter, and his expression changed. 'Of course, Peter's right,' he said. 'He has something. I give it him. It's unfunny. Don't you think, sir?'

'Yes,' I said, 'it's unfunny, all right. Don't you disapprove of Chaffey yourself?'

'Are you kidding? Certainly I do. The bastard did it for a five-pound note. He's a traitor to his class.'

'What class, Tarpark?' I was interested in this changed note.

'The clerks. The clerisy.' Tarpark, a well-read buffoon likely to be a credit to Talbert in the end, had taken a jump from Keats to Coleridge. 'Us.'

Peter didn't make much of the clerisy. But the Third World was in his head, and he insisted on saying a number of serious things about it. He was capable of literally losing sleep, I imagine, over Biafra and similar intractable problems. Not greatly to my surprise, Tarpark fell silent and listened to him respectfully. If Peter Lusby had probably never before met a George Tarpark it was equally probable that George Tarpark hadn't before met a Peter Lusby. So here, I told myself comfortably, was Oxford education going on. I was quite sorry when a bell banged, and we set off for hall and our respective dinners.

But in fact I wasn't altogether comfortable about Peter, for I had sensed that he had something oppressive on his mind closer to hand than Biafra or Bangladesh. Perhaps his Lempriere self-assignment was getting on top of him. He didn't look too well.

Quite late that night he knocked on my door and stuck his head in—plainly anxious not actually to pay me a third visit in the day. I had to order him into the room.

'It's only this,' he said nervously. 'I don't quite like to put it to Mr Gender. He might get me wrong. So can you tell me what the arrangements are for going down for a bit? Just for a week-end—that sort of thing. There's a book of rules they give you, but it seems rather vague on the subject.'

'Probably because the subject's vague itself.' I looked warily at Peter, feeling in the presence of something unexpected and possibly ominous. 'In my time it was clear-cut. You had to get a chit from your tutor and take it to the Provost himself before they'd let you hook it for the night. In an earlier age, incidentally, you'd have had to get your tutor's permission if you wanted to go for a quiet country walk. However, things are more flexible now. If you're thinking of going home for a few days——'

'Yes, that's it.'

'Then I'd just mention it to Mr Gender, or send him a note—and that will be that. Nothing wrong at home, I hope?'

'Oh, no—nothing at all. Thank you. Thank you very much.'

Peter turned and made for the door—a state of affairs too unsatisfactory to let pass. Over the trivial circumstance of Peter Lusby being prompted to make a break for home there hung the enormous shadow, as it were, of Paul Lusby's having once so fatally felt the same compulsion. There must be something wrong with Peter to make him come out with such an inquiry. But even as I realized this I realized, too, that it was something quite simple as well. Until coming into residence, Peter had never been away from home in his life. He was home-sick now. There was nothing for it but to plant this commonplace fact squarely on the carpet between us.

'You're home-sick, Peter.'

'Yes, I suppose that's it. And it's insane! I've so wanted to come. And now there's this. I suppose I'm being a fool. I suppose it will go away.'

'If my own experience is any good, it certainly will.'

'*You* were home-sick, sir?'

'Yes, of course—although, oddly enough, I succeeded in blotting the fact from my memory for nearly twenty years. But I've recovered it.'

'I see.' Peter was silent for a moment, and I was afraid that he saw no reason to attend to my thus breaking into idle reminiscence, even if in a well-meaning way. 'Tell me,' he said.

'There's not much to tell. You know I once had rooms on this staircase? There's a man called Watershute in them now.'

'Yes.'

'If you went into the bedroom, and threw up the bottom sash of the window, you'd just be able to distinguish a small kilted figure with a bubble coming out of his mouth that tells him he must put up with it.'

'And you drew it yourself?'

'Yes. And I must have been home-sick to do that, mustn't I? Most of the people round me, you know, had been away at boarding-school since they were nine. I'd never been away from home except for holidays with relations. So I was entitled to my small spot of trouble.'

'Were you enjoying almost everything at the same time?'

'I was certainly taken to be doing that. I don't know that I was altogether unlike your friend George.' It struck me that this was an immodest assertion. 'Not so witty, of course.'

'Not so much bounce, you mean.'

'Let's say *élan*. It's a more dignified word.'

Peter consulted his French, and actually produced a rather wan grin. I had no faith that he could be much cheered up by chat, but perhaps chat was better than nothing.

'There are troubles,' I said, 'that come and go in a very unaccountable fashion. But home-sickness is something that can't last in Oxford for more than a maximum of eight weeks flat.'

'Yes, of course.' Peter sounded doubtful. 'Only it may be just one expression of a general weakness that will always get me down one way or another. I'm sometimes afraid of that.'

'It's nothing of the kind, Peter. Only there are times when one just has to hold on for a bit.'

'Yes, I know. And, of course, I know the right text.'

'What's that, Peter?' Rather unexpectedly, Peter had produced a gleam of fun. He understood very well that I thought of him as excessively well-seen in scripture.

'He who endures to the end shall be saved.'

'That's every wise man's text. And now it's about time that two wise men went to bed.'

# XIII

JUVENILE HOME-SICKNESS is not a mortal disease, but it did seem as if Peter required help. Whether consciously or not, his turning up on me with his question about college rules had been a call for it. I knew by this time that there was held to be a standard treatment for the malady. It consisted in the removal of the sufferer to within a domestic circle, for a day or a week according to the severity of the case. You yanked your afflicted pupil from beneath the bedclothes and took him home with you. In no time he was playing rounders with your children, or responding to your wife's request that he should pull up a few carrots. When he returned, his sanity restored, to college, nobody thought the worse of him. Undergraduates, having a clear view of themselves as passing through the most desperate of all phases of human life, take nervous disturbances among their number as nothing out of the way, and will visit a friend in a madhouse with as much unconcern as if he were in a holiday camp by the sea.

The Genders were the right people to deal with Peter in this way, and Anthea Gender would be briskly competent on the job. But Peter had taken his trouble not to Jimmy Gender but to myself, a friend having no official connection with him. It was clear that the last thing he wanted was to reveal any lame-duck quality to Jimmy, who was the man who had taken him on.

At this point the McKechnies came into my head. Being a professor, Ranald McKechnie had no undergraduate pupils. He was not one who felt no concern about undergraduates in general. He was known to hold strong views on what and how they should be taught. But individual undergraduates had ceased to play any part in his life, and I felt it probable that Janet regretted this. She would have enjoyed having young people coming and going around her. I didn't doubt that with Peter Lusby she would be very good indeed. I resolved that the McKechnies it should be. And a further thought came to me; I could mask the plainness of my design upon Peter by bringing his friend George Tarpark into the picture.

So on the following morning I rang up Janet, explained the situation, and asked if I might run both boys out for a day in the country. With luck something might develop from this. Janet agreed.

'I say!' Tarpark exclaimed as we turned off the main road. 'Is this their private drive?'

'Yes,' I said. 'And pretty bumpy.'

'Are they country gentry? All dogs and shooting-sticks and things?'

'Nothing of the kind. They live in an old rectory.'

'Then is this Mr McKechnie an old rector? That will be just right for Peter. They can have a quiet chat about the tridentine mass.'

'George, you just haven't been listening.'

'It's because he talks too much.' Peter said this with distinguishably recovered spirits from his seat at the back. He was acquiring proper notions of undergraduate candour.

'Yes,' I said, 'that's it. Ranald McKechnie is a professor of the university, George. And he's a fellow of the college as well. He and I were at school together, and I knew his wife at that time, too.'

'He got married when he was still at school? Some kids at my school had to marry. It was that or a bastard's lot for somebody. But I didn't know it happened in Scotland in the olden time.'

'Sir,' Peter said, 'I feel we'd better put George out. He's going to be impossible.'

'I think we'll just risk it.' Peter's suggestion had been offered facetiously, and I was increasingly convinced that Tarpark was proving a wholesome educative influence upon him. 'George may go off the boil when he finds himself in the presence of a man even more learned than Mr Talbert. By the way, the McKechnies have no children. The Talberts have the advantage of them there.'

'Peter and I will stand in for the day,' Tarpark said—thus touching the fringe of something scarcely in any conscious focus in my mind. But it did occur to me that much of Tarpark's present foolery was being turned on with the aim of cheering Peter up—not that he had hinted an awareness that Peter stood in need of anything of the kind. 'Is that him?' he now asked suddenly. 'He looks just like a country gentleman to me.'

I didn't know that I could agree. McKechnie, following his usual habit or addiction, was pottering about with a barrow and broom. His clothing suggested less a country gentleman than an agricultural labourer in some sombre story of rustic life. But at least a barrow and broom weren't lethal, and he had every reason, it seemed to me, for putting in long hours in the garden and grounds of his vicarage if the place was to be livable in at all. Even at this time of year—which I thought of as no more than a kind of tidying-up season—it was evident that there was a great deal to do. It could scarcely be that the McKechnies were too poor to employ hired labour of an appropriate sort. Probably there was none to be had. Or conceivably Ranald McKechnie nourished views of a high-minded but vexatious sort on the morally elevating effect of doing all one's own chores.

Becoming aware of our presence only as we tumbled out of the car, he greeted us in his customary way. Glancing from one to another of us, that is to say, in the most friendly fashion, he said 'Oh, yes!' in a tone of mild surprise, and then left the ball in our court.

'This is Peter Lusby,' I said, 'and this is his friend George Tarpark. I expect Janet told you about our invasion?'

'Oh, yes. Oh, yes—indeed. How very nice. I'll find her.' These utterances came with disjointed effect, but the resource represented by the last of them seemed to cheer McKechnie up. 'She'll be in the kitchen,' he said. 'So come along.' He turned and started off towards the house, and then checked himself and turned round again. 'How do you do?' he said. 'How do you do?' He shook hands jerkily with the two young men. 'My wife will enjoy seeing you. It's sometimes rather dull for her here. Of course she has plenty to do.'

'We can help,' Tarpark said promptly. 'And I like this place. Oh blest seclusion from a jarring world! Cowper, I think. He was a bit off his head, so it was sensible of him to opt for a country life. Do you keep tame hares, sir?'

I suppose McKechnie was surprised upon this first brush with George Tarpark's style. It was impossible to see anything unexpected in that. What was unexpected was the fact that McKechnie took a liking to Tarpark on the spot. It had been in my mind that Tarpark would amuse Janet, and that Peter Lusby's seriousness might commend him to the serious McKechnie. The following half-hour was to show me that I had got this the wrong way round. Janet was to find Tarpark a little tiresome (as more than a modicum of him could undoubtedly be), but Peter appealed to her at once. Correspondingly Peter didn't really get across to McKechnie, whereas Tarpark drew out a curiously boyish streak in him.

'So what shall we do first?' There hadn't been more than a few exchanges round the kitchen table before Tarpark made this demand—much like a child at the beginning of a party.

'We'll have a division of labour,' Janet said promptly. 'Duncan, you and Mr Tarpark——'

'George,' Tarpark said promptly.

'You and George will help Ranald with the chestnut leaves. They're much the worst, because they've gone so mushy that the machine won't gather them. Peter can stay here and peel the potatoes. And then lay the table.'

'Oh, yes!' Peter said. 'But I'd like to work in the garden too. After the washing up.'

I was pleased with myself, for here was a sign that the domestication-therapy was going to work. The McKechnies' vicarage—spacious in an ingeniously ugly way, and proliferating with pinewood panelling, expanses of encaustic tiles, and improbable Gothic windows—wasn't at all like the Lusbys' tiny ground-floor flat in Bethnal Green. Nor was Janet at all like Peter's mother, a woman inclined in her admirable fashion to stances yet more severe than Peter himself. But the vicarage was a home, and Janet commanded it, and Peter found these things good. By the time we came together again in the kitchen for a glass of sherry before luncheon he was relaxed and happy. The change wasn't dramatic, and didn't make him talkative, but it was as decisive as if he had been given a potent shot in the arm. I told myself that two or three further such occasions during the remainder of his first term would render him immune to at least one disease for keeps.

Most of the talking was still being done by Tarpark, but this didn't get in the way of his exercising an observant eye. When we went into the dining-room he halted before the chimneypiece and examined the picture hanging there.

'But look!' he said. 'It's a Pattullo. It's the lone shieling of the misty island. I'd know that man's stuff anywhere. Wouldn't you, sir?' He had turned to me. 'Why didn't you become a painter too? Pattullo the younger. It would sound awfully well.' For a moment he was silent, and studied the picture soberly. 'I love it,' he said to Janet. 'Have you had it ever since you knew Mr Pattullo at school?'

'Not quite. And we weren't at the *same* school.' Janet was amused. 'But we went to the same church—didn't we, Duncan?' Janet pointed Tarpark to a chair. 'Mr Pattullo's father gave me the picture as a wedding present. On my first marriage, that is.'

I believe that both young men were a little embarrassed by this explanation, as if it were indelicate to mention a first husband in the presence of a second. McKechnie was sufficiently aware of their reaction to offer some casual remarks about my father's picture himself. I suppose he didn't want Tarpark to form the notion that he had hit upon a tactless topic. How McKechnie felt about Calum Grant I didn't in the least know. He must have been conscious that he was himself not at all Grant's sort of man. But he could never have set eyes on that drowned fisher-lad. (Nor had I ever done so, although Ninian had.) There was no reason to suppose that jealousy or discomfort entered into his feelings about Janet's past. And marriages come in all shapes and sizes, and the unlikeliest-seeming are sometimes the best.

There wasn't much leisure for reflections of this sort, since the meal was a lively and at the same time slightly hurried affair. McKechnie had taken with surprising enthusiasm to the notion of a band of under-gardeners, and was working out a plan for the afternoon. I was beginning to form a further plan myself—one to bring Peter regularly under Janet's eye. Once a week, and whether accompanied by Tarpark or not, Peter would come out to the vicarage on a bus, and there perform a day's labour for an honest wage. Peter could use the money, without a doubt. It was true that what might be called campus employment didn't much happen in Oxford: less because there weren't plenty of undergraduates prepared to cook breakfasts or shovel coal than because conservatively inclined authorities feared that the spectacle of such activities being thus undertaken might upset the sensibilities of the full-time menial classes. But such considerations were of no relevance in this corner of darkest Berkshire.

McKechnie, meanwhile, although eager to get back to his garden, felt it proper that the meal should conclude with coffee, and that this should be drunk in his study. I hadn't been in the room before, and it was perhaps his idea that young students should be allowed any glimpse that offered of the life of learning. Most of the vicarage was sparsely furnished. Making our way across the hall, I was aware of our voices echoing through the house in a manner that hinted a rather disheartening emptiness: and this was the more evident because what was at the moment being produced there was a good deal of cheerful noise of a sort that seemed to generate itself naturally in the vicinity of Tarpark. But the study was sobering. It was probably the only crowded room in the place. I was reminded of that earlier luncheon party at the vicarage, when McKechnie had remarked that books were becoming a problem, but that the house fortunately ran to a vacant nursery wing which he proposed to use for their reception.

Even Tarpark looked round him respectfully, although not without being prompted to a challenging question.

'Books!' he said. 'And I'll bet they're not just loads of learned lumber, either. That's Pope. Thousands and thousands! Another contrast with the Talbertian scene. Sir, have you read them all?'

At this I could see that Peter had another of his moments of unease. McKechnie seemed to consider the question an excellent one.

'Do you know,' he said, 'I believe I can almost say I have? My father—he was a philosopher, although originally a Classical man—had a rule about books which I myself have followed on the whole. When he came by a new one by one means or another he never shelved it until he'd read it through. It lay on his desk until then. What do you think of that, George?'

It surprised me to hear McKechnie thus address a young man by his Christian name, since it must have been contrary to his habit. And Tarpark was obviously pleased.

'Shall you be coming by many more yourself?' he asked. 'Or are you near to winding up?'

'I suppose that here and there I'm approaching the end of a road.' McKechnie was delighted. 'But one can always learn another language. Portuguese, for example. I don't know a word of Portuguese. Do you? Or do you, Peter?' This bringing in of Peter's name instanced a sensitiveness to personal relations which one would scarcely have predicted from McKechnie's frequent awkwardness of manner and absence of mind. 'There's an extensive literature in Portuguese. And all those translations one's familiar with probably do only indifferent justice to their originals. Camoens in particular, no doubt. I must look round for a Portuguese grammar. But now about this afternoon. I have my eye on all that scrub on the south bank of the stream.'

Half-an-hour later, McKechnie's monster had been brought roaring from its lair, and the contraption called a scrub-cutter attached to it. There was a whole stable of these auxiliary devices; and some it was proper to hitch to the monster's snout, and some to its tail. Many of McKechnie's difficulties resulted from his inability to remember which went where. I imagine that a manual of instructions had originally come with each, but that these (since they belonged to the category of *biblia abiblia*) had been lost. Peter, however, proved unexpectedly apt with mechanical contrivances, and the scrub-cutter was hitched on in its correct position. 'Scrub' is a vague term. It looked to me as if the cutter—which was painted a lurid red with green stripes—would make no bones about demolishing young trees if they came its way.

'You'll both want to have a go,' McKechnie said to the young men. 'But I'll just show you the hang of the thing first.' He scrambled on to his familiar perch, and the monster jumped and shuddered into life. 'It's as powerful as a Jag,' he shouted over the roar of the engine. 'It takes really stiff slopes with no difficulty at all. Only you must remember to go straight up and down. Moving along an incline tends to unbalance it.'

I felt rather alarmed. We were now at the top of the bank. At its bottom, and before the stream, there was perhaps just room for one of the monster's celebrated U-turns. McKechnie was proud of its flexibility in performing this manoeuvre, and I had seen him successfully thus direct it before. But that had been on the public road at the foot of the drive, where the hazard had been from other traffic hurtling by. There might be difficulties of a different kind here.

McKechnie let in the clutch. The machine went at a reasonable speed down the bank, hurling out a maelstrom of scrub, thistles, mare's tails, hog-weed and hedge-parsley before it. McKechnie turned without difficulty, and the machine came up-hill again as effortlessly as it had gone down. Again he turned it, and then came to a halt.

'You see?' he shouted above the continuing racket of the engine. 'It's perfectly simple. I'll just do another couple of swathes.'

'Sir!' Tarpark's own shout was urgent. 'You might skid, I think. It's muddy underneath. Perhaps——'

But McKechnie was off again—not without taking a hand from the controls to wave at us. I was remembering this confident gesture, of which he was again obviously proud, when the monster did skid. It slewed through an angle of forty-five degrees, and proceeded for a couple of seconds in the longitudinal manner deprecated by its owner. Then it tilted up and rolled over and over like a nursery toy down the bank. I had a glimpse of evilly whirling steel before the monster was in the stream, and McKechnie with it. Already as we scrambled down the bank the water was stained with whorls and skeins of blood—as the Corry burn had seemed to be long ago when I covertly poured into it the factor Alec Mountjoy's unacceptable gift of sticky Kola. There were

139

further numbered moments before we realized the full dimensions of the accident.

I drove the two young men back to Oxford in the wake of the ambulance and of Janet in her own car. It wasn't the arrangement I had wanted, since it seemed dreadful to me that Janet should be alone hard upon the catastrophe, even if only on a short journey. She had refused to travel in the ambulance itself, saying that she would merely be in the way, and that in any case she would do well to remain as independently mobile as possible. It hadn't been a moment for argument. In any case, her nurse's training—for she had followed that profession in the long stretch of time between her marriages —lent authority to this disciplined decision. I wanted to go with her and let Tarpark, who could drive, bring back my car, with Peter as his passenger. But Janet turned this down too. It soon appeared that, although not in the ambulance, she was determined not to lose sight of it, and she clung to its tail as it went sirening first down the open high road and then through the environs of Oxford. At a roundabout outside the city I lost my own place in this breakneck cavalcade, and had at once to drive much more slowly. When we arrived at the hospital the ambulance had vanished, and I was told that Janet had accompanied her husband into the casualty department. We waited for half-an-hour, and at the end of that time an ominously reticent message was sent out to us. There was then nothing to do but return to college and go on waiting there.

During the later part of that afternoon I found that my mind, unlike Janet's, was behaving in a very unruly fashion. I may initially have been in what newspapers call a state of shock; if so, what followed would better be called a state of confusion. My mind kept on straying from the central situation—flicking over, as in a brutally cross-cut film, to peripheral or even irrelevant matters. I suppose this kind of dissociation is a protective mechanism, and well-known to those in constant contact with violent events. I worried about having involved Peter Lusby and his friend in so harrowing an episode. I remembered with horror how Albert Talbert, with his genius for misinformation, had once fallaciously informed me that McKechnie had been killed in a road accident. And I kept on presenting myself with a bizarre visual image in which Talbert—all the Talberts, indeed—again figured: that moment on Old Road in which an elderly dog (Thunderbox, successor to Boanerges) had met his end beneath a motor car. And behind all this I was conscious there lurked an enormous question. If Ranald McKechnie died what would Janet do? What might I do? Beyond this, again, there harboured thoughts so monstrous at such a time that I had to resist the final ignominy of seeking refuge in a decanter of brandy.

Instead of this I must have gone to sleep in my chair, since a moment came when I was abruptly conscious of Robert Damian as being in the room with me.

'Good evening, Duncan,' he said unemotionally. 'You've been mixed up in quite something, haven't you?'

'Yes, I have. Is there any news?'

'Not much that I've got hold of. It's not a pie I have any finger in, thank God. Or fist, rather. For it's the hell of a shambles, by all accounts.'

'Then you've had an account?'

'Sketchily, from a man I met a few minutes ago. It's clear you all did everything you possibly could on the spot. Only McKechnie lost the devil of a lot of blood.'

'If they get hold of him while he's still alive don't they just pump more in?'

'Yes, of course. But it mayn't be exactly plain sailing after that, I imagine.' Damian was looking at me curiously. 'You're making heavy weather of it, Duncan. I haven't seen you quite like this—not even when poor old Timbermill moved on. Are you a close friend of Ranald McKechnie's? He has always seemed to me rather a shy and retiring chap.'

'We were at school together, but never intimate. Hardly knowing one another, in fact. He was a high-flying scholar—all that sort of thing—even then. Of course, we've picked up a bit since I came back to Oxford. I know his wife better. We were friends as children. No, not as children. As young people.'

'Yes.' Damian uttered this monosyllable inexpressively, but I didn't think he was at sea. It was an understood thing among certain of the ladies of the college that between Janet and myself there existed a faded romance—the rumour having reached them, it seemed, by way of my late Aunt Charlotte's kinsman, Arnold Lempriere. 'Have I heard,' Damian went on, 'that Mrs McKechnie lost a first husband in an accident donkey's years ago?'

'Well, she's not quite that old.' I found myself offended by Damian's choice of phrase. 'But she did—and two sons as well.'

'Christ!' Damian, whose manner masked an amount of feeling inconvenient but perhaps prizeable in a physician, was silent for a moment. 'Well, one just has to wait and see. I suspect—although, mind you, I'm almost totally ignorant of the facts of the case—I suspect it may be for a long time. If McKechnie survives the next few days, that's to say. It might turn into one of those big team jobs.'

'Robert, do you mean——?' I think I knew what Damian meant, but failed momentarily of the means of expressing it.

'I've heard it called violating Clough's canon. About there being no need to strive officiously to keep alive. Striving has become fashionable nowadays. I go in for it myself with all that ancient mummy flesh in North Oxford.'

'Will you have a drink, Robert?' I asked this because I couldn't think of anything to say.

'No thanks; I must be getting along.' Damian moved

towards the door, took another look at me, and appeared to decide that he ought not to leave without attempting some change of subject. 'I say, Duncan, is it true that your colleagues have decided to go after that chap Watershute in a big way? To deprive him, or whatever their jargon is?'

'I don't know. But, yes—I think so. I don't care a fuck for Watershute. I believe he's in a mess—or several messes. Unfortunately, he has a very decent son on this staircase now.'

'I see.' Damian again spoke indifferently, but he hadn't failed to mark my dipping into language not habitual with me. 'You'd better go in and eat a decent dinner,' he said brusquely. 'And then have a bit of a jabber with the crowd till bedtime. When I hear anything more about McKechnie I'll let you know.'

## XIV

I took Damian's advice to the extent of not ringing up
and signing off hall, which was the course I had been disposed
to. When I set off through the early winter dark it was in the
company of Giles Watershute, who had come downstairs as
I stepped into the quad. More often than not he or Mark
Sheldrake joined me in this way. Giles looked quite cheerful,
so that I reflected on the resilience of youth. It would have
taken me some time, I thought, to recover from an entertainment like that lately offered by his mother. Being in
need of any heartening I could find, I fell into step beside
him.

'I believe you know a man called Mogridge,' Giles said.

'Yes, I do.' Giles's remark had startled me. 'We were
contemporaries here on Surrey Four.'

'He didn't mention that. But he said he'd met you at a
Gaudy.'

'We certainly ran into one another again at a Gaudy—only
the summer before last. Have you yourself known him for
long, Giles?'

'Oh, no—no time at all. And we got acquainted in rather
an odd way.' Giles evidently felt that he had something
amusing to tell me. 'It was in a bookshop, where I wanted the
last *Nouvelle Revue Française*. I'd put out my hand for it—
there was only one copy on the table, you see, although, come
to think of it, they may have had a pile of the things at the
back. I'd put out my hand for it in the precise moment that
this chap Mogridge, as he turned out to be, did the same
thing. It was really rather funny. We each made polite noises,
and then he said he'd buy it, and read it that night, and deliver

it to me at a knock-down price the following morning. It seemed a bit eccentric, but he was so very nice that I couldn't possibly snub the idea. And of course there was money in it in a small way.' Giles paused on this, and I had time to wonder whether his father's improvident courses had resulted in his giving increased thought to such matters. 'So that's what we did. He turned up in college next morning—it seems he's doing a good deal of work in Oxford—and we had quite a chat. He's a frightfully interesting man, although he talks at times in rather a laboured way.'

'So he does.'

'And we've met several times since.'

'I see.' As I said this I wondered whether what I did see (and had already been believing myself to glimpse) could be other than quite mad. 'Have you read any of his books?'

'Yes, of course—although I didn't tumble to it at first. *Mochica*. That's a tremendous thing. I felt it quite exciting to meet a hero. Being young and naïve, I suppose.'

'There was certainly something heroic about it all.' In a general way I felt doubt about the second quality that Giles had claimed for himself, but perhaps it was genuine enough in the specific instance.
around quite a lot since then, and I suppose he has seen a thing

'And, of course,' Giles went on, 'Mogridge has travelled or two. You might say he has an inquiring mind. He wants to know quite a lot about one. It would almost be cheek, if he wasn't so senior and distinguished a man.'

'He knows quite a lot about me,' I said. This must have been a confused attempt at humour. The more I looked at this thing which I seemed intermittently to be brushing the fringes of, the more I doubted my present sanity. From what tangible spring-board of fact had it propelled itself into my imagination? I wasn't even one, I told myself, who read himself asleep on sensational fiction.

'We none of us know much about other people, I suppose,' Giles said. 'That must be what literature—plays and novels and that kind of thing—flourishes on the strength of. It cons us that our fellow-mortals can be made sense of.'

'I suppose so.' As we passed under one of the big lanterns that create uncertain patches of light in the Great Quadrangle I glimpsed Giles's face and saw that he was no longer cheerful. His breezy account of the encounter with Mogridge had been a whistling in the dark. We walked on, and were again in near-darkness ourselves.

'Parents and children,' he said. 'Would you say they make head or tail of each other in a regular way?'

'I'm not very well-equipped to judge, Giles. But, yes, I'd suppose so, on the whole. Patches of obscurity, perhaps, and outbreaks of cross-purposes.'

'All that. There's said to be a traumatic phase when it begins to dawn on one that daddy isn't God and that some people find mummy rather absurd. But later, I'd suppose, a relation of confidence builds up again.'

'Yes. On the whole, something like that.'

Giles and I were now nearing the spot at which our paths towards dinner would diverge. We walked on in a silence that somehow took us past it. We were going to continue right round the quad, as we had ample time to do. My impression that Giles needed a fresh confidant had been reinforced in these last few minutes. And the very fact of my own preoccupation with another matter somehow drew me towards Giles and his answering unhappiness. But responding to it was a large and hazardous step to take.

'I usually made out my own father,' I said. 'More or less. Once I'd got the hang of what an artist is.' But this was temporizing. 'Giles,' I said into the darkness, 'is your father a bit of a puzzle to you?'

Giles took his time before answering this. Perhaps it was

only because a group of young men was walking past us, laughing and putting up a show of scuffling.

'Yes,' Giles said. 'Rather a puzzle. Just lately.' He paused for a moment. 'Do you remember my asking you why so many people have to work in universities? I had my father in the back of my head then. Since I've come to take a good look at dons, you see, it has come to me that he's not one. In temperament or something, I mean. Intellectually, he's a very high-powered one indeed: and I've never heard anyone doubt it.' This had come with a flash of pride. 'But he might have done other things. *Mochica,* now. My father, it seems to me, could have brought off what one reads of there.'

This view of the elder Watershute as a potential hero—or as a Mogridge—it wasn't for me to comment on. And even a brief silence seemed now to upset Giles.

'But I'm boring you,' he said. 'I'm sorry.'

'You're doing nothing of the kind. And don't imagine I'm at all pleased at your coming out with such a remark, Giles.'

'Sorry again. Shall I go on?'

'Tell me where you think the bother lies.'

'Well, there's money, for one thing. It seems to be in very short supply. It's far from very nice tackling one's father on a financial crisis in the family, particularly if there may be something not very nice about the explanation as well. All I managed was to say I wanted to go down from the university and find a job.'

'And your father didn't agree?'

'He was quite furious. He tried to make me promise not to mention such a thing again for a year. By that time, he said, things would be all right. But there was no explanation, you see, and I didn't think it was a promise he was entitled to exact from me. So it was all rather unsatisfactory.'

'Yes, it must have been.' I noticed that Giles's mother

didn't figure in these confidences, and I resolved to steer clear of her myself for the present.

'You know,' Giles said on a reasoning note, 'I don't see why one need be hard up in quite so flamboyant a way.'

Recalling the missing piano and carpet on the one hand, and the champagne on the other, I could have concurred in this readily enough. But I risked silence again, feeling that I had already gone a little far in drawing Giles out.

'And then there's this other thing,' he said. 'It's really very worrying. My father's away a lot. I think perhaps it's more than it ought to be from the college's point of view. One or two of his pupils have been a bit odd with me. Going out of their way to be friendly without lingering. You know what I mean?'

'Yes, I think I do.'

'However, he's at least back in Oxford now, and dining in college tonight. It's a relief that he's turned up again.'

I might have said, 'Let's hope it's not like the bad penny'. What I actually managed was, 'We'll keep in touch, Giles'. For we were at the foot of the hall staircase and about to part. Giles said nothing more, but gave me a swift glance and bolted, taking the shallow treads three at a time. I could only hope he wasn't regretting—or even panicked by—this strange conversation.

It proved true that William Watershute was dining that night; he was among those waiting in common room to go into hall, and standing alone in a corner of the big room with a glass in his hand. As I made to join him I noticed that what the glass contained wasn't sherry. He must have called for some alternative not customarily on offer. I had a notion that one might do this by way of consulting the taste of a guest, but that it was regarded as slightly tiresome when one was on one's own. In many trivial ways we were a curiously old-fashioned society.

148

'Good evening,' I said—and I am afraid I put into the greeting a cordiality I didn't feel. Curiosity, in fact, rather than charity was at work. 'I've just walked across the quad with Giles. He thinks that you and I and everybody else are unknowable. Perhaps he ought to be reading Philosophy.'

Watershute's reply to this not very pregnant remark was to wave his glass at me. Then he steadied the glass, and might be said to have waved himself instead. I realized that he was drunk to the point of being unsteady on his feet.

In certain other perfectly reputable places—a green-room, say, or a theatrical club—this state of affairs would have struck me as regrettable but as nothing out of the way. But here, I knew at once, we were on the verge of enormous scandal. Nobody drank too much in this common room until late at night—and even then you had to be both very senior and very able to carry your liquor in certain prescriptive ways if your excess wasn't going to be regarded as censurable. You could become boisterous but you mustn't hector; you could be vehement but you mustn't repeat yourself. All that. And here was Watershute very tipsy when about to dine in the presence of some three hundred undergraduates.

'You bloody man!' Watershute said loudly—and tapped me on the shoulder as if to leave no doubt that it was I whom he addressed. 'Oh, you bloody man!' Disconcertingly, he followed this up with a charming smile, so that I had to acknowledge that I was being greeted in the friendliest spirit. 'Dear old bloody Duncan!' he elaborated. 'Scots wha hae! The pride of the kail-yard school!'

'Nice to see you back,' I said—and managed to make a half-turn which brought the other men in the room within my view while avoiding the appearance of breaking off relations with the problem confronting me. 'Your wife gave a very pleasant party while you were away. I enjoyed it thoroughly.'

'Liar!' Watershute said.

As this was both true and again offered in the most amicable fashion, I found it difficult to find a reply. There were about a dozen men at the other end of the room, and I'd have expected them to be clumped together in consternation and consultation. But nothing of the kind appeared. Bedworth was talking to Gender at a sort of earnest leisure. Gender, with his head cocked consideringly to one side, was listening courteously and occasionally giving a grave nod. It was as if Bedworth had incubated a plan for turning a music-room into a seminar-room or a seminar-room into a music-room, and Gender were giving the proposal even more attention than its weightiness deserved. Other men were similarly engaged. There didn't appear to be any guests—which was a small blessing—with the exception of Dr Seashore, the university's Keeper of Pictures, much in favour among us as the discoverer of Piero's Madonna. Seashore was temperately admiring on the wall a drawing by George Richmond of some anonymous Victorian don. He was being assisted by our archivist, Christian Burnside—so that this extravagantly retiring man was having the ill-luck to be making one of his rare appearances on what promised to be a sticky occasion. The Provost hadn't yet turned up. I wondered whether Mogridge would join us.

David Graile was standing apart, reading a newspaper. He glanced up from it; caught, as I think, Bedworth's eye; went on with his reading. Then he put down the paper; seemed to notice, as he did so, some further item of interest; picked it up again and satisfied himself about this; finally abandoned it, and strolled across the room towards Watershute and myself. I stepped back a couple of paces, divining that I wasn't a useful element in the scene.

'Evening, William,' Graile said. 'A pretty dull crowd, wouldn't you say? Let's slip away. I've got a bite in my room. A bottle of Lafite, too, as it happens. And '61 at that.'

'You're drunk already,' Watershute said.

'Come, William——'

'It's becoming a habit. We have our eye on you.' Watershute swayed on his feet. 'And now it's solitary tippling in your own rooms, is it? Nothing more dangerous. Friendly warning, old boy.'

'Look, now, don't be an ass.' Graile spoke with more good humour than was habitual with him. 'Whether you come with me or not, you'd much better stay out of hall.'

'Stay out?' Watershute appeared to pick up the words in a hazy fashion. 'No, no, David. Far better get yourself safely inside. Might take you in a damned awkward way. Little girls—heaven knows what. And I can recommend a thoroughly discreet place. Passes as treating liver complaints. Lashings of booze around, but they fix it so that there's a vomit in every dram. So don't give up hope, old chap—and here's to your health meanwhile.' Watershute raised his glass so enthusiastically that most of its remaining contents slopped on the floor.

It would have been difficult to find any encouragement in these disobliging remarks—unless it was in the fact that they were most affably delivered, and that Watershute was no longer shouting. His manner had become heavily confidential. And now he turned away and wandered uncertainly across the room.

'What the devil are we to do?' Graile asked me as I came up to him. 'The man's capable of making a bloody fool of himself at high table. And—think of it!—his son may be dining.'

'His son is dining. We walked across the quad together.'

'Damn and blast the fellow! The very worst sort of drunk is the one the stuff turns to clowning.'

'I don't think so, David. Some turn berserk, and have to be classed as homicidal until they sober up again. That would be much more awkward. Look! I think he intends to have a go at Seashore.'

'Bother Seashore. I'm going to try to catch Edward on his way across. Give him a word of warning.'

Graile made for the door, no longer feigning leisure. Seashore was now alone in front of the Richmond; he was lavishing on it the kind of sad and fatigued approval he went in for. Watershute joined him, and for some seconds assisted in this respectful scrutiny. Then he began murmuring circumspectly in Seashore's ear. For some further seconds Seashore accorded him a mild and courteous attention. Then his features registered progressive surprise and dismay, and he was clearly relieved when Watershute strolled away again. He glanced round the room, caught sight of me, and approached by a circuitous route that gave Watershute a wide berth.

'How very remarkable!' he said to me. 'I had no idea! Watershute tells me that the Richmond over there is a portrait of Dr Butcher, the college murderer. I've never heard of him, I'm ashamed to say. It seems he killed and dismembered a boot boy, concealing the remains on the roof of the chapel. But he was a most eminent Arabist—I think Watershute said an Arabist—which is why the portrait continues to be exhibited. It must have been a most difficult decision to arrive at.'

'There wasn't any decision, and nobody knows whose portrait it is. Watershute was having a little joke. It was no way to entertain a guest. I apologize.'

'My dear Pattullo!' Seashore received this prompt civility (which showed how adequately, in those months, I was taking on the colour of my surroundings) rather as if it might be a little joke itself. 'Is it possible that Watershute has been drinking?'

'It would appear so. And I'm afraid everybody is a shade upset. That's why they're all not-attending like mad.'

At this moment the Provost entered common room, accompanied by Graile. The Provost preserved his usual air of regretting he might be a little late, while perfectly well knowing he was not. He was far from betraying alarm, and at once entered into conversation with Dr Burnside, who was an old friend. It was evident that he had already decided against any precipitate action. His endowments, I had sometimes thought, brought him within bow-shot of the character desiderated by Kipling in 'If——'. He would certainly wait and not be tired by waiting.

But now there was, at least, no more waiting for dinner. We straggled into hall with our customary informality, and disposed ourselves in a random or random-seeing fashion down the only side of the long table which had to be put to use on this not very well attended night. The undergraduates, on the other hand, represented a fairly full house, as seemed to happen towards the end of term, when people were hard up. A few had brought in girls. It seemed to me that this liberty, gained almost without a struggle after centuries in which the mere notion could scarcely have got into anybody's head, wasn't creating much of a revolution in Oxford life. I wondered whether mixed dining in a college hall had proved on experience to be an unpromising prelude to intimate relations between the sexes.

It was understood that while most of us consulted our own inclination in the matter of placing ourselves at table the Provost ordained his own more immediate company. Exercising this prerogative deftly now, he secured Seashore on his right hand and then—quite firmly—Watershute on his left. Thus, one might have felt, does a courageous commander elect for himself the position of principal hazard on the field. Burnside sat down next to Watershute in what seemed a vague and unrecognizing way. I posted myself on Burnside's other hand. On Surrey Four we were neighbours after a fashion, since he kept his archives in its attic chambers. It would scarcely have surprised me, nevertheless, if he now hadn't known me from Adam. But this at once proved not to be so.

'My dear Pattullo,' he said in his unexpectedly deep voice, 'I am delighted to have the opportunity for a word with you. I have made another of my little discoveries in those invaluable Allsop papers. And I feel it is bound to interest you. It is a record of a performance in this hall, and in Christmas week 1589, of Richard Puttenham's *Lustie London*. As you doubtless are aware, the play is a lost one, and hitherto there has only been Puttenham's own word that it ever existed. So I am venturing to hope that the discovery may be received as not unimportant from the point of view of theatrical history.'

'Yes, indeed!' My response to this information was designed to convey alert enthusiasm. 'And it must greatly interest Talbert. He's our prime authority on the lost plays of the Elizabethan period.'

'No doubt, Pattullo.' Burnside, the most gentle of men, spoke with a sudden grimness which told me that I had said the wrong thing. 'We all recognize Talbert as a great scholar. I think I may claim that his reputation has even penetrated to the recesses of the B.M.' Burnside allowed himself a relaxed chuckle at this joke at the expense of his place of employment. But then the note of asperity returned to his voice. 'But Talbert, I am sorry to say, entertains the most extraordinary notions about the Allsop papers. He asserts, and most dogmatically, that Theodore Allsop was an unscrupulous forger! Imagine, Pattullo, my indignation when he first propounded to me so monstrous a calumny. He seemed sublimely unconscious that he was slandering one of the most eminent antiquarians of the eighteenth century. I was greatly upset.'

I extricated myself from this unfortunate topic as well as I could, and Burnside's composure quickly returned to him. He displayed no sense of any threat to the general seemliness of things less remote than the learned pugnacity of Albert Talbert. This, at the moment, distinguished him from almost everybody else at high table. During the earlier part of the meal, indeed, Watershute's behaviour was subdued to a point at which irritation or tolerant amusement would have been the normal reaction to it on the part of his colleagues. Yet it was impossible that he had actually sobered up. (Tony Mumford was the only person I had ever known to possess the useful power of flicking out of drunkenness at will.) A single glance, moreover, revealed a man not quite adequately in command of his knife, fork, and wine glass. Once or twice he laughed loudly enough—or at least oddly enough—to attract the attention of two or three of the young men sitting nearest to us in the body of the hall. It was this kind of notice that we were all (perhaps rather comically) afraid of. Or we might have been indulging the dreadful vision of Watershute breaking out anew in some picturesque fashion, and of being thus caught for the instruction of the outer world by Boswell Chaffey and his flashlight camera.

That no disaster had happened so far was due to the efforts of the Provost, who had concentrated all his faculties on keeping Watershute reasonably quiet. Policemen are said to be trained to chat up drunks rather than to bundle them into a van, and Edward Pococke owned an analogous command, perhaps quasi-hypnotic in character, of the powers of persuasion rather than compulsion. Or so I reflected. It seemed to me at the same time that what was going on at high table in a general way was a kind of war of nerves. There was a diffused uncomfortable feeling of teetering on some perilous verge.

The Provost, however, was a man as punctilious in the discharge of one duty as of another. The moment came when he must attend to Dr Seashore, the guest on his other hand. This had the consequence of turning Watershute and Burnside into interlocutors, so that I had to direct my own attention elsewhere. I tried to spot where Giles Watershute was sitting in the body of the hall, being a good deal more concerned over the possibility of his suffering a humiliating experience than with any present discomfiture being felt by my colleagues. By the time I had made this search in vain, and exchanged a few desultory remarks with the voraciously hungry young man called Ralph on my other hand, it had become apparent that something was developing between Watershute and Burnside.

Burnside had once spoken of himself in my hearing as having been 'a rowing man'. Unlike the majority of that fraternity, he was not only a shy person but constitutionally timid as well. Had he not, at our first tête-à-tête amid his dusty archives, charmingly confessed to me that he had turned down a fellowship and plunged into the womb-like security of the British Museum out of a feeling that he was not up to the 'rough and tumble' of academic life? It was only too probable that he might fall a ready prey to the freakish impulses possessing William Watershute on this harassing night.

Watershute was now certainly directing upon him the confidential murmuring technique which had perturbed Seashore when suddenly confronted with the myth of the murderous Dr Butcher, that eminent Arabist. I tried to overhear what was going on. Ralph, less absorbed in his platter than might have been supposed, appeared to be attempting the same thing.

I caught from Watershute the words '. . . *last year it was pubs used by the troops*', and then '. . . *raising their sights*', and '. . . *stepping it up*', and '. . . *class-war element*', and '. . . *luxury London hotels*'.

It was a time at which one would have had to be very much a recluse not to be able to give these fragments an immediate context. But Burnside, as a remote scholar, was sufficiently near that condition to be looking considerably bewildered. And he was looking notably uneasy as well.

'. . . *what they think of as centres of the Establishment*', Watershute said.

'Jesus, Pattullo! Do you hear that?' Ralph asked this question in an uncharacteristic because cautiously muted voice. 'He's scaring the lights out of the old geezer with a load of crap about urban terrorists. Queer sense of fun.'

'So he is. I'll try to stop it.'

But this wasn't easy. Watershute had already said '. . . *actually under the Provost's car*', and was now pointing dramatically to a contraption like a portable oven used to keep plates and dishes warm for us.

'. . . *only have to open the doors*', Watershute said. '. . . *or under this very table, for that matter*'.

Burnside's expression was now one of uncontrolled alarm. Even so, there was something unexpected in what immediately succeeded. Burnside jumped to his feet, knocking over a wine glass and uttering a loud cry. It was in his confused head, no doubt, that he was alerting us to imminent and dire danger. And certainly everybody in the hall was aware of some untoward event. This would have been very embarrassing indeed but for the extraordinary presence of mind of the common-room butler. Observing a respected senior member gone thus abruptly out of his mind, he promptly let the tray he was carrying drop on the floor. There was a splendid crash of splintered crockery and glass. The fraction of time elapsing between Burnside's cry and this admirable diversion it would have been almost impossible for those sitting in the body of the hall to mark. I managed to grasp Burnside's gown and get him back to his seat.

'It's all right,' I said. 'The man's talking nonsense. He's drunk.'

As Burnside stared at me in bewilderment, I became aware that it was now Watershute who was on his feet. He pushed away his chair and began staggering past the backs of his fellow diners. His uncertain progress might have been interpreted as owing to the cramped space in which he moved. Reaching the end of the table, he stopped, and gazed down the hall. It seemed his intention to direct his further progress through it to the screens at the far end—in which case his condition would be immediately apparent to all. Then he turned and disappeared through the nearby door leading directly to the senior common room. I supposed that he had spotted Giles.

# XV

IF I LOST sleep that night it wasn't over the problem confronting the college in the person of William Watershute, or even because chance had presented me with a view of the matter radically different from any held by my colleagues. Watershute, the Watershute family, hardly came into my head at all. What I was busy with in the small hours was willing Ranald McKechnie not to die.

Scratch a man, however 'civilized', and he becomes a primitive being at once. The postulate has been a standard resource of psychological fiction at least since the age of Racine, and in our own time it has become alike one of the lessons of modern history and a dogma of analysts of the mind. In terms of it we are prone to build up pictures of ourselves which may be in large part mythological, and in which our lineaments may appear in some very disadvantageous lights.

It was a kind of myth in my family—and one largely invented by my father—that Ranald McKechnie and I had been rivals as boys, and would remain so. In actual fact our awareness each of the other had been intermittent and almost nugatory. Two boys heading respectively for a professorship in the University of Oxford and the scramble of the London stage have no reason to barge into one another. And it hadn't been McKechnie who had beaten me for Janet Finlay in a fair fight; it had been a man whom neither of us had ever glimpsed, and who by all accounts was well qualified for victory in any contest there had been. McKechnie's eventual turning up on me as Janet's second husband had certainly been a little thunder-clap of sorts. But it had happened only after ages passed, and my relationship with both of them had almost immediately sorted itself out in a wholly amicable way. McKechnie himself, although knowing all our histories, would scarcely have been aware of a problem. And Janet had controlled any difficulty there was. That here and now I was in any sense jealous of McKechnie surely belonged much more to the mythology than to fact. Yet I didn't know. Here I was, lying in the dark and desperately wishing—or telling myself I was desperately wishing—that McKechnie should live. Perhaps I was clinging to proper feelings in a laudable manner. On the other hand it was possible that there was obscurely at work the sexual funk of which Fiona had indicted me. I went to sleep while engaged in this inglorious self-examination.

The following morning began unpropitiously with one of Plot's more massive breakfasts. As he had carried it across a couple of rainy quads, and was now busy flapping a duster around me as I ate, there was nothing for it but to display an appetite I didn't feel. Before the toast and marmalade, however, release came to me in the form of my telephone bell. The caller was the Provost's wife.

'Duncan, is that you? This is Camilla Pococke. Can you possibly come over to the Lodging? There are matters to discuss.'

'Yes, of course. Straight away, Camilla?' I didn't doubt that here was a summons prompted by William Watershute's behaviour the night before. The last straw had been loaded on the Provost's forbearing back, and the informal committee he had proposed to me on our walk to Iffley was being summoned to meet and deliberate on the matter. I hadn't wholly shed my reluctance to have anything to do with it. And I felt particularly indisposed to it now.

'Yes, at once, Duncan.' (Edward Pococke would have added '—if you can possibly be so very kind'. His wife was

no waster of words.) 'There are several things to get clear.'
And Mrs Pococke rang off.

I wondered whether the members of an informal committee
wore gowns. Perhaps, being virtually conspirators, they
ought to have hats plucked about their ears, like the associates
of Cassius in *Julius Caesar*. I decided against a gown, and took
my umbrella instead. The door of the Lodging was opened
not by Honey, the melancholic butler, but by Mrs Pococke
herself. She took me into a small office-like room in which I
imagined she transacted business affairs.

'Janet,' Mrs Pococke said, 'is asleep.'

'Janet? She's here in the Lodging?'

'Certainly she is.' Mrs Pococke didn't scruple to indicate,
very justly, that my question had been unnecessary. 'We
couldn't have her dashing to and fro that none too cheerful
vicarage. I collected her from the hospital a couple of
hours ago. She'd waited there all night, and I hope she'll
sleep for at least a little longer.' Mrs Pococke paused for
a moment. 'Edward,' she said, 'will join us in a few
minutes.'

I wondered whether the Provost was still discussing his
breakfast, and with a better appetite than I had commanded
for mine. It now looked as if the McKechnies, and not
Watershute, had been the occasion of Mrs Pococke's
summons. Had it been otherwise the Provost would not have
thus deferred his entry on the scene.

'One gathers, Duncan,' Mrs Pococke said, 'that you were
there when the accident happened?'

'Yes, I was. I'd gone out to lunch with the McKechnies.'

'With two undergraduates?'

'Yes.' I was a little surprised by this inquisition. 'Two
boys called Peter Lusby and George Tarpark.'

'Lusby—the young man who defended the Piero?'

'Yes, indeed.'

'That is most reassuring. Edward will be reassured.' I

161

thought I caught a glint of amusement in Mrs Pococke's eye. 'Edward has been in some anxiety, as you may imagine.'

'My dear Camilla, whatever do you mean? Aren't we all anxious about poor McKechnie? I'm sure you are.'

'Yes, of course. But, Duncan, please be quite clear. There was no involvement on the part of those young men? They didn't contribute to the disaster by any sort of fooling around?'

'Certainly not.' I must have been staring at Mrs Pococke in astonishment—and perhaps indignantly as well. 'As a matter of fact, Tarpark, who is a sensible as well as lively lad, tried to warn McKechnie that he was doing something dangerous. And when the thing had happened, Camilla, both the young men did uncommonly well.'

'I'm glad to hear it.' Mrs Pococke left me in no doubt that this was true. 'And I think I must go and hurry Edward up.'

At this, Mrs Pococke left the room without more ado, and I was delivered for a couple of minutes to my own thoughts. They were characterized by wonderment. Why should the Provost's wife conduct this odd interrogation—which was clearly on her husband's behalf? But I had scarcely asked myself this question when the answer to it swam up out of memory. Hadn't it been I, when an undergraduate and accompanied by two other undergraduates, who had 'fooled around' on a golf course to the effect of our almost maiming, if not braining, Edward Pococke himself? The incident had lingered in his mind (as why should it not?), and I was associated there with the general notion of young men thirsting for their seniors' blood. That the Provost recognized a certain irrationality in this line of thought was demonstrated by his having set his wife to resolve the matter. In doing so, he had acted with his customary sagacity. Had he himself raised with me the possibility that I had let two young men behave in a manner endangering our host's safety, I'd have been very angry. Nobody was ever angry with Mrs Pococke.

But now the Provost was in the room—relieved that no scandal lurked in the misfortune that had befallen a Regius Professor, and greeting me with a courtesy even a shade more pronounced than usual. During these exchanges I probably betrayed some absence of mind. Mrs Pococke's questions, I found, had been curiously upsetting. What I had told her about the circumstances of the accident was strictly true, since neither the two boys nor myself had remotely contributed to it. Yet 'remotely' wasn't quite right. I had initiated the luncheon party, and in a sense it had been its very success that had precipitated the disaster. The company of the two boys—and particularly of Tarpark—had been unexpectedly agreeable to McKechnie. Just as he enjoyed general society once he had been dragged there, so—and more pronouncedly—did he enjoy the company of the young when confronted with it: I remembered how, on Janet's river picnic, he had so unexpectedly applied himself to manufacturing bows and arrows for Johnnie Bedworth. It was because McKechnie had been in high spirits that the accident had happened. And I had been the agent in bringing those high spirits about.

I knew that there was a great deal of nonsense in this. On the very first occasion that I had visited the McKechnies in the country Ranald McKechnie had behaved rashly with his monstrous engines, and it was improbable that this had been other than his habitual way of treating them. Had I been an insurance agent on that day I'd have insisted on a pretty stiff premium if required to estimate the hazard of McKechnie's electrocuting himself, or chopping off a limb, in the course of trimming a garden hedge. I hadn't, therefore, the remotest occasion to blame myself for the catastrophe. Yet I knew I was going to continue to feel irrational guilt, all the same. So here was the super-ego at work—and evidence that my id, or whatever it was, had it in for McKechnie, after all. But I saw that this analysis in terms of faded intellectual formulations wasn't going to cheer me up. Only Janet's being relieved of hideous anxiety would do that.

'A terrible misfortune,' the Provost was saying. 'But how lucky, Duncan, that you and those two capable boys were at hand! Lusby, of course, one would know one could rely on. And Tarpark, it would seem, is a young man with a great deal of vitality. I recall his tutor describing it in last term's report as *élan*. *Élan* can have its vexatious side. But there is much to be said for it.'

'No doubt, Edward.' I didn't feel that these remarks, designed as a species of palinode for the misgivings on the Provost's part lately messengered to me by his wife, required any lingering on. 'But what one wonders about is McKechnie's condition. Have you any news?'

'A telephone call only a few minutes ago. His life is no longer in danger but his condition is exceedingly grave.'

The relief I felt at the start of this speech obscured for a moment its oddity when received as a whole. Then my mind cleared on the point.

'Do you mean,' I asked, 'that there may turn out to be some fearful permanent disability?'

'That is what *they* mean, if I have not misinterpreted what I was told. Certainly I didn't feel that I was receiving any very reassuring report.'

'Does Janet know this?'

'Yes, she does.' It was Mrs Pococke who answered the question. 'Something of the kind emerged during the examination, or emergency operation, or whatever took place. It's a dreadful possibility—and a good thing that Janet is a courageous woman.'

'She has been through suffering before,' the Provost said. He frowned, as if displeased with himself for thus superfluously uttering what must be in all our heads. Then he made a small, helpless gesture of a sort not habitual with him, and therefore rather touching. 'It's deeply distressing. And what can we do?'

'We can consider some of the practical issues,' Mrs Pococke said. 'That's what Duncan is here for. And before Janet wakes up and I have to attend to her.'

'Yes, indeed, Camilla. One hates to think ahead in a way that envisages the worst, but it is prudent to do so, all the same. So we must tentatively predicate incapacitation—mental incapacitation—and nothing less. Needless to say, Duncan, McKechnie's academic emoluments come almost entirely from the university and not from the college. All the more reason that we should be on our toes, and see that the ball is set rolling in the right direction from the start.' The Provost paused on this, perhaps conscious that he had stumbled on an image of some oddity. 'Strictly speaking, the McKechnies' personal circumstances are irrelevant, but it may be useful to be clear about them, nevertheless. Duncan, I believe you must be well informed about the family backgrounds of both of them.'

'Within limits.' I wasn't entitled, I told myself, to dislike this conversation. The Provost was being perfectly sensible, and in feeling his way into university administration he must be on firm and familiar ground. 'I can't think they either of them have much money, Edward. They are both the children of professors in Edinburgh, and that isn't a monied trade.'

'Indeed it is not. How often have I to remark nowadays that academic people with little of their own are disgracefully poor. But quite happy on it, most of them. Dangerously happy! A man like Ranald McKechnie may see little out of the way in possessing nothing but a mortgaged house and a few hundred pounds in a bank. But there was his wife's first marriage. Would that——?'

'Janet married very simply, and when there was the tragedy you are aware of she was left quite penniless. She trained as a nurse.'

'An admirable woman,' the Provost said, and again wasn't quite pleased with himself. 'At least there's no family to bring up. Not that, in human terms, that doesn't make the thing worse.'

'So it does.' I felt the Provost must be awarded a good mark for this perception. He himself had children, now out in the world. 'There couldn't be any question of actual penury?'

'Good God, no!' The Provost, as a clergyman, didn't often permit himself this ejaculation. 'We have to keep an eye on the situation, all the same. For instance, effective medicine can come uncommonly expensive, even within the context of our blessed social-service state. Let alone outside it. Suppose poor McKechnie's man turned out to be in, say, Geneva or Turin. What then?'

'I rather believe, Provost, that you'd think something up.' I said this out of an enhanced regard for Edward Pococke. He was a man who looked warily ahead—and allowed (as it seemed to me at the moment) for the most unlikely contingencies. It was this that was in my mind as I saw Mrs Pococke cross to the door of her little room, open it, and listen.

'I think that's Janet,' she said. 'Duncan, it was very good of you to come in.'

I got to my feet, aware of being (very sensibly) dismissed. I badly wanted to see Janet, but this wasn't quite yet the moment for it.

'Duncan, I am most deeply grateful to you,' the Provost said, and led me to his front door. 'Most deeply grateful,' he reiterated, and showed me out.

As I walked across the Great Quadrangle I felt that Janet, for the moment, was in reliable hands. The Pocockes, butts of our juvenile humour back in those gay, those foolish 'forties, were a well balanced pair.

That afternoon I went to tea with Arnold Lempriere. This had become a weekly occasion, taking the place of our former perambulations of Oxford, which it seemed now improbable that he would ever resume. The vacation lay immediately ahead of us, when I understood it to be his custom to endure a week's exile from Oxford in order to be with his sister in Northumberland over Christmas. Whether he was proposing to make the journey this year I didn't know.

'I never expected to see you with a dish of tea,' I said—for I knew the old man liked to be rallied in this way. 'You used to say you never touched the stuff. Just like our young kinswoman Fiona Petrie, who starts in on her whisky at four o'clock.' Lempriere by no means approved of Fiona, whom he judged to have adopted an unwomanly course of life. He did, on the other hand, enjoy any invoking of consanguineous matters.

'I hold no brief for tea,' he growled. 'But young Damian says my liver is coming away in little bits. If I don't cut down on honest liquor in time, he says, it will be either the water wagon or the hearse. And which, he asks, would be worst? I like Robert Damian, thank God. The family's of no antiquity, but one of them did well at Waterloo.'

'Your tea's very good tea,' I said.

'So it ought to be. Gall understands these things, I'm glad to say. I expect he was at Waterloo too.' Lempriere gave his throaty chuckle at this joke, the only point of which lay in the fact that Gall, who was his servant, looked almost as old as himself. 'This equipage belonged to my grandmother, and the fellow knows how to handle it.'

I looked at the utensils thus described, and concluded that the silver dated from the reign of Queen Anne. And Queen Anne—I thought with almost Junkin's chronological haziness—mightn't have been dead all that long when Lempriere's grandmother first acquired the stuff. Lempriere himself looked very old and very sick this afternoon, but having an instinct for doing a thing in style he had got himself up in what was itself a grandmotherly way. He was sitting supported by cushions in a fireside chair, with a shawl draped over his shoulders and his hands in fingerless mittens against the winter season. He poured the tea with as much precision as if it had been a daily task with him since the turn of the century. But since his eyesight was failing the result wasn't always quite right. Gall—habituated to hearing all sorts of absurd things said about himself—was vigilant in a corner of the big dusky room.

'The lad Lusby,' Lempriere said. 'He's coming to read aloud uncommonly well. Improves with practice.' Lempriere paused virtuously, as if his only object in allowing himself to be read to was an honest endeavour after Peter's better education. 'Intellectually immature, but not a hopeless proposition by any means.'

'What are you making him read to you now, Arnold?'

'Suetonius.'

'Good Lord! In Latin?'

'Neither of us would be quite up to that, Dunkie.' Lempriere chuckled happily at this admission. 'First class translation by a young fellow called Robert Graves. I remember him very clearly.'

'Doesn't Lusby find Suetonius rather shocking?'

'Of course he does. Part of the idea. Broaden the mind and extend the sympathies.'

'Extend them to Nero and Vitellius?'

'We tried the *Satyricon*.' Lempriere had ignored my question. 'But we found it dull. I clearly remember, come to think of it, finding the *Satyricon* dull long ago. Stupid made-up stuff. *The Twelve Caesars* is another matter. Full of fun. And good clean fun, some of it. Or a little of it. Do you remember the emperor who had elephants trained to walk the tight-rope? Domitian, I think it was. No, probably it wasn't Domitian. Anyway, Lusby and I both found it uncommonly funny.' Lempriere paused in this rambling, and suddenly glanced at me with his old sharpness. 'The boy just looked in on me this morning,' he went on. 'Something wrong with him, I thought. He hasn't got at odds with Jimmy Gender, has he?'

'I'm quite sure he hasn't. But he has been a little home-sick, for one thing. And, for another, he had rather a shaking experience yesterday afternoon.' I hesitated for a moment. It hadn't been my intention to tell Lempriere the rather grue-some news about Ranald McKechnie, who probably meant little to him, anyway. But, having stumbled on it in this fashion, I thought I'd better go on. So I told him the whole story as briefly as possible. I couldn't have been certain that his mind hadn't wandered from it, but as soon as I'd finished it became clear this wasn't so.

'He'll probably die,' Lempriere said comfortably. 'And then you can marry the widow, Dunkie.'

'Why ever should I marry the widow, Arnold?' I was horrified by this echo of a voice muted deep in my heart. 'Don't be absurd!'

'Handsome woman, and about ages with you. Peasant stock, I'd suppose, but first class of its kind. Keep you out of mischief later on.'

I must have been unable to conceal that I was displeased. Lempriere, although with the mists gathering round him as they were, was aware of it at once. His eyebrows briefly rose and then fell again.

'Beg your pardon, Dunkie,' he said. 'Frivolous idea, and the subject's serious. Besides, it's a foolish thing to marry a widow when you may have a maid.'

'I don't think Samuel Johnson is much of an authority on marriage, Arnold. But I'm not going to marry a widow, if only because there isn't going to be a widow in the case. So think again.'

'It's what I'm doing now.' Lempriere was pleased with this retort to what had been a careless turn of phrase. 'It must be the girl, Dunkie. That's the long and the short of it. And make her toe the line.'

'The girl' had become Lempriere's way of referring to Fiona, so that I knew I was going to be in for another uncomfortable inquisition. It wasn't the less uncomfortable for being conducted in the continued presence of Gall. I hadn't been bred up to the belief that there exists a small class of confidential servants who are both deaf and dumb. Lempriere plainly had.

'Yes,' he said, 'it's the appropriate thing. Good people, the Petries. Hold up their heads with the Glencorrys any day. All that about King Gorse, you know. Wholly unhistorical. Sheer bosh.'

'I don't doubt it is.' With the exception of my Aunt Charlotte, no Lempriere, so far as I knew, had ever crossed the border even from neighbouring Northumberland. But it was a foible of Lempriere's that he was as well up in Scottish families as in English ones. 'And I don't doubt, either, that the Petries go in for being rather sane, whereas the Glencorrys go in for being rather dotty. But it doesn't add up to the propriety of my marrying my Petrie cousin.'

'Rubbish, Dunkie. I never heard anything against a man's marrying his uncle's granddaughter. Most natural thing in the world.'

'I doubt whether Fiona thinks so.'

'So you've asked her, Dunkie?'

'No, I haven't. But Fiona has made a kind of joke out of it, all the same. She's elusive.'

'You mean she's elusive when you go courting her?'

'In a fashion, yes.'

'Good heavens—pull yourself together, man!' Lempriere,

who would himself have courted a tightrope-walking elephant as soon as a woman, showed every appearance of being ashamed of me. 'Perhaps you'd better go about it in a more formal way. Take yourself off to Garth—if that's what their place is called—and ask her father for her hand.'

'Not possible. He's dead.'

'Dead!' Lempriere was outraged at having to receive this news from me. No degree of kinship more remote than his with the Petries could well be conceived. But he had decided that Fiona was related to him, and felt there was an affront in his not having been informed of her father's death. I judged it unnecessary to tell him that I hadn't been promptly told either—but only belatedly and by Margaret Mountain. It was Miss Mountain who came into Lempriere's head now. 'You'd have to get the girl clear of that little scribbling woman. Thoroughly unwholesome stuff, I'm told.'

'I don't know if it should be called that, Arnold. But she's certainly no Mrs Humphry Ward.'

'And then winkle the girl out of that young ladies' academy.'

'But Fiona's a very good scholar. Women *can* be that, you know. We have to face it.'

Lempriere produced an ambiguous noise, not exactly his chuckle, which I took to signal his understanding that he was being made fun of, and his willingness to put up with a modicum of this from a kinsman.

'Have one of those silly sandwiches,' he said. 'Gall makes them for his budgies, but brings them to table on visiting-days.'

I took a sandwich. 'Visiting-days' belonged to a vocabulary Lempriere was evolving to mark his semi-hospitalized condition. He had become fond, too, of referring to himself as an 'inmate', as if he had been reduced to incarceration in some antique Poor Law institution.

'What sort of fellow was the girl's father?' he demanded.

'Andrew Petrie? I never met him.'

'Good God! Then what does his daughter say about him?'

'Very little. Or almost nothing at all. She made a dash to Scotland lately on some sort of family business, but I don't think she's very much in touch with her people. She had to fight clear of them in order to get herself the education her brains deserved, and the struggle seems to have left its mark.'

'I don't like the sound of it at all, Dunkie. Perhaps you'd do better to look elsewhere.'

'I'll think about what you say, Arnold.' I don't suppose I offered this undertaking seriously. My distant cousinship with Lempriere had never seemed to me more than a harmless fiction, and I didn't feel it entitled him to any great freedom of admonishment—particularly as he was becoming increasingly prone to propound now one course and now its opposite. So I steered our conversation elsewhere. It appeared to be part of his code that this was something that had to be acquiesced in even with his intimates. We gossiped for another half-hour, and then Gall showed me out. As he handed me my umbrella his glance fell upon me only momentarily and totally without speculation. It was impossible to believe that he had allowed himself to overhear a word spoken on this odd occasion. But as he opened the door he spoke to me himself.

'Mr Lempriere always enjoys your visits, sir. And those of that young gentleman, Mr Lusby, as well. There aren't many others call.'

'I'm sorry to hear that.'

'It may tend to make time hang a little heavily on his hands. Of course he has his interests. He spends a good deal of time in the toilet.'

'Does he, indeed.' I was disturbed by this seeming reference to some purely physiological aspect of Lempriere's distressed condition. I was also surprised that Lempriere permitted Gall the use of a term which he would judge absurd. But

Lempriere, who said all sorts of outrageous things to his servant, would regard correcting his vocabulary as impertinent.

'It's the only place from which he can see the work being done on the tower, sir. Mr Lempriere is very much taken up with that. Only it's an awkward little place, with one of those narrow turret windows. He can see out only by standing on the convenience itself. It's not at all safe, to my mind.'

'It doesn't sound so. Does he lock himself in?'

'Not of late, sir. We've come to an understanding there, I'm glad to say. Thank you, sir.'

Gall bowed me through the door, and closed it softly behind me.

# XVI

THE ONLY RESULT of Lempriere's so blithely canvassing alternative matrimonial plans for me was to make me fight shy of Fiona for several days. I knew she had returned from Scotland, having been told so by the well-informed Mrs Firebrace during an encounter in the street. I found it impossible, nevertheless, to make my way to the little house on the Woodstock Road. I scarcely knew why. There was no rational ground for what I felt: that in the present circumstances there was a kind of indecency in moving from Janet to Fiona or from Fiona to Janet. I did see Janet several times during this period of her husband's state of coma, as in fact it appeared to be. She treated me, very simply, as the closest friend she had. But this didn't mean that she was going to weep on my shoulder. She was rather reticent, and it was from Robert Damian that I had to extract what possibly faced her. McKechnie wouldn't have to be kept alive on machines. He would almost certainly become self-supportive at a physiological level. But this mightn't be accompanied by a great deal going on inside his head. There were people in Chicago, Damian said, who were reputed to have made some progress in reversing the irreversible in that particular department. But it was way-out stuff so far.

This dreadful information was what, in some strange fashion, kept me away from Fiona. When we did meet, it was on a staircase in the Bodleian Library. Nowhere in the Bodleian is it possible to conduct a conversation other than in a muted fashion. The place carries a weight of learning that presses down on one like the lid of a box. Equally daunting is its smell: the smell of universal knowledge embalmed in books—but decomposing, if ever so slowly, all the time. Individuals prompted to any communication do well to get out into the open air. Under this impulsion, Fiona and I had left the building in silence and passed into the Schools Quadrangle. And again in silence we walked through the little tunnel leading into Radcliffe Square. I wondered whether she was displeased with me, or whether the Scottish trip had seriously upset her. The journey had been brought on by some family dispute, and I already knew that, even at the best of times, she wasn't fond of the whole ethos of Petrie family life. I felt that it was far from a good mark for me that we were cousins.

'How did you get on with your brothers, Fiona? Did you compose matters with them?' This seemed a question I might decently ask. But Fiona proved not to like it.

'How do you know about that?' she demanded. 'I've hardly ever mentioned my brothers to you.'

'That's true. We're neither of us very hot on brothers. Ninian and I hardly ever see one another.' I must have said this, which didn't fairly represent my own family situation, by way of trying to make a little common ground with Fiona. The attempt didn't come off. Fiona looked stony. 'I only know,' I went on, 'what Margaret told me when explaining your dash to Scotland. Why didn't you tell me you were going?'

'One can't tell everything to everyone.' Fiona had the grace to dislike this speech as she uttered it. 'I'm sorry—but it was at such short notice. And I'll at least tell you another short-notice thing now. I'm exchanging with Steenstrup.'

'Who on earth is Steenstrup?'

'I took you to his lecture at Burlington House. You can't have much attended to him.'

'I didn't. I was thinking of our dinner afterwards.'

'Belt up, Duncan.' Fiona snapped this out in a manner unfamiliar with her. 'It's for next term. But I'm going early, because of their library.'

175

'I don't know what you're talking about, Fiona.'

'I'm talking about a term's exchange with Professor Steenstrup of Copenhagen. You don't even listen. I'm going to lecture there. As a matter of fact, it's quite a thing, and you may congratulate me.'

'Then I certainly do.'

'As for my brothers, it ought to blow them out of my head. They've certainly been rather tiresome. In fact they came at me in a bloody low-down way. But I expect all that will sort itself out.'

'I hope it will.' It didn't seem to me I could inquire what 'all that' was. 'Margaret also told me about your father having died some time ago. I'm sorry.'

'And I didn't tell you about that, either. Well, I don't much talk about my family—or think of them, I suppose. I just never felt right at Garth, and always wanted to get away from it. Let's say that's the whole thing. But at least I feel I ought to have done better by my mother. We've agreed, you and I, that she's terrifyingly ignorant. But she's a decent woman enough. And she had a rough spin, after all.'

'Of course she's a decent woman.' It was easy to concur in this moderate encomium, but what Fiona meant by 'a rough spin' it was impossible to say. 'And I expect your father was a decent man. But, Fiona, it seems to me natural to grow away even from one's parents, if their interests and abilities are totally different from one's own.'

'That's what Margaret says—and acts up to. She hardly ever sees those parents of her in Paris.'

'Bother Margaret and her parents. Look, Fiona—your father's death hasn't landed you with a sense of guilt, has it?'

As I asked this question, I saw that we were now leaving Radcliffe Square and nearing the High Street. I wondered whether our ways were going to diverge there. Fiona was lengthening her stride as if something of the sort were in her mind.

'Guilt? Yes, I expect it has. I used to dislike him quite a lot—if only because he was so terribly mindless, and so pig-headedly determined I'd grow up that way too. But he *was* decent. For he did—didn't he?—do the decent thing.' Fiona looked at me searchingly. 'Rather a long time ago.'

The former Mitre Hotel, now a chop-house, was on my right. The former city church, now a library, was on my left. In front of me was the High Street, which hadn't yet changed into something else. But what had chiefly changed was Fiona, since a new and transforming piece of information had come to me with those last and not particularly dramatic words. I'd sometimes wondered what, if anything, Fiona knew about the circumstances of her arrival in the world. Here suddenly, replacing conjecture, was a piece of hard fact. Somehow it had come to her knowledge that her mother's marriage had been hasty and a matter of social necessity; that young Petrie of Garth had done 'the decent thing' by wedding the neighbouring girl he'd got with child.

It wasn't so very terrible a history, but it looked as if the awareness of it, however and whenever obtained, had come to colour Fiona's relations with her family in rather a drastic way. She was taking it for granted that I knew the story, but she had brought herself to refer to it only in so oblique a fashion that it was clear how little she was at ease with it. I now suspected, too, that her brothers knew the small but no doubt humiliating fact, and hadn't failed of some unseemly reference to it in the course of a family rumpus. But even if the dates on Fiona's birth certificate and her mother's marriage lines weren't what they ought to be, it was scarcely something for a clear-headed young woman to be uncomfortable over.

'Fiona,' I said, 'I do know what you're talking about. But is it so awfully important? Even if something slightly shameful is involved, how many people know anything about it? A small chunk of our family history certainly doesn't seem of the slightest account to me.'

I probably made this speech impatiently. My mind was more inclined to return to Janet than to linger over any supposed troubles of the sort that this conversation had stumbled upon. And it was stupid to offer Fiona, upset as she clearly was, well-meaning avuncular remarks. Even so, I didn't expect her instant reaction.

'Enough's enough,' she blazed out at me. 'I don't seem to have as much taste for the ludicrous as I imagined. Let be.'

'Fiona——'

'And look—I'm late. I'm going to catch that bus.' And like a child in sudden panic, Fiona dashed across the High and ran for Carfax.

That evening I dined with Martin Fish in a hotel at Woodstock. Fish had been looking at a Paris Bordone in some country mansion near by. 'A gaggle of tarts in a bawdy-house' was his description of it. But it was nicely done, and the owner willing to consider a reasonable price. It seemed a suitable canvas, Fish said, to 'touch them up a bit' in Adelaide or Perth.

I asked Fish whether he remembered Tony Mumford's Victorian masterpiece, *A Languid Afternoon,* a composition of somewhat similar erotic appeal. Fish remembered it very well, and didn't fail to remind me of how, through the agency of Robert Damian, it had so injuriously greeted the Provost and his guests from the position over my mantelshelf where *Young Picts* ought to have hung. I then told Fish of that later night upon which *A Languid Afternoon* and Ivo Mumford had departed from Oxford together.

This relaxed chat was assuaging and composing: ministrations of which I stood in some need. And upon this it almost necessarily followed that Fish became my confidant once more, with my beginning to tell him in some detail of the present state of the case between Fiona and myself.

'The key word is "ludicrous",' Fish said.

'What do you mean by that, Martin?'

'That we're back with Thomas Hardy. I reread that novel last week. It's ludicrous to be courted by a man who courted your mother. A sensitive girl wouldn't like it, at all. I suppose Fiona *is* a sensitive girl?'

'There's something rather hard about her, as a matter of fact. But, yes—of course she is.'

'Very well. The thing has got round to her. It's ancient history, Duncan. But that's it.'

'Look, the thing isn't there to *get* round. I *didn't* court my cousin Anna. I simply——'

'Yes, of course. But if you offered to marry her without so much as having kissed her in the gun-room or whatever of your blessed Corry Hall, that just makes the thing more absurd still. Hadn't it ever occurred to you that Fiona might have got hold of the story?'

'Yes, it had. But it's not really possible. Who would conceivably tell her such a thing?'

'Haven't you told me that the Glencorrys are all a bit mad? What about that uncle?'

'My Uncle Rory goes really and truly mad from time to time. Fair enough, Martin. His telling Fiona the story isn't wholly inconceivable.'

'Or the girl's mother herself?'

'Anna is so stupid that almost nothing would be beyond her.'

'So the possibilities multiply.'

'Well, yes. But, Martin, listen. The story of the generous young cousin would be meaningless without its necessary complement: the initial backwardness of Andrew Petrie after seducing Anna. Surely nobody——'

'I thought you said you'd been already wondering whether that part of the thing wasn't known to Fiona—and had perhaps been chucked at her again by her brothers?'

'That's true. I can't say that I myself think "ludicrous" is the word for all this.'

'That may be a failure in point of view. And I'm wondering, Duncan, whether, even now, we've got quite everything on the table.' Fish paused on this and found himself having to wave away a hovering waiter who had overheard his last words and failed to comprehend their metaphorical nature. Fish, I could see, was laudably anxious to sort me out. At least we were both in our right minds, which hadn't been so when I had attempted to perform the same service by him a long time before. 'This ancient business of your juvenile piping up,' he went on, 'and offering the betrayed maiden your hand. There's something oddly sudden about it.'

'Of course there is! It was sheer impulse, Martin. Just one of those things.'

'What I mean is, hadn't there been anything between the two of you before? Something that might have planted in your head—perhaps quite irrationally—the notion that you bore some responsibility to the girl, and that might have acted as a trigger. You see?'

'Yes, I do see.' I was staring at Fish in astonishment. 'There *was* something. But it was two—no, it was probably three—years before the Petrie business, and when I was the merest kid. It had nothing to do with the case.'

'What happened, Duncan?'

'Anna and I—Anna already grown up, and I nowhere near it—used to go tumbling in the heather. Wriggling over and under one another, and puffing and panting. All that. But it faded out ages before Anna and Andrew Petrie got together. It's just not in the picture.'

'Who would have known about them—those tumblings, I mean—apart from the two of you?'

'Nobody. Or, no! Anna's sister Ruth might. I fact I'm pretty sure she did.'

'Might she out with it, long afterwards, to her niece Fiona?'

'Again, it sounds inconceivable, Martin. But I'm not sure that it is. Anna and Ruth are rather like elder sisters in a fairy story. Only they're not ugly or positively malign. Just stupid. One has to come back to that. Simply not knowing the impact of what they come out with.'

'So you agree there would be an impact? Here's a young woman knowing she's attractive to a man—a kinsman—much older than herself. And she doesn't, on her part, find him *not* attractive. But she already knows—or somebody suddenly chucks at her—some quite *ludicrous* stuff about his past. He was petting her future mother in the heather long before she was born. And later, when another young hopeful went from petting to poking on those wild wide moors, forward the gallant wee mannie strode and declared that all might yet be well. It's *funny*, Duncan. Keep that in your head. And it's what this Fiona has to face whenever she looks at you. *The Well-Beloved* simply isn't in it as an achievement in the absurd. It would put any nice girl out of temper.'

'And now she's bolting to Denmark.'

'Very well. Say she is, and face up to it. Why shouldn't a girl bolt from a man, Duncan? It's her own affair, isn't it? Or it is unless she happens to have made some very definite commitment. Fiona hasn't engaged herself to you?'

'Of course she hasn't.'

'Then you must just wait and see what happens—and without starting to nurse a grievance. It doesn't seem to me you've been all that positive and whole-hearted in this affair. I think you did better among those tumps of heather long ago.'

'What do you mean, Martin—did better?'

'You haven't been tumbling with Fiona, I suppose. Have you ever kissed her—apart from that upper-class cousinly stuff?'

'No.'

'Shall we have another half-bottle of this wine—instead of brandy or that sort of thing?'

'Yes.'

By this time I'd had enough of Fish's stiff talk, although I was aware that it was both just and salubrious. And Fish himself now seemed content to leave his argument in air—or perhaps to incubate, as it were, under the straw.

'I'm taking the family to Rome at the end of the year,' he said. 'And then straight home, because of schools and things. But I'm going to be back in Europe on my own for a few weeks in spring. Your spring, that is. And do you know what I'd like to do?'

'Buy up the Louvre, perhaps.'

'Do a little tour with you, Duncan.'

'The art cities of Italy again? Who'd have guessed what lay ahead of you, Martin, when we prowled the Brera and the Uffizzi, boyish hand in hand.' Fish's suggestion must have cheered me up a good deal. 'I'm your man.'

'Bonzer!'

'Don't be silly.'

'You're a real cobber, Duncan.'

'Oh, Lord!' Fish and I didn't seem to tire of this ancient ritual nonsense.

'But not Italy. Scotland, Duncan. Do you know? I've never been there.'

'Then you've never seen the best Raeburns and Allan Ramsays—or the best Lachlan Pattullos, for that matter. So Scotland it must be, Martin. Until we fix just when, I'll keep the whole Easter vacation free.'

'That's fine. By the way, did I tell you I ran into Gavin Mogridge again?'

'No, you didn't. Was it in a book shop?'

'A book shop?' Fish was surprised. 'No, it was just in the street. As a matter of fact, I've run into him twice. The second time was on the departure platform at Paddington, and we travelled up to Oxford together. Gavin's very conversable in that slow-motion way of his. Did you say you know *Mochica*, Duncan?'

'Of course I did.'

'Did it ever strike you that the Mogridge who went through all that gives the impression of being a man with a *quick* mind?'

'Yes, it most certainly did. Did Gavin put in your train journey chatting about old times and old pals?'

'Just that. Bill Watershute, and so forth.' Fish glanced at me with a well-bred lack of curiosity. 'Shall we go and have the rest of the wine and our coffee by that fire in the other room?'

## XVII

WHEN INDULGING THAT gloomy self-absorption which
is a kind of vocational risk for lives without domestic ties, I
had more than once told Janet that I didn't in the least
understand the academic society in which I had landed
myself. That I wasn't like my colleagues was proved by the
fact that when I tried to forecast their reactions or decisions
I always guessed wrongly. In particular, the men around
me would suddenly be in a great hurry over something
I thought not at all urgent, or they would begin taking
their time in situations I'd have expected to bring them right
on their toes. This was now happening over William
Watershute.

I'd expected that Watershute's late disordered conduct, and
more particularly his luring the unfortunate Burnside into a
public exhibition of panic, would precipitate those consulta-
tive processes which the Provost had appeared to have determined upon. But nothing of the kind occurred. Term was
over; there was a general effect of packing up for Christmas;
the Governing Body held a final meeting of a prescriptively
brief sort. It was only after this that the Provost got together
his 'informal committee'. I gathered the inwardness of this
timing from Bedworth. Anybody now prompted to take the
bit between his teeth and demand that the college forthwith
proceed to some solemn corporate act would be balked until
the next meeting of the Governing Body some eight weeks
ahead. The informal committee would of course have no
executive power whatever.

When at length it met, it proved unexpectedly populous.
The Provost, I thought irreverently, must have been taking

no end of quiet walks to Iffley and expressing his particular confidence in no end of colleagues. Bedworth had the college Statutes on the table in front of him. Gender—wearing, so to speak, his barrister's wig as another hat—had prepared a document doubtless dealing with High Court precedents and the deliberations of the Queen in Council. There was provision for our recruiting ourselves with tea and buns when it was all over.

'We must bear in mind from the start,' the Provost said, 'that our Visitor is a difficult man. Of course all Visitors are difficult. That's a well-known fact of Oxford life. But some are more difficult than others. And bishops are the worst, without a doubt.'

This exordium, so strikingly without orotundity, represented Edward Pococke essaying an informal note. At the same time it came straight to the point. It might even have been said to skip several points in doing so.

'Have you visited the Visitor?' Adrian Buntingford asked. 'There might be something to be said for sounding him.'

'No, Adrian, I have not. One must be chary of sounding a sounding board. The bishop might reverberate one way or the other in all too noisy a fashion. Anybody who knows him will understand me. And he doesn't like us. It's as simple as that.' The Provost paused upon this further adventure into the colloquial, and seemed to judge it went a shade too far. 'It were idle to pretend,' he went on, 'that the posture of our affairs is other than delicate and difficult. So may I begin by advancing one or two considerations that appear to me important? I would hope for some measure of agreement on them. And at least they will have been ventilated—and in an amicable spirit, I am sure. May I continue?'

'Provost,' Bedworth said with solemnity, 'please go on.'

'First, then, we have to remember—it is a little difficult to remember—that we are not a club.' The Provost smiled round at us benignly. 'We cannot take corporate notice of purely personal aspects of a colleague's life simply because they may not be agreeable to us. I wonder whether I am right?'

'Right enough,' Buntingford said. 'But there are questions both of kind and of degree involved. A college might elect into a fellowship a man who proved to be far and away the most crashing bore in Oxford—which is to say a lot, God knows. But the college couldn't then turn him out; it would have to resign itself to him for life. In that instance degree of boringness wouldn't count, simply because an initial distinction would have to be made between moral and social turpitude. Now take a chap who hastens to get into bed with a colleague's wife. That's very improper and immoral and ungentlemanly and all the rest of it—entirely to be distinguished from being a bore. But again you couldn't sack him —or not straight away. Degree comes in. The dog's allowed several bites. Jimmy, isn't that right?'

'I don't think I'd express the matter in quite those terms.' Gender disapproved of Buntingford's tone. 'But it's certainly true that "immorality" is an uncomfortably compendious and indefinite word. Our Statutes—and I see Cyril looking at them now—speak of "flagrant immorality" as an occasion for the Governing Body's petitioning the Visitor to deprive a man of his fellowship. The adjective has without doubt been carefully weighed by those whose wisdom framed our rules for us. Sexual immorality becomes flagrant, I imagine, only when obtruded and reiterated and persisted in.'

'Exactly,' Buntingford said. 'Three bites or thereabout. Cyril, what are you digging out of that stuff?'

'I've just noticed rather an interesting thing.' Bedworth looked round as if to collect our attention. ' "Flagrant" occurs several times in our Statutes in their present form. In the seventeenth century the word was "heinous" in every case. It's a curious semantic point."

' "Heinous" is a stronger word than "flagrant", as well as of distinctly different connotation.' This came from Albert Talbert, whose presence had surprised me. 'I recollect Dr Johnson as judging it not a heinous sin, but merely a sin, to get a wench with child.' Talbert, who was strong on Johnson, paused with the air of one who has contributed a point of quite shattering relevance to a debate. 'Are we to understand that Watershute gets wenches with children *pertinaciously*? That would appear to be the point.'

'Certainly not,' the Provost said with some asperity. 'And nobody must suppose Watershute to have been improperly involved with any lady know to us. Rumours of such irregular courses there have been, but not in Oxford. Nor, such as they may have been, are they properly to be taken cognizance of. That, indeed, is the consideration with which I began. Only if sexual ill-conduct becomes a matter of open and, as it were, local scandal——'

'That's it,' Buntingford said. 'You're all right if you're not found out—or rather if you avoid being too much gossiped about by the neighbours. It's a shameful ethic, but it's the drill. Provost, I think we'd better pass to some other aspect of this affair.'

'Quite right,' Penwarden said. 'The man has become a damned nuisance about the place. During this past year, it's been as if sheer nuisance-value had become his aim in life. Adrian, don't you agree?'

'Yes, I do, Tommy. But you're still piping up—aren't you?—with the voice of what the Provost calls the club. If this *were* a club the man would get frozen out and that would be an end to it. But we can't go to the Visitor and say, "Bishop, we are minded to petition you in the perplexed matter of the bad manners of Dr William Watershute at bed and board", or something like that. The venerable prelate would simply have us shown to the door of his palace. The only point worth debating at a college council like this is the extent to which the man isn't performing his duties. When does the thing go beyond cutting his corners? The problem lies there.'

' "Contumacious disregard",' Gender said, looking up from his papers. 'That's what Cyril will find in the Statutes. It's a fairly testing definition. Is Watershute behaving in contumacious disregard of his duties as a fellow and tutor? We might have to prove he is.'

'Does a fellow have duties?' Buntingford asked. ' "Attendance at divine service upon all proper and convenient occasions." There used to be that one, but it went out rather a long time ago—and just as well for many of us. Tutors have duties. But I'd reserve my opinion about fellows.'

'An important distinction,' the Provost said. 'We may have to return to it. Are there any other preliminary views?'

'I agree that doing an honest teaching job is the crux of the matter,' Geoffrey Quine said. 'It is I who have to sign the man's cheques, you know. And I always have auditors looming ahead. I'd look a proper Charley—Provost, you'll permit the expression—if it proved I'd been paying a man who lived more or less permanently in Peking or Kamchatka.'

'David,' the Provost asked, 'can you help us in any way?'

The appeal was directed to Graile—who, like myself, had contributed nothing to this weird discussion so far.

'Only with a question at the moment, Provost. I presume you have attempted to discuss the problem with Watershute himself?'

'Indeed I have. I wrote to Watershute some time ago, asking whether he could drop in on me at some convenient season and discuss his plans. Unfortunately my letter would appear to have miscarried.' The Provost seemed pleased with this subdued sarcasm. 'I then took occasion to be informed by the porter on the gate of his next coming into college. When this occurred I called on him in his rooms.' The Provost paused again, as if to mark his full awareness of this sensational breach of protocol. 'He asked me to go away.'

'To go away?' Graile repeated blankly.

'Just that. And I fear I must divulge that he made use of an indecent colloquialism which I will excuse myself from repeating. It must be presumed that some degree of inebriety was a factor in his availing himself of it.'

So startling a disclosure produced silence. I caught Buntingford's glance, and Buntingford very improperly winked at me. Penwarden was breathing heavily. Bedworth looked extremely distressed; he might have been feeling that the college's last days had come. Gender had taken refuge in his papers. Talbert, having made his one pregnant contribution to our discussion, had apparently gone to sleep.

'I shall now ask the Senior Tutor,' the Provost said with sudden formality, 'to provide us, so far as he is able to do so, with a chronicle of the occasions upon which Dr Watershute has brought about inconvenience and a disruption of his pupils' studies through neglect of his tutorial functions. Senior Tutor, if you will be so kind.'

Bedworth produced what appeared to be a diary, and addressed himself to this disagreeable task. He made a thorough job of it. When he had finished, and had sat back looking thoroughly unhappy, a ragged discussion developed. Men who had not spoken hitherto said one thing or another. This went on for what seemed a long time. Eventually I became aware of the awkward fact that I was the only person left in the room to have said nothing at all.

'Duncan,' the Provost said inexorably, but with a return to his less formal manner, 'you have that fresh eye for our perplexed affairs. Does anything occur to you?'

'I gather, Provost, that depriving a man of his fellowship is a complex process. It makes me feel that we ought to do everything possible to get Watershute into another job more agreeable to him. But would anyone consider him a good buy? When I look at the present picture of the whole man I rather doubt that.'

'Perfectly true.' David Graile spoke sharply. 'Theoretically considered, the Provost is correct in saying that Watershute's private life is irrelevant. But it wouldn't be so if he were on the labour market—our sort of labour market.'

'That's my point, more or less.' I was grateful to Graile for chipping in, and rather hoped that I'd be judged to have said my piece. But this wasn't so. Men I hardly knew were looking at me attentively. 'Here's a distinguished physicist,' I had to go on, '—a nuclear physicist in a pervasively disorganized state. He must be very much his own problem as well as ours.' I hesitated for a moment. 'It does just occur to me to wonder whether he may be at risk—and our own reputation at risk as a consequence—in ways that mighn't readily come to mind.' Here I stopped, quite clear I wasn't going to say more—although this much it had been my duty to say. By this time I hadn't the slightest doubt that it was in his confidential professional character that Gavin Mogridge was interested in William Watershute. But this was something I couldn't possibly divulge.

The discussion continued, but without my hint being taken up. I had the impression that one or two people for whom the penny had dropped were feeling it prudent to keep silent. As for the Provost, he was doing little to direct the talk. He was seeing how the land lay, and nothing more. It was his instinct, too, that it is almost always desirable that land should stay put. Begin actively shovelling it, and landslide may follow. Having those reasons of my own for judging that the Watershute affair was going to prove uncommonly ticklish, I sympathized on the present occasion with his point of view.

This state of the case encouraged my mind to wander—until it was abruptly recalled by James Gender.

'We'll do no good by hounding the man,' Gender had suddenly said—and with much less than his usual mildness of manner. I instantly felt that here was a first hint of sharp fission. The college was going to divide over Watershute, and some men would be bobbing up on the unexpected side of the fence. Thus I'd have judged Gender, who as a matter of temperament went in for the proprieties, to be all for short shrift being meted out to our peccant colleague. It wasn't so. Gender was a conformist, but he was a very fair-minded man as well. He was also, of course, a lawyer, and disliked any hint of a kangaroo court.

'He's in a fix,' Gender went on. 'He's in a number of fixes, and we can call them all of his own making. But we don't yet know that he hasn't the sagacity to get out of them off his own bat.'

'Quite right.'

Graile uttered these two words sharply, and then held his peace. It was another surprise. Graile had been the first man to mention to me the trouble about Watershute looming ahead; he had predicted that it would be in the open within a month; later, he had declared absolutely that Watershute would have to go. He had attempted to humour Watershute when drunk, but it hadn't appeared to me to be in a friendly spirit. He alone, after the trying party in Northmoor Road, had revealed to me some sense that the affair might have dimensions we hadn't got a grip of. He had now—with these two words—abruptly shifted ground. Or so it seemed to me. I wondered whether his supposed understudying of Arnold Lempriere's role was going to run to a wayward movement of mind now in one direction and now another.

There was a moment's uncertain silence. Bedworth had put aside his Statutes and produced a newspaper.

'I think,' Bedworth said, 'people should see this.'

The Provost was the first man to examine the fresh document in the case. I was reminded of the occasion upon which he had similarly studied Ivo Mumford's *Priapus* when that graceless youth had impertinently obtruded it upon him.

A noble distaste had marked his expression then. It was doing so now.

'What the Senior Tutor has handed me,' he said presently, 'has the character of what I believe to be called a gossip column. I will so far test your forbearance as to read the title-line aloud. It is *"Dons on the dole—but the champers still flows"*. By "champers" is apparently meant champagne. With your further indulgence, I will give a moment to digesting the gist of the thing.' Composedly, the Provost let his eye travel down the news-print in front of him—his colleagues gazing at one another in some perplexity the while. 'The piece begins,' he then said, 'with a few perfunctory remarks on the present paucity of academic emoluments. That is harmless enough. It then proceeds to a ludicrous account of a party held in North Oxford. The furniture is in pawn, there are bailiffs in the house, the host is absent since he has been imprisoned for debt, but there is abundance of champagne. I confess myself at a loss before such a rigmarole. Cyril, what significance can this hold for us?'

'I understand, Provost, that it travesties an actual party given by Mrs Watershute a short time ago. And it is the work—for I think there can be no doubt of it—of an undergraduate member of the college called Chaffey.'

'The man who impudently took that photograph in hall, and sent it to the press?'

'Yes, Provost. It appears that he aims at a career in journalism.'

'There can be little doubt that he will go far.' The Provost pushed the paper to the middle of the table, as if for anybody who cared to read. 'But it is improbable that it will be from a continued base in this college.'

'I take it the article isn't signed?' Gender asked.

'It is anonymous—needless to say.'

'Then the editor is unlikely to divulge its authorship—particularly as it is equally unlikely that anybody will threaten to take him into court. If the young man, being taxed, were to disclaim the thing, there would really be little to go upon.'

'Perfectly true, Jimmy. I am most grateful to you. And it is, of course, the wider implication of this rubbishing lampoon that we must reflect on. The avoidance of publicity must be almost our first care in solving the problem ahead of us.'

'And which we'd better get back to now,' Penwarden said. 'Go quietly about it if you like. But the sooner we take means to part company with Watershute the better.'

'I'm afraid I don't find myself in agreement with you, my dear Tommy.' The Provost said this with perfect equability; he had been counting heads and knew his ground. 'Circumspection must be our watchword still.'

'I support the Provost,' Bedworth said swiftly. 'We must be prepared for action, but avoid going at anything head-on.'

'It is true that we must not confuse caution,' the Provost said, 'with a supine acquiescence in the unacceptable. But the stage at which we have arrived is that requiring—in the modern phrase—contingency planning. Let me recur to the very valuable distinction which we were reminded of by Adrian at the beginning of our talk. It is the distinction between fellows and tutors. It so happens nowadays that nearly all fellows are tutors, and nearly all tutors are fellows. But a radical difference in tenure remains. A fellow is elected by the Governing Body, subscribes to our Statutes under oath in the college chapel, and from that moment is in the enjoyment of his rights until he reaches retirement age. A tutor is simply appointed by the Provost, and the extent of his tenure is in fact as the Provost deems expedient in the interest of the educational function of the society. Were a Provost to terminate a fellow's tutorial status, his decision would be final—always subject, I need hardly say, to his retaining the confidence of the Governing Body. It is as a tutor that Dr Watershute is disappointing us, and it is therefore his tutorship that must first come in question. And there, I submit, the responsibility lies with me. I shall give the matter the most careful yet urgent thought, and hope to have your further invaluable help at a subsequent meeting. And I am most deeply grateful to you all for sparing time to assist me so generously this afternoon. Honey will now bring in tea.'

This sudden essay in autocracy went like a bomb. The majority of those present were relieved, and the disaffected held their tongues. The college council had concluded.

# XVIII

My own over-cautious speech had apparently gone under the mat, and I now felt oddly cut off from my colleagues. To them Watershute was simply an embarrassing problem, and their only concern was to resolve it while preserving a fair degree of unanimity among themselves. But I saw Watershute as a mystery, which was another matter. It was even possible to view him as on the verge of a precipice from which it might just be feasible to snatch him back.

My obvious course was to seek out Mogridge and insist on being told whether or not I was romancing to myself. But Mogridge was not around, and I had no notion how to find him. His name didn't occur in the London telephone directory. In *Who's Who*, where he figured as the author of half-a-dozen books, his address was given as care of his publisher, and I knew it would take some time to break through that. Moreover I was still chary of presuming on my knowledge of his true vocation in any interest whatever. I felt it to be an unspoken agreement between us that I'd never do that.

There was only one man possessed of the slightest good-will to the college whom I was conscious of as also in possession of Mogridge's secret. That man was Tony Mumford. Tony's father was also in the know, but could scarcely be regarded as well-disposed to us. I decided to contact Tony. A former Cabinet Minister ought to be familiar with the ropes in an affair like this. I waited until the morning following the Provost's council, and then rang Tony's London number.

A male voice said, 'Lord Marchpayne's residence'—a form of words with which I had endowed stage butlers in my time, but which I found off-putting when actually fired at me. His lordship was not at home. I gave my name, and asked where he might be run to earth. There was a pause which I imagined to be occasioned by a need to consult some list of reputable callers. I was then informed that his lordship was at Otby, and not expected home for quite some time. I rang Otby. Tony's own voice answered me.

'Is that Mr Cedric Mumford's residence?' I asked.

'Yes, you idiot. What do you want?' Tony had recognized my voice too.

'I want to run out and see you. It's about something rather important. Can I come now?'

'Yes, I suppose so.' Tony seemed oddly hesitant. 'But yes—why not? You may be of some use, I suppose. Providential, even.'

'Good.' I didn't pause to elucidate these remarks. 'I'll be there within the hour.'

'We'll be breathless,' Tony said. 'Stay to luncheon.'

Being accustomed to Tony's brand of humour, I didn't expect him to be waiting on the doorstep of the elegant Brobdingnagian doll's house that was Otby Park. A figure, however, there was. A female figure. Distrusting my senses, I glanced up at the big golden ball that glittered above the mansard roof. Then I looked down again. There could be no mistake. The female figure was Penny's.

I almost turned and drove away. I was furious with Tony for not having forewarned me—except in the most oblique fashion—of this strange encounter. I was also puzzled. There recurred to me an occasion upon which Tony had once referred to my former wife as a bitch, but I could remember no other connection between them at all. I climbed out of my car. There was nothing else to be done.

'Darling Duncan,' Penny cried, 'welcome to Otby! Welcome a thousand times!' She was running down the steps, and with the plain intention of embracing me. Only the sudden appearance of a hovering maidservant seemed to restrain her.

'Hullo, Penny!' I said, no doubt sufficiently lamely. 'How are you?'

'Tell Lord Marchpayne'—Penny had turned to the attendant woman with an air of considerable grandeur—'that Mr Pattullo has arrived.'

At one of my unsatisfactory encounters with Ivo Mumford, the heir of Otby, I had gathered that his father, like his grandfather, was a widower of a good many years' standing. Now, rather wildly, I expected the maid to say 'Yes, your ladyship', or something of the kind. Any such inference seemed possible. But if the maid uttered, I didn't hear her. She seemed merely to vanish obediently.

'But, of course, you have been here already,' Penny said. 'And long before me. How very, very strange!' And Penny produced that tiny motion of the lips—a *moue*, I suppose it should be called—that had once made me think of her as a very Helen of Troy.

At this moment the front door opened and Ivo appeared. He didn't seem surprised to see me, but he came down the steps with marked reluctance all the same.

'Oh, hullo, sir!' Ivo said. He produced his own facial spasm: the nervous tic that seemed now habitual with him.

'Hullo, Ivo—nice to see you.' As frequently before, Ivo struck me as in need of support which in all probability he didn't particularly deserve. 'Still in that Discount House?'

'Packed it up.' Ivo might have been more communicative had not Penny, baulked of embracing me, embraced him instead. It was in a mock-maternal fashion that didn't strike me as agreeable. Whether the young man relished it or not remained problematical. Penny, kissing his ear, apostrophized him as her dearest, dearest boy. I remembered the Sheldrake twins. Everything was as ambiguous as could be.

Tony now joined us from the house. It was my impression that—most uncharacteristically—he had been skulking in the hall before nerving himself to greet me.

'Hullo, hullo!' he said with false exuberance. 'Quite a reunion, Duncan. Jolly decent of you to come. All you dons are still busy, I expect. Not just sitting on your bottoms reading *Julius Caesar*, as the old ruffian likes to think of you.' Tony hadn't lost his habitually affectionate manner of referring to his father, the venerable head of the family.

'The term's over,' I said shortly. 'But it has left a bit of a puzzle behind it. That's why I've come to see you.'

'Excellent! You couldn't consult a more reliable man. We'll have it out as we look at the pigs. Ivo, help Penny to fix the drinks. I'm going to introduce Duncan to the prize Otby porkers. They're expecting him.'

Having uttered this nervous nonsense, Tony led me round a corner of the house. The Otby pigs may or may not have existed. Even if they did, I judged it improbable that there was really to be an inspection of them. And Tony came to a halt as soon as we were out of sight and ear-shot.

'Duncan,' he said, 'could you perhaps take her away?'

'Penny? Certainly not! She's no affair of mine. And how did she get here in the first place?'

'Ivo asked his grandfather whether he might have her down, and of course the old dotard agreed at once. Didn't even ask her name, I imagine—and had no idea she'd prove to be a gorgeous widow.'

'Penny isn't a widow. I believe the word is divorcée.'

'Well, you know the general idea. As a matter of fact, it was some time before I tumbled to her connection with you. Former connection, that is. No offence, Duncan.'

'Ivo kept mum?'

'Oh, I shouldn't say *he* knew much about her. Picked her up pretty casually, I'd say.'

'Wouldn't it be a matter of her picking up him?'

'You have something there.' Tony laughed uneasily. 'Anyway, here she is—and with a wardrobe that looks as if it might last her till Easter. I'm inclined to think the boy's a bit bored with her. Made the round of her, you know.'

'You mean he'll have slept with her here at Otby?'

'Oh, he'll have had it off with her, all right.' Tony's uneasiness grew, as was shown by this drop into the idiom of the public bar. 'Ivo's apt to get moody, of course, and the situation is really turning awkward. The old man's turning difficult. Couldn't you propose a brief reunion with her, Duncan? Nothing the least serious. A week in gay Paree, or something like that. She'd jump at it.'

'Tony, don't be so stupid and offensive. And what do you mean by saying your father's becoming difficult? Does he object to such goings-on at Otby? I wouldn't blame him myself. Still, it's said to be a common feature of country-house life.'

'Good Lord, nothing like that! The fact is that he's after Penny himself. Gruesome, isn't it? He can't have much jump left in him—can he? He pesters her, and she seems amused by it. But he can get so frightfully indecent, you see. Priapic, you might call it.'

'He did put his money into *Priapus*.'

'Oh, God—that! We pretty well have to drag him away. We've got Jiffy Todd in the house—you remember Jiffy Todd?—because he's the only chap can cope with the old satyr. The servants are bound to be talking. And it will be all over the village. I don't like it. I don't like it at all.'

'Perhaps you ought to shack up with Penny in Paris yourself.'

'Do you think I could?' Tony had again come to a sudden halt, and I realized to my astonishment that my foolish remark had been by no means alien to something already in his head. And now his expression had become frankly wistful. 'I expect it would be a good deal of fun with Penny.' He looked at me in shameless interrogation. 'Isn't that right?'

'Well, yes. In a way. Or several ways.'

'Of course she's getting on.'

'That's what Ivo's beginning to think, perhaps.'

'But it's a good age, actually, if you know your way around. Having her on one's own would be quite something. Here, you see, it would be all a bit difficult—because of one thing and another.'

I was silent. By 'one thing and another' I understood Tony to mean his father and his son respectively. The situation was, I suppose, less shocking than merely farcical. It was also the product of a side of Tony Mumford's life that I knew nothing about. And he was a coarser man than he had been a boy. Perhaps he held some affinity with Penny there. But Penny— I had to tell myself in fairness—deserved something of a salute for having brought off so notable an instance of her sort of thing. Twin brothers were nothing compared with this. Grandfather, father, and son. If I quite peculiarly didn't like it—and I didn't—it was because of the grotesque way in which it again hove Thomas Hardy's blameless *The Well-Beloved* within my horizon. Muddle the generations, and you may have the devil to pay.

'Well,' Tony said, 'that's the pigs.'

'Yes, indeed.'

'And now we'd better go and lunch.'

'Listen, Tony. I've told you I've something on my mind— and I reckon it's a sight more important than Penny's love life. Shall I tell you now?'

'Go ahead. We'll walk round the house.'

In fact it took a couple of circuits of Otby for me to expound the Watershute affair. Tony turned into another man, listening intently and without interruption, and, when I had finished, speaking at once and with complete confidence.

'Absolutely clear,' he said. 'I took means to find out about Mogridge after Ivo's affair. His isn't a line of business that stray Ministers are supposed to get curious about—but I managed it. He's high up, all right, as we guessed at the time, and he wouldn't be sent chasing after peanuts. So Watershute's nuclear physics or whatever is of a sensitive kind. He's not a don stuffed with *Julius Caesar*; he's a don stuffed with classified material. And he's been going to pieces in what you might call a copy-book way. Open to blackmail, open to mere bribery, and probably with some now concealed ideological slant. Fortunately they have tabs on him, and that's an end of it. Suppose he's thinking of defecting; he has no more chance of bringing it off than of reaching the moon. So you have nothing to worry about. Certainly there may be a scandal, and the college won't like it. They'll have to lump it, all the same. I advise you to forget the whole thing.'

'I'm in an awkward position, Tony. There are all those chaps mulling over the man's academic sins, and not one of them except myself will acknowledge having a glimpse of this dimension of the matter. Do you think I might properly tell the Provost about it?'

'Certainly not. Gavin Mogridge broke cover to help Ivo, and that's dead against his book of rules. If you tell Pococke he has Watershute under surveillance, the old donkey will hurry off to the Prime Minister or someone, and the whole thing will be blown.'

'Pococke will do nothing of the kind, if I stipulate against it. The man has his airs, but his standards of personal rectitude are positively terrifying.'

'Bother his rectitude. And just keep your mouth shut. See?'

'Yes, Tony.' I had received the advice—or injunction—I'd

expected, and was finding it hadn't much relieved my mind. Perhaps I had come to Otby on a fool's errand. Certainly I was landed with a social occasion so *outré* that it couldn't conceivably have come into my imagination at its most inventive moment.

'Shall I be seeing your father?' I asked, somewhat apprehensively, as we entered the house.

'If you don't see him you'll hear him,' Tony said.

I was indeed going to hear Cedric Mumford. We entered the dining-room upon the spectacle of a scared parlourmaid hastily removing from the head of the table the cover that had been laid there. The discomposing incident didn't perturb Jiffy Todd. Jiffy, once more attired as for the stable, greeted me with his customary urbanity. From somewhere overhead came a muted thumping and banging—suggestive, perhaps, of a demented plumber taking a short way to demolishing an unsatisfactory heating system. I wondered whether the squire of Otby had in fact possessed himself of a sledge-hammer.

'One or two badly affected elms in the park,' Jiffy said to me on a note of small-talk. 'Rather spoil the view from that window at the far end of the room. Care to have a look, Pattullo? Odd term, Dutch elm disease. Blame the thing on your neighbour, eh? Like French disease for the pox. Slightly awkward situation at the moment. Fortunate that you're an old family friend.' These last remarks, offered with no change of tone, coincided with our arriving in front of the window. The park, although sunlit, had a bleak winter look. Elms were in evidence, but as they were leafless it was impossible to estimate the extent to which the scourge had attacked them. 'Simply have to turn the key on him from time to time,' Jiffy said. 'It's either that, or have them come and take him away.'

'Like my Uncle Rory.'

'Ah, yes. I was sorry to gather, my dear fellow, that things were like that down at Glencorry. Pleasant memories of the place in your grandfather's time.' Jiffy paused on this correct degree of commiseration. 'However, we make out all right at the moment.' He glanced warily over his shoulder. 'Lady may go away, I suppose. Ease things.'

'Undoubtedly. But I'm afraid I can't weigh in. It would probably be counter-productive.'

'Not a thought of it in my head.' Jiffy hastily disclaimed having hinted any sense that I bore a responsibility in the matter. 'Some minor inconveniences, of course. Deprives us of the services of Cedric's butler for most of the time. He's upstairs now. Admirable man. Old soldier in every sense. Will know just when to nip in with a cutlet and a peg.' Thus indicating an Anglo-Indian hinterland I hadn't suspected, Jiffy led me back across the room. Our progress towards what promised to be a sticky refection was accompanied by a sudden crash of breaking glass directly overhead. 'Window, I'm afraid,' Jiffy said composedly. 'Chap around, fortunately, who can cope with that sort of thing. Everything done by direct labour at Otby now. Regularly constituted firm, and all that. Taxes. Pays off even on a moderate-sized estate like this. Does the lady call herself Mrs Pattullo?'

'I haven't the faintest idea.'

'They all three of them call her Penny. Don't seem able quite to manage it myself. The servants call her Mr Ivo's guest. Ridiculous expression. Hard to keep a decent face on the damned thing. Tony gone on her too, you know—although at the same time he's scared and would be glad to be rid of her. Out of office, but still afraid of scandal. No good telling him half the houses in the county turn themselves into brothels from time to time nowadays. Riff-raff of townees in most of them. You should see the bastards trying to sit a horse. Tony edgy ever since Ivo's confounded gang bang.'

These robust remarks—slightly surprising from Jiffy

Todd—brought us to table. The nervous parlourmaid was already making a noisy business of ladling soup.

Penny's line during the meal was that of the great lady who is the soul of tact. Since nobody else seemed prepared to do so, she directed the conversation herself, and for the most part through decorous channels. This effect, however, she counterpointed from time to time with glances now at Ivo and now at Ivo's father such as no lady, great or small, customarily indulges in on public occasions. I imagine she had in her head some picture of the manners of Regency society in aristocratic houses of an emancipated cast. I was intensely depressed. Had I been the poet Henryson's trew Knicht Troilus stumbling upon the leper-woman Cresseid begging alms I'd have been less abased than by this final vision of Penny Triplett encapsulated in sheer silliness. Not that she had ceased to be attractive. In fact she was still Cresseid in, so to speak, her heyday with the sudden Diomede and others. Tony goggled at her. Ivo was in a state of confusion I couldn't fathom. Jiffy remained his manful self, concerned to avoid a *débâcle* which it didn't seem to me would have mattered a bit. The food was well up to the indigestible Otby standard.

For a time the imprisoned Cedric Mumford appeared to have calmed down, so that I supposed he must be discussing his cutlet. But this gustatory event, if it had occurred, proved pacificatory only in the shortest term. Hitherto, Cedric's displeasure at his immurement had manifested itself only through the instrumentality of bangings and stampings such as might have been achieved by a poltergeist of gargantuan size. Now, his voice made itself heard. Nothing articulate, indeed, was conveyed by it, and this may have been just as well. What came to us was a howling, animal rather than human in suggestion, so that one might have been prompted momentarily to wonder whether Otby had set up with a 'wild life park' in the manner of some greater houses of its kind.

'Cedric's toothache,' Jiffy said firmly. 'It's becoming unendurable, I fear. But he simply refuses to see the dentist.'

'The poor darling!' Penny said expansively. Her eyes sparkled as she spoke, and it was impossible to doubt that she very well understood and appreciated the peculiar nature of her host's pathological condition. Had Apollo been a savage god of the jungle and not a well-bred Hellenic divinity he would have produced just such noises if trammelled in his pursuit of Daphne.

'Smuggle in the dentist,' Ivo said, 'disguised as the man who comes to wind the clocks.' On this wild witticism Ivo jumped to his feet, and I saw that he was looking quite desperate. 'Can I take Pattullo into the garden?' he asked his father. 'I've had enough. And I expect he has too.'

Tony only nodded dumbly, and with a helplessness such as I had never known in him. He might have been one of the feebler companions of Odysseus, passively awaiting transmogrification into an Otby porker. I followed Ivo as he stormed out of the room.

We went into the garden without pausing to pick up overcoats. It looked as if Ivo, at least, would be kept warm by his own vehemence. I myself would have to rely on keeping up a brisk pace. But Ivo, for that matter, was almost running. The gardens at Otby were much more extensive than I'd imagined. It looked as if he wanted to put the whole lot, and much of the park as well, between ourselves and the house as soon as possible.

'It's disgusting!' he cried. 'It's quite revolting! I suppose you think I was an all-time shit to bring her here?'

'I think nothing of the kind. I'd say Otby's rather a nice place for a love affair. Of course the result has been a little unfortunate. We have to face that.'

'It wasn't even much fun!' Ivo's familiar sense of injury

was suddenly in control. 'I suppose I mucked it. I suppose I mucked it twice. It wasn't a bit like what chaps say, or one reads about. It's all a bloody fraud!'

'Good heavens, Ivo!' Naïvely, I stared at the young man in astonishment. 'Do you mean that Penny is the first woman you've slept with?'

'Yes, she is.' Ivo, in whom there was much honesty, glowered at me furiously. 'I never got near that village trollop, you know.'

'No. And I recall your grandfather being displeased by the fact.'

'It's something one keeps dark about, isn't it? Never having had much sex, I mean. And I'm nineteen.' Ivo hesitated and flushed—impelled to yet more shameful confession. 'I'll quite soon be twenty.'

*How soon hath Time the suttle theef of youth* . . . Across the years, I was conscious of a source of strong fellow-feeling with Ivo. It is very terrible to feel that only old age lies ahead, and that so far one has done no more than muck things in bed—or even in a barn. But it was never rewarding to make sympathetic noises to Ivo.

'You must look on the cheerful side,' I said. 'Penny's pleasure at least must have been increased by your unseasoned condition. She's something of a rapist, really. And goes in for collecting maidenheads.'

'But it's too late for my father's, isn't it? Not to speak of my grandfather's. It's all too utterly disgusting. *Old men!* They're positively nymphomaniac.'

'Nymphomania works the other way on.' I was amused by this cropping up of Ivo's defective education. 'And don't you exaggerate the thing a little? There's nothing disgusting or unnatural in your father's being attracted by Penny. She's a very attractive woman. But I agree that your grandfather's manner of feeling the flame is another matter. Jiffy Todd's an admirable friend, but a bit too anxious to cover up. I'd say it's your job to get the old man into reliable medical hands.'

'They wouldn't listen to me.'

'Your father will do pretty well anything you tell him, Ivo —I'm rather sorry to say.'

'It's been one of my troubles, hasn't it?' Ivo managed the less unattractive of his smiles. 'All right—I'll try. But what about Penny?'

'What about Penny, indeed. She's your problem. And if you land yourself with her as a stepmother you'll have no case for complaining.'

'That isn't true. It would be disgusting—a man's stealing his son's mistress.' Enunciating this last word appeared to give Ivo confidence. 'It might be better, mightn't it, after another try or two?'

'Almost certainly.'

'If she let me. You never know where you are with Penny.'

'That's true, Ivo. And it's sometimes a rude shock when you do.'

'Don't you think this is a funny conversation for you and me to have?'

'No.'

'Her having been your wife made it seem more of a lark at first. That was pretty foul.'

'Nothing of the kind. Don't dramatize yourself, Ivo. You've been involved—you *are* involved—in a totally commonplace affair. A very young man and a much older woman of predatory habit. To the outside world it's entirely boring.'

We were now in a remote and somewhat untended corner of the grounds. There were thick beech leaves on the path, and Ivo began scuffing through them viciously like a sulky child.

'All right,' he said—suddenly and surprisingly. 'I'll take all that. I don't *love* Penny, or anything of that sort. Mostly now I wish she'd get lost. But then it comes over me again. You can't quite have forgotten how.'

'Indeed I haven't.' Ivo's touching an impertinent note was a sign that his father's resilience was working in him.

'And I'd rather it ended with a bang than a whimper. Or just a few bangs. Of course I couldn't think of getting tied up to somebody who's——'

'Old enough to be your mother.' Ivo had hesitated, and I completed what was clearly his thought. 'And now I feel we've about finished this talk. I must be thinking of getting back to Oxford.'

'But there's something *else* I wanted to talk about.' Ivo had come to a halt, and was looking at me awkwardly and strangely. 'It's about that man's brother.'

'Paul Lusby's brother?' I had understood this at once.

'Yes—Peter Lusby. We met in that bloody Discount House. It was very odd. He'd come in as a temporary office boy.'

'And was making the tea as well as licking the stamps. I know all about that.'

'Oh, I see.' Ivo was disconcerted. 'The point is that I don't think I was very nice to him. It was quite some time, as a matter of fact, before I discovered who he was. And he knew the facts. Or got to know the facts.' Ivo's face twitched. The Furies, I saw, still held a niche in his mind.

'He had the story from me, Ivo. Fairly, I hope. He came up to Oxford to ask me.'

'And he's an undergraduate there now?'

'Yes. He's reading Law. Paul's School.'

'He left the office, and then he wrote me a letter.'

'I know that too.'

'I'd said I was sorry about Paul, you see. And he wrote me this letter.' Ivo was now having enormous difficulty in expressing himself. 'As a matter of fact, we've been in what you might call correspondence.'

'Pen friends?' I regretted this cheap irony as I uttered it.

'It might come to something like that.' Producing this strange prognostication, Ivo had gone very pale. 'It's difficult, of course. We haven't at all the same ideas, as you can guess. He wouldn't like a thing like this Penny business, would he? He wanted me to do something religious with him. But of course I don't believe in religion. Nobody does.'

'You may be exaggerating again there. In fact you must be. For he does. Peter Lusby, I mean.'

'And now he wants us just to go walking somewhere in the Easter vac. The Lakes, I think. The elevating influence of Nature.' Ivo produced the jibe wanly.

This revelation of Peter's determined missionary zeal oughtn't to have surprised me. It did so, all the same.

'Well?' I said.

'I don't know. I'd like to help him, you see.'

'You'd like to help Peter Lusby?' My reaction to this must have been a blank look. 'Good God, Ivo! How can you help Peter Lusby? He'd be a damned sight better able to help you.'

'But he's just a penniless pleb, isn't he? Has to go and lick stamps.' Ivo looked quite bewildered. It wasn't the first time I'd felt the confusion of his mind to be daunting.

'Look,' I said. 'You and Lusby are about ages, I suppose. Of course he's not in the Uffington.' I cursed myself for having again said something cheap. 'But there are one or two things in which he's ahead of you, all the same. Purposiveness. A sense of responsibility. Matters of that kind. You'd have to begin there, Ivo. It would be a nonsense otherwise. He wants to manage a practical instance of the virtue of forgiveness as it ought to be operative in a Christian society. That may sound priggish. But it's the fact.'

'Another guardian angel.' Ivo's face twitched more violently than before. And then, amazingly, he smiled. 'I'll take that too,' he said. 'And thanks a lot.'

This was a stiff moment for me. I was like a character in a

novel of sentiment: an exemplary curate, perhaps, who feels himself to have wrestled successfully with the evil of jealousy in an elderly female parishioner. The ludicrous image probably helped me not to overestimate what was no more than another hopeful hint of a regenerate man conceivably lurking in Ivo. I turned back towards the house.

'Well,' I said, 'I'd better be off.' We walked in silence till the elegant façade of Otby was before us. I stopped beside my car. 'Things being as they are,' I said, 'perhaps you'd better say my good-byes for me. Will you?'

'Yes, of course. But your coat's inside. I'll fetch it for you.' And Ivo, plainly glad of this diversion, bounded up the steps and vanished.

My coat was brought out to me not by Ivo but by Penny. She must have taken it from him in the hall and ordered him into the house. Now she came down the steps hugging the garment affectionately, like a faithful and snug little wife of a fetishistic turn of mind. It was a tiresome performance, and I'd have expected myself to do no more than find means to get away from it unregardingly and without fuss. But this wasn't the effect that Penny's appearance now had on me. Perhaps because thrown off balance by that glimpse of grace in Ivo—although Ivo had little to do with the case—I was suddenly moved by the spectacle of my former wife confirmed in a kind of nemesis of the absurd. I had already registered my sense of Penny's mounting mere foolishness; now I was stricken by the recovered knowledge (for it had the feel of something I'd been haunted by often enough before) that Penny today was my yesterday's fault. I didn't understand just how I'd failed her. I did understand that she had failed me. But that second fact didn't affect the tormentingness of the first. I'd always felt guilty, I'd always feel guilty, about Penny. I'd been too close to her once not to be responsible for her now. And there came back to me with a sort of horror the few but crude words I'd used about her to Ivo only a few minutes before this encounter.

'That's very kind of you, Penny,' I said, and made to take the overcoat from her.

'I'll help you on with it.' Penny held up the coat like a commissionaire or a servant in a club. I turned my back on her obediently and began to feel my way into the thing. I was still in this position when I spoke next.

'Have you got a maid with you?' I asked. It must have been the generally archaic character of the set-up at Otby that prompted this ludicrous question.

'Of course not.'

'Then go upstairs and pack your own bags.' I had turned round again and was facing Penny. 'We'll clear out together.'

*Uncle Rory, I'll marry her* . . . Not since thus proposing to resolve my cousin Anna's predicament had I spoken, I suppose, more irrational or less premeditated words. Penny gazed at me wide-eyed.

'Duncan, whatever do you mean?'

'To Paris, say. For a week. Just as old friends and travelling companions.'

'Travelling companions?' For a moment there had been something drawn and almost tragic in Penny's face. Now, as she took in the implication of this chaste proposal, she relaxed into gaiety. 'Duncan,' she cried, 'what lovely, lovely nonsense! And now get into your car and drive away.'

'But I really mean——'

'Do as you're told! You used to, you know—rather too much.'

I climbed into the car. Penny advanced to the window, and signed to me to lower it. I thought she meant to kiss me. But she didn't.

'I knew Duncan,' she said, 'but I never knew Dunkie. The successful playwright, yes; but the honest Scottish boy, no. Too late to begin, darling. Good-bye, good-bye!'

Penny turned and ran up the steps. I drove away. At a turn at the foot of the drive Otby came momentarily into view again. The great golden ball crowning it appeared to wink at me mockingly. It was a very disorderly house, I told myself. How incredible that my only other visit to it had been in company so decorous and august as Edward Pococke's. I summoned up various useless thoughts of this sort and clung on to them until I reached Oxford. It had been a confused day.

THERE WAS AN envelope perched in front of *Young Picts*. It said *Duncan Pattullo Esq.* in Janet's neat hand. My heart pounded as I tore it open, for I thought it far less likely to contain good news than bad.

> Dear Dunkie,
>
> I scribble this in a great hurry in your room. I've looked in but you're out, and Plot tells me you have gone off for the day. Have you noticed that Plot is putting on weight? The Plot thickens, one might say.
>
> The doctors have been rallying round splendidly—but now rather alarmingly as well. They've named the best team for some long and tricky treatment, and it turns out to be at a clinic in Chicago. That's so unexpected as to be daunting, rather. But it has to be faced and somehow it's heartening too. They've organized the best conditions for the journey and we fly out in three hours' time. I'll let you know how goes. Please thank the two boys again for being so staunch when it happened. And, Dunkie, thank *you*.
>
> Love,
> JANET

I read this letter with dismay. The vision of Janet and her husband caught up in a world of modern medicine so strange that they could suddenly be hurtled across the Atlantic into a total unknown made me feel quite desperate. I was horrified, too, by my own behaviour. On what had turned out to be one of the most harrassing days of Janet's life I'd been fooling around at Otby, meddling ineffectively in some sort of spy story and almost involving myself in a freakish Quixotism that would have been of no use to anybody. And before that I'd been tagging after Fiona to what seemed no good purpose at all.

I read Janet's letter a second time, and saw that she had risen to her occasion as I'd expect; the fact was apparent even in the crazy joke about Plot. As the Provost had remarked, she had been through things before. Strangely perhaps at this moment, I was conscious of a certain envy of Janet: the envy, it might have been called, of the untempered for the tempered spirit.

I woke up on the following morning to a dim sense of having forgotten something, trivial in itself, which nevertheless I ought to be remembering. Plot—the corpulent Plot— didn't appear. I dozed off again, having had only an indifferent night's sleep. When I next awoke a clear dull daylight was filtering through the bedroom blind. Everything was very quiet. I got up and went into my sitting-room; the quality of the light there told me what to expect when I walked to the window; Surrey lay under a light carpeting of snow. A few flakes were still falling in a slow discouraged manner. There was nobody moving. There weren't even any footprints to be seen. I glanced at the calendar on my writing-table and saw that it was Christmas Eve.

I now remembered about Plot. He had been worried on learning that I had made no plans for the holiday period, and anxious to turn up at least on Boxing Day. This I had firmly forbidden. There would be meals somewhere around college if I wanted them; I could make my own bed; I could even polish my own shoes. So as far as Surrey Quad went, I was on my own for the next three days.

I made myself a cup of coffee, and then took a walk round the college. In common room a temporarily promoted pantry boy was kindling a fire which nobody except myself seemed likely to seek the comfort of. A dining-list revealed that

Adrian Buntingford and I would be tête-à-tête that evening—
which meant we'd rehearse yet again those tedious jokes
turning upon my juvenile insufficiency before Latin unseen
translation. One night of this would be bad enough, and the
prospect of two was insupportable. I remembered that
Lempriere was still in college, and it occurred to me that I
might propose myself for dinner with him on the following
evening. Gall, I had been told, was an excellent cook. But
Lempriere was not in Northumberland only because he was
so very far from well, and a midday call on Christmas Day
was probably as much as I should venture on.

I wished the pantry boy a merry Christmas, and returned
to the Great Quadrangle. In the fountain Neptune and his
rout were crowned and garlanded and cuffed with snow. The
great chub, also numerously attended by minions of his kind,
floated motionless in water already fringed with ice. But if
the fish held their usual station in the great stone basin there
was missing from its dark surface the reflection of the college
tower. The tower had now entirely vanished, leaving a broad
open wound in the west front of the Great Quadrangle.
Standing where I did, I could see across the street and
down a short vista to the very spot where Lempriere and I
had stood—less than a year before, although it seemed longer
ago than that—and observed the tiny scraps of fractured glass
that presaged the structure's doom. All, of course, was to be
well. But what would be returned to us was not the old tower
but a new and identical one. The great chub and Bernini's
Neptune would be a novelty to it, and it to them.

This fancy held me for a moment, and then I noticed that
the large hiatus itself was even barer than before. The
scaffolding too had come down, since it would be in the way
of the next phase of the intricate plan going forward. Gender's
anxiety over the presence or absence (I'd forgotten which it
was) of water beneath the original foundations was being
obviated by further deep excavations on the site. Concrete

laced and braced with steel was going to fill this vacancy in a big way. At present, however, nothing was going on, since the workmen's Christmas holiday had begun. I lingered for a moment, idly identifying the spot, now empty air, where Piero's *Madonna of the Astrolabe* had lain hidden and unharmed for centuries, and then I returned to Surrey. I was becoming reconciled to my rather eccentric continuance in residence. Over the remainder of the vacation, I told myself, I'd get a good stretch of writing done. Blessedly, a new play was simmering in my head. I wasn't happy; thinking of Chicago, I couldn't be that; but I could retreat behind my typewriter without disgrace and a little solace myself that way.

My sitting-room looked a bit bleak, all the same. The snow outside threw an unusual light on the ceiling, and to a chilly effect. I looked at the bare bottom of the young Pict who was Duncan Pattullo and had a notion that it had turned a shade blue with the cold. Then I sat down to type. I'd put *Act One, Scene One* in an old-fashioned way at the head of a page, and see what happened.

There was a knock on the door—or rather the particular bang which normally told me that Nicolas Junkin would be sprawled on my sofa within a second thereafter. This time, however, when the door opened Junkin simply stood framed in it. I realized that this was a visit to which a certain amount of protocol attached.

'I hope I'm not interrupting you?' Junkin asked.

'Not a bit, Nick. Do come in.'

Junkin came in, sat down rather stiffly, and looked around him.

'We've heard you're staying up over Christmas,' he said. 'A bit of a dull hole, isn't it, at this time of year?'

'It certainly doesn't seem to be exactly lively.' I thought that Junkin was going to relax, but it wasn't immediately so.

'It would give my wife and myself great pleasure,' he

enunciated formally, 'if you would dine with us tomorrow evening.'

'I'll be delighted to, Nick. Thank you very much.'

'If none better's offering,' Junkin said more easily.

'Certainly it isn't.'

'We haven't got a turkey, because it wouldn't go in the oven. But we've got a couple of ducks—formerly a coople of dooks.' Junkin was becoming uneasy at the pressure upon him of what is called Received Standard English (although Upper Class Cockney would be as accurate a term) and had taken to sardonic jokes of this kind. 'Half seven,' he added. 'That should give Moggy a chance. Do you know Walton Street?'

'Moderately.'

'It's more or less industrial. There seems to be some sort of big printing works.'

'Good heavens, think what you say! That's the Oxford University Press.'

'The university prints things? How very odd!' Junkin sounded genuinely surprised. 'As a matter of fact, I thought it was the nick at first. Dungeons masked by a dignified classical thingummy.'

'Portico. Or façade.'

'You've been a marvellous tutor. I wish you'd take on Moggy, Duncan.'

'Moggy is already a much more widely informed person than you are, Nicolas Junkin.'

'Of course she is.' Junkin's acknowledgement was immensely cheerful. 'It comes of not having to mug up all that stuff about Oudenarde and Malplaquet. Who cares who belted whom in the Hundred Years' War?'

'Marlborough didn't.'

'Ah—there's a catch in it. There always is.' Junkin tumbled to his feet. 'Half seven for eight, then.' With this evidence of further assimilative pressures, he made his way to the door.

And then, as if reading what was in my mind, he added with broad irony, 'By the way, we don't change.'

'Not in that sense, anyway. I'll be there.'

'Seeing you,' Junkin said again on a more casual note. And the door banged behind him. It banged so vigorously, indeed, that I thought it had made my telephone bell ring. But it was a genuine call, and I heard Mabel Bedworth's voice.

'Duncan, Cyril has only just told me you're still up. Cyril's hopeless. Can you come to dinner tomorrow? Plum pudding but no crackers.'

'I'd have loved to, Mabel, but I've just this minute promised to go somewhere else.'

'New Year's Day, then?' Mrs Bedworth's voice had its usual faintly disturbing quality. It went, somehow, with her mysteriously exciting downcast gaze. I could see her eyes shamefastly on the floor even as she talked into her telephone.

'Yes, indeed. I'll look forward to it.'

'Half-past seven, then. We're so glad. Good-bye.'

I felt less gloomy for the rest of the day.

Buntingford and I dined in common room. The promoted pantry boy, still on duty, was our sole attendant. He exhibited an alarmed deference, as if some quirk in time had landed us back in the Victorian age and he felt that all his fortune might depend on a single word of approbation or disapprobation from above. I'd rather have talked to him than to Buntingford. At the moment, however, that wouldn't have done at all.

Having watched our butler at work, the boy was chiefly attentive to our glasses; and as Buntingford believed that a glass stood in front of him only to be briskly emptied this began to affect the character of our evening quite soon.

'My dear Prudentius,' Buntingford said, 'you and I

haven't sat at table together like this since those intimate little luncheons long, long ago.'

'There weren't any intimate little luncheons, Adrian. There was only madeira—but a good deal of that.'

'You astonish me. Weren't you an amazingly attractive stripling? Most people seemed to feel it was your floppy hair.'

It struck me that I knew very little about Adrian Buntingford—that once young don now so sunk in the stupidity of his middle years as to think it funny to address me as Prudentius. Unlike Ninian, who had escaped or been denied warfare by a matter of months, or myself who had been at a year's further remove from it, Buntingford had been just of military age. But some disability had kept him from any firing line; Latin and Greek were no qualification for the role of a boffin; he had been too young to be sucked into Whitehall. He might have helped to crack ciphers in some secret country mansion. But it was my impression that he had simply stayed in the college and taken a precocious part in running it. Conceivably having missed out on what our seniors were fond of calling a 'good war' had marked him in some way. Certainly his life had remained tied to the college, rather as Lempriere's had done. But the two men were quite different. In spite of his rubbishing chatter about floppy hair (inconceivable from Lempriere) Buntingford took no particular interest in young men. In his relationship with the place a kind of lazy discontent predominated, and his attitude of good-humoured tolerance ceased to be slightly factitious only as it became tinged with cynicism. He was greedy at table in the manner of a man obscurely undernourished elsewhere. I wondered whether I could manage somebody like him in my shadowy new play.

'An Unpredictable Element,' Buntingford said, 'in the Movement of Public Opinion.'

'Oh, Lord! Give over, Adrian.'

'Not a reminiscence of dotage this time.' Buntingford chuckled as if he had caught me out. 'It's a thought bang up to date. Occasioned by our nuclear-minded friend.'

I was about to say 'Watershute?' on an interrogative note when I realized that this periphrasis had been prompted by the continued presence of the pantry boy, who was anxiously fiddling with the port and sauterne he would presently plant before us.

'What about him?' I asked.

'You don't run through the newspapers?'

'*The Times* at breakfast. That's about all.'

'Ah! But you should keep more in touch. Always take a look at the gutter ones. They're laid out in this room. The yellow press, as our fathers said.'

'What have they been up to now?'

'Another scandal-piece of local application, just a few days ago. Absentee dons.'

'It sounds bad. And actually slanted at us?'

'Not specifically. But that nasty Chaffey's work, without a doubt. Sheer twaddle. But the point is that it has been taken up by a pro. He must have had some private low-down from the egregious contributor and decided to do his own look-see. Pumping the seniors of young Ganymede here.' This was plainly a reference to our attendant. 'Heaven knows what.'

'Worse and worse. But what has it to do with that Unknown Element?'

'If it comes to something further in the public prints it will undoubtedly swing things drastically.'

'Adrian, just what do you mean?'

'If the thing turns into an impertinent inquisition into our ways, my dear Prudentius, it will produce a closing of the ranks: a solid swing—if swings can be solid—behind our wandering friend. You'll see.'

I did see. I'd have been a poor observer of 'our ways' if I had not. And I was suddenly prompted to a certain lack of

caution. I had attempted, with no apparent success, to alert
the Governing Body to a conceivable truth about Watershute,
but Buntingford was one of those whom I suspected of not
quite having ignored what I said. If I now embroidered a little
on the theme—but still without any suggestion of special
knowledge on my own part—it might be possible to explore
the state of the case.

'It's an interesting idea,' I said. 'The team spirit gets to
work. But there would be limits, wouldn't there? Imagine
this one. Imagine that our nuclear friend isn't just a common
don like you and me. He's stuffed with secrets of state, you
might say. And suddenly he doesn't take off for blameless fun
in the Bahamas or tatty Capri or whatever. He beats it for the
Kremlin or some such place. We'd have to quit, don't you
think, being old school pals, solid against the outrages of the
gutter?'

'It would be a facer for poor old Edward. But he'd think
round it—or think he was thinking round it—before he'd
budge.'

'Our Provost is certainly a deliberating type.' I now sensed
that Buntingford, whatever the movement of his inner mind,
was simply too lethargic for any serious discussion of
Watershute's case. 'Let's forget about our colleague,' I said.
'All the same, there's a general issue of some interest. What
has come to be called "defecting"—meaning swopping
horses or changing camps. It is a crime? Oughtn't a man to
be entitled to go where he likes and say what he likes and
communicate anything he has a mind to?'

'You're a born subversive, Duncan.' Offering this surely
inaccurate opinion, Buntingford poured me port and then
filled his own glass. 'Here's to treason. Hurrah!' He sniffed at
the wine. '*Not* to be sniffed at,' he said. 'Taylor 1945, I'm
given to understand. Far from despicable in hard times. I
think I'll just step into the garden.'

Upon this euphemism Buntingford left the room. The

pantry boy remained, and was producing coffee cups. I wondered when he would judge it proper to go home to bed.

'Do you like it here?' I asked.

'The man at the job-creation said it can lead to catering. Collect the right refs, and I can go to the Polytechnic and do catering there.'

'And that would suit you?'

'It's nice work if you can get it.' The boy grinned at me as he produced this current wry phrase. 'Sir,' he added as an afterthought.

Buntingford returned, and I resigned myself to another hour with him. Two hours after that it would be Christmas Day.

## XX

CHRISTMAS DAY ARRIVED, and with it more snow. Looking out of my sitting-room window as I got myself a coffee and toast breakfast, I was surprised to see that a snow-man had turned up in the middle of Surrey. Had there been any undergraduates around, its appearance would have been natural enough, since snow prompts to the behaviour of schoolboys even in third year men. But there wasn't an undergraduate left in college—so who had turned to in this juvenile fashion? But what I was looking at—I instantly discovered—was simply the statue of Provost Harbage, transformed by the elements. The abraded character of this effigy was due to some centuries of such treatment by wind and weather. And now a chunk of snow slithered off the head of Provost Harbage as I watched, so that the effect was of that doubtless pious scholar's having determined to exhibit himself in the white sheet of a penitent. Could one make anything of that on a stage? It wasn't my sort of thing. But the idle question at least told me where my thoughts were turning. A second cup of coffee, and I'd really begin on my new play.

This resolution holding, I did sit down and work. Most of my starts are false starts, but absorbing all the same. It was noon before I remembered my resolution to pay a Christmas call on Lempriere. The Provost would certainly do so, perhaps accompanied by his wife. But there would be no crush of visitors. Thus thinking of Lempriere in his isolated condition, I felt it would be becoming to take him a Christmas present, and in this interest I looked vaguely round my room. It was a pity I was no scholar. Lempriere was scarcely a scholar either, but he had lived with scholars nearly all his days and understood what they valued. Were I properly learned myself, I could pick from the shelf some small thing—a Virgil that had belonged to a former Provost, a polemical pamphlet circulated by a bellicose fellow of the college at the time of some long-forgotten rumpus—which would be exactly right. Having nothing of the sort at my command, I walked over to Lempriere's rooms empty-handed. At least I had become rather fond of Lempriere, which was probably the main thing.

Gall had by no means gone off duty on account of the festive season. He received me so much like a character of my own (answering a telephone or putting the finishing touches to a dinner table as the curtain goes up) that I found myself asking him whether Mr Lempriere was at home. It isn't a form of words customary on a college staircase, but Gall found it in order nevertheless. Even so, he hesitated for a moment before replying, and I feared that Lempriere was perhaps not well enough—or even in too much pain—to be seen.

'Why, yes, Mr Pattullo. But, as it happens, a sitting is in progress.'

'Mr Pattullo' instead of 'Sir' represented an enhanced intimacy between Gall and myself, and was therefore gratifying. But for a second the meaning of the words accompanying it eluded me.

'A sitting, Gall?' I repeated.

'Yes, indeed.' Gall was now reproachful. 'The portrait, Mr Pattullo. It's understood to be going very well, I'm happy to say. But whether we should——'

'Gall, don't be a damned fool.' Lempriere's voice made itself heard, not robustly, from his sitting-room. 'Show Mr Pattullo in.'

As Lempriere had uttered the first of these injunctions precisely as he would have uttered it to myself or to the Provost, Gall was unoffended, and even indicated to me with

224

a slight bow that I might proceed. The sitting-room, the normal condition of which was crepuscular, now appeared oddly lit, and I supposed for a moment that, as with my own room, this was an effect of the snow-covered terrain without. But in fact it was occasioned by a concealed lamp at play upon the concave surface of an enormous white umbrella. What my father would have made of such a contraption (currently much favoured by photographers of artistic objects) I don't know. Nor, for that matter, do I know what he would have made of the canvas perched on its easel at one end of the room. But it was undoubtedly the portrait of Lempriere commissioned by the college (somewhat tardily) as a mark of its esteem. I had a fleeting impression that the sitter was represented, appropriately enough, in the middle of a snow storm. And then Lempriere spoke.

'My cousin Duncan Pattullo. Had a father in your line, Bobby. Sir Robert Buffin. Old chum.'

Sir Robert Buffin put down a maulstick and shook hands. He looked a very old chum indeed, being demonstrably aged with Lempriere himself and not noticeably in a better state of repair. Here, in fact, was a feature of the artistic life of Oxford which I recalled having been told about: if an aged man has to be painted he commonly stipulates that some old friend of his should undertake the job. The eminent Buffin (for he was that) had no doubt once been a little boy sitting next to Lempriere in a prep school, covertly drawing tanks and Fokkers and Zeppelins in an exercise-book supposedly dedicated to Latin nouns and verbs. And now here were these two ancients cheek by jowl again.

'Perhaps an unseasonable activity for Christmas Day,' Buffin said to me. 'But we can't afford to waste any time, you know.' He glanced at his contemporary and appeared to sense that this was a remark of unfortunate implication. 'Fact is, I like to put these things aside for a few months before there's any question of the *vernissage*. So it's a matter of catching this year's Academy, you see. It wouldn't do to miss that. Oceans of people will want to see Arnold in his habit as he lived.' The random dip into *Hamlet* was not too happy either, but this time Buffin didn't appear aware of the fact. 'I wanted him in Doctor's robes. Rose with madder facings: something like that. Go with the greenish tones of the complexion. But Arnold says he isn't a Doctor—not yet. Undiscriminating place, Oxford, wouldn't you say?'

I agreed that Oxford hadn't done the right thing by Lempriere. Lempriere himself contributed his throaty chuckle; it indicated his enjoyment of the situation.

'I suggested a shroud,' he said. 'Some old poet or preacher had himself done that way.'

'Yes,' I said. 'A very distinguished one. He was Dean of St. Paul's. John Donne.'

'That's right. I used to be fond of his stuff. Poetry's tedious if it isn't a bit rum. Have a look at Bobby's daub, Dunkie.'

Brought up, as I had been, to the etiquette of the studio, I knew that this invitation ought to have been left to Buffin himself. Buffin, because he knew this too, made haste to take me by the elbow in a friendly fashion and lead me up to the easel. The snow-storm was confined to one side of the canvas, and the snow-flakes were small rectangles and parallelograms. This was perplexing. I glanced round the room, and saw that it was festooned with Christmas cards. It looked as if all England had been turning them in. I realized that if Lempriere's colleagues and a present generation of under-graduates had forgotten him whole generations of former pupils had not.

'There's one from your learned friend Junkin,' Lempriere said abruptly, and as if interpreting my glance. 'Nice of him. And one from the youngest of the Mumfords. You couldn't, could you, get much more impertinent than that? But no doubt Ivo meant well. I sent him a thing called a greetings telegram at once. Gall took it over to the post office.'

'Just thought of the cards this morning,' Buffin said. 'They're only roughed in.'

I didn't know what to say about the taste of this inspiration, which seemed a shade on the sentimental side. Nor did I know what to think of the regenerate Ivo Mumford's latest performance. But Buffin spoke again, obviating the need for comment.

'The window surprises you, eh? But I thought of that invention from the start.'

The portrait included in its background a large window in a wall where no window existed, and through it there was a glimpse of that area in space which the tower normally occupied. The scaffolding was represented as still in position there.

'Adds a note of historical interest,' Buffin said, and chuckled rather in Lempriere's manner. 'Catch the eye of future generations when all four of us have been forgotten about.'

I understood that this computation was offered in an egalitarian spirit as designed to include Gall. Gall was at this moment bringing in sherry for Buffin and myself, and for Lempriere a cloudy and repellent draught in a large medicine glass. But Lempriere brushed this refreshment aside. The *motif* of the window had agitated him, and he was struggling to his feet.

'It's a disgraceful state of affairs,' he said. 'Hordes of workmen scurrying about all day, and no end of dust and racket. But not a damned stone gets laid. Come and look.' He shuffled slowly and painfully from the room, and we followed him. I had no doubt where he was heading for. It was the lavatory which lay beyond his bedroom, and which Gall had assured me contained the only position from which the site of the tower could be viewed. It naturally proved a far from spacious chamber when we reached it. Lempriere went in, and left Buffin and myself standing by the open door. What

Gall called the convenience was a substantial affair; it had a broad and solid mahogany seat and a heavy mahogany flap or lid that came down on top of that. Even so, it was a hazardous perch for an infirm man. But Lempriere scrambled up on it, opened the small window, and stuck his head out. It would have been an absurd sight if it hadn't simply been a painful one. 'Nothing at all!' Lempriere's voice came back at us. 'Damned vacancy.' Suddenly he swayed dangerously, and I had to take a hasty step forward and grab him by the thighs. Seconded by Sir Robert Buffin (who proved surprisingly spry), I got him safely to the floor. 'Up you get, Dunkie,' he said. 'Up with you!'

I did as I was told, obediently sticking my head out. It was true that there was nothing to be seen—or nothing except the top of the deep excavation where the new foundations were going to rest. I got down and attempted to explain this to Lempriere. Up to the previous day, I insisted, there had been a great deal going on, and it was an activity that would begin again the day after tomorrow. In a few weeks the lowest range of the restored tower would become visible even from this perch. Meanwhile, why didn't Lempriere come down into the quad and take a look at such progress as had been made?

I put this to Lempriere as the entirely feasible suggestion that it was. If he could scramble on top of a privy and there stand on tiptoe, he could certainly with proper assistance get down one flight of stairs and up again. But Lempriere rejected the idea impatiently. I persisted for a time, and at one point was almost prompted to say 'You know, Arnold, there's not a soul around the place'. For I had realized that the complete seclusion in which he had now chosen to live was in large measure a matter of pride. He couldn't bear to think of himself as under observation in his debility; as an old pensioner shambling through those spacious courts that he had once commanded. This being the state of the case, I abruptly shut up. In any event, he was plainly determined to live until he saw the tower begin to rise again. And he was a sufficiently determined old creature to have a good chance of managing it.

We returned to the sitting-room, and Buffin took his leave. He was engaged to lunch in the Lodging. I wondered whether, as on the occasion of my father's first sitting down to a meal there, the Provost would discourse on the genius of Albrecht Dürer. I could still spend half-an-hour with Lempriere without getting in the way of his own midday meal, and this I decided to do. He had been almost resentful of my attempt to lure him into open air, and I hoped to manage a little friendly and composing talk. But it was less easy than it used to be to gossip with Lempriere, partly because he seemed to have lost interest in college affairs. This was discouraging. There had been a phase, not long before this time, in which he had exhibited an almost fussy interest in such matters, even although he no longer took any formal part in the running of the place. His succeeding rapid switch to an absence of concern was ominous. I had managed quite recently to engage his attention with an account of McKechnie's accident, but only to the extent of eliciting rambling speculation about my own possible marital future. It now occurred to me that he was feeling the college to be passing him by; feeling that he hadn't been told things he ought to have been told; nursing a determination not to accept new information that it was humiliating he hadn't received already. But if I went far enough back, I thought, I must be on territory that he had known well. Unless his memory was failing badly—which was a possibility—that ought to be an area for comfortable talk.

'William Watershute and I,' I said, 'must just have missed each other as undergraduates. I expect you missed him too. You'd still be in Washington when he went off somewhere to his first job.'

'Watershute?' It didn't sound as if Lempriere was much interested in Watershute. 'Yes, that would be so. He had the start of a pretty decent war, I think, but got knocked out early and came up to the college. And of course I knew him from the time he came back as a junior don. Back room boy: that's been his line. Takes up with the other lab boys mostly. Always plants himself down beside one when he dines. No instinct for civilization, you might say.'

'I've been told he has—or used to have—lively political interests.'

'Never heard of them. Finish the sherry in that damned decanter, Dunkie. No use to me.'

'Now that he's in this trouble you've heard of, one's naturally interested in his personality.'

'Ah, his trouble—yes!' Lempriere looked at me warily. 'Well, there must be different views of it—and even about the facts of the case. How do you see the thing?'

It was clear that Lempriere knew nothing whatever about the Watershute affair, and was applying his familiar primitive guile to eliciting the situation from me while dissimulating his ignorance. I resigned myself to going along with this—which made a discussion of the matter a slow-moving and un-profitable task. I confined myself, needless to say, to the common view of it, and I expected Lempriere to be con-siderably outraged as he got hold of the picture. Scandalous neglect of college duties would surely strike him as a very great sin. But Lempriere was unperturbed. It pleased him to take the view that, as the university's competitive examina-tions were stuff and nonsense anyway (an old dogma of his) a tutor did small harm in paying no attention to them. This was the Lempriere who liked to contradict majority opinions —although he was doing so with nothing of his old sardonic flair.

'But the Governing Body doesn't like it,' I said. 'There's talk of depriving him of his fellowship.' I felt sure that this would horrify Lempriere, since such a virtually unheard of event could not be regarded, I had gathered, as other than a deep disgrace to any college. But once again I was wrong.

'Plenty more where he came from,' Lempriere said. 'And plenty of other jobs for a fellow like that, whether he's reliable or not. Has no end of mischief at his fingertips, I'll be bound.'

I saw that this was a useless discussion. Lempriere would afford no fresh view of Watershute, and moreover by this time I had probably tired him out.

'Well,' I said, getting on my feet, 'at least it will be tough on his son, who's only in his second year with us. When undergraduates are turfed out they have a knack of turning disgrace to glory. But when dons——'

'Certainly the man has a son—a nice lad called Giles. You ought to make his acquaintance, Dunkie.'

Lempriere's speech was far from matching his manner, which had become agitated. I saw that he had forgotten the existence of Giles Watershute, and that it had suddenly come back to him. The sons of colleagues and old members were so much Lempriere's thing that this forgetfulness spoke sharply of more than a physical decline. But at least his mind was now vigorously engaged with the Watershute affair.

'It's disgraceful!' he said, and made to struggle to his feet again. 'Misconducting himself under the nose of a son in residence. And a promising lad, they say. I'll speak to him.'

'To Giles?'

'To the fellow himself, of course. Damn it, Dunkie, I'm his most senior colleague. I'll tell him what I think.' Lempriere was now looking round his room as if seeking to conjure up an overcoat and muffler.

'You could try, Arnold. The Provost did, and was sent away with a flea in his ear.'

'He wouldn't get from Edward what he'll get from me.' Lempriere, who five minutes before had been treating the insufficiencies of William Watershute with ironic indifference, was now speaking as of a reprobate character of the darkest hue. But it seemed to me unlikely that his indignation was going to be useful to anyone. Watershute would certainly not mend his ways as the result of a confrontation with a man he probably regarded as a superfluous dotard, and Lempriere himself was in no fit state for anything of the kind.

'At least there's nothing to be done at the moment,' I said. 'He won't be around. Nobody's around. It's Christmas Day.'

'Then I wish him merry of it.' Lempriere had sunk down into his chair again, incapable of producing these words as more than a mumble. 'And send in Gall,' he added. 'He insists on keeping those blasted pills.'

# XXI

THE SMALL HOUSE in Walton Street ran to two door-bells, beside the upper of which was a card announcing Mr & Mrs Junkin. I pressed this and walked into a narrow hall. It was brightly lit, oppressively orderly, and smelt of furniture-polish. A discordant note, however, was struck by another card, this time large and sprawling, which said *Nick & Moggie: backstairs folk* and added the further guidance of a red-ink arrow pointing into the depths of the house. Although the whole place was on a modest scale there really was a second staircase, a social absurdity which could have been contrived only in the Victorian age. I climbed. The bell must actually have rung (although such bells commonly didn't), since Junkin was standing hospitably at an open door when I reached the top.

'Hullo, Nick,' I said. 'Who's down below?'

'Our landlady. She's the widow of a head porter some-where, and naturally a bit high. If she'd heard you, she'd have come out and told you to wipe your feet.'

'I have. I had to kick off quite a lot of snow.'

'It's nice of you to venture out, Duncan.' Junkin said this as if I had been his late tutor Lempriere himself. 'Come in, come in. Let me take your coat. I hope it's reasonably warm. Would you care to wash?' A slight effect of previous memorization attended these utterances, but at the same time Junkin wasn't at all lacking in ease. 'Moggy's dead on schedule,' he went on with satisfaction when we had matters sorted out. 'But I'm a bit behind on my own jobs. Haven't laid the table even, I'm afraid. It's this insurance. I'm trying to get it clear. Only it's rather perplexing.' We had entered a very small sitting-room. It provided a setting in which Roy Lichtenstein's *Whaam!* and Bosch's *Garden of Earthly Delights* —transported along with the bug-eyed Ishii Genzō from Junkin's former abode in Surrey—showed as on the restless and clamant side. Everything else, however, was domestic, and the general effect was snug. Culinary noises and odours came pleasingly from what looked like a cupboard. 'Have some sherry,' Junkin said.

'Yes, please. What sort of insurance, Nick?'

'Life insurance. My auntie's been on about it. She's going to pay.'

'The sweet-shop auntie?'

'That's right.'

'And with the houses as well.'

'Fancy you remembering that, Duncan. And it's the point, you see. The superior urban properties.' Junkin grinned happily. 'Come to mark her, it has. Moggy's found a word for it in the dictionary. Difficult to pronounce, although the meaning's plain. Bourgeoisified. It was invented by Marx or Lenin or somebody. Moggy says the old soul is that. She says—auntie, I mean—that Cokeville Grammar School was a credit to the town when I was there, but where is it now? And she says that, if you know how to go about it, you can still put money by for education in a way that offers a shrewd deal tax-wise.'

'I see.' I was impressed by this challenging response in a northern city to recent trends in social legislation. 'She doesn't want the next generation of Junkins to be comprehensively uneducated. But I'm not sure about calling it bourgeoisification. Your aunt sounds to me to have belonged to the bourgeoisie already.'

'*Petite* but not *haute*.' Moggy had emerged from her kitchenette to exhibit this brisk command of a foreign tongue. 'And it's only the *haute* that dabble with private education. The old woman's daft, I'd say. But she means well.' Moggy, although thus masterful in speech, was looking at me shyly and without formal greeting. I saw that she wasn't managing to comply with some instruction issued by her husband.

'Moggy,' I said, 'say *Duncan*. If you need to, say *Duncan, Duncan, Duncan.*'

'Duncan, Duncan——' Moggy broke off, laughing. 'Oh good, there's Giles!'

'Giles Watershute?' I asked. The door-bell had rung, and Junkin had hastened from the room to receive his new guest.

'Yes. We discovered he was another Christmas waif, Duncan, just like you.'

'I realize you're being very kind to me, Moggy dear. But what makes Giles a waif?'

'He's all alone in that house in Northmoor Road. His parents have gone off to Switzerland, skiing or something. You'd think they'd be too old for it.'

I almost said 'Or too poor'—which would have been a reasonable comment in the light of what was known or conjectured about the Watershute finances. Indeed, William Watershute was by now firmly lodged in my mind as a person in whom any evidence of a sudden access of wealth would have to be regarded as sinister. But if I was startled it was chiefly on account of the mere information that Watershute had gone abroad. My recent conversation with Tony Mumford came back to me. I even wondered whether Gavin Mogridge might be trailing the Watershutes in some bizarre disguise.

'Didn't they offer to take Giles with them?' I asked.

'I don't know. Nick thinks he hasn't been making out with them too well lately. But it's natural, of course. Didn't you have rows with your parents, Duncan?'

'Not exactly. But we'd all of us—my parents and my brother Ninian and I—get furious, every one of us, with all the rest of us at the same time. It was noisy, but impressed the neighbours. We felt it was useful for my father's reputation to have a good deal of artistic temperament blowing around the house. In Edinburgh that *haute bourgeoisie* held a firm belief in the artistic temperament and the *vie de bohème* in general. It came from reading novels like *Trilby*.'

I may have produced this chatter because still slightly perturbed. But now Giles was in the room, and he and Moggy were kissing each other. I took this to have become a form of salutation prescriptive among the young—or at least among the young of Junkin's set. Certainly Junkin presided over it in this instance with the largest approval. I made a mental note myself to kiss Moggy when I came away.

Giles greeted me with satisfaction. He looked very well and wholly unstrained—something he had scarcely done since my first acquaintance with him. I wondered whether this was merely the result of being clear of his parents for a while. He couldn't have provided himself with a girl friend—or not officially, as in that case she'd have been here now. But such arrangements are commonly incubated in a period of privacy during which public notice may not properly be taken of them. Perhaps this was Giles's present condition, and perhaps the empty house in Northmoor Road was a factor in it. This was to turn out a baseless speculation. One is prone in middle age to a pan-sexual view of one's juniors. As it happened, a quite different aspect of sexuality now bobbed up on us.

'Nick,' Moggy said, 'do give Giles his sherry. I want us to be sitting down in ten minutes. And clear and lay the table, for the love of mike. I'm going back to those birds.'

Moggy disappeared into her little kitchen, but not before Junkin had jumped to obey orders. When abroad in Oxford with her he was inclined to adopt a masterful form of address, as if giving notice that here was a husband who knew how to make his wife toe the line. But this old-fashioned comportment evaporated at home. Here—he had plainly worked it out—Moggy was to rule in her own kingdom.

The table was littered with soft woollen stuffs and sewing materials. It was a moment before I saw that Junkin was removing them with a certain ostentation, and another moment before I realized why. Moggy was engaged in making baby clothes, and her husband regarded the fact as one proper to be noticed and commented upon. I hastened to indulge this wholesome complacency.

'When's the baby due, Nick?' I asked.

'Oh, not for ages.' As usual, Junkin eschewed chronological exactitude. 'But not an accident, you know. There'll be a written guarantee that it was conceived in holy wedlock.'

'How absolutely marvellous!' Giles, expressing this opinion with no effect of extravagance, jumped up and dashed into the kitchen. I supposed he was intent upon kissing Moggy again. He might have been the Junkins' best friend for years. As I tried to convey my own adequate satisfaction I reflected (as my situation frequently constrained me to do) on the bright speed of youth. Junkin began laying the table, giving particular care to the positioning of wine glasses. He was as proud as Punch and Judy rolled into one, much as if he were a man conscious of having achieved a task of the utmost difficulty. Giles returned to the room, sat down, and gave himself up to looking awed.

'Are you going to have a large family, Nick?' I asked.

'Enormous. Moggy's going to be that old-fashioned mother of nine. And one ought to start early. It helps to cut down the generation gap.'

'I'm sure it does,' I said, and felt that here was an arithmetical calculation of unusual accuracy on Junkin's part. I also wondered what other calculations he and Moggy were capable of. What on earth were they going to live on? Perhaps the rich auntie would provide part of the answer.

'Of course we have to be thinking about jobs,' Junkin said

more prosaically, and as if reading my thought. 'Summer will be here in no time, and the young graduate will be on the street. Thought is definitely required.'

'You're going to produce plays,' Giles said stoutly, and turned to me. 'Isn't that right, sir?'

'Yes, it is. But there's rather a crush at the start.'

'Nice work if you can get it,' Junkin said. And he produced a bottle of wine and uncorked it with care.

Moggy's first dinner party (as it may have been) was a success and ended late. Perhaps this was why Giles, although his own route lay north, thought it proper to walk me back to college. Mugging seemed lately to have gone out in Oxford, so he can scarcely have been thinking seriously about my personal safety. Perhaps he was just being polite, and didn't reflect that his insistence cast me somewhat in the role of an apprehensive maiden lady. But the fact that we walked in silence for a time (and this after several hours of lively talk) made me think he had something to confide to me. If so, it must be about his family situation: a topic on which we had so far failed to touch. I now took the initiative myself.

'Are your parents going to be in Switzerland for long?' I asked.

'Oh, no—definitely not.' Giles's answer came quickly. 'Only for ten days. My father says he has to do a lot of work that he's behind on. He wants to give an extra course of lectures next term. And he was busy up to the last moment getting out reading lists for his men in college. They've been getting slack, he says, and he's going to drive them hard. Several of them are quite good, and he's dead set on a couple of Firsts in Schools this year. The college in general has been doing damned badly lately. He's determined that Natural Science, at least, is going to get a stiff kick in the pants.'

'What about Modern Languages, Giles?'

'Well, that's another year off.' Giles took no offence at a

question plainly of personal implication. 'I think I have it taped now, as a matter of fact. The alphas keep rolling in on the model tutee. Of course I know it's all utter nonsense.' Giles paused on this robust assertion of the gospel of Arnold Lempriere. 'Still, it would be quite fun to bring it off.'

'So it would. No particular credit to you, of course, in jumping through the hoops you were born to. Fun, all the same.'

This response, which I felt would have done credit to the deftest tutor, was again received by Giles in good part. We walked on for a time in a renewed silence, and through softly falling snow. Gloucester Green, untenanted even by the most belated bus, might have been a deserted football field. All Oxford was already sleeping off the fatigues of Christmas Day.

'As a matter of fact,' Giles said, 'my father has to be thinking of the Summer Term's work as well, because of this Peking business in the Easter vac.'

'He's going to Peking?'

'Yes. He's due to read a paper at a conference there.'

'I see.' I hoped I hadn't sounded more than mildly surprised. Into my head had come a vision of Mogridge in a pigtail, keeping tabs on Giles's father in the Forbidden City. 'Isn't it frightfully hazardous for an eminent physicist to venture into the heart of China?' A note of whimsical concern struck me as being at the moment my best policy.

'Oh, but it's quite monumentally respectable. I expect the whole thing is an anti-Russian ploy thought up by the CIA. My father says some of the top Americans are going along. I wish I was. But a family jaunt is out. My mother isn't going either.'

'It would certainly be interesting. But it's said they don't really allow one to see much—except in a show-case way. The Chinese resemble the Russians there.' I wondered how to continue this conversation. The picture of a reformed William

Watershute didn't come to me wholly convincingly—any more than did the picture of a reformed Ivo Mumford. But it was Giles's state of mind rather than his father's that interested me at the moment, and I decided on cautious exploration. 'You've struck me,' I said, 'as being a bit worried about things lately. Would you say, Giles, you've now cheered up?' This didn't sound at all cautious as I uttered it. I must have been fairly sure that there was something more Giles wanted to say.

'Yes, that's true. But explaining might be a bit of a bore. You'll have had about enough of kids for the day.'

'For pity's sake, Giles! We've had the generation gap once already.'

'All right. And it *has* been worrying. I was coming to feel that odd things were happening to my father. I couldn't get square with him about them. And not with my mother either. They were almost ganging up on me—or that's how it felt for a time. Shutting me out of something.' Giles's voice had now become hesitant and embarrassed, and I understood that he didn't go in for talk of this sort at all readily. It was possible that Junkin, not yet a friend of long standing, was the nearest thing to a confidant he yet had in Oxford—and he probably didn't have the girl friend I'd been imagining either. 'Do you remember,' he asked abruptly, 'that bloody awful party?'

'Of course I remember that party. And I agree that it wasn't altogether comfortable.'

'You knew my mother long ago. So you saw that she was putting on a turn, didn't you?'

'She has a sense of theatre.'

'It was more than that. There was something bogus about the whole thing—including my father's champagne. Christ! This is a rotten way to talk about one's parents.'

'Not if it helps to get things in a clear light.'

'Well, I think it *is* in that now. I think my father had some sort of bad patch that's now behind him. And that I was imagining things.' Surprisingly, Giles kicked out savagely at the slushy snow beneath our feet—much as Ivo had kicked out at the fallen leaves at Otby. 'I can't forgive myself for the things I was imagining. They were too absurd! You're sure you don't mind this jabber? It's getting it off the chest stuff, I suppose.'

'Go on, Giles.'

'Well, it was like this.' But now Giles hesitated. We had crossed the Cornmarket, and in front of us was St. Michael-at-the-North-Gate with its little outdoor resting-place: the spot where Lempriere and I had once come upon the aged J. B. Timbermill seated amid a bunch of juvenile *Wandervögel*. The wooden benches were deep in snow. Surprisingly again, Giles swept the snow off the nearest of them with a vigorous arm and sat down. I did the same, although I was quite certain it wasn't going to be comfortable. We were like a couple of benighted tramps, gathering strength to struggle on to a doss house or a Salvation Army citadel.

'Did you ever do any thinking about treason?' Giles asked.

The nearest street-lamp was some distance off—so if I'd looked startled Giles hadn't perhaps noticed the fact. It would do no good to betray any immediate understanding of what he was talking about.

'Gunpowder treasons and plots?' I said. 'Not really. They've never come my way. But why?'

'It's the role in which I was coming to see my father. Of course it was quite lunatic. You probably think I'd been reading too many spy stories.'

'It would be one explanation.'

'It wasn't that. I believe it was the way dons talk. I've had to listen, you see, to an awful lot of dons talking. You know how. Being open-minded. And arguing points of view and asserting tenable positions. All that.'

'Do you mean, Giles, the rights and wrongs of acting out the consequences of ideological convictions—all *that*?'

'That sort of thing exactly.' Giles was relieved by this comprehension. 'Particularly scientists. Allan Nunn and Klaus Fuchs. Chaps like that.'

'Yes.'

'Or Kim Philby, who isn't a scientist at all. There was a man came to dinner at home once who said there were grey areas. I don't remember his name, but I was told he was one of the top philosophers in the place. He could talk marvellously. And he said there were those grey areas, and a *gradus*—by which he must have meant a slippery slope. He tackled me about what he called class traitors. He meant Etonians and Wykehamists and so on who have had it pretty good from one sort of society and then turn into left-wing politicians wanting to subvert it. They're regarded as perfectly respect- able—as the heirs of the philosophic radicals and so forth. But are they any different in essence, he asked, from chaps who take similar stores of trained intelligence and privileged know-how to helping not another class or faction in their own country but——'

'Yes, Giles; it's interesting table-talk. But how did you manage to take a jump from it to this other thing?'

'My father has always loved talking that way too. All sorts of paradoxes and heresies. And he was always, quite seriously, no end hot on keeping scientific knowledge moving across political barriers. You see? And here he was, in some sort of queer disrepair and seeming to have taken a great deal too much on his plate. And my mother playing ball with him in some way I just didn't understand. So I got that crazy notion for a time. I see now that it was the most utter balls, and I'm enormously relieved. But I can't tell you how ashamed I am to have had such notions. Or rather I can and I have.' Giles smiled wanly. 'I say! My bottom's soaking. Is yours?'

'Yes, I'd say it is.'

'Then we'd better be moving on.'

'So we had. Or rather we'll take our several ways, Giles, into our several hot baths. And I do appreciate your confiding in me as you have.' Even although I said this honestly I feared I must have said it lamely. My position was wretched. There appeared to be no basis upon which I could—or could without being disingenuous—congratulate Giles upon having returned to his right mind. Nor did I know to what extent, despite his air of regained confidence, unresolved doubts might not linger in his head. That William Watershute was showing signs of returning to his role as a conscientious teacher seemed to be all that his son had to go on in point of hard fact, and at least it must be comforting to a boy who had to look his father's pupils in the eye from time to time. But Giles must be aware of a good many puzzles as left in air.

We parted, then, not awkwardly, but with some sense of inadequacy on my side. Walking the short stretch back to college, I thought again of the possibility of tackling Mogridge on the Watershute enigma. But I doubted whether any comfort would result. If Mogridge believed as I believed he believed, he would be far from puzzled by the spectacle of Watershute appearing to pull up and become a model character. There are walks of life, I knew, in which strict instructions may be issued to act that way while in cold storage.

# XXII

On the following morning Provost Harbage had ducked beneath his sheet again: there had been a high wind as well as further heavy falls of snow, and against these outrageous elements he had muffled up his face, like Julius Caesar beset by his assassins. Beyond him the off-white façade of the library had turned to a deep cream by contrast with the snow which, piled up high between the huge Corinthian columns, seemed to turn the building into a multipedous monster ploughing through foam. And the monster belonged to an era not yet pestered by the emergence either of *homo sapiens* or of his forbears. For again there was nobody about. After breakfast I walked adventurously round Long Field and then through empty thoroughfares. It was as if Oxford lay under an enchantment: a terrain of great white spaces like so many pages blank in a diary in which there is nothing to record. And some such impression was to stay with me throughout this Christmas vacation and beyond. Uneventful days glided stealthily, like a sledge on silent runners, into uneventful weeks. The vacation was literally a vacation: it had drawn on a vacancy.

For me the highlight of this period was my dinner at the Bedworths' on New Year's Day. I'd hardly have expected it to be an occasion destined to become brightly lit in memory—nor was it except for the unexpected presence of the Sheldrake twins at Mabel Bedworth's table. Prior to this appearance, I don't think I'd set eyes on an undergraduate, nameable or anonymous, since saying good-night to Giles Watershute. It didn't seem to be a season at which the need for working educative overtime was at all apparent to junior members of the university. Examinations of any importance were reassuringly far off. And Mark and Matthew Sheldrake made it clear that they were in no technical sense 'in residence'. It was simply that their home was no more than thirty miles away. They were, in fact, fairly close neighbours of the Mumfords of Otby Park—a household, however, with which they appeared not notably intimate. Matthew Sheldrake, although not a censorious boy, threw some light on this. The Mumfords were, of course, Catholics, and the first Mumford to own Otby had given out a dubious claim to be of a family firmly recusant in a respectable antiquity, and in support of this idea had built himself a private chapel which an uninstructed eye might have supposed to belong to the age of the Blessed Edmund Campion. A Sheldrake given to antiquarian studies had publicly deplored this architectural deception, and between the families a continuing coolness had ensued.

These historical facts, although they reminded me of analogous feelings obtaining between family and family in the neighbourhood of Corry Hall, were less interesting than was the puzzle constituted by the presence of the two boys at this family board. Cyril Bedworth had an explanation which he offered me as soon as he had opened his front door and rescued me from the wintry blast. It seemed to be his feeling that I might regard the company of a couple of under-graduates as vexatious and in need of apology. At one or two parties to which they had been invited, Bedworth said, the Sheldrakes had greatly taken to Mabel. They did, he went on, have a mother living. But she was a magistrate, and much occupied with that and other public duties, so that her sons saw little of her. Mabel, therefore, was mothering them a bit. Bedworth thought they appreciated it very much.

It would have been difficult not to feel sceptical about this. It was true that I had cast Janet for a role in relation to Peter Lusby similar to that in which Bedworth was now casting his wife. But the circumstances were different. The Sheldrakes were back home for the vacation, so it wasn't plausible to regard them as home-sick. Nor were they in the least the sort of young men to fall into a despondency because their mother was having a busy time.

We hadn't been at table ten minutes before I was convinced of the unsurprising truth of the matter. The twins were madly in love with the Senior Tutor's wife. They were hard at work adoring her. One could almost see their heads swimming above their white collars and old school ties whenever Mrs Bedworth addressed them, or whenever she dropped her gaze modestly to her plate or to the floor. Only Bedworth (or perhaps, I asked myself, Ranald McKechnie in a similar situation?) could have got the state of the case so ludicrously wrong. But I didn't feel alarmed, and I did feel instructed. It wasn't that I had no cause for alarm. Less than a year ago, these two young men had been at enmity over the favours of Penny at her vicious best—or worst. But there wasn't a shadow of such feeling between them now. Wandering love's orchard, they had been returned, so to speak, to square one: a region of the imagination where all is grace and awe. It was comical—as comical as it had been in me with Janet during our earliest days—but there was nothing in it for Cyril Bedworth to grind his teeth or bite his knuckles about. I tried to imagine Bedworth performing either of these actions. It wasn't easy.

'I'm afraid,' Mabel Bedworth said, 'I hear the children again. They won't settle until they've seen both of you. It was a kind of promise. So—Mark, Matthew—do you mind? The pudding will keep; it's that kind of pudding. But be quite firm. Not more than one game of Ludo or Snakes and Ladders.'

The Sheldrakes jumped to their feet and departed upstairs like young knights granted by their lady the boon of an enthralling errand. Mabel glanced at her husband (who was favourably affected by these motherly proceedings); glanced at me with the faintest gleam of fun; and then consulted what would have been her toes had her toes not been invisible beneath the table.

'Mabel,' I asked, 'do you have to send a lot of young men to play Snakes and Ladders with Johnnie and Virginia?'

'It's a resource, Duncan. And it's useful to have resources when one has problems.'

I was sure about the problems, since I still couldn't listen to Mabel Bedworth's voice without feeling a bit of a problem myself. There must always be a score of undergraduates in love with her. What was new to me was the discovery that she took the thing on and saw the love-lorn youths through. The presence of the Sheldrakes tonight witnessed to that. They weren't here to be flirted with. When they returned to the dining-room—laughing and rumpled from what had clearly been a romp rather than a sedate game with dice, and to the sound of much valedictory shouting from the children above —they had been exposed to commonplace domestic sanctities in what was doubtless a steadying and maturing way. It was curious that although Bedworth hadn't a clue as to what was going on the influence of his character was apparent in the conduct of his wife when this particular sort of problem blew up. Mabel was genuinely shameful and unflirtatious, and it would have been her instinct to take rapid evasive action at the first sign of a young man's being prompted to drop on his knees before her. But it wouldn't be conscientious thus to bolt—and conscientiousness came very high in Cyril Bedworth's reckoning of the virtues.

Bedworth began to speak of serious matters. He was drawing up a scheme to stiffen the conduct of the college's beginning-of-term collections. These tests of vacation study, he explained to me, were treated far too lightly at present.

Whether Bedworth's improved plan came into operation

at the end of January I don't know. Hilary Term began with its customary air of confronting us with the stretching part of the academic year. The snows had departed, but the days, the weeks, were cold and muddy. In the hideous excavation where the tower had been pumps chugged and hiccuped day and night. The racket ought at least to have reassured Lempriere that work was going on. But his privy must have been a noisy and confusing place, supposing that he was any longer able to frequent it. Towards the middle of term I was twice told by Gall that his employer was too ill to receive me, and I had to wait a week before a chance meeting with Damian gave me any news of his patient.

'The old chap's determined to go home,' Damian said.

'To Northumberland, you mean? Good Lord! I thought he was determined to die here in college.'

'Precisely not. He says he's had his life here and it would be excessive to have his death as well. I suppose it's what he obscurely feels to be the right thing. To die on your own property is to die with your boots on. He's just waiting for his old chum Muffin, or whatever his name is, to finish his daub, and then he'll pack his bags. Or Gall will pack them for him.'

'Buffin ought to have finished the thing weeks ago.'

'Something went wrong—an idea that didn't turn out too well.'

'Christmas cards.'

'Christmas pudding, for all I know. But it has meant a lot of repainting. And the eminent artist has been down with some senile disorder of his own. I shan't take the responsibility of letting Arnold travel without a consultation with the big-wigs of our little medical world here.'

'The big-wigs managed to send McKechnie to Chicago. By the way, Robert, have you had any news of him?'

'None at all. I thought you might, as a matter of fact.'

'I've had one letter from his wife. It said he was coming

into very fair physical shape, but that she wouldn't write again until she had something more definite to report. Somehow, I didn't like the sound of that. Tell me, Robert— was packing him off there just some local consultant's gimmick or fad? My father used to say Chicago was famous only for corned horse.'

'Rather a sweeping generalization, Duncan, about a sizeable place. But, no—medicine's like that now. At its growing points, that is. Sometimes the surgeons shuttle around in a global fashion. And sometimes the guinea-pigs.'

'You wouldn't care to become a guinea-pig yourself?'

'Only if it looked like helping towards a break-through of a sensible sort. Otherwise I'd hope to notch up a decent acquiescence in my own end.'

This was the bleak voice of science, and to be soberly received. Damian and I went our respective ways.

The quiet of Hilary Term (quiet except for the builders, who in its final weeks took to churning thousands of tons of concrete in revolving cauldrons) was congruously marked by the regular presence of a quiet William Watershute among us. Whether the piano and carpets had returned to Northmoor Road we didn't know, since there had been no more parties there. But Watershute's industry was undeniable. He had once more become a model tutor—and according to his young colleague Lenton, moreover, he was lecturing and demonstrating like mad. I'd have expected, therefore, that on that front too all would be quiet, at least for a time. But this wasn't so. Among members of the Governing Body a powerful party had formed in the plain interest of refusing to let bygones be bygones. Watershute's past behaviour had been unforgivable, and they wanted to see him tried and sentenced. It seemed a weak position. Any such penalty couldn't be regarded as reformative in aim, since the man was reformed already. It could only be retributive or deterrent.

The first of these purposes could be represented as illiberal. The second appeared to assume that there were others among us liable to turn grossly negligent. Despite all this, the punitive party held on. There was even considerable bad temper in common room. Bedworth, conscious of this, went about looking as if the end had come. The Provost, on the other hand, gave the impression of believing that our society had never been so united and harmonious before.

Gavin Mogridge continued to turn up from time to time, and it had to be assumed that he was achieving a considerable depth of research in the Banbury Road. Suspecting that this labour would have been concluded had the Watershute affair revealed itself as a mare's nest from his point of view, I continued to fear the worst—and the worst wasn't, as with Bedworth, the dreadful spectre of the college 'split' in a scandalous fashion. I even took to buying (in a semi-surreptitious way) all the paperbacks I could lay my hands on concerning espionage and related activities. It was a field that had sophisticated itself since the distant time when Pattullo Minor, the Secret Service Boy, had enthralled his schoolfellows with his hazardous escapades—even troubling the rational and superior juvenile mind of Ranald McKechnie. But the essentials remained the same. Invisible ink was *vieux jeu*, having been replaced by whole messages microscopically concealed within full stops. Spies were no longer known as $X$ and $Y$; they went around under *sobriquets* like Teapot and Biscuit. But the underlying rules were as I had picked them up from boys' adventure stories long ago. I came on nothing useful in the course of these renewed researches.

I had several after-dinner conversations with Mogridge at this time, but it was only with the failed 'cellist, and with the author of *Mochica* and a number of stodgier subsequent books, that I was permitted to be in contact on these occasions. I accepted the fact that Mogridge didn't doubt my discretion and was merely obeying his, rules. Or rather I half-accepted this, feeling that he had an intelligent man's ability to subscribe to such a code only with rational reservations which might well have been brought to bear in the present case. His rules no doubt took account of the miraculous power and range of bugging devices, and even of the possibility that some elderly don asleep in a corner of common room was operating something of the kind. But Mogridge could surely have tipped me a shade more than the ghost of a wink that I had to be satisfied with? I came to feel that I was being subjected to the operation of a sense of humour which only considerable knowledge of Mogridge could distinguish as harbouring in him at all.

But at least there was no obligation upon me to treat the very existence of William Watershute as taboo. As soon as this reflection occurred to me I acted on it.

'I suppose you're aware,' I asked, 'that there's been a certain amount of trouble blowing around here over that chap Watershute?'

'Oh, yes. I'm rather preoccupied just at the moment, you know, but I have had a bit of an eye on the college scene. And I have rather gathered that Watershute has been too interested in physics at a level far above undergraduate capacities. I once had a music-master who was rather like that. It wasn't at Marlborough, but at my prepper. Do they still say "prepper" for "prep", I wonder? They're both short for "preparatory school", of course.'

'So they are.'

'This master at my prepper expected us all to be little Mozarts. Or Schuberts, perhaps I should say. For Schubert was even more precocious than Mozart. Mozart didn't come along quite as fast as Schubert did. They ought to make Watershute a professor. Professors don't have to bother with undergraduates. Undergraduates are bothered over by tutors.'

'It's a solution that has been considered, I believe.'
Mogridge, I thought, was coming increasingly to parody
himself—or to parody the public one of his two selves. As a
relief from the presumed hazards of his profession he was
entitled, I supposed, to indulge this peculiar sense of fun.
'But the trouble seems to have abated,' I said, 'and Watershute's being very industrious. Only there are people still
out for his scalp. They say he'll always be a useless run-
about. And it's true he's off to Peking in a couple of weeks.
It will be in the vacation this time, of course. But there are
men who insist he's a flighty character as well as a viewy
one.'

'He's off to Peking?' Mogridge registered vast surprise.
'Why, I'm going to Peking myself in about a fortnight's time!
When that sort of thing happens it's quite a coincidence,
wouldn't you say, Duncan?'

'Yes, Gavin, I would. What's taking *you* to Peking?'

'Well, what's taking Watershute?' Mogridge paused on
this unwontedly brisk challenge, and I thought there was
almost a communicative gleam in his eye.

'I understand he's going to read a paper at a conference. I
don't know whether it's just in physics, or whether it will
have some political slant to it. He's said to be keen on letting
scientists from either side of the Iron Curtain forgather at
will. That sort of thing.'

'That's rather surprising. I had no idea Watershute had
any political interests. It's highly creditable, of course—
although not my kind of thing, Duncan. Still, I'll try to
contact him when I'm there. Before I set off.'

'Set off, Gavin? Where for?'

'I'm thinking of that interesting walk along the Great
Wall.'

'The Great Wall of China?'

'Yes, that one. I've always found it very pleasant, walking
along walls. I expect you've walked along Hadrian's Wall,

Duncan. Of course the Great Wall of China is longer, but the basic idea is the same. It's what I've been reading up in rather an interesting place out on the Banbury Road. The Great Wall of China.'

'But mayn't it be rather difficult—dangerous, even— roaming free through contemporary China? Even, Gavin, if you have no political interests. Why, you might be taken for a spy!'

'Oh, I say, what an alarming idea! But I don't think so, Duncan. There's a great deal of continuity in Chinese society. The scholars go and labour in the fields from time to time, of course. Yes, there's all that. There's all that to the Cultural Revolution. But the Cultural Revolution has its cultural side. That's why it's——'

'Yes, I see. You'll be received by learned people, and so forth, and sped on your way. Quite a long way, too.'

'Well, not all *that* long.' Mogridge was heavily judicious. 'Perhaps not more than three years. Good Lord! It's ten o'clock and I must be off. Yes, I must be on my way, I'm afraid. I'll try to remember about Watershute, Duncan, and look him up. Of course I've been in China on a good many occasions before. I expect I could show him one or two things that would surprise him.'

'I expect you could. Shall I tell him, Gavin, to look out for you?'

'Oh, yes, do. Not that he knows much about me or may be particularly interested, of course. But do mention it, by all means.'

For the fraction of a second Mogridge looked at me (or rather at some indefinite object over my right shoulder) with detectable mockery, so that I almost felt that he judged me to be under some ludicrous misconception. Then he gave a casual nod and wandered vaguely from the room. I wondered whether there had been a word of truth in the statement that he was going to China himself, or whether it had been a mere joke at my expense. If he was going, would he have the slightest power to keep tabs on Watershute there? I was more bewildered by this whole unsatisfactory colloquy than any former Secret Service Boy ought to have been.

# XXIII

OXFORD IN VACATION (although celebrated by Charles Lamb in an essay greatly admired by Talbert) has not much to commend it to unattached persons. At Christmas I had been accurately described by Moggy Junkin as a waif, and I looked like being a waif again at Easter. The McKechnies were beyond the Atlantic, and Janet still silent. When Fiona proposed returning from Denmark I didn't know; I'd written her a Christmas letter directed to the University of Copenhagen, but nothing had come in reply. So I was wondering once more about the vacation problem (and by implication about my whole course of life) when I heard from Fish. Fish held me to my promise to visit Scotland with him in early Spring. This was excellent news, and solved part of my difficulty. But Fish made a further suggestion. He'd fly not to London but to Naples; I'd meet him there; we'd have a fortnight in Italy before proceeding with our original plan.

What prompted this nostalgic proposal, and so lavish a bestowing on me of a busy man's time, I was never quite to discover. Perhaps I shied away from doing so. Long before, we had helped to sort one another out. Fish may have decided that I needed sorting out again now. Alternatively, some hitch had conceivably developed in what appeared to be the smooth tenor of his own domestic life, and he was seeking a little detachment from it for the purpose of reflection. I was prone, I suppose, to see other people's lives that way. But however this might be, the plan fell in with some quite practical sorting out that I'd been meditating for some time. The Villa d'Orso, acquired because *a buon prezzo* by Penny and myself long ago, was still the major piece of property I possessed, but I had been making less and less use of it as the years went by. At the moment it didn't constitute any sort of financial problem, if only because the lira was as sick as the pound sterling. But mightn't some radical change in my condition (such as I dimly lived in the consideration of) make this no longer so? Besides which, there was surely something almost unwholesome in hanging on to a house which, although delectable in itself, held associations obstinately of a raw and painful order. I decided that Fish and I should begin our Italian jaunt by making the same run from Naples to Ravello that we had made as undergraduates, and that after a brisk tidy up I'd put the villa on the market—whether *a buon prezzo* or not. This being decided, everything was easy, and a series of telephone calls saw the details of the plan arranged. On the last day of term I packed my bags, gave Plot the Villa d'Orso as a forwarding address, and drove to Heathrow. Within a couple of hours I was across the Alps.

When I reached Naples Fish was there before me and had hired a car: a somewhat imposing Lancia which witnessed unconsciously to the prosperity of the Australian pastoral interest. Our first exchanges consisted of juvenile badinage over this circumstance. It was immediately apparent that we were going to get on well. Italy took instant hold of us, as it commonly does. The country was virtually without a government at the time. An economist or politician would no doubt have distinguished imminent disaster attendant upon this, but only an enhanced sense of well-being was the result to any superficial view. There were odd minor inconveniences I'd hardly met before. Coins had almost vanished from circulation, and in the shops one took one's small change in single cigarettes or in *gettoni* with which one could make telephone calls if one wanted to. If one tackled a shop-assistant or a tram-conductor about this he would explain that all the coins—and the 100 lire pieces in particular—had been carried off by tourists because they could readily be converted into handsome trouser buttons. I supposed that if one had the misfortune to fall very ill or to be put in prison the general administrative shambles might bear on one hardly. Short of that one was all right.

In Ravello we could have camped comfortably in the villa, or even organized a regular *ménage* there at short notice had we wanted to. Fish, however, was anxious to put up in our old hotel, and we drove there at once. The newspaper photograph of D. H. Lawrence, much faded, still hung in the hall, and this prompted Fish to reject the well-appointed modern cubby-holes we were severally offered and insist on our once more sharing the large and antique apartment which we had believed (erroneously) to have been slept in by Lawrence and Frieda. This was perhaps to carry nostalgia rather far. I even became apprehensive that Fish might whip a *Lady Chatterley's Lover* out of his suitcase and entertain me to more of Mellors's dark thoughts on women. But this didn't happen. And we had a very good dinner.

It came to me during the next few days that winding up the Villa d'Orso represented a final closing down on Penny. The house was my last remaining physical link with her. Perhaps it was because of this—although all unconsciously—that I'd held on to it. It was even true to this day that my experience of Penny was something I wouldn't care to lose utterly; to purge from my being with the help of some potent drug. She'd had a share in shaping my life, even in forming my character, and she had her right to a continued lurking place deep inside my head. But I didn't want to view her in any theatre of active memory ever again, and parting with the villa was a symbol of that fact.

All this was only in the back of my mind, for there were numerous small practical things to decide. What, for example, was to be done with the big Rauschenberg collage which Penny had given me as a birthday present?

'You must part with it,' Fish said firmly. 'There's a lot of pop art that has its place in a gallery but won't do in private hands. Or, anyway, not in *your* private hands, Duncan. Do you remember this chap's stuffed goat all tangled up with a motor tire? You wouldn't sit down to dinner with that, would you? And you can't have this thing, although rather good of its kind, hanging cheek by jowl with a Pattullo. You'd better sell it to me, and I'll find it a good home.'

'It's a benevolent thought, Martin. But not on your life. I'm going to send it back to New York, where it belongs.'

'You say Penny gave you the Rauschenberg,' Fish said. He had decided that talk of this sort was of wholesome cathartic effect. 'Is there anything around the house that you gave her?'

'I shouldn't think so. She'd probably have taken anything of that sort away with her. I left her in possession here, you know. Uncommonly abruptly. And then lawyers took over—English ones and Italian ones as well—and settled it all up. It was a mess. Look, let's get out of this and walk around. Or up and down those *scale*. We'll have to get some exercise if we're going to go touring in that great fat car.'

'And lock up here?'

'Yes. We've done everything useful. People can come in and sell up the lot.'

We went into the little *giardino*. Lizards and cyclamen, rock cress and green helebore and euphorbia. These were what Penny had seen here—and on a day not unlike this, when there was a first warmth in the air and a faint haze veiling Capo d'Orso where it showed westward over the roof of the Palazzo Rufolo.

'We'll take a dekko at the Cimbrone,' Fish said. 'Remember that inscription? I'd like to see it again.'

We walked to the entrance of the Villa Cimbrone and rang the clattering little bell. More than a quarter of a century before one had feared that a single incautious tug would bring it down, but here it was still. We handed over a 500 lire note. No *gettoni* or cigarettes were forthcoming—which rendered Fish's curiosity a shade expensive. We walked through the long formal garden and duly found the poem which our hotel had appropriated for Lawrence's Muse. *Lost to a world in which I crave no part* ... The incised quatrain above the rustic seat was a little less legible than on the last occasion of my studying it. We went on to the garden's end, and to the little Belvedere perched on the verge of the tremendous cliff that drops sheer to the Gulf of Salerno incredibly far below. It was here that I had come upon Colonel Morrison and my Uncle Rory's factor Alec Mountjoy sitting hand in lover's hand. The Belvedere differed a good deal from the image of it I carried around, even although I had seen it frequently enough in the interval. Colonel Morrison and Mountjoy I had never seen again, and it was possible that I might recognize neither of them were he to present himself to me.

'Let's do Amalfi,' Fish said. 'I forget—can we go straight down?'

'Not unless we're proposing suicide. But we can go back into the town, and then down a series of *scale* to Atrani, and then along the coast road. It's nothing once one's down, but quite a step before that.'

'Well, let's do it. We can probably get a bus up again in time for dinner.'

I wasn't sure that I wanted to revisit Amalfi. There was a sense in which it was almost literally no more than a stone's throw from where we now stood, but on terra firma it was sufficiently far away to be avoided without eccentricity. When staying in Ravello I had formed the habit of dropping down to Maiori instead, and of doing my shopping in Salerno. But this irrational distaste was no reason for damping Fish's ardour. So we retraced our route through the deceased Lord Grimthorpe's deserted garden, and then made our jolting way down endless flights of stony steps until we reached the sea.

Amalfi, although in fact a populous little place, always appears rather empty except in the tourist season, and there was as yet no sign of that beginning. But the afternoon was sunny and therefore hot; here and there along the front idle people were sitting outside cafés; there was even some stir of life on two or three of the small yachts at anchor close inshore. We leaned against a railing and gazed out over the Mediterranean. I was wondering what Fish would say if I suggested a swim or paddle when my attention was caught by something familiar about the largest of the craft immediately before us. There was activity I couldn't quite distinguish at the stern, and on the roof of a small deck-house two fair-haired children were sitting, intent upon what may have been some sort of mechanical toy. And then in a second vague familiarity turned to certainty so complete that I could almost feel the boards of the *Ithaca* beneath my own feet. There she floated—in different colours but otherwise unchanged. But it hadn't been children who were amusing themselves on her deck-house when my binoculars had turned upon her from the *Piccolo Gallo* some twelve years before.

'Let's go and find a drink,' I said abruptly.

Fish gave an acquiescent nod accompanied by a quick glance; he was a man regularly aware of what Nick Junkin called the vibes. We moved along the front, past shuttered booths and cheap sprawling restaurants not yet painted up for the season. Amalfi, I supposed, had been a small resort of some elegance when Ibsen had settled down in it to write *A Doll's House*—a fragment of literary history, this, unearthed by Penny on our wedding journey. Nowadays, no doubt, the populace of Naples poured out to it during the summer months: endless *seicento* on the tail of *seicento* along the agreeably lethal *corniche* through Sorrento. As this was not yet happening, we crossed the road without difficulty to an almost deserted café. It appeared, indeed, to have only one customer: an elderly man in what were obviously good English clothes fallen into disrepair. He regarded me fixedly and sternly as we approached, like one resenting intrusion. But this wasn't so, for suddenly I saw that he was blind, and that there was a white walking-stick laid across the pavement table before him. And then I saw that the man was Ulric Anderman.

He was somebody who had passed entirely from my ken. I may vaguely have supposed him dead, like his companion Henry Tindale, the White Rabbit. But in this moment of recognition—recognition on one side only—I behaved oddly. It would have been quite simple to pass Anderman by; to move on to a part of the café where even a possibly familiar voice couldn't reach him. But—face to blind face as we now were—I couldn't manage this; couldn't manage taking this advantage of his condition. He had, after all, been my host, and it was only casually due to his former way of life that Penny and Frediano (Penny far more than Frediano) had misconducted themselves on board the *Ithaca*. I was even indebted to the man for a revelation which had happened on what might be called a sooner-the-better basis.

'Good afternoon,' I said. 'You may hardly remember me, but I am Duncan Pattullo. And this is my friend Martin Fish. Martin—Sir Ulric Anderman.'

'How are you, Pattullo? Mr Fish, how do you do?' Coldly correct, Anderman held out a chilly hand. And we found ourselves seated beside him.

We ordered drinks. Or rather Anderman ordered drinks, remarking with finality that he was on his home ground.

'My domestic situation is such,' he said, 'that I hesitate to regard myself as my own master in such matters. Otherwise, I need hardly say, I would hasten to offer a more adequate hospitality.'

It was Fish who managed an appropriate reply to this. There was really no social situation that could get Fish down. I myself was left searching for something to talk about, and I found it only when I realized that it would be absurd to ignore Anderman's affliction.

'I'm extremely sorry,' I said, 'about the disability I fear you suffer under.'

'Ah, yes! Doubtless it is what they call a retributive disease.' Anderman paused on this—which probably shook even Fish. 'It interferes with various pursuits of mine which, Pattullo, may be within your recollection.'

'Yes, indeed. You were very much the field naturalist, Anderman. I remember your taking me in search of—I think—a blue and black lizard. Is that right? There was a small island it had been reported as to be found on.'

'*Lacerta muralis faraglionensis*, Pattullo. It is of marked zoological interest. The island may have been the *Piccolo Gallo.*'

'So it may.'

'It would give me great pleasure to take you on a return trip to so agreeable a spot. But unfortunately my sailing days are over.'

'I notice the *Ithaca* at anchor out there. Have you parted with her?'

'The *Ithaca* remains in the family. And I continue to live, I may say, in my old house. My wife finds it somewhat inconvenient, but we are both attached to it. I see you are a little surprised. Or I should rather say I assume you are.'

'I'm sorry, Anderman. I'm afraid I'd forgotten you were a married man.'

'That is very understandable. The fact is that my wife and I decided to come together again. That, I believe, is the common phrase. She must be an exceptionally devoted woman.' Anderman said this as if recording a surprising fact that had just occurred to him. 'Of course she has her children, and now her grandchildren—and our circumstances are such that I have to make provision for the lot. We live together in a positively Asiatic way.'

'What's now called an extended family,' I said.

'No doubt, Pattullo. I am much behind the times in such aspects of social change. But here we all are, Anglo-Italians recalling a past age—and in a house, as I have hinted, a damned sight too small for us.'

'Would those be your grandchildren on the deck of the *Ithaca* now?' I asked.

'They are, indeed.' Anderman paused again. 'And I am sitting here to keep an eye on them.'

I felt that this savage irony was intended as a curtain-line, and that Anderman was indicating that his entertainment of us was concluded. Not much wishing to prolong the encounter myself, I got to my feet and said something about our bus. Without rising, Anderman held out a hand to each of us in turn.

'Ah, the bus station!' he said. 'If you go that way, it might interest you to glance at Innocenzo's shop on your right. You might even make a purchase there, should you judge the proprietor to merit your support. Good-bye, Pattullo. Good-bye, Mr Fish; I am delighted to have met you.'

We walked away, and in silence for a time. Fish, feeling there were unknown factors in the case, would certainly offer no comment until I had taken some explanatory initiative myself. But when I did speak, it was merely to ask a question.

'What the devil do you think he meant about Innocenzo's shop?'

'I haven't a clue, Duncan. But there it is. And what it seems to sell is candy-floss.'

'I'll go and have a look,' I said, 'while you make sure of that bus.' I waited while Fish nodded and walked away—entirely as if he weren't in the least surprised. I myself *was* surprised, but only at my discovery that I wanted to cope with this one alone. For I suddenly hadn't the slightest doubt about what Anderman had directed me to; I was certain of it even before catching sight of the sign above the window. *Frediano Innocenzo,* it read, *Cartoleria, Picture Postcards, Confetto.* I hadn't known that Frediano's surname too was a little out of the way. I entered the shop.

Twelve years isn't twenty-five. When Fish walked into my room in Surrey it had been moments before I recognized him. But I recognized Frediano instantly, and he me. He advanced upon me with outstretched arms: a young man in his early thirties, stout and out of condition, puffy-faced but for the moment with a smile I remembered very well.

'*Signor Duncan! Come sta? Siete il benvenuto!*' Having embraced me, Frediano shook hands and looked hospitably round his shop. 'American candy?' he asked.

I declined American candy, and felt that Frediano had me at a disadvantage. Indeed, I was rather at a loss, and wondered why I had wantonly added this encounter to the sufficiently disturbing one I had just concluded. At the same time, I felt easier with Frediano than I had done with Anderman— perhaps because Frediano was entirely easy with me. He now dropped into an instant nostalgic vein which would have done credit to Tony Mumford and myself in our cups. The *Ithaca!* His honoured *protettore, il signor Tindale!* Those divine Calabrian days! Frediano was presently expatiating so copiously and rapidly on what I took to be the theme of our first innocence that I had difficulty in following him. Had not the serpent, he was asking, entered the garden in the form, as always, of *il bel sesso?* The theology of this was a shade confused, but the leading idea was clear. Penny had been the occasion of expelling us all from our paradise.

When Frediano reached this point I felt I'd had enough of him. Not that I wasn't rather liking him at the same time. Except for having once been almost as good-looking as the Sheldrake twins, he was, and always had been, as common as they come. Or was that quite true? Had there been, perhaps, some strain of sensibility in him? Had he been honestly devoted to his bewilderingly indecisive *protettore*? I couldn't remember. I only saw that I bore Frediano no ill will; that I merely had to bring Penny into the picture, indeed, and there became apparent a certain sympathy and even complicity between us. But this didn't mean that I wanted any more of Frediano, either now or ever again. I moved towards the door of the shop. Frediano halted his harangue for a moment, again casting round for the purpose of endowing me with some material token of his regard. Responding to this insistence, I grabbed a picture postcard at random, and managed to speak just as Frediano was proposing to hold forth anew.

'*Si, si, Frediano,*' I said. '*Come son crudeli, le donne.*'

Frediano's volubility stilled. He laid a hand upon my arm— as one philosopher, deeply read in the sorrows of the world, might do to another who has said some pregnant thing. I was blessedly in open air before his mood changed again.

'*Addio, addio, signor Duncan!*' he cried enthusiastically. '*Arrivederci, amico mio, caro mio! Arrivederla!*'

'Good-bye, Frediano,' I said, and I shook hands and walked away. Fish was waiting for me at the bus station.

'Well,' he asked, 'did you buy some candy-floss?'

'No, I didn't. But I've brought you a postcard. It was for free, with the compliments of the proprietor.' I handed Fish the card. He glanced at it and appeared amused.

'Well, that was clever of you, Duncan,' he said. 'You did recognize it, didn't you?'

'I didn't think to look, Martin.' I looked now. The brightly coloured view of some corner of *la costiera Amalfitana* was certainly familiar. In fact Fish himself had bought the identical card on one of our first days in Ravello long ago.

'I say!' I said. 'Do you think on the back it still says——?'

Fish turned the card over. And there it was. *Angolo*

*suggestivo, Suggestiv Ort, Fascinating noow*. I tried to recall the ingenious indecencies we had contrived to extract from this well-meant polyglot effort. But they failed to come back to me.

'It is odd,' I said, 'how this and that bobs up again.'

We climbed into the bus. That night—being without the possibility of readings from *Lady Chatterley's Lover*—I gave Fish a more detailed account than hitherto of the concluding phase of my married life. He called it, comfortably, filling up the corners of the canvas.

We drove off in the Lancia on the following morning. Fish must have decided that bobbing up was something we'd had enough of, for we wandered among places unfamiliar to either of us. Finally we returned to Ravello for a single night, and I signed some papers authorizing competent persons to close with the first reasonable offer for the Villa d'Orso that came along. Fish was disappointed at the non-arrival of a letter about some picture he'd heard of as on the market. Come bush-fire, come flood, he said, the mail invariably turned up punctually at Wangarra, and he didn't see why it shouldn't do the same thing in Basilicata or Puglia. He was put in better humour by an amiable Italian, encountered in a trattoria, who explained that there was no money available to pay anybody to sort and deliver anything of the kind. The mail-trains, therefore, went quietly round and round Italy, ending up at a factory where there had been a shortage of the materials for making cheap papier mâché suitcases, with the result that these were now once more in abundant supply. This was the same sort of Italian joke as the one about the trouser buttons.

# XXIV

## WATERSHUTE: THE INSIDE STORY

### *by Boswell Chaffey*

I STARED UNBELIEVINGLY at the headline in the newspaper I'd picked up on board the Trident. It was the first
English paper we'd either of us bothered to look at since
leaving England. The run of the thing was obscure and
muddled in Chaffey's best manner, and a sub-editor with an
interest in the law of libel hadn't made getting hold of the
situation any easier. But an outline emerged. Watershute had
set off for a conference in Peking. The conference was now
known to have existed only in his own head—a statement to
this effect having been issued by the Chinese Embassy.
(There was a smudgy photograph of the Embassy in Portland
Place.) Then, somewhere in the Middle East, he had eluded
surveillance (Chaffey was emphatic that there had been
'surveillance', but unfortunately of an incompetent order) and
travelled straight to Moscow. That he had arrived there
didn't admit of doubt, since he had been the star exhibit at a
conference—a real conference this time—at which he had
made a speech denouncing the West and all its ways. The
conference had concluded with a party at which he had talked
in the same vein to several western journalists who had met
him on previous occasions. There was a great rumpus in
Oxford (this, Chaffey treated with a satiric pen), and furious
questions were being asked in parliament.

'A friend of ours in the news,' I said to Fish, and handed
him the paper. Then I watched him read it through, which

he did composedly. 'What on earth do you make of it, Martin?'

'Not much. Is Watershute dead silly? You have a fresher acquaintance with him than I have.'

'It hadn't occurred to me that he was exactly silly.'

'Was it the prospect of this blowing up, Duncan, that made that chap Graile try to pump me about Watershute? I remember feeling he was doing that.'

'I doubt whether Graile was looking ahead to just this. It was simply that Watershute had turned unreliable and negligent, and everybody was cross and puzzled about it.'

'Do you think he's all that important—I mean as a man able to give away top scientific secrets? And doesn't that kind of thing tend to happen uncommonly quietly, at least at a start?'

'Spy-stuff obviously has to be hush-hush. But this isn't that. I suppose it's what's called defecting.'

'Yes—and if he really gave somebody the slip it looks as if heads may roll in MI5, or whatever it is.'

'Yes,' I said rather grimly. 'It does.'

'Defecting organized in the interest of this bit of brouhaha in Moscow. Noisy stuff. There are plenty of scientists in Russia who'd be quite glad to move to gentler climes. Everybody knows that. And here's a show-piece designed to exhibit the process in reverse. It's something like that.'

'Well, at least that allows one to suppose in the man some degree of serious ideological persuasion. But think of your glimpse of him in Venice! The story begins with a man falling into extravagant and dissolute courses, going completely disorganized, and then briefly turning quiet and respectable and unnoticeable again. Isn't that much more like the picture of a person who has been spotted as vulnerable because in desperate difficulties, and has cracked under pressure and turned merely venal as a result?'

'Fair enough, Duncan. But what has come of it seems to be a mere charade.'

'Exactly—"seems". The charade may be a front for something else. We're offered the picture of a futile political gesture. But he may still have taken something in his pocket with him.'

Fish appeared to judge this worthy of thought, since he fell silent for a while. During this interval the note of our plane's engines changed. We were beginning to drop down to Heathrow.

'Martin,' I said on a sudden impulse. 'Do you know? I think I'd better get back to Oxford. Just for a day or two, and to see what's what. I'm not really in on this. But the man has a wife who was the foundation of my fortunes in an odd way. And a son who's an undergraduate at the college now, and whom I've got to know quite well. He's just above me on Surrey Four. There's even something I know about the business that perhaps nobody else in college does. It's connected with Surrey Four again, oddly enough.' As I made this perhaps foolishly mysterious speech I think I almost heard the distressing strains of Gavin Mogridge's 'cello coming through the floorboards as long ago.

'That will suit me very well, Duncan.' Fish had received my last speech without a flicker of overt curiosity. 'I've one or two pictures to hunt down in London, as a matter of fact. So let's put off Scotland for the inside of a week. Ten to one, you know, Watershute won't even be a nine days' wonder. Fasten seat-belts. Here we are.'

My first contact was with Plot, to whom I had sent a telegram announcing my return. Plot, accordingly, was helpfully engaged in turning my rooms upside down when I did arrive.

'You'll have heard this shocking piece of news, sir,' Plot said on a positive note.

'One's always hearing shocking pieces of news nowadays, Plot. It's the character of the times. So just what do you mean?'

'It's this Dr Watershute's levanting that I'd have in mind.' Plot, although not commonly an ironist, had indicated that he was unimpressed by my attempt to play down the situation. 'It's causing a lot of trouble—what with one man saying one thing and another man saying another. At a regular sixes and sevens the place is. And that although we're nearly three weeks into the vacation, which is usually a time that's quiet enough.'

'It's bound to disturb things a little, Plot. But perhaps the newspapers are treating it in rather a sensational way. Dons don't much care to see their concerns aired like that.' I was taking it for granted that Plot's reference had been to my colleagues. But this proved to be not so.

'It's the college servants I'm thinking of, Mr Pattullo. They're the people I naturally hear talk about the matter.' Plot had said 'college servants' with an unforced confidence and dignity. To an outsider's eye this body of men—for they were nearly all men, or boys—must have appeared a rag-tag crowd in an income-group rightly to be despised by all. In fact they regarded themselves as *soldats d'élite* in any comparison with the more prosperous regiments on the conveyor belts. 'There's that Mr Gall, now,' Plot went on, 'who has been with Mr Lempriere for many a year. We're in the vacation, he says, when a man has a right to go where he pleases. And Dr Watershute, being a deep scholar in his line, has a duty to say what he thinks when he gets there. But very subversive, Gall is felt to be by most.'

'So I'd suppose, Plot.' It struck me that Gall must have been speaking with his master's voice, since Lempriere's habit of contraverting majority opinions was unlikely to desert him on his deathbed. I wondered whether David Graile was proving himself the industrious apprentice in this latest exigency too.

'And those that are commonly quiet enough are all uptight about it.' Plot may have had this vogue word from one of his juvenile charges. 'There's a little chap working in the S.C.R. who's usually as mild spoken as you could please. All for bettering himself in catering and the like.'

'I think I know him.'

'Well, this little chap says to watch the kind of people who go off like that. What they have in Russia and such places is people's democracies and workers' republics. But those that bolt there are men like Dr Watershute who are the hired lackeys of capitalism and imperialism. You never hear of a worker levanting, he says. Perhaps, I tell him, it's because they haven't got the cash. Not even them shop stewards have the cash. Nor the secrets to sell either.'

'It's a valid point, Plot.' I was a good deal impressed by this revelation of debate below-stairs in college. It was only too likely to be going on above-stairs as well. Between Plot and myself it had now perhaps been given a sufficient airing. So I changed the subject to something that had been a good deal on my mind before Boswell Chaffey's contribution to public knowledge had suddenly come my way. 'By the way, Plot, did you forward any letters to me in Italy?'

'Yes, Mr Pattullo. It might be half-a-dozen of them—to Ravello, as you said.'

'Would there have been one from America?'

'Yes. One was from America.'

'Did you happen to notice the postmark? Would it have been Chicago?'

'That might be. But I didn't take note of it.' Plot was intimating that it wasn't his place to exercise this sort of scrutiny. 'No doubt those letters, if they missed you, will come back to Oxford.'

'It's possible.' I thought of the papier mâché suitcases. 'I have to go out now. But please don't trouble to do much more here today.'

'Very good, sir.' Plot picked up his Hoover with a slight air of unrequited devotion. 'I'll be here in the evening as usual. Just give that shout, Mr Pattullo, if anything's required of me. Time on my hands, in a manner of speaking, with all them untidy lads well out of the way. Not that there isn't a lot of thoroughing to do.'

'Thank you very much. And I'm sure there is.'

I walked over to the post office and sent a cable to Janet in Chicago. Having letters forwarded to Italy had been a stupid mistake by which I'd been caught out in the past. And I couldn't bear to have Janet suppose that I hadn't at once responded to news from her, whether it was good or bad. Having got this off my mind, and on returning through the college, I went into common room to put myself down for dinner, and there I came upon Charles Atlas. He was poring over a fat volume which I distinguished as being the Statutes of the University of Oxford. It had lately become possible to peruse these in other than the Latin tongue.

'Hullo, Charles!' I said. 'How nice to see you back. thought your leave was for the whole year.'

'I flew back as soon as I heard.' Atlas looked at me severely. 'It seemed the proper thing to do.'

'Heard? Heard about what, Charles?' This was the technique I had tried out on Plot.

'Don't be a fool, Duncan, with your bloody superior "academic-storm-in-a-teacup" line of talk. This is serious.'

'I'm very sorry.' Even by Lempriere, I had never been snapped at in this fashion in this room before, and I wondered whether it portended what might be advancing upon us on a broad front. 'I quite agree it's serious.'

'So what do we do here and now? That's the question.' Atlas, swiftly mollified, put this to me as if I might really have an answer. 'I'd be extremely grateful to hear what you think.'

'Well, I'd say there are two issues in this Watershute affair. They are really quite distinct, and of differing magnitude.

The first is his having gone to pieces as a tutor, and having scandalously absented himself, and so on. As you'll have heard, there wasn't finally much dispute over the degree of his ill-conduct. But people were still wondering what to do, when he suddenly turned into a reformed character. There was a whole term of that; his negligence, or whatever it's to be called, was distancing itself; a debate did start up as to whether or not the college ought to let bygones be bygones. There was certainly room for a reasonable difference of opinion. And it hasn't been resolved yet, so far as I know. What's your feeling, Charles?'

'That a man who has indulged himself in a series of aberrations as Watershute has must always be a potential liability thereafter, and ought to be got rid of as humanely and with as little publicity as possible. But this is only to deal with the first of your issues, Duncan. The second is quite simple. It turns on where Watershute is, and what Watershute has been saying, here and now. That's plain common sense, isn't it?'

'Oh, yes, Charles. Of course it is.'

'But I can see it being said that the problem's *not* simple. Preferring one social system to another, and spending a holiday jabbering to that effect in Moscow or Timbuktu, isn't grave immorality, is it? Equally, it has nothing to do with non-observance of statutes—whether ours or the university's, so far as I can see. Perhaps it can be called misconduct. But that's a pretty nebulous term. Ask Jimmy Gender.'

'I don't need to ask Jimmy Gender. And the whole problem isn't legalistic. It's moral or philosophical.'

'Yes, I agree, Duncan. But what if Watershute has been making his new friends a present or something?'

'Well, Charles, if the something were in the sphere of official secrets, the man would have committed a felony. And in that case his fate would be out of our hands.

'But we can't sit back and just fold them! The university

has its eye on us, and the country has its eye on the university. There really is the most frightful stink. Everybody's talking. As you're just back yourself perhaps you haven't gathered that.'

'Indeed I have. Even the college scouts are talking—and on very much the lines you and I are huffing and puffing over now.'

'Don't be gamesome, Duncan.' This time, Atlas was entirely friendly. 'But I repeat, what can we do?'

'Think about Watershute's wife and son, for one thing. Do you know anything about them?'

'Nothing whatever. I'm afraid they've scarcely entered my head. But I expect Camilla Pococke——'

'Yes, of course. She'll be doing the right thing. A little briskly, perhaps—but the right thing. However, I knew June Watershute long before she did. I think I'll go up to Northmoor Road now.'

I went to get out my car, and found Buntingford similarly engaged.

'Hullo, Duncan,' he said. 'Off for your round of golf with Edward?'

'Adrian, for pity's sake! You get more and more like an old cracked gramophone record.' I believe I said this with real asperity; if so, it was another small instance that edginess was around. I didn't know how it had come about that a luckless episode on a golf course in the year 1947 or thereabouts had established itself in a distorted form as a small common room legend. 'As a matter of fact, I'm running out to North Oxford to see the Watershutes. Mother and son, that's to say.'

'You may see the mother, but I gather you won't see the boy. Giles Watershute has vanished. Put it, perhaps, that the young Telemachus has gone off to seek papa. In which case anything may happen. He may even marry Circe, supposing

274

that there's a Circe in the story. And there always tends to be, wouldn't you say? What sort of a boy is this Giles Watershute? Is he *like* Telemachus?'

'I don't know anything about Telemachus.'

'Liar! But I can remind you that he was a somewhat timid and diffident youth, who proved however to have considerable stuffing in the end. He quite astonished his mama by taking a difficult domestic situation in hand.'

'I don't think that would be beyond Giles, Adrian. But I suppose this wretched business will confront him with a difficult college situation as well.'

'Not if he faces up to it.' Buntingford was suddenly serious. 'His friends and mere acquaintances will be absolutely solid for him. And everybody else as well, for that matter. It always happens that way when something totally shocking turns up in a man's background. And if any of those news-hounds come hunting him down, they'll find themselves in the fountain before they can get out their bloody scratch-pads. Incidentally, that disgusting Chaffey will get the hell of a time if he ventures back into residence. Not that Edward will let him, I imagine.'

'Edward will be all for treading carefully—and quite right too. Has there been a lot in the way of news-hounds?'

'You must be joking. They're all over the place. Well, be off, young Pattullo, and hold mama's hand. She's one of those celebrated old flames of yours, isn't she?'

'We had a profitable professional association at one time, Adrian. Good-bye.'

Contrary to Buntingford's persuasion, it was Giles and not his mother whom I found at home. He opened the door for me, said 'Hullo, sir!', and glanced quickly round the untidy garden and up and down the road. There was a police car at the nearest corner, with a couple of uniformed men sitting in it impassively. At the garden gate were standing three bored reporters. I'd had no doubt they were that as I skirted them to gain the house.

'Come in,' Giles said. 'The fuzz are quite good. They keep all that within bounds. And interest has slackened since I got my mother away. Still, I generally have one of those pests following me around. Every now and then they come and walk alongside and ask the same questions over and over again. I just shake my head. I ought to feel furious, but actually I feel rather mean. But scared, too, to tell the truth. They'd torture something out of me if they could.'

This last remark, which had taken us into June Watershute's still denuded drawing-room, had been lightly uttered. I felt it to emanate, all the same, from some not very comfortable corner of Giles's imagination.

'I hope you don't mind my coming out,' I said. 'I thought I ought to try to see your mother. Somebody told me you were away from home yourself.'

'I have been. I went off to arrange a hide-out for her. And that's fixed up now, thank goodness. You see, she's had to carry rather a lot for rather a long time. She did it frightfully well, I think. Now that I know about it I think that. I suppose that being an actress helped. We've talked about that party before, haven't we?'

'So we have, Giles.' I was puzzled by the drift of these remarks, and felt that Giles had changed in a fashion I couldn't work out at all. I had seen comparatively little of him since the Junkins' Christmas dinner. He had been in good spirits then—and confessedly on the score of what had appeared to be his father's reformed courses. All that he'd had to contend with was the memory of having almost suspected his father of treason. Now, it must surely seem to him as if his darkest fears had come true. There was certainly a new gravity, a sternness, about him. He seemed older. Telemachus, I thought, in his second phase.

'It became a whole lot better,' Giles said, 'when I'd been

told.' He might have been reading my thoughts. 'Being shut out of something that was obviously deadly serious: it was that that was rather hell. But about my mother. Somebody thought she mightn't quite manage to continue to stand up to it. She might let something slip. So I've got her off to relations in a thoroughly hush-hush way. And—well—I've taken over, really.' Giles paused for a moment. 'What do you think about it all?'

'Well, Giles, I arrived thinking things must feel pretty desperate, both for you and your mother. Do they?'

'Yes, of course. I try to feel it will come right, but the odds seem desperately against it.'

'It's difficult not to feel that.' I was still much puzzled by Giles, and I now felt that he on his part was puzzled by me. It was almost as if we were at an obscure cross-purposes. And this effect immediately increased.

'But it's as if you're not with it, sir. Hasn't he *told* you?'

'I don't know what you're talking about, Giles. And I sometimes think that nobody ever tells me anything.'

'Then it's a good thing he told me *I* can tell you. If you happened to turn up on me first, he said.' Giles had actually produced a mischievous and care-free grin. 'I say, would you terribly mind if I joined the Junkin family and called you Duncan?'

'High time.'

'Good! Well, about Mogridge——'

'Mogridge, Giles?' I oughtn't to have been startled, but I was.

'Yes, Mogridge. You must have thought it funny how he came after me, cultivating my acquaintance in that way. The *Nouvelle Revue Française,* and all that.'

'I didn't think it at all funny, Giles.' As I said this I felt like a man upon whom a strange dawn breaks. 'I didn't feel it funny, because there was something I happened to know about Gavin Mogridge.'

'Yes—and I know too, Duncan. The whole ploy was a kind of security check. He was vetting me. And he decided I was reliable—in which I modestly think he was quite right. So in the end he came in the clear. I was enlisted, you might say—just as my mother had had to be from the start.'

'From the start? What I supposed, Giles, was that Mogridge was cultivating you because—suspicion being his line of business—he was suspecting your father of steering for the port he seems so definitely to have arrived at now. And that wasn't funny at all.'

'Yes—and so Mogridge was at the beginning. Whatever the thing is, you see, it was my father's private initiative. Not Mogridge's people at all. Or that's how I've worked it out. But then they adopted it, and made it what you might call official. Duncan, does this sound completely dotty?'

'Completely. But then, from all I read of it, it's a dotty area of human activity. Highly ingenious often. But always clean crazy.'

'I don't think my father's clean crazy. He's a very sane man among them, if you ask me.' Giles said this with one of his occasional flashes of pride. 'Among all those agents and spies and spy-masters, I mean.'

'I'll take that, Giles. But just what *is* it all in aid of?'

'I don't know. I just don't know.' Giles looked perplexed. 'We have to call it a secret mission. My father's gone off on a secret mission. And it all seems so mad that I have to struggle desperately to keep any faith in his ever coming back again. And there's another thing that's terrifying.' Giles was talking very fast now. 'The elaboration! It's kind of double-agent stuff, it seems to me. But, for a long time at the start, private enterprise on my father's part. Building up a deceptive picture of his own character and situation. And doing some pretty rum things, if I haven't got them wrong.'

'No doubt.' I felt this to be an aspect of the matter that Giles and I need not enter upon. William Watershute might well have allowed himself a certain amount of authentic and unedifying licence in building up, under the eyes of an observant foreign intelligence, the picture of a scientist personally disintegrated to the point of being on the market. 'So there he is, Giles, in Moscow and being treated as a regular pet by all. And what we have to do—I understand it now—is just wait and see. Let's face it. It's a nerve-stretching thing.'

'You're telling me. And there's something more, Duncan. Mogridge says a build-up has to continue. There have to be mounting howls of rage and panic—as if my father had carried off there all the blasted atoms and molecules in the universe.'

'It's a cheerful prospect.' I got to my feet. 'Tell me, Giles, have you any notion of the sort of ploy your father would have thought up in the first instance—regardless of how Gavin Mogridge and his crowd may subsequently be exploiting it?'

'Yes, I have. It would be something to do with personal honour.' Giles stopped, as if surprised by the absoluteness of his own words. 'I mean, you know, not scoring a futile trick in a cold war, or anything of that sort. Something he felt as a personal and private challenge. That's it.'

'Mogridge would back that.' I said this, I believe, with a sudden conviction matching Giles's own. 'You've read *Mochica,* I seem to remember?'

'Yes.' Giles stared at me. 'Yes, I have.'

'The Mogridge of *Mochica* wasn't much more than a boy. But he took charge of men; organized them; persuaded or inspired or commanded them to endure incredible things. It was a thoroughly down-to-earth job in a way. But what enabled him to put it through was a high romantic imagination. And Mogridge would always respond to anything of that sort in another man. In short, Giles, I think he and your father might hit it off quite well.'

## XXV

THE ACTIVITIES OF William Watershute, although still
attended by mystery, had been certified to me as not disreputable. Indeed, since whatever he was up to had presumably
exposed him to considerable personal hazard, he must be
said to be displaying a hardihood which in itself was wholly
admirable. I wasn't very pleased that Mogridge had left it to
Giles to admit me to an inside view (or at least glimpse) of the
matter, but I accepted it as no doubt only an instance of the
general obliqueness favoured in the peculiar world he
operated in. What troubled me much more was a consciousness of the increasing awkwardness, as it seemed bound to be,
of my position *vis-à-vis* my colleagues. It had been bad
enough to be in possession, seemingly, of a more sinister
slant on the thing than they were aware of. It was going to be
even more tricky now that there had been an ironical reversal
of this situation. Moreover, according to Giles, we were to
suffer a factitious intensification of alarms and despondencies
over Watershute's supposed defection. For if Mogridge felt
there had to be a further build-up, a further build-up there
would assuredly be.

Thoughts of this sort possessed me on the following
morning as I drove up the motorway to Scotland. I was to
join Fish for dinner in Edinburgh that evening. By this time
I had established Fish in my head as a kind of tutelary spirit—
summoned from the vasty deep of the Indian Ocean or the
Great Australian Bight to guide my steps through the
regions of my nativity. I didn't expect anything portentous
to attend our forthcoming foray, but I had been so long
expatriate, and during recent years my visits even to Ninian

and his family had become so infrequent, that a lack of ease commonly assailed me as soon as the line of the Pentland Hills came into view.

On this occasion the Ninian Pattullos were away on holiday, and I scarcely possessed a handful of acquaintances in my native city. Outwardly little would disconcert the memory; every street and building would be familiar, yet every street and building feel dispeopled; I would be beset as I went here and there less by specific recollections of this or that than by elusive states of feeling the long-past sources of which were lost to me. It was my awareness that I was heading into this that made me glad I was to have Fish as a companion.

We devoted our first morning to the Scottish National Gallery. Such places, and for that matter scenes of outstanding natural beauty, can hold a disheartening aspect if revisited after a long period of years. One may know more about the history of art than one did as a boy, one may now be able to compare what one views with Sunium's marbled steep or the Bay of Naples. But what one remembers is a sharpness of aesthetic sensation which will not come back to one. I was aware of this in front of the Vermeer; I remembered, too, that it was in front of the Vermeer that I had first kissed Janet. Reflections of this sort made me moody; Fish, although more interested in the Raeburns and Wilkies than in me, observed the fact; he must already have detected me as feeling entitled to disturbed emotions on returning to the haunts of my childhood. He asked whether I had prowled around this building often. I made the dark reply that, apart from my father's studio, I regarded it as having been the only place of education open to me in the city. Fish was amused, and promptly announced that we were now going to pay a visit to my old school. Although I didn't judge that he was likely to gain much enlightenment from this, I fell in with the proposal, perhaps because the myth of the tutelary spirit was at work.

'I'm as much under your thumb,' I said, 'as Dante was under Virgil's in hell. It's not wholesome, Martin.'

'Of course it is—and that's fine. So come on. And our mood being one of wild extravagance, we'll take a taxi. If they've got beyond hansom cabs in this town, that is.' Fish was indicating that gentle melancholy was not to be the key-note of our pilgrimage. We took a taxi to the verge of the New Town. And there the school was.

We stared at the severe Doric building through a gate— which was as near as I had got to it for many a year. Fish remarked that it must be an older foundation than Geelong. I said that this couldn't be other than probable. Fish said that it looked the sort of place in which any sensible boy would get a good deal of education.

'The grand old fortifying classical curriculum,' I muttered, and continued to stare. Here was the birthplace, it might be said, of Ranald McKechnie's learned career. It was also the deathbed of the first fantasies of the Secret Service Boy. Ninian, very usefully, had walloped them out of me. Or scrubbed them out of me. I could feel his knuckles on my scalp now.

'I agree it doesn't look quite *like* you,' Fish said conces-sively. 'Not exactly the cradle of a deft playwright, Duncan.'

'It's much more the cradle of deft lawyers, Martin. I'm sorry you're not going to meet Ninian.'

'Is his law deft?'

'I expect so. He's the most impressive person I know. But turning a bit on the grim side. He's preparing to be something called the Lord Justice Clerk.'

'I'm sorry I'm not going to meet that.' Fish turned away. He wasn't going to insist on our entering the pebbled yards around which I'd thwacked tennis balls with a wooden implement like a large flat spoon. 'Am I going to meet anybody?'

'Yes, of course. It's clear to me we must go to Glencorry.

That's where my mother was born. It's approximately in the Highlands, and the Highlands are part of what you've come for. I've neglected my surviving relations there for longer than is decent. No Raeburns. But the place does have several Allan Ramsays.'

'What did you tell me the place is called?'

'Corry Hall.'

'Fairly remote—so that you'd propose yourself for a stay there? I don't think you can roll up, Duncan, after what appear to have been neglectful years, with a strange colonial in tow.'

'You'll get on very well with my uncle—if he happens to be sane at the moment. I thought we might go to a hotel—there's a tolerable one, I believe, about twenty miles from Corry—and I could send a letter from there and see what happens.'

'I have misgivings, Duncan.'

'Rubbish! It can't be as bad as the Inferno. And I must have my good genius at my side.'

'Very well, since you put it that way. We abandon hope, and set off tomorrow.'


I knew that it was to my cousin Ruth that I must write, since upon the death of Aunt Charlotte she had become the mistress of Corry. Conceivably because of my failure to invite her to Oxford and surround her with returned warriors, Ruth had lived on into her thirties as a spinster in her parents' house. Her elder sister Anna was established in some consequence at Garth, which was an estate of very much the same size as Glencorry. Neither property would have been impressive by merely squirarchal English standards, but in their own and indeed in a general local esteem their lairds were veritable Monarchs of the Glens. But Anna having married the heir of Garth (or, as she would have liked to say, the Master of Garth) was ahead of Ruth, who was only the unwed daughter of the Glencorry. Ruth's life had thus become, one could suppose, a matter of mounting discontents—such as I might have foreseen as lying in wait for her when I knew her fresh from school. Eventually she had adopted the desperate measure of marrying the parish minister.

There had been nothing difficult about this in any doctrinal regard. The Glencorrys were episcopalians (it had never occurred to my mother to cease being one when she married a minister's brother) but Corry Hall was a long way from any episcopal church, and for some generations they had judged it seemly to worship along with their presbyterian tenantry from time to time. So Ruth's difficulties were social rather than ecclesiastical, her marriage being much the same sort of *mésalliance* as my mother's had been. The minister, moreover, was a good deal older than Ruth, and a widower into the bargain; and it appeared that the mild indelicacy commonly imputed to a second marriage was regarded as much enhanced when the person concerned was a pillar of the Kirk. Ruth's minister had crowned all this by rather promptly dying of a dim but distressing disease, leaving her in a manse which she was required to quit as soon as might be. Aunt Charlotte's death had, in a sense, rehabilitated her, since she was back in Corry Hall and commanding it. But as she lived there alone with an intermittently demented father, aged and incompetent servants, and a slender budget, it didn't seem wise to look forward to her company as invigorating.

Many years having elapsed since Ruth had heard more news of me than would go on the back of a Christmas card, I awaited her reply to my letter with misgiving. It turned out, however, welcoming after a fashion, although it did obscurely touch in what seemed intended as a 'let all be forgiven' note. I must come over and stay at Corry at once, bringing my friend with me. Her father had vague recollections of there being Glencorrys of a cadet order in Western Australia, and

284

might be interested in meeting somebody from that part of the world. At the moment, he was in quite good health. The tailor had gone on holiday, but the hatcheries were a resource. Anna was now settled in the dower house at Garth, and I must go over and see her there. It was a dwelling of mean appearance (Ruth added with distinguishable satisfaction) and excessively inconvenient. At Garth itself Robin Petrie was behaving as might be expected.

Robin Petrie I supposed to be the elder of Fiona's brothers, with whom she had gone on record as having a row. Who the tailor was, and what the hatcheries were, remained obscure. Nor did I feel any great stir of curiosity about them or anything else at Corry Hall—the Glencorry connection being something that had long ago ceased to hold much interest for me.

But here I was deluding myself. As Fish and I took a final turn through the heathery windings of Glencorry itself, and the whitewashed pepperpots and crenellations of David Bryce's mansion came into view, I felt an unexpected excitement. Ninian and I as we grew towards manhood had affected to regard both the house and its inhabitants as absurd. But in our earlier boyhood we had been a good deal in awe of the Glencorrys and their home, and secretly proud of the feudal aspect of our ancestry that they represented. And this hadn't entirely rubbed away. It hadn't even rubbed away from Ninian, so soon to be Lord Justice Clerk.

Ruth received us in the hall: a gloomy chamber so festooned with stags' heads (now sadly moth-eaten) and other trophies of the chase as to suggest an Aeaea in which a somewhat uninventive Circe had laboured for a long time. Ruth, however, was scarcely Circean. She had been a heavy girl (in this resembling Anna, whose heaviness when on top of me in the heather could come upon me as a physical sensation still), and as a middle-aged woman she was approaching the lumbering. But what I was chiefly aware of as I introduced

Fish was the sharpness of the covert curiosity she directed on me. And this, if it wasn't exactly resentful, was obscurely jealous. Was it possible, I wondered, that the ghost of an Edinburgh schoolboy lingered around Corry, and that Ruth was capable of recalling that, in episodes entirely juvenile and substantially innocuous, her elder sister had got ahead of her? I wasn't confident that something uncomfortable in her attitude to me was to be accounted for in quite this flattering way.

Uncle Rory appeared, stringy within his knickerbockers as I remembered him. He welcomed Fish politely but vaguely— so vaguely that I saw that here was a bewildered old man who would have been pathetic had there not been detectable in his eye still a hint of the sacred strangeness I remembered in him. He wasn't 'confused' in the sense in which gerontology uses the term; he was bewildered because he hadn't yet lost the saving knowledge that the world is bewildering.

'Ah, Duncan,' he said, 'this is very timely. You will help me—and Mr Fish will too. Tinker is away, you know, so there is leisure to consider a little. To draw back and consider.'

'Tinker is the tailor,' Ruth said, as if this explained all.

'Calls himself a court tailor,' Uncle Rory went on. 'Means he can put you into knee-breeches and so forth. But Tinker is a military tailor too. And that's the point, of course.'

'Of course, Uncle Rory.' Light on this particular mystery had come to me instantly.

'I wish, Duncan, we had your father here. I'm afraid he didn't come to Corry very frequently. We may have been neglectful, I'm afraid. But he would be the man now. Which colour goes with which, you know. Just his line. We'll go and look in a minute, and you'll take your choice. But, Mr Fish, a little whisky first. Ruth, the Glenlivet. It's our habit here, my dear sir, when a guest arrives. A mere dram.'

We had a mere dram (except that Ruth, when judging her-

self unobserved, had two). Uncle Rory, although punctilious
over this observance, was impatient to carry us off to quarters
peculiarly his own; he was like a small boy who, having
a new toy to exhibit to friends in his nursery, is all eagerness
to carry them away from the more formal apartments in which
grown-ups are receiving them. Ruth, who had her own ritual
requirements, insisted that we must first be shown our bed-
rooms: surprisingly distant chambers to which our suitcases
had already been transported with a considerable appearance
of effort by two octogenarian female retainers. But when we
were reunited again downstairs, Uncle Rory immediately
carried off Fish and myself to what I recognized as the old
stable block in which Mountjoy had formerly had his
quarters. Here there was a long narrow room down either
side of which was ranged what I took at first to be an exhibition of waxworks. I then saw that they were tailor's dummies
of the shop-window sort, and all male. A few of them were
unclothed, a circumstance which I registered to myself as a
novelty. For it is surely a fact of experience that, whereas
female figures of the sort are occasionally exposed to the
public gaze in a nude condition, carelessness or whimsy
never seems to achieve a similar effect with male ones: and
in this there appears to be an inversion of the degrees of
impropriety which convention severally assigns to the exhibition of masculine and feminine nudity respectively. By the
time I had concluded this reflection I had realized that we
were in the presence of a new phase in the creation of my
uncle's standing army. For all the clothed figures were in
garments of unmistakably martial if often bizarre suggestion.
The phase of mere sketches and designs of galligaskins and
the like was long since over. Uncle Rory's dream of successful
rivalry with his neighbour the Duke of Atholl was a big step
nearer fulfilment. And Tinker was the instrument—it must
have been the expensive instrument—of this achievement. I
was to learn from Ruth later that she (and Ninian, who now

largely controlled the march of events at Corry) possessed medical authority for the view that this strange fantasy was to be indulged as of therapeutic value in my uncle's case.

I had happened never to mention to Fish Uncle Rory's persuasion that a lineal descendant of King Orry (or King Gorse) was entitled to a military establishment; and Fish, although a man quick in the uptake, required some minutes before orientating himself to the situation. Initially, he supposed that we had been conducted into no more than the sort of dusty collection sometimes to be found in provincial museums. When the true explanation came to him he at once engaged my uncle in a rational discussion of the comparative merits (regarded alike from an aesthetic and an active service point of view) of these brain-children of the Glencorry's and Mr Tinker's invention. And it seemed to me that Uncle Rory, although full of pride in what he had to display, was not without an underlying sense of embarrassment on the occasion. This particular foible belonged after all to one of his less commonplace phases, and at times like the present when he was being rather sane he seemed to be puzzled by the whole thing. So our lunch-hour, when it arrived, was a relief, and during the meal Fish succeeded in turning the conversation in the direction of cattle, sheep, and freshwater trout. Uncle Rory possessed, as I had discovered long ago, curiously little exact knowledge—so desirable in a landed proprietor—of these lores; and I was constrained to wonder who had taken over from the sexually aberrant and exiled Alec Mountjoy their superintendence at Glencorry. Ninian, no doubt, had arranged things as they ought to be.

Ninian had certainly created the hatcheries, the mystery of which was explained by the time we had arrived at the rice pudding and prunes. Sizable ponds had been created in the glen, fed by the Corry burn, and the trout were one day to effect a marked improvement in the economic viability of a sadly run-down estate. But here too a therapeutic intention became evident. Uncle Rory had got hold of the cardinal point that if fish are to be farmed successfully they must not while reaching their maturity consume protein to as great a value as they will themselves eventually yield. Uncle Rory now spent much time netting and weighing trout, and parcelling rations of whatever they were fed on. It was arranged that he would provide his Australian guest with insight into this scientific pursuit on the following day.

Fish, I believed, had agreed thus to go off with Uncle Rory on the supposition that I'd myself want either a morning's confidential chat with Ruth or an opportunity to visit other of my kinsfolk in the neighbourhood. In fact, of course, Fiona's mother was the only such person there was. I had mixed (or even mixed-up) feelings about Anna, that heroine of the heather, but I couldn't possibly do other than contact her. So after breakfast I rang up the dower house at Garth and asked for Mrs Petrie. A maidservant, whom I conjectured to be of the resigned all-purposes sort maintained by gentlewomen in reduced circumstances, replied with some satisfaction that Mrs Petrie was out.

'Do you know when she'll be back?'

'I dinna' ken. She's for doing the messages.'

'This is Mr Duncan Pattullo speaking. Will you please tell her I'm walking over to Garth, and hope she'll be able to have me to lunch?' I felt that this was an admissible informality in a cousin. 'I'll arrive before one o'clock.'

'Verra weel, Mr Pattullo. But there won't be ower mickle on the board.' This was again announced with satisfaction. 'Would you be one of them at Corry?'

'Yes. I'm Mr Glencorry's nephew.'

'Weel, there might be a hen on the ashet. But it's no a promise, mind.'

'That would be a fair treat,' I said. With this concession to the vernacular I rang off.

It had been a raw morning, with what my late interlocutor would call a haar over the moors. But this misty drizzle was starting to clear as I set out, and intermittent shafts of sunshine were playing on the graceful summit of Schiehallion to the south. My memories of the terrain were far from fresh, but I didn't think it likely I'd get lost, and by the time I'd walked for an hour the mist had concentrated itself into small cloud-like puffs and curtains that came and went around me to odd effects of swiftly enlarging and contracting visibility. I might have been advancing—it came to me in a figure no doubt prompted by my uncle's martial interests—through an ill-directed smoke-screen provided by artillery hidden among the braes. It was under these conditions that I became aware of another wayfarer: a man clad in an antique coat and cape who was walking towards me on the barely distinguishable moorland path I trod. The man halted as I looked, and appeared to raise his arms in front of him. It seemed to me that I was being studied through binoculars. Then a dollop of mist rolled between us like a gigantic snowball, so that I walked on slowly and blindly for perhaps a couple of hundred yards. The dollop drifted upward and vanished; the wayfarer had come to a halt in front of me; he was an old man, spare and upright, with binoculars slung across his chest. It was twenty-six years since I had last seen Colonel Morrison in the garden of the Villa Cimbrone. But I had no doubt of him, nor he of me.

'Duncan!' Colonel Morrison said. 'What a splendid surprise.'

# XXVI

I HAD EVEN more cause for surprise than Colonel Morrison had. I was simply on holiday where I had often been on holiday before. But nothing had seemed clearer to Colonel Morrison on the occasion of that brief encounter on the dizzy height above Amalfi than that he had left Scotland for ever. His unfortunate association with my uncle's factor—or rather its having become known to the small society of these glens—had made that inevitable. But here he was, taking his accustomed all-weathers walk from the home of his ancestors, as if disaster had rolled away as the mists were finally rolling away from the Corry moors now. Here he was with all his old cordial regard for me: as cordial as my regard for him. And there was an immediate warmth of feeling between us which, at the moment, seemed even to be affecting the climate of Scotland. Spring sunshine was pouring down on us; the heather was almost dry; there were convenient boulders which, if not quite dry themselves, weren't going to soak the bottom as Giles Watershute's bottom and my own had been soaked on the bench outside St Michael-at-the-North-Gate. So we sat down companionably together and took our bearings.

'I'm so glad that you're back home,' I said. I had decided that it would be absurd to ignore the circumstances of the case as a mere acquaintance might have felt obliged to do. I remembered enough of that last encounter to know that I'd said or done nothing then to be ashamed of, and it would be sadly retrograde to turn evasive now. 'Perhaps you've been home for some time? I've been very neglectful of most of my old associations in these parts, I'm afraid.'

'My dear boy, you've had your career to make—and very distinguished it's proving to be. But you will do well to return regularly to Scotland from now on. Never starve your roots, Duncan. I remember once reproaching Willie Maugham for living so much abroad. He was a dear man—although something of a cynic in his writings at times, I'm afraid—and he took it very well.' Colonel Morrison paused briefly on this recrudescence of an ancient foible. 'But, yes— I have been home again for some years now. Things get forgotten about—or almost forgotten. And attitudes change. There's a great deal of tolerance now. And one ought not to disparage tolerance. It's a very minor virtue, indeed, if it's a virtue at all. But it's a kind of second cousin to charity. Of course I don't go much into company. Society up here is as you remember it to be. It's not as in the circles I used a little to know. I used to talk about these sexual things to Wells. He was perfectly understanding, although he came of a class of society in which a great deal of prejudice exists about deviant behaviour. It was a credit to him, of course. Getting as far as he did, I mean, with the novels and scientific thinking and so on. I don't suppose anybody reads Wells now. Or Bennett, for that matter. I never greatly took to Bennett somehow. But they used to say he had sterling qualities.'

'I don't think that either of them—Wells or Bennett—has altogether passed out of currency.' Colonel Morrison and I had used to hold conversations like this about eminent writers, but I didn't feel we ought just to stray off among them now. 'But what about Alec?' I asked. 'What's happened to him?' I had almost said 'Mountjoy' instead of 'Alec' and felt, I'd had a narrow escape from insensitive behaviour.

'We parted, Duncan. What had been between us was very real, you know, but I suppose that a parting was inevitable all the same. It was Alex's youth that I loved in him, I think— so how could I complain that it was youth he loved too? Yes, it was much younger people that attracted him. You attracted him yourself at one time, Duncan, although he can't have given you occasion to suspect the fact. That was so, wasn't it?' Colonel Morrison was suddenly anxious. 'He'd never, for instance, said anything to you about your hair?'

'Definitely not. And if he glanced at it—well, I expect I merely thought he felt I needed a hair-cut.'

'Yes, of course.' Colonel Morrison was reassured. 'We travelled about the continent a good deal when we were together, and Alec became rather indiscriminating in his choice of young companions. We had a bad time in Naples. I won't go into that. But in the end we had to go our several ways. And I seemed to have nothing left in the world, Duncan, nothing at all. So all I could do, I felt, was to come home and face up to things.'

'It was the right decision, I'm sure. What has happened to Alec since then?'

'He had employment in the merchant navy for a while. But he had to leave it quite suddenly. He was always sea-sick, it seems, and they grew tired of it and turned him out.'

'I see.'

'So he has no very regular employment now. Of course there is no money problem. I see to that, Duncan, but it doesn't relieve the terrible sense of responsibility I feel. A sense of guilt, really. It was through me that Alec came to lose an honourable career.'

This produced silence, since I could find nothing to say. Colonel Morrison had been the older man, and one with wealth and position. But Mountjoy had been no raw lad; he must have been in his thirties, indeed, by the time that his irregular connection with his employer's elderly neighbour began. And I wondered about Mountjoy's feelings and motives throughout. At Ravello he had been totally inscrutable to me. Anderman, Tindale, Frediano: these I felt I understood pretty well. But Mountjoy was a mystery—although not perhaps a very interesting one.

These were unprofitable reflections, and my business now was to find something else to talk about.

'I'm walking over to Garth,' I said, 'to lunch with my cousin Anna in the dower house. Just as with you, I haven't seen her for ages.'

'It's understandable, perhaps.' Colonel Morrison spoke with a sudden diffidence I didn't in the least comprehend the occasion of. 'Of course, Duncan, it must be easier there—in the dower house, I mean—than it would have been in Garth itself.'

'Well, yes—I suppose so. I never knew the Petries at all well. In fact, I never knew any of them at all.'

'You're staying at Corry Hall now?'

'Yes, but only for a night or two. And with an Australian friend.'

'How do you get on with Ruth Glencorry, Duncan?'

'Oh, fairly well, I think.' I was surprised by this question. 'I sometimes imagine I alarm her, as if I were a kind of Legend of the Glen. The Curse of the Glencorrys, or something like that.' I don't know what prompted me to this nonsense; perhaps I merely felt that the greater part of my conversation with Colonel Morrison had been painful, and that I should aim at a whimsical note. 'However,' I went on, 'my uncle takes me quite in his stride. Perhaps the dark Legend has gone out of his head.'

'Well, yes—I'm afraid a good deal has. Yes, that will be it. His faculties come and go, Duncan. A sad thing.' Colonel Morrison rose from his boulder as he said this, perhaps feeling that he was detaining me from my cousin's table too long. 'Come back, Duncan. Come back to Glencorry soon.'

'I'll come straight over to see you when I do.' I stood up too. 'We could have a lot to talk about.'

'Yes, indeed.' For a moment, Colonel Morrison hesitated. 'How is your daughter, Duncan?'

'I beg your pardon?' I thought I had misheard.

'I've never met her, you know. But I'm told she is having a brilliant career at Oxford. How is Fiona?'

'Did you call Fiona my daughter?'

'Duncan, I'm deeply sorry.' It was very clear that Colonel Morrison was also deeply hurt. 'I ought not to have mentioned her. I ought not to have been the first of us to mention her. But I am an old man, my dear boy, and almost as old a family friend. Of course I know the story. The history, I ought to say. But I'll never mention it again.'

For a moment I told myself that Colonel Morrison was merely crazy. But instantly I knew better. Small scraps of fact were tumbling about inside my head with the effect of physical objects. Or like fragments of glass in a kaleidoscope they were perhaps coming together to form a pattern. If so, it looked like being a pattern of a lurid sort.

'Do I understand,' I asked, 'that you believe—and that it is widely believed—that Fiona Petrie is my daughter?'

'Not widely, Duncan; not widely at all.' Colonel Morrison made this reply in a voice so agitated that it ought to have warned me to be calm myself. 'Only your family——'

'It's untrue—do you hear me? Absolutely and utterly untrue! There was a grotesque circumstance long ago that might get distorted into such rubbish. But it's a monstrous fabrication. Do you see?' I suppose I was furious. I suppose I was even in a panic.

'Yes, yes—I do see, Duncan.' Colonel Morrison was looking at me sadly, as one looks at a man one knows to be demeaning himself with bluster and lies. 'As I said, I ought not to have spoken of it. And we shall meet on a happier occasion, I hope.' I now saw that Colonel Morrison was trembling all over. I had almost made a scene, and a scene was something he no longer possessed the nervous vitality to stand up to. I also saw that something he had long believed was something it wouldn't be easy to drive from his mind, and that it was quite a different effort that was now required of me. For his condition had become pitiable; he was confused, meaninglessly apologetic, even afraid. For a moment I was afraid myself—I suppose with that terror of death which a sudden revelation of extreme debility in another can bring. Timbermill had made me the same parting gift; Lempriere would perhaps yet do so. I stepped forward and took Colonel Morrison's slight figure in my arms.

'I'm sorry I shouted,' I said. 'It's all nonsense. We'll forget it. May I walk home with you?'

The words held little meaning, but my action was of some effect. Colonel Morrison smiled at me and straightened himself, so that I wondered whether one of the strange mechanisms of age hadn't for the time wiped the whole perturbing incident from his mind.

'Duncan,' he said—and almost with the gaiety I remembered in him—'how kind you are! We must have another meeting soon. Meanwhile, good-bye, good-bye!' As he said this, he in his turn clasped both my arms—and with surprising strength. Then he turned and walked away. He walked away so steadily that I judged it best not to attempt to accompany him. I sat down on my boulder again—almost as prostrated as this very old man had been.

Of course—I thought, when I began to think coherently—there was little that was mysterious about the origin of the outrageous misconception I had just been made acquainted with. What was astounding was that such a piece of nonsense should perpetuate itself and proliferate over nearly half a lifetime. The rash offer of my hand (if it might be so described) to the mysteriously pregnant Anna had been made to my Uncle Rory when I was eighteen, and no mischief had seemed to ensue. But something—was it my uncle's insanities, an aberration of the jealous Ruth's, the general mythopoeic genius of the Highlands?—had turned everything upside down. Anna Glencorry, it had come to be believed, had been got with child by her schoolboy cousin from Edinburgh, and nothing had seemed in prospect except an absurd and humiliating shot-gun marriage until young Petrie of Garth had chivalrously stepped forward as a highly eligible suitor and married Anna himself.

How far had this disastrous fiction carried? Not, surely, to Anna herself, or she would not have permitted it to survive. But naturally Anna wouldn't have heard it; nobody was likely to have brought her a piece of impertinent comment about the supposed illegitimacy of her eldest child.

And another person who was unlikely to have been treated to anything of the sort was Ninian. One glance at my brother would tell anybody that he was unlikely to be entertained by slander. It seemed certain to me that Ruth knew and believed the story—believed it even if she had invented it in the first place; this explained the effect of my being the Legend of the Glen. And Fiona's brothers must be possessed of it: they had turned nasty about property or whatever not because they knew her to have been conceived out of wedlock but because they believed her father was not theirs. Robin Petrie and his brother couldn't be very agreeable young men.

It was surely strange that all these thoughts passed through my head before Fiona entered it. But when this did happen the effect was like the exploding of a bomb, since I was confronted by the likelihood that Fiona herself had been told the story and believed it. For a moment this had the status merely of a wild thought in my head, and then I saw that it could be true. All too much became explicable in the light of it. I'd already entertained, and even discussed with Fish, as it were the outworks of the idea: that Fiona knew the embarrassing story of my inept offer to marry Anna—and knew, too, of those earlier indecorous capers on unchaperoned picnics. And now, following upon Andrew Petrie's death and her recent visit to Garth, she had been told and had accepted the fable that we were father and daughter. Hence her flight to Denmark.

Confronted by this revolting nonsense out of the blue, I suddenly felt very sick. But at least I was on the spot where I could make a start on demolishing the myth. Anna Petrie was only a couple of miles away, and I must begin with her. I got to my feet and walked rapidly on across the moor.

The dower house may have been of mean appearance, but I didn't notice it. I rang a bell, and expected to be admitted by the retainer with whom I'd talked on the telephone. The door was opened, however, by Margaret Mountain.

'Talk of the devil!' Miss Mountain said. 'Come in.'

'Margaret, how nice to see you.' I produced this formula automatically, although I suppose 'confounding' would have been more accurate than 'nice'. 'Is Fiona here?'

'Of course she is. It's not likely that I'd have wandered into these parts on my own. She said she needed support. Quite untrue. Fiona's as hard as nails. Did you know that?'

'Do you mean that——'

'Come inside, for heaven's sake.'

'No—wait a moment, Margaret. Have I arrived in the middle of some sort of show-down?'

'At the tail-end of it. Fiona felt she couldn't take it any more. So we came to Garth so that she could have it out with her mother.'

'*It?* Listen, Margaret. Is *it* a notion about whose child she is?'

'Of course. About her being your daughter.'

'And what has Fiona's mother said about that?'

'That it's nonsense. What else would she say?'

'You mean you don't believe her?'

'Of course I believe her.' Miss Mountain (who, as the author of *The Orrery,* could be expected to take such incidents as the present in her stride) looked at me coolly. 'But my state of mind is neither here nor there. The relevant point is that Fiona herself has been believing the story for some time. You don't have much luck, Duncan, do you?'

'Never mind my luck. What do you mean by "some time"?'

'You'd better have that out with her yourself.' Margaret had hesitated for a moment on this reply. 'Have I to keep on telling you to come inside? There's to be a boiled fowl. Almost as elderly as its cook, I imagine.'

'Margaret, do you mind if I don't? I'd like, I mean, to talk to Fiona alone, and straight away. I expect I can face her mother later. But now I'll walk up the glen a little way, and wait for her. Send her after me. I believe she'll think it a good idea, on the whole.'

'Quite probably. Very well.' Margaret Mountain, who continued composed in the face of our strange conversation, shut the door on me.

I walked away from the dower house, and hoped it wasn't in the direction of Garth itself. The neighbourhood was unfamiliar to me, and in this at least matched my situation. Then Fiona appeared from the house, walking rapidly to overtake me. She seemed to have no disposition to waste time. She looked very young.

'Fiona,' I said without preliminaries, 'did they put this thing in your head when you came up to Garth before going to Copenhagen?'

'No—although my brothers started making a bit of capital about it then. About being willing to keep quiet under certain conditions, so as not to distress our mother.'

'Conditions about family property, and so on?'

'Yes.'

'How bloody awful. Then for how long, in fact, have you known the story?'

'And believed it? Oh, for ages. I ought to have tackled my mother about it, only it didn't seem decent.'

'You've tackled her now? That's why you're here?'

299

'Yes.'

'And you've believed her?'

'Good God, yes! I'd know when she was lying. I've had practice at it. She's not honest, you know, any more than she's clever.' Fiona paused and eyed me, amused at my disturbed look on receiving this dispassionate appraisal. 'It ought to be an enormous relief, wouldn't you say? Actually, I feel a bit flat.'

'Can we be rather more precise?' In my turn, I tried for a dispassionate note. I ought to have been relieved myself—triumphant, even, at the glimpse of a green light before Fiona and myself. But it wasn't so. I hadn't liked the suggestion that the innocence of our situation when revealed to Fiona had left her feeling 'flat'. Indeed, an odd unfocused horror was threatening to invade my mind. 'Precise about dates, I mean,' I said.

'I know you do. Well, then, Duncan, I knew what I probably had to believe about you on the afternoon you introduced yourself to me in the Woodstock Road. It was quite a moment. I'd sometimes had dreams about its happening one day.'

'Fiona!'

'Yes, yes.' Fiona was impatient, brisk. 'It came from my Aunt Ruth first—and long before you and I met—in a kind of whispering way. I didn't believe her at the time, because everybody knows she gets odd ideas in her head. But I came round to it—rather irrationally, I can now see. You know how I never felt right with the Petries. They didn't seem to be my sort of people. I even actively disliked Andrew Petrie for being so pig-headedly determined that I'd grow up his sort of kid. So I thought I'd found the explanation. And when I poked around cautiously, other people seemed to confirm it.'

'Fiona, believing such a thing, was it wise to let me fall in love with you?'

300

'You did nothing of the kind!' I couldn't tell whether Fiona was amused or angry, but I was acutely aware that Miss Mountain hadn't been wrong in describing her as being as hard as nails. 'You began flirting with me, which is quite a different thing. It didn't seem more at first—that sort of talking and behaving—than a tacit agreement to get some fun out of ignoring our relationship: a kind of sophisticated make-believe. Then it developed and became perversely exciting, I suppose—although I must have produced a decent uneasiness often enough. In a way I think I was trusting you, Duncan, not to break through the rules of an outrageous private game. And the kinky *is* fascinating, don't you feel? One mustn't underestimate its pull. And the prosaic truth— not that it's quite prosaic—seems quite dull after it. Anyway, it all packed up. It all packed up as soon as it looked like turning physical, didn't it?' Fiona smiled rather wanly. 'I suppose I'm not an Orrery type.'

'Of course you're not.'

'And then suddenly there was a grain, several grains, of doubt. I suddenly saw something quite hideous: that you were perhaps that first cousin once removed, and nothing more, after all, and that I'd been making a fool of myself not in the least in the way I'd thought I was. That's why I came up to Garth. Anyway, it's all over now.'

'Of course it is! And you do now realize, Fiona, that I hadn't a notion that this monstrous fabrication was in your head? And you see where we now stand? We're in the clear. We can——'

'Duncan, stop. I *mean* that it's all over. And you just don't understand how I feel about myself. What I look back on is a mix-up of silly naughtiness and silly sentimental make-believe. So here's a simple and brutal question: do you think I could marry a man who's old enough to be my father, and is believed to be my father, and once went cock-teasing with my mother in the heather, and who proposed absurdly to throw his school satchel over the burn and marry *her*?' Fiona pulled up on this staggering speech, and then went on quite quietly. 'And, Duncan, have this humiliating history between us for keeps? Have some sense, and go away.'

'Fiona, surely——' I broke off, persuaded, against my better sense, of being unjustly treated; even remembering how Fiona had once taken the initiative in discussing our possible marriage in a freakish way at some sherry party. 'Surely, Fiona——'

'Just stop, please. I declare a prior attachment, if you like.' Fiona's tone had switched swiftly to a familiar one of simple fun. 'To a gorgeous Dane. A Great Dane! He's six-foot-six, and twenty-five. He's all white teeth and flaxen hair and bulging muscle.'

'I don't believe in him.'

'Neither do I. But please, please, go away and don't come back.'

Fish and I drove south again rather sooner than we'd proposed. But we were beyond Carlisle before I told him about this strange interview. Fish listened without interrupting, and remained silent when I had concluded. It wasn't a disapproving silence, but it scarcely suggested commiseration either. His only comment, which came when we had stopped at a wayside pub for beer and a sandwich, drew, not inappositely, upon the past.

'Awful experiences of women, Duncan,' Fish murmured. And he raised his tankard to mine.

# XXVII

I SAID GOOD-BYE to Fish at Heathrow with a promise to come out on a visit to Wangarra. My state of mind was such that the other side of the globe held a considerable attraction for me. But for the present I returned to Oxford, where the final week of the Easter vacation was slipping past. I was dismayed to find that there was still no word from Janet. I'd expected at least a letter from her in reply to the cable I'd sent to Chicago: a cable explaining that a letter from her must have gone astray in Italy. There didn't seem any further possibility of errant correspondence; I'd made no arrangement to have anything forwarded to Scotland, and all my mail had be stacked neatly on my writing-table by Plot.

I was so upset by this that I fell to wondering whether I could have offended Janet in some way, and my perturbation was increased when I detected this feeble thought in my mind. In the light of the desperate character of Ranald McKechnie's illness it seemed much more likely that something had gone badly wrong.

The thought of illness put Lempriere into my head, and I decided to go over and call on him at once. He would take pleasure in hearing that I had been colleaguing with Glencorrys, and I needn't be too specific about the calamitous issue of my Scottish journey.

The Great Quadrangle already held a scattering of under-graduates, many of them trundling to their rooms trunks of unnecessary size. (When engaged in coming up or going down undergraduates are mysteriously incapable of travelling light.) These were supposed to be exceptionally industrious youths, annoying their scouts and the kitchens by a premature arrival in the interest of intent study. In fact, it was more likely to be rowing or cricket or Junkin-like theatrical activity that was in question. I noticed this; I noticed that great stone bastions were beginning to peer above ground level in the excavations; and then, on Lempriere's staircase, I ran into Anthea Gender.

'Good morning,' Mrs Gender said. 'We haven't seen you for some time.'

'I've been visiting relations in Scotland.'

'I understood you paid no attention to them. Well, what you've been missing, Duncan, is a terrible confuffle, with everybody at jar and by the ears.'

'The great Watershute scandal?'

'Yes, of course. Mabel Bedworth says your colleagues are behaving like a pack of frightened old women. All except Cyril—and Jimmy, of course, when it's me she's talking to.'

'Of course.'

'Mabel says the Governing Body ought to have half-a-dozen women on it. They'd stiffen its morale.'

'These seem to be massively contradictory statements. But excessive feminism conduces to confusion of mind. How is Arnold? I'm going up to see him.'

'Arnold has departed.'

'You don't mean——'

'No, no. Arnold has simply departed to Northumberland. He insisted on it. There was a great to-do, with Dr Damian gloomy and misdoubting, and an ambulance carriage hitched on to a train, and heaven knows what. But Arnold got home in one piece, it seems, and will die in tranquillity. He did put off the journey until rather late, because he was determined to wait until he saw the tower starting to rise up again. He has that man Gall with him, and I suppose Gall will look after him. Only Gall doesn't approve of Northumberland. He has been known to say that he regards it as provincial. There will at least be nothing provincial about Arnold's next destination. I've been up in his rooms, incidentally, doing a little tidying up. A kinswoman's part. I felt he'd approve of that. There was a pile of Christmas cards awaiting attention. Arnold doesn't approve of Christmas cards, but it seems he writes a letter to everybody who sends him one. Among others, it involves half the Cabinet, no end of schoolmasters, and a large chunk of the higher nobility.'

'He has had a good many pupils in his time.'

'Yes. But if Arnold has departed, the McKechnies have arrived.'

'They're back in Oxford?' I was staggered by this news.

'Only a couple of days ago, it seems. I came across Janet in the covered market yesterday afternoon. She asked about you, Duncan.' Mrs Gender looked at me quizzically. She was one of the stoutest adherents of the faded romance theory.

'And Ranald is restored?'

'Very decidedly, I'm inclined to imagine.' Mrs Gender continued to look at me speculatively. 'Janet said she was worried about letters and a cable chasing around in vain. Something to do with Italy, and with their moving on to California. Ranald recuperated there. He wanted to do some work at Stanford or Berkeley or some such place.'

'I see. Then his mind is quite all right? Even what might be called his intellectual faculties?'

'Oh, all that! Yes, without a doubt.' Mrs Gender paused. 'Janet had some news she was sorry you hadn't received, I gather. She didn't seem to feel any need to give it to me.'

'I think I'll run out to the vicarage now.'

'Good. A wonderful thing, the vacation. Dons with nothing to do except wander loose all over the place. When they're not in a panic about the KGB.'

With this rather tart remark, Anthea Gender left me.

The vicarage was bathed in spring sunshine. I parked my car, and walked round to the front of the house. Janet was sitting under a verandah. She was sewing, and had a work-table in front of her. I looked at it, and it was as if I were back in the Junkins' sitting-room. There could be no doubt about the news Janet had to tell me. For she was making baby clothes.

'Don't goggle, Dunkie.' Janet stood up, came round the table, and then—a rare event—kissed me. She drew back, laughing but detectably shy. 'And it's quite all right, so don't start being alarmed. Ranald being alarmed is enough.'

'I'm not being alarmed. I'm delighted—and rather overwhelmed. It's a tremendous event.'

'Is it?' Janet was amused. 'The American doctors were worried, just for a time. They felt I was a little out of practice, I suppose. There was even one old dear who felt it might be prudent to terminate the pregnancy. But that blew away, and they became confident I can go to full term. I'd like Ranald to have rather a bouncing babe.'

'Where is he? I want to congratulate him.'

'Oh, he's in Bodley, working like mad on some new inscriptions. They're always digging up new inscriptions, and Ranald's determined not to fall behind on them. He's marvellously vigorous. They really did their job in Chicago.' Janet paused. 'All round,' she added tranquilly. 'Come in and have a drink.'

We went into the house, and its large emptiness already seemed subtly altered.

'Ranald's going to have a problem with his books,' I said. 'That nursery wing will no longer be available.'

'Notionally not.' Janet laughed happily. 'But a single child of middle-age doesn't take up all that room. So we'll make do.'

'Cots and play-pens,' I said. 'Tricycles, bicycles, schools, O-Levels, A-Levels, Oxford, a profession. It's such a long road! I find it hard to imagine.'

'I wish you had to, Dunkie.' Janet looked at me seriously.

'Have you and Fiona got any further?'

'Yes—right to the end of the road.'

'Meaning?'

'That we were messing around for kicks in an equivocal family situation. Or that is what it would always feel like now.' I found I had to stop at this. '*Schluss!* Just like that. You never liked her, did you? You took a hard look, and disapproved of her.'

'I suppose I disapproved of *it*. It didn't feel right.'

'Nor was it. You said, I remember, that I'd do better with Margaret Mountain.'

'One always regrets saying things like that. It was quite stupid. I'm sorry.'

'Janet, we mustn't have talk like this at what's a celebration. For it is, isn't it? I mean, you really are content to live it all again?'

'You're a funny old bachelor, Dunkie. Daunted by nappies.'

'Ranald won't be.' This suddenly came to me with complete clarity. 'He'll be a devoted father.'

'Even in rather too concentrated a way, perhaps.' Janet said this gravely, and I saw that she had been thinking things out. 'I may decide'—she was suddenly gay again—'to adopt four or five baby refugees from Indo-China or somewhere. Just to keep Duncan company.'

'Duncan?'

'But of course. Ranald and I are both certain it's going to be a boy.'

## XXVIII

THE ROW OVER William Watershute had been running on predictable lines, and it continued to do so as the summer term gained momentum. A number of observations to which I had been treated about it turned out to be true. There was certainly a confuffle, as Anthea Gender had said. Buntingford had been right in predicting a swing in our wandering physicist's favour as a result of the witch-hunt in the popular press. It wasn't, indeed, a solid swing, which I remembered as Buntingford's term. What had emerged was a small but not uninfluential group of fellows determined that the college was not going to be stampeded by noisy journalists and members of parliament. David Graile had come down on this side of the debate, and was no longer predicting that Watershute would go. This was an accession to the side of caution (or obstinacy, as the other faction regarded it) which carried some weight. Lempriere, to whom somebody had officiously written in Northumberland with an account of the development of the affair, sent a telegram to the Provost to the same effect. It was read out to the Governing Body and created a deep impression—almost, indeed, a sensation: it was as if we had been called upon to listen to the dying voice of a John of Gaunt.

The Provost, being (as Plot in his aquatic character might have put it) something between a canvas and half-a-length ahead of the rest of us in point of diplomatic skill, was far from greeting the formation of this faction with cries of joy. He had to keep his options open, and busied himself with being as temperate and open-minded as a judge on (as Buntingford put it, following Milton) the Royal Bench of

British *Themis.* His informal committee had become a formal one—and had in consequence shrunk in size, so that I had been happily released from it as a person of only minor sagacity after all. Its deliberations were nothing if not deliberate.

Another man who had spoken a true word was Fish when he had remarked to me (hyperbolically, indeed) that the Watershute defection would prove something less than a nine days' wonder. It hadn't quite done that, but it had rather notably attenuated itself, so far as public interest went, while our term was still young. It was, I suppose, only because —once more—I knew some things that others didn't that I sensed behind this an element of arcane manipulation. It was as if Authority—Authority remote from the obscure deliberations of an Oxford college—had decided that Watershute was a lost cause and not all that important either. By this time I had come to think of Mogridge as a master mind, and probably accountable only to the Prime Minister himself. Mogridge was shoving his pieces around on a chess board invisible to the rest of us. But I had no opportunity to tackle Mogridge on this. He was as invisible as the chess board itself. His studies in the interesting Institute in the Banbury Road had to be thought of as having come to an end. I judged it only too likely that Watershute had come to an end as well. Whatever he had been up to had obviously been as hazardous as could be conceived. Had it been possible to bet on the matter in the common room wager book, I'd have been reluctant to risk a five-pound note or a bottle of claret on the likelihood of his ever turning up on us again. I was more upset by this than by the spectacle of Cyril Bedworth's nightmare coming true and the college being 'split' in an unprecedented way.

From the legitimate point of view of immediate college interest one fact became incontrovertible before the first week of term was behind us. We were again without our tutor in physics. It was no longer a relevant argument that what a man did with himself during a vacation was his own affair, even if it extended to visiting a far from friendly country and making speeches objectionable to the majority of his fellow-citizens. Formally considered, a foreign power *isn't* unfriendly if one isn't at war with it, and in the present case the foreign power was one with which full diplomatic relations obtained. But this high ground was cut from beneath the feet of Watershute's supporters as not so much fallacious as beside the point. What must concern us was the simple fact that the man wasn't in residence and doing his job. We had to deal with this before peering into the vast hinterland constituted by the fact that there are certain men who carry round 'classified information' in their heads. The defence of the realm wasn't directly our affair. But that young Lenton (the youth with ambitions in the science-fiction line) had to be called upon to interrupt his postgraduate studies in order to teach Watershute's pupils was. The college must at least get round to sorting out that. It wasn't difficult. As Buntingford had pointed out, fellows are fellows and tutors are tutors, and which fellows are to be or remain tutors is the Provost's business alone.

Here, then, was Edward Pococke's final temporizing resource, and he adopted it, with quite splendid composure, at a meeting in the middle of term. In the circumstances at present obtaining, he announced, he had thought it expedient to remove Mr Watershute from his position as Tutor in Physics. He had appointed Mr Lenton, a highly competent young graduate, to act in that capacity during the remainder of the academic year.

At this the storm broke. Half-a-dozen normally mild men endeavoured to speak simultaneously. The noise was confusing, but its purport was clear. The scandal had continued long enough, and steps must be initiated forthwith to deprive Mr Watershute of his fellowship. There could be little doubt as to what a vote on this matter would reveal as the will of the Governing Body.

It was at this juncture—and when the Provost (almost unbelievably) betrayed some sign of wavering—that Cyril Bedworth did an incredible thing. He stood up. Never in living memory (I was to be told) had anybody addressed the Governing Body from such a stance before.

'Both as Senior Tutor,' Bedworth said, 'and from strong personal conviction, I support you, Mr Provost, in the action you have taken in this matter. Were a resolution to the contrary to be carried, I should regard it as an expression of no confidence in the college officers as a body. I should therefore be obliged to resign my fellowship.'

Silences are sometimes described as 'stunned', and the silence as Bedworth sat down had a fair claim to the adjective. Into it David Graile spoke.

'Mr Provost,' he said, 'you have told us of the arrangement you have made. May we now pass on to the next business?'

And that is what the Governing Body did.

It was about a fortnight after this memorable event that I encountered Geoffrey Quine in the Great Quadrangle. He was viewing with satisfaction the now quite perceptible progress being made in the re-edification of the tower. As Bursar the spectacle gave him no headache, since the money to defray the cost of the operation had arrived so miraculously out of the blue—the wonderful misty blue, it might have been said, of a Madonna's robes. 'Quite a bomb' was Quine's way of describing the size of the cheque. He turned round as I approached.

'Have you heard about Watershute?' he demanded.

'No, I haven't.'

'Do you want to, Duncan? I'm damned if I do ever again.' Quine was firmly one of the anti-Watershute party. It went against the grain with him, he would assert, to deplete the college revenues in order to pay out a salary to an invisible man.

'Yes, I do, Geoffrey. I'd like to hear anything about him, short of news of his funeral.' This was an indiscreet speech. But then I'd been occupied in being discreet about William Watershute for weeks.

'Not a funeral but a feast. He has sent a telegram to the Provost, saying that he's going to turn up for the Gaudy.'

'Well, well! I suppose he's entitled to?'

'Certainly he is. He's a fellow of this large madhouse still. But there's another thing. He says he's bringing two guests.'

'Odder and odder. And I didn't know one could invite one's own private guests to the summer Gaudy.'

'No more one can, in a general way. Or rather there's a convention one asks them only to the minor binges. But nothing in this place is more than a convention or a custom or an understanding. Unless it's in those nonsensical Statutes, of course. And I believe people have from time to time proposed to bring a guest on their own initiative. But two is a bit much. However, that's neither here nor there. The main thing is that, in the circumstances of his case, the man's turning up at all is bare-faced impertinence. There's bound to be an awful shindy.'

'Perhaps people have had enough in the shindy line, Geoffrey. What does Edward say about it?'

'I can't make him out. He's quite unperturbed.'

'I see.' It occurred to me to wonder whether Mogridge had taken the Provost belatedly into his confidence. 'Imperturbability is Edward's forte, wouldn't you say? Didn't you watch him the night Watershute was as drunk as a lord at high table?'

'Perhaps he'll turn up drunk at the Gaudy too. And his precious guests as well.'

'Come, come, Bursar. Don't take so gloomy a view. Do you know, by the way, where Watershute's telegram came from?'

'It came from Helsinki. And he said he'd just make it.'

'A dramatic touch. I wish him *bon voyage*.'

'I wish him further,' Quine said with vigour, and walked away.

The Gaudy promised little liveliness. Revolving in its three-year cycle, the system had gathered in again the most senior generation of old members. Some of them were very old indeed. Had Cedric Mumford accepted his invitation (and I was thankful that he had not) he would have appeared a tender juvenile in comparison with a score or more of the diners. These, in fact, were the ancients about whom Plot delighted in the most dire forebodings. Dr Damian, he told me darkly, was likely to have a busy night with 'apoplexies and the like in them that ought never to have been let leave their beds'. I gained from him the impression that stretcher parties had already been organized.

Aware that I'd probably be unacquainted with a single one of the guests, and that I'd have to converse either with colleagues or with persons hard of hearing, uninterested in my existence, and perfunctorily introduced, I planned not to arrive too early at the preliminary sherry-drinking in the Great Quadrangle. In fact I rather overdid this precaution, and turned up only as the Provost and the grandees emerged from common room and made their way in an indefinite sort of procession towards the staircase leading to hall. The inferior orders stood and admired the while. This it was very proper that we should do, the superior gathering being notably august even by the customary standard of the occasion. In addition to the eminent *savants*, native and foreign, whom the university had been honouring that day, various odd notabilities, including the Prime Minister and the Archbishop of Canterbury, had turned up. Most august of all was the urbane and unassuming retired statesman who was Chancellor of the university at the time.

313

We all found our way into hall—bumping into one another because our noses were in the brochures (as they might be called) telling us where we must now sit, what we should presently eat and drink, and to whose eloquence we should eventually listen when the speeches came round. Finding my way to the modest station appointed me, I was pleased to discover on my one hand young Lenton, whom I could at least question about how science fiction (or the simple thriller) was getting on. We were all still standing, the elaborate sung grace was still a minute or two off, when Lenton suddenly clutched my elbow.

'My God!' he said. 'It is! It is, I tell you. Just look at them.'

I looked as directed. What I saw, on the dais far up the hall, was William Watershute in tails and his doctoral robe. On either side of him were his guests: two rather small men in plain black suits, who struck me at once as pale and strained but at the same time composed. These three were some way down the long table. And now the Chancellor appeared to have called an unrehearsed halt to the proceedings. Painfully and slowly, since he walked with the aid of a stick, he made his way past the other guests, followed by the Provost. The Provost (not entirely out of his element) introduced Watershute and the two small men. Watershute gave a brisk nod to the Chancellor, and the two small men produced deep and formal bows. Brief and polite exchanges followed upon this, and the Chancellor made his way back to his place. The singing began, and it appeared to be a long time before I could question Lenton.

'Well,' I said, 'who are they?'

'Vladimir Simonson and Anatole Kriltsov.' Lenton seemed entirely awed. 'There's not a doubt of it.'

'Physicists?'

'And dissidents. They've been kept in a bin for years. I can't make head or tail of it.'

'I can, Lenton. Your boss has brought them out.'

'Brought them *out?*'

'Yes—and I think I know who came to master-mind the operation. Call it Scarlet Pimpernel stuff.'

As soon as the speeches were over I went straight back to Surrey. It was to find Mogridge established in my sitting-room, drinking my whisky, and listening (wistfully, no doubt) to Suggia on my record-player. I took this complex of facts as indicating that Mogridge's book of rules had been tucked away for the time being, and that confidential communication was proposed. This proved to be correct.

'Oh, Duncan,' Mogridge said (with his gaze apparently on a far corner of the room), 'I hope you don't mind my barging in and making free.'

'Very far from it, Gavin.'

'And keeping you rather in the dark. You see, if one's obliged to keep nearly everyone in the dark, it isn't easy to go shedding light all round.'

'I take the point. What about this whole exploit? Was it easy?'

'It began to straighten out, I'd say, when we took hold of it. Some friends of mine, that is.'

'Quite so. Some friends.'

'Once you've got a thing straight, you can begin to see your path some way ahead. I must say this one was a bit sticky at the start. But as an amateur's effort one might expect that of it. Professionals know a good deal that amateurs don't, wouldn't you say? In fact it's what makes them professionals. In music, for example.'

'Yes, of course. Are you saying that Watershute began this as a one-man show?'

'Entirely. He's a very enterprising person. A little given to excessive thoroughness, perhaps.'

'Overkill?'

'Well, that's not a bad term for it. He even ran an entirely bogus and recklessly extravagant amour in Venice. Or rather it was certainly extravagant and possibly bogus. Not our business.'

'Definitely not.'

'He made his wife put on a turn, too.'

'So he did. I was there. There was a bit of overkill about all that as well.'

'I'm not surprised. He was a bit erratic, I'd say, and the thing became viable only when we'd spotted what he was about and joined in. And I'm quite pleased with it, really. It's been a model of effective penetration at a high level. And the advantageousness of your penetration being at a high level is rather a dogma of mine. As often as not, it's going to earn you an extra half-hour at the end of the road.'

'And it's half-an-hour extra that may be vital?'

'Oh, decidedly. *Il n'y a que le premier pas qui coûte.*' Mogridge smiled with innocent pleasure at having achieved this witticism. 'Literally, it can be, when you're bolting for a tunnel. That's a metaphor, of course. It's not a factual statement but a metaphor. The Finland tunnel, say. It means a journey underground. But that's a metaphor too.'

'Can you tell me anything more about it, Gavin?'

'I'd say there's very little to tell. They thought they'd got that chap where they wanted him. Spotted him in difficulties, chatted him up, did him a hand-out or two, chatted him up again, and then told him to lie low and hold himself *en disponibilité* for his sensational defector's act.' Mogridge seemed to have taken a momentary fancy to the French tongue. 'All fairly routine. And then they loosed him on those unfortunate chaps who'd been shut up for quite some time. Old colleagues of Watershute's they'd once been, somewhere or other. So he was to have a pull with them and bring them to a better frame of mind. After that it was easy. Watershute's new paymasters were trusting him like mad, and he only needed to say that a certain relaxation of surveillance would help things along. Quiet and reflective country walks or something. The rest must be quite clear to you, Duncan.'

'Absolutely. But, Gavin, what was the object of the exercise, so far as your lot went? Was it just to help William Watershute bring off a humane and quixotic exploit? Or has there been something else: deep scientific secrets, and so on?'

'I believe deep scientific secrets are rather rot.' For a moment Mogridge appeared at a loss. 'There's an element of rot, they say, about deep scientific secrets. But, well, it showed some other chaps we keep our muscles flexed. They show us *they* do that from time to time.'

'It's the Great Game?'

'Oh, Duncan!' Mogridge said. He was suddenly deeply stirred. 'Fancy your remembering *Kim*.'

# XXIX

ARNOLD LEMPRIERE WOULD have considered it a little over-dramatic, I believe, to go home and promptly die. And since between the event and his memorial service a prescriptive interval had to elapse, the service was held early in October, in the first week of the new academic year. It was a day on which the Provost and his supporting clergy had a busy time. We gave thanks for Lempriere's life in the college chapel in the afternoon. During the morning Duncan McKechnie had been christened there. The christening was a small domestic affair, and quiet except for the infant's yelling loudly. There was a modest party afterwards, with glasses of madeira and a nibbling of biscuits. I thought Janet looked about twenty years old, but as I didn't check up with anybody on this, it may have been a subjective conclusion.

McKechnie looked exactly his age, which was within a few months of my own. He also looked even more pleased with himself than the occasion demanded, and this would have annoyed me if he hadn't demonstrably been so pleased with me as well. It was almost embarrassing. He might have been treating me not merely as a godparent at the solemnity but as a collaborator in the whole enterprise. He told me that on the previous day he had moved a good many books.

From this party I walked back to Surrey with a pleasant sense of something still to do. I had remembered the picture hanging in the dining-room of the vicarage: my father's wedding present to Janet long ago. There was something I hadn't done then that I could do now. I took down from above the mantel-shelf *Young Picts watching the arrival of Saint Columba*, made a careful parcel of it, and addressed it to my godson as his christening present. At least it was something: partly because it was by a great artist, and partly because I'd miss it quite a lot.

I went into common room to lunch, and talked to Albert Talbert. He was the bearer of calamitous and obviously fallacious news of something that had happened to an eminent English scholar at Yale.

For the memorial service the chapel was crowded with men most of us had never seen before. Many of them were almost as old as Lempriere himself had been when he died. One got the impression that it was his earliest pupils who remembered him best.

When the service ended I went for a walk round Long Field. There were many cars parked on the broad path traversing it, for the congregation had not yet driven away. Variously known to one another, they stood around in groups, conversing with the temperate cheerfulness proper to the occasion. Through them threaded small files and bunches of young men in rowing kit, going down to the river at the double, unprompted to wonder what their seniors were about.